THE ~~REAL~~ LIFE OF GREY MONROE

CATHERINE LYON

THE ~~REAL~~ LIFE OF GREY MONROE

CATHERINE LYON

CANNON VALLEY BOOKS

MUSIC

As you read this book, enjoy these original songs that accompany the story. Use the QR code below to access the YouTube playlist:

wilderbluebells
NOOOO!!! RIP ME
greymarcshipper
They did NOT just kill off LeMarc! I can't breathe right now...
realgreymonroe
Wait... did someone murder him? WHAT IS GOING ON?
wilderbluebells
I can't believe we have to
GREYWATCH

Grey

1

L *iar, liar, pants on fire.*

Grey Monroe, slumped in the backseat of her family's sleek black Mercedes, would have thought the text was a prank if it weren't for the number that had sent it. She'd entered the contact into her phone as *Lucy from Algebra* just in case her mother ever saw a text coming through, but one glance at the chat history would have raised even Astrid Monroe's perfectly plucked eyebrows.

LeMarc is dead, Grey told herself. *The text couldn't be from him.*

She leaned her head against the glass of the car window, wincing in the sunlight as she looked out at the crowd in front of St. Andrew's. Everyone had donned their finest black attire and porcelain masks of sorrow for Collin James LeMarc. *Lucy from Algebra*. Grey could almost picture him amongst the somber guests, those dancing eyes full of mischief.

In the front seat, her mother tugged on a pair of black silk gloves. "You'd think they would have picked a better time for it. Right in the middle of the day! In this heat, we'll all melt before they get the coffin in the ground."

Astrid's blonde hair was piled high today in an elegant twist, her lace-covered black dress barely long enough to be decent. "Not that I'm complaining. The world's that much brighter with one fewer of those wolves in town."

Grey closed her eyes against her mother's words, but the back of her eyelids only played back memories she didn't want to see. LeMarc, fingers grazing her cheek, whispering in her ear. The flash of an impish smile, that scar just above his top lip. The necklace he'd given her, gold shining in the moonlight. Blood on her clothes. Blood on her hands. Blood everywhere.

"Astrid, try to have some compassion," she heard her father say. "I know their family and ours have had our share of strife, but he was just a kid."

"He was a LeMarc, Oscar." Astrid waved the funeral announcement back and forth like a fan to cool herself off. "Heaven knows the only reason I'm here is to see that old crone and her greedy thug of a husband on the worst day of their lives."

The feud between the LeMarcs and the Monroes had been going on since before Grey's older brother Danny was even born, but a funeral was hardly the time for her mother's venom.

"Mom, can you please just stop?"

"Why do you care? You hated Collin. He used to pick on you in grade school."

"No one called him Collin," Grey muttered to the window, but her mother didn't hear.

If Danny were here, he would have done something outrageous to set their mother squawking: make up ridiculous internal monologues for all of the stuffy guests outside, or recite a list of the top ten ways to put the "fun" back in "funeral." It would have been a nice distraction from yet another of Astrid's tirades about the LeMarcs.

Grey's phone beeped again, another text.

Did I say pants on fire? I meant you, Grey. You might have killed me, but I'm still going to see you burn.

Grey gasped and dropped the phone. It clattered down to the car floor, landing underneath her mother's seat.

Her father met her eyes in the rearview mirror. "Everything all right?"

Grey nodded and forced a shaky sound through her lips she hoped he'd take as a yes, clutching at the seat with her fingers to keep herself upright.

It's not him. It can't be him. It's a prank. Just a cruel joke.

Whatever the person behind the text was implying, she hadn't killed LeMarc. She *hadn't*.

And once she remembered who the real killer was, she'd be able to prove it.

Several hours of time were missing from her memories of that horrible night. Grey could close her eyes and be right there next to LeMarc by the river again—feel his hands, his lips, hear his voice soft and sweet and low—but then there was nothing. It was all blank until the moment she'd woken up in her bed, groggy and covered in blood. But even if Grey didn't remember what had happened, she knew she would never have done anything to hurt LeMarc. Never in a million years.

So who thought she had?

The phone beeped again, but Grey left it on the floor of the car, closing her eyes. *Who would be this cruel? Who even knew that LeMarc and I were together?*

The phone didn't buzz again.

Her father found a parking spot, and Grey left her phone behind, trailing after her parents to join the flock of mourners making their way to the massive oak doors like an unkindness of ravens. The LeMarcs were well respected in Heringford, so the funeral was just as much a chance to make an appearance as to pay respects. There were lots of kids from LeMarc's prep school in the crowd and even a few from her own. She and LeMarc hadn't just been from rival families, but rival schools as well.

She wondered if any of these people cared that LeMarc's favorite smell was the salty tang of the ocean, or that he'd read the stars like a mystery novel, always guessing at the ending.

Through the fabric of her purse, she could feel the hard outline of a book. She had no idea how she would manage it, but it would be with him when they lowered him into the ground.

Janice and Phillip LeMarc stood at the entrance to the church, welcoming each person as they entered the funeral. "Look at them, reigning supreme," Grey's mother muttered. "They don't even look sad."

Grey didn't usually agree with her mother about anything, but the LeMarcs did look more like the hosts of a dinner party than mourners at their own son's funeral. If it weren't for their black attire, there would be no indication that their son was dead.

Grey studied Janice LeMarc as they stood in line, biting her lip as she took in as many details as she could. Janice was small and pointy, but she had LeMarc's familiar eyes and hooked nose. What was she feeling right now? Did her smile and polite nod hide depths of untold grief? Whatever pain she was in, the woman didn't show it.

Then again, no one looking at Grey would see anything more than a bored teenage girl, not someone whose world had just imploded.

Mrs. LeMarc didn't have her son's phone in her hand. Grey hadn't expected it, that his mother would send Grey menacing texts from his phone minutes before his funeral was set to start. But who *did* have it, and how? Had he had it on him when he was killed?

If only she could remember *something* from that night.

It took forever to reach the doors. Grey's black heels sank into the lush grass as they stood waiting. The day had gone from hot and dry to hot and sticky, and her tight black dress felt like saran wrap. She'd wanted to look pretty for LeMarc one last time, but she regretted the decision now.

He wasn't there to see her dress.

Janice LeMarc's eyes went wide when they approached, as though she hadn't seen them standing in the line for the last ten minutes.

"I never thought I'd see the day when the Monroes would sink so low." Her thin voice carried through the dead summer air. "How dare you come to my son's funeral trying to stir up trouble?"

Grey felt her mother stiffen beside her, and she knew an argument was brewing. Tears pricked at her eyes. Who cared now about some feud no one remembered the start of? She just wanted to say goodbye to him.

"No matter what our history, the loss of a son is a tragedy," Grey's father responded, cutting off his wife's retort. "We know that better than anyone. We've simply come to pay our respects."

"We don't want you here, Oscar," LeMarc's dad said sharply. He was so unlike his son, all brawn and bravado. The man was the size of a bear, and his deep growling voice just magnified the effect. "Just go away."

Grey felt a sudden, sharp panic, a need to get inside that church. She had to say goodbye, or he would haunt her forever.

For never was a story of more woe than this of Juliet and her Romeo.

"Please." Everyone looked at her in surprise, and she shuffled her feet. Everyone thought she'd hated LeMarc. She wasn't about to correct them, but she couldn't leave, not now. "I want to... I have to come in," Grey said, conscious of the herd of people listening in. "Please."

LeMarc's mom studied her face, and for a moment, Grey thought she saw a glimpse of her son's compassion there, his depth of understanding.

But then the moment was gone. She waved her hand in disgust.

"Fine. You'll sit in the back." Janice nodded them on, and they passed through the thick arched doors into the chapel.

The stained glass windows scattered the light into dancing glimpses of color as they settled into the back pew. Grey had attended weddings and baptisms and christenings here at St. Andrew's, and the church always seemed to be watching, nurturing its little flock. Usually its air hummed with the sighs and prayers of people long forgotten.

Today, even packed with people, it felt empty.

"The impudence of that woman," Astrid muttered as they sat down. "Trying to police people's grief like that."

Grey ignored her. At the very front of the center aisle was a photograph of LeMarc covered with flowers and ribbon. She stared at it, trying to burn the image into her memory. She wanted to remember him smiling.

Pastor Davies began his eulogy right away, his dry voice ringing through the church. He described a boy who was dutiful and loyal, who was eager to follow in his father's footsteps and continue a beautiful family legacy. LeMarc would have laughed at that. He'd had a low laugh, a deep chuckle that always made her grin. Now, the memory of it stabbed at her gut like a knife.

It might have been the dust floating through the air, or the lifeless sermon Pastor Davies was trying to deliver, but Grey couldn't keep her mind from wandering, circling down into the darkness that drew her imagination like a deadly magnet.

That night, LeMarc hadn't cared about duty. When he'd kissed her, his hands tightening against her waist and his lips searching against hers, he hadn't cared about family loyalty or legacy or some feud that said they shouldn't be together. She'd clung to him, her hands in his hair and lips hot against his skin and her very soul melding with his. He'd whispered into her ear, his fingers tracing across her lips.

Grey had kissed plenty of boys in her lifetime, but she'd never experienced anything like LeMarc. Every time he kissed her, it felt like she could finally breathe.

The night LeMarc was murdered, Grey knew she'd never be able to breathe again.

By the time Pastor Davies had finished his remarks, she'd managed to stop the tears from falling. Her mother was too absorbed in scanning the congregation for gossip to notice her daughter surreptitiously wiping her eyes, and Grey had dealt with enough tragedy to know how to keep her emotions buried deep.

There was a line afterward to approach the coffin, and Grey stood behind her mother and father, heart beating in mingled dread and anticipation. She hadn't expected an open coffin, not when he was murdered and autopsied. The body hadn't been released until the coroner's report was finalized.

She was staring at a bit of pulled lace on the back of her mother's dress when, without warning, it disappeared. She was suddenly looking at the stone floor of the church.

Whirling around wildly, she realized *everyone* had disappeared. The crowd, the coffin, even the altarpiece at the front of the church. The quiet murmuring of the people around her had cut off, too. She was alone in the gutted-out sanctuary.

There was a buzzing noise to her left, like a mosquito. She turned and caught the quick gleam of a shiny black orb hovering nearby, peering down at her...

It only lasted a second. Grey blinked, and suddenly everyone was back. The hushed conversations around her returned, and her mother's pulled lace was just where it had been before. The strange buzzing orb was gone.

"What just..." Grey started, trailing off. No one around her was acting like anything was amiss.

Her father turned around. "Everything all right, sweetheart?"

Grey swallowed, blinking away her strange vision. "Um... yeah. Yeah, I think so. I just got dizzy for a second."

"It's this heat," her mother said. "This church is too stuffy. They should have known the place would be steaming at this time of day."

Heat and grief were a lethal cocktail, apparently. She needed to hurry up and get out of here or she was going to go mad.

The line took forever, but when she was finally able to stand before the coffin, Grey was surprised at how easy it was to pretend it wasn't LeMarc lying before her. It didn't look like him, this wax figure. LeMarc had been a great many things, but never empty.

"If you could keep moving please," Janice LeMarc said sharply to Grey's mother, standing in front of Grey.

It was as though Astrid had been waiting for an opportunity. She immediately snapped back with a call for patience. "I need time to mourn," she said through clenched teeth.

"Like that black heart of yours could feel any emotion other than spite," Janice spat. She took a few menacing steps towards Grey's mother. "You've never had a single positive thing to say about my son."

Astrid lifted her head, the light from the stained glass window creating a mosaic of colors across her face. "Obviously I should remedy that. Here's one: He's dead."

A *crack* resounded through the church as Janice's hand slapped across Astrid's cheek.

The whole church stood in silent shock for a moment, except for one loud bark of laughter sounding from the back of the chapel.

With a cry of rage, Astrid flung her clutch at the grieving mother. "How *dare* you lay a finger on me, you wretched woman!"

She lunged forward and pushed Janice backwards with both hands.

Grey stared in horror as her mother and Mrs. LeMarc collapsed into a fit of slaps and scratches. What was her mother thinking? It didn't matter how many times her mother made a scene, it still always took Grey by surprise. Astrid wasn't even drunk this time.

Shaking her head, she pulled a slim volume of *Romeo and Juliet* from her purse. This was her chance, and she wasn't likely to get another one. With a desperate, silent goodbye, she tucked the book into the coffin, fast as she could.

At first she thought no one had seen her. Everyone was staring at the two spitting women facing off over the casket, not at Grey.

But glancing behind her at the crowd watching her mother's break-down, she thought she caught a pair of dark eyes watching her.

When she looked again, the crowd had moved and the eyes were gone.

Grey

2

*T*ap tap tap tap tap tap tap tap...

Grey eyed Kalie Fuller's tapping pencil, wondering if it was unpresidential to grab it and throw it across the room. If a girl couldn't do the important things, what was the point of being student body president?

Right now, she wished she had the power to cancel school for the day. It was only 7:08, the first official student council meeting of the year, and already it felt like Grey had been here for hours.

From across the table, Kamilla was avoiding her eye, though Grey caught her sneaking a guilty glance every now and then. Grey clenched her jaw, her mind flashing back to the last time they'd spoken—though it'd been more yelling than speaking, at least on Grey's part. She so rarely lost her temper, but with the magnitude of Kamilla's betrayal...

Kamilla and Grey had been best friends ever since they'd survived a tornado together in the third grade, though for Kamilla, *friend* and *competitor* often went hand in hand. Now Grey wasn't sure if she was either. They hadn't spoken since the spring.

Could the sudden fissure between them make Kamilla bitter enough to send the cruel phone messages? She was smart enough to figure out about her and LeMarc, and Grey knew better than anyone how she could be single-minded in pursuing what she wanted. But she wasn't vengeful, and the texts were another level of heartless.

It'd been months since LeMarc's funeral, and Grey still had no idea how to process the third text sent from his phone.

As Todd Milkins, the student council vice president, began his proposal to introduce a dunking booth at the homecoming carnival, Grey pulled out her phone to look at the message again, stark white letters against a blue background.

You have until the Christmas gala to tell the truth, or I won't be the only corpse in this town.

How could she tell the truth if she didn't know what happened? And if the texter thought she was guilty of murder, why not go to the police?

And that third message hadn't been the last; there were more threats, vicious taunts about the night LeMarc died. They came at random intervals, lighting up her screen in the middle of the night or buzzing during her teeth cleaning appointment. Every time her phone pinged, her shoulders tensed and her breath caught. Every text might be a fresh torture.

I didn't kill him, she'd texted back a hundred different ways, along with pleas for the messages to stop, angry demands to know the identity of the sender, requests for evidence or information. But the texter never answered, just held silent until the next pointed threat.

Grey felt a sudden, sharp, longing to sit down in the fold of LeMarc's arms like she used to when something was bothering her, to tell him how hurt she was about what had happened with Kamilla, how scared she was about what she didn't remember, how much she *missed* him.

His eyes, those green eyes, would light up at the idea of the murder mystery. He would drag her all over the city looking for clues about the strange black emptiness in her head where her memories of the night should be.

Romeo meets Sherlock Holmes.

Grey put her head down on her arms, trying to stop herself from crying in front of her classmates. *He isn't gone. He's getting ready for school, putting on that terrible orange jersey he loves, thinking about how much he wants to see me.*

"Grey, you're not even listening," Todd Milkins complained.

Startled back to reality, Grey raised her head and looked around the table, where everyone was waiting expectantly for her to answer a question she hadn't heard. The student council met in the office conference room, cluttered with mismatched chairs and stuffed into the back of the office like a broom closet. Usually she didn't mind the posters with their cheery slogans, but today the room felt blank and cold.

Kalie's pencil was still tapping out an incessant beat. *Tap tap tap tap tap tap tap tap...*

"Sorry, I spaced out there for a second. What was the question?"

Todd rolled his eyes, and Grey sunk in her seat a bit. There was that flutter, the one she felt anytime she didn't put on a star performance. Todd always made her feel out of step, like she was a dance move behind everyone else. Incredibly smart, with a body chiseled out of marble like a breathing Michelangelo statue, he was easily the most popular boy in school. He'd asked her out a few times the previous year, but then she'd met LeMarc, the midnight moon that overshadowed Todd's sun in a total eclipse.

LeMarc had made her feel like she was good enough even when she wasn't perfect.

"You know, Grey, as student body president, you shouldn't be spacing out an entire meeting."

"I know, I just—"

"It makes the rest of us feel undervalued," he interrupted. "We all work hard here."

Grey felt like melting into a puddle right there in her seat. "I get that, Todd, I do."

Her treasurer, Grant, opened his mouth to speak, but Todd cut him off, basking in the glow of his own self-righteousness. "You didn't come to the opening bonfire last week, either. Everyone was expecting you. And now that you're here, you might as well be absent. What's the point of a student body president who doesn't care at all about the student body?"

Grey wrapped her arms around her middle, face flaming. She looked over at the faculty advisor, Mr. Partridge, but he was asleep in the corner. "The end-of-summer bonfire isn't a school-sponsored activity. And I'm sorry I spaced out for a few seconds, but I have a lot on my mind."

"A few seconds? I bet you can't name a single idea for the homecoming carnival out of all of the ones we've discussed for the past ten minutes. It's like you don't even care."

Tap tap tap tap TAP TAP TAP TAP...

"I don't!" Grey cried. "I don't care about any of the pointless things this council does!"

Kamilla's eyes widened, and several class officers' jaws dropped.

Grey put her head down on her arms, face burning.

She'd just said that. She'd actually just said those words in front of the whole student council.

Todd cleared his throat. "I don't think that's surprising to anyone here. You don't care about this council or this school."

Grey slowly raised her head, trying not to burst into tears. Todd had his chest puffed out, his head cocked in defiance, arms crossed. She glanced around to all of the other faces in the room: her treasurer, Grant, who was biting his lip; Mary Shelton, who as usual was clearly entertained by the drama; Victor Green, who was glancing back and forth between Grey and Todd. Kamilla was playing with her phone, as though she didn't care about the fight at all.

When she answered, she surprised even herself. "You can have it."

The room stopped dead still for a moment, her statement hanging in the air.

"Have what?" Todd asked, his brow furrowed.

"The presidency. Class president. You can have it."

And then everyone started talking at once. All of the members of the council started babbling, asking Grey to reconsider.

"Grey, you're an amazing president," Lindsey said, putting an arm on Grey's shoulder.

"Don't let Todd just take it, he's awful," Grant urged.

Kamilla met Grey's eyes briefly, and Grey could see the calculations taking place behind those amber irises, could practically hear her ex-best friend's mind whirring. Of all people, Kamilla knew how hard Grey had fought to be president. The three-way fight between Grey, Kamilla, and Todd the previous year for student body president had been fierce, and Grey had edged out Kamilla and Todd by a tiny sliver of votes. Kamilla had accepted defeat as gracefully as Kamilla ever accepted any defeat, which was not very, but they were both used to the give-and-take competition that made up their friendship. They even had an old, tarnished play tiara they passed back and forth for each victory. It was currently stuffed into Grey's dresser drawer.

Todd was just standing there, his mouth hanging open at Grey's declaration. Surprisingly, he looked more unsettled than smug.

"You're right," Grey said to him, standing up from the table. Her chair made a loud screeching noise, and Todd winced. Everyone else quieted. "My heart isn't in this. You would make a great president. So take it."

She grabbed her bag, stuffed her notebook inside, and left the room, trying for silent dignity but landing somewhere closer to trying-not-to-cry.

As the door closed, she heard Todd say, "Now what are we supposed to do? The carnival kissing booth thing was supposed to take up a whole episode. I better not be fired."

It didn't make any sense, but there was a good chance she had misheard; she wasn't thinking clearly right now.

It was still early enough that the hallway was empty, only 7:20. Grey leaned her forehead against a locker, letting out a shaky breath. She wasn't upset to not be student body president anymore. She hadn't been lying when she said she didn't care about carnivals and dances. But she did care about what people thought of her. She cared about staying in control.

"You okay?" came a voice from behind her.

She composed her face into a smile before turning around. "I'm great!"

She tried to sound chipper as she turned, but it came out sounding a bit manic.

Her eyes landed on a boy standing in front of her with a worried expression, and her smile almost fell in surprise. Even with LeMarc's death so fresh, she could take a moment to appreciate a pair of dark eyes like these ones. The boy looked Middle-Eastern, with thick Disney-prince hair and broad shoulders.

At her overeager answer, he grinned. "Good. You looked upset at first."

She shook her head. "I was just thinking."

He stuck out his hand. "I'm Yusuf Abdullah. I just transferred over from Hilton Prep."

LeMarc's school. Grey sucked in her breath as she shook his hand. "Grey Monroe. I'm glad you escaped the dark side."

He laughed, his eyes lighting up. The way he was looking at her made her stomach turn a few flips, a feeling she hadn't felt since the night LeMarc died. He still hadn't let go of her hand.

And then the fire in his eyes dimmed a bit, and he pulled his hand back, getting serious. "I saw you this spring at LeMarc's funeral."

It was getting hard to breathe in this hallway. She wanted to drop her gaze, but there was something magnetic about his eyes as they searched hers. She was finding it hard to lie as smoothly as she usually did when talking about LeMarc.

"I didn't really know him. My parents wanted to make an appearance."

Yusuf looked like he was going to say something, but then stopped.

"What?" Grey asked softly. "What were you going to say?"

Yusuf gestured to her to start walking with him, and she pushed off from the lockers, trailing him slightly. They walked slowly, meandering toward the gym. He stuffed his hands in his pockets.

"When I said that I saw you... I saw you put the book in his coffin. And I saw the expression on your face when you did it."

The dark eyes. She'd seen someone watching that day. Grey was grateful he'd started them walking, so he wasn't looking at her face as he said it. Marty Shumacher called out a greeting from his locker, and she tried to smile at him.

Yusuf continued, "I don't know what LeMarc was to you, but to me he was a friend. I'm sorry for your loss."

She nodded, unable to speak through the lump in her throat.

"I have to admit, I asked around about you. I'd never seen you hanging around LeMarc before, and I was curious."

"How'd you know my name?"

He grinned. "As you might imagine, several people were... ah... *discussing* your mother after the funeral."

Grey rolled her eyes. Of course everyone had been talking about Astrid Monroe after she got into a catfight with a woman burying her son. "And did you hear the whole sordid tale of the Monroe vs. LeMarc feud?"

"And so much more. You survived a tornado, fought off a kidnapper last year, your friend and that coma, your brother missing in action... And now losing another friend so violently. Honestly, hearing it all, I just thought..."

"That someone, somewhere, has a very powerful voodoo doll and a grudge against me?"

He shook his head. "No, I thought you sounded like someone who could use a friend."

They reached the corner of the hallway and stopped walking, facing each other again. Grey looked down at her feet. "I have to go meet someone, but this was..."

Yusuf winced. "A total downer? I'm sorry, I shouldn't have mentioned all of those things that have happened to you, I just wanted to tell you how amazing I think you are to still be going after everything you've been through."

She bit her lip. "Thanks."

Most people pretended that everything that had happened to Grey was no big deal, that she should just get over it. LeMarc had been the only one who hadn't needed her to be perfect even after everything she'd been through, who was okay with her being just a little broken. After losing him... She wasn't just a little broken anymore. She was drowning, and she'd gotten so good at pretending to be fine, no one had even noticed.

No one except for this unexpected boy, with his kind smile and eyes that saw far too much.

"I have to run," she said, "but it was really nice to meet you."

Yusuf smiled that Disney-prince smile. "It was nice to meet you, too, Grey Monroe. Don't be a stranger."

Grey watched him walk away, biting her lip again.

Just as he disappeared around the corner, her phone rang. When she saw her friend Ellie's name on the screen, Grey panicked. Ellie texted, Ellie messaged, Ellie posted on social media. Ellie did *not* use her phone to make actual phone calls.

"What's wrong?"

Her friend's scratchy voice was three pitches higher than normal. "*What's wrong*? What's wrong is that Victor just told me that you quit being student body president! Do I need to stage an intervention here? You have been acting weird all summer."

Speak for yourself, Grey thought. Ellie had been in a horrible accident the previous fall and in a coma for two months, and ever since she'd awoken she'd been a different person. The basics were the same, and she had all of her memory back, but there was some part of Ellie, a light she'd carried, that was lost in the accident.

At least she wasn't keeping secrets and going behind her back like certain *other* friends, so Grey would take what she could get. "I'm fine. No intervention needed, I'm just over student council. I can't handle being in the same room as Kamilla, anyway."

"I already told you, I'm not taking sides. I am Sweden."

"You mean Switzerland?"

"Whatever, one of the snowy ones."

Grey let out a sigh. World History wasn't really Ellie's strong suit. "Where are you?" she asked. "I'm by the gym."

"Ugh. Still in morning detention. Mr. Krueger fell asleep. Can you stop me the next time I decide to make out with a football player in a boy's bathroom stall?"

Grey wrinkled her nose. "First, ew. Second, I *did* try to stop you this time, and you completely ignored me. Third, I don't think there's anyone left on the football team you haven't already made out with, so you should be fine."

She could hear Ellie laughing on the other side of the phone. "I can't help it. When they throw those big eyes like the puppies from those TV commercials, I just can't say no."

Grey smiled absently at a few people who nodded hello to her. The hallway was starting to fill up with students getting ready for the school day. "What's a TV commercial?"

There was silence on the other end of the line.

"El? You still there?"

When Ellie answered again, she was whispering. "Mr. Krueger woke up. Sorry, gotta go."

Confused, Grey pulled up a search on her phone. *Teevee commercial*, she typed in.

No results found.

She tried a few variant spellings, all with the same result. She even tried T and V as just letters, but nothing pulled up. She would have to ask Ellie about it later.

"It was you, wasn't it?" came Kamilla's voice from behind her.

Grey whirled around to see Kamilla standing there, hand on her hip and phone in the other.

It was you. Just like the texts.

Grey backed up against the bank of lockers behind her, squeezing her books tight in her arms. "It wasn't... I didn't do anything. Whatever you're accusing me of, I didn't do it."

Kamilla shook her head, her thick dark ponytail bouncing behind her as she stuck out an accusing finger. Did she really think Grey would *kill* someone? "You're the only one who knew about us. Me and Danny."

Grey grimaced. *Kamilla and Danny.* It wasn't that one of her best friends had dated her brother. It was that she'd lied about it, kept it a secret until after he'd been declared MIA.

Grey flashed back to that rainy autumn afternoon when Danny had left for basic training. He'd looked so much older in his fatigues and short hair, his dog tags jingling around his neck.

"You're never going to lose me, Grey," he'd said, his usual goofy smile replaced with a somber expression for once. "No matter what happens, I'll meet you in your best dreams, 'kay?"

It was something he'd said when she was little and afraid of the dark. *Go to sleep, and you'll see me in your best dreams.*

But he'd lied. He'd been missing in action for months, and he hadn't shown up in any of her dreams, the best or the worst ones.

It was the day after LeMarc died that she'd found the photograph: Kamilla's scrunched nose as she grinned at the camera,

Danny's smiling eyes as he planted a kiss on her cheek, arm around her shoulder. Seeing him happy like that, so soon after she found out he was missing...

They'd both lied to her, but she couldn't be mad at Danny, so Kamilla got the anger for both of them. Here in the school hallway, after years of sleepovers and school lunches, Grey might as well have been looking at a stranger. She crossed her arms. "What does you seducing my brother have to do with anything?"

Kamilla did everything with confidence—she went for what she wanted and got what she went for—but suddenly there was an unfamiliar hesitancy in her stance and her voice. "I didn't *seduce* him. I was the one who broke it off before he left for the army, because I didn't want to hurt you."

"You were seeing him for *months* and you said nothing!" Grey responded, keeping her voice low so as to not attract the attention of the whole school hallway.

Kamilla's hand tightened around her phone. "So you sent the texts as some sick sort of revenge? Do you really hate me that much?"

"Texts?" Grey's heart was suddenly racing, pounding out a flurried beat. "What are you talking about?"

Kamilla's eyes narrowed. "You're seriously going to pretend you didn't send them?"

"You've received threatening texts?"

The hallway around them was filling with students, and this wasn't a conversation Grey wanted to have in public. She grabbed Kamilla's arm and dragged her out the front door of the school into the sunshine.

"What are you doing?" Kamilla asked.

Grey pulled her underneath a tall poplar tree, where there was no one around. "How long have you been receiving texts?"

Kamilla yanked her arm back and rubbed her elbow. "They started not long after you found out about me and Danny," she said pointedly. "I'd have to be an idiot not to know it's you, Grey."

"Give me your phone."

Without waiting, Grey snatched Kamilla's phone out of her hand and keyed in the password, which she'd known for years. Kamilla's texts were already open. She opened up her phone as well, pulling up *Lucy from Algebra*'s profile to get LeMarc's number.

"I hope you've been practicing your surprised face, because you're not a very good actress," Kamilla said, leaning over her phone in Grey's hand. She pressed on a recent text strand. The contact was just labeled *DM*.

"It's not LeMarc's number," Grey muttered as she opened the contact info, disappointed.

"Collin LeMarc? The kid from Hilton Prep who was murdered last spring? Why would he be sending me texts?"

Grey held her phone out to Kamilla. "Lucy from Algebra."

Kamilla pressed on the chat, opening the text strand. Grey bit her lip. If she wasn't careful, she'd give herself a bloody lip with all this biting. "The last three texts. Lucy from Algebra is really LeMarc. We grew... close this past year."

Kamilla raised her eyebrows. "You were dating a *LeMarc*? How could you not tell me? And how did your mother not kill you?"

"I didn't tell anyone, *especially* my mother. That's what the *Lucy from Algebra* pseudonym was for. But after he died, someone sent me these texts... You should just read them."

Kamilla ducked her head to read, and Grey held her phone up to scan the texts from *DM*, scrolling to one dated the night of LeMarc's murder, 4:00 AM. That was during Grey's lost time.

You broke me long before the bullets did.

Her breath caught in her throat. *DM*. Danny Monroe.

The next was dated on the morning of LeMarc's funeral, just like the ones sent to Grey from LeMarc's phone.

Now it's my turn to break you.

She scrolled down a whole series of texts that mirrored the awful ones she'd been getting all summer, stopping at one not far down the list. *You have until the Christmas gala to tell the truth, or you'll be missing, too.*

Grey was fine. The tightening in her throat was allergies. She was fine.

She leaned over, putting her hands on her knees. Kamilla's phone slipped to the ground, but she didn't reach down to pick it up. "Who else knew about you and Danny?"

Her voice sounded far away.

"No one. Not even Ellie."

"This is impossible. Danny took his phone with him on his deployment, and they haven't sent his things back. It's somewhere in the Middle East right now."

Grey's throat tightened, an odd heaviness settling in her chest.

You broke me before the bullets did. There were no bullets. Danny wasn't dead. Danny was just missing, and missing things could be found. He was coming home.

Grey looked up at Kamilla, who was watching her with a tense expression. "What is going on?"

"That's exactly what I was just thinking," Kamilla answered. "This person is accusing you of *murder*. You didn't have anything to do with LeMarc's death, did you?"

"How could you even ask that? I don't know who killed LeMarc."

"Well, this mystery texter sure seems convinced."

Yes, but *why?* What did this texter remember that Grey didn't?

The bell rang, but the girls both stayed right where they were even as students from around the schoolyard streamed into the building.

Kamilla sunk down onto the grass. "So you didn't send them."

Grey shook her head. "No. And I think I can officially rule you out as the person impersonating LeMarc, too."

After a moment, Kamilla spoke again. "Two texts from two dead boys."

Grey winced. *One dead boy.*

"The Christmas gala is four months away. What is it this person wants us to tell the truth about?"

Grey shook her head. "I don't know."

Whoever was tormenting them with these messages, they were trying to scare them.

It was working.

"I think," she continued carefully, "we may need to put aside what happened between you and Danny to find out."

Kamilla's lip quirked up into the hint of a smile. "I'm game if you are."

Both phones suddenly pinged at the same time. Still kneeling, Kamilla handed Grey her phone and retrieved hers from the grass where Grey had dropped it.

Even before she clicked on the notification, Grey knew who it was from. Kneeling down on the grass next to Kamilla, she held her phone up so both screens were visible, side-by-side.

The senders were different, but the message was the same:

Better hurry! Don't want to be late on your first day.

"That's worse than the threats," Kamilla muttered as she stood, brushing the dirt off her school uniform.

"Way worse." Grey scanned the gray windows peering out from the school's ivy-laden facade, the parking lot full of tinted windows perfect for hiding a pair of watching eyes.

Just as she stood, their phones pinged again with a follow-up to the first message:

Never know if it could be your last.

Wilder

3

Wilder Blue wiped his sweaty palms on his jeans as he padded down the rickety stairs to Luke Dime's basement. As always, it smelled of weed, unwashed bodies, and blueberry muffins. The dark cave, packed with a jumble of ratty furniture and tech equipment, had become a home for Wilder over the last few years, its occupants a family of sorts. He'd left that family behind to become LeMarc, the leading man on *The Real Life of Grey Monroe*. Now was the moment of truth to find out if he was still welcome here.

None of Luke's Padawan hackers had seen any part of his home other than the dank basement, but it stood in stark contrast to the home's wholesome exterior. Hanging plants, a picket fence, a light blue mailbox, and windows with white curtains: the perfect suburban abode. Wilder strongly suspected it was Luke's mom's house. Occasionally, the twenty-something hacker would come down with a lemon cake or loaf of banana bread in one hand, his white cane in the other.

When Wilder got down to the basement, he saw Carly right away. His best friend's hair had grown longer since he'd last seen her, and she was wearing more eyeliner than she used to. She was typing on her computer, eyebrows scrunched together in concentration.

He noticed with surprise that she was sitting on Abe Goodson's lap. That was new.

Luke wasn't down, but there were a few other friends in the room, and one new girl that must be a freshman.

"The prodigal has returned!" Mark Haderly, a heaving brute of a hacker, called out when he spotted Wilder. "Dude! I saw you making out with that girl on TV. Well done, bro. Grey Monroe is hot."

Tag Hughes piped up from the corner, half hidden behind two massive screens. "It helped that she didn't see your real face."

Wilder picked up a pillow from the ripped plaid couch by the stairs and threw it at Tag, trying not to notice that Carly was ignoring his entrance completely.

"Hey, watch the equipment, man!" Tag called out.

He could have been less of a jerk about it, but Tag was right. Though Grey's eyes and smile were etched in Wilder's memory, she had never seen his real face. LeMarc had different features than Wilder did, and dark curls instead of Wilder's blonde. Most of the avatars on the show were created to look like the actors behind them, but when an actor quit or got fired, someone new started with the same avatar. They'd switched out Grey's best friend, Ellie, after a coma plotline the previous year, and they'd been through about a billion Astrid Monroes. The original LeMarc hadn't wanted to return last season, so Wilder had gotten his role—and his face.

"Seriously, welcome back to the fold," Tag added. "We were worried you'd gone all corporate on us."

The new girl smiled timidly at him. She had a bubble-gum pink computer with an anime sticker on it. Her hair was the same shade of pink as her laptop. "I'm Tanya. I'm a huge fan of yours, Wilder. I love the show, and I think you and Grey are the cutest couple ever."

"Thanks," he said, and then turned to Carly and Abe.

"It's good to see you, man," Abe said. He didn't have a computer, but in one hand he was holding half a blueberry muffin.

"You too, Abe. How's football going?"

Abe was a good guy. Too good, some would say, to be interesting, but Carly apparently disagreed. Wilder chatted with Abe for a few minutes about the team's chances of going to state, and Carly didn't acknowledge his presence once.

Finally he grew too fed up to remain quiet. "Seriously Car, you're not even going to say hi?"

"To who? I don't see anyone I know." She didn't even look up from her computer.

"Just your best friend."

"You're not my best friend, *LeMarc*."

Wilder had been friends with Carly long enough that he'd encountered her temper before, more times than he'd like to count. She'd called him every curse word the English language had to offer, and just about all of the Spanish ones, too, but somehow now she managed to make his character's name sound like the worst of all.

"C'mon, Carly, don't be like that," Wilder said, wishing they didn't have to have this conversation in front of everyone.

Carly finally stopped her furious typing, crossing her arms. Her heavily-lined eyes narrowed into slits. "Like what? Like I'm looking at the jerk who skipped town without warning to star in the most disgusting TV show ever made? No phone calls, no texts, just *gone*. I had to beg your awful dad to tell me where you went. And your mom... Do you have any idea how angry she is with you? She's been fighting against that show for years, and you go and join the cast. And your sister told me you haven't even gone to see her since you've been back."

"Uh, well—" Wilder was saved from having to answer by Luke's appearance in the doorway.

"Wilder!" he called, a fresh plate of blueberry muffins in one hand, his white cane in the other. As always, he was wearing his sunglasses. "I thought you'd left us for good."

"Yeah, I'm hoping to start coming around again."

Carly scoffed, but Wilder ignored her. He walked over to grab a muffin. "There's actually something I wanted to ask you about in private."

"Say no more. Step into my office, Blue," Luke said, gesturing to the small room where he had his stuff set up. With one last long look at Carly, Wilder followed him inside.

Luke's equipment was seriously next-level; he had some gear in this room that rivaled Monroe Studio's setup. Wilder didn't know hardware nearly as well as he knew coding, so he wasn't actually sure what some of it did. The whole room flickered with blue, red, and green lights. As a blind man, Luke didn't need to turn the overhead light on, so his equipment was the only source of illumination.

Wilder knew Luke through Carly. Her older brother, Mario, had gotten into coding, and then hacking, when he was in high school, and he'd introduced Luke to the languages of programming. Mario had gone on to get a degree in software engineering, and Luke had stayed here on April Street to guide and mentor the next generation of hackers and database architects.

The first time Wilder had come, he'd made the mistake of commenting that he was impressed that a blind guy like Luke could use

the Internet, let alone work it the way Luke could. Luke had turned
to Mario and asked, "What is this? You brought me a moron."

Mario had shrugged. "At least he's a smart moron."

Wilder still remembered Luke's horrified response: "That's the
worst kind."

After that first day, Wilder was hooked to the feeling of reading
the Internet like a storybook, full of open doors and calls to action.
Now, he closed the door and parked himself on the raggedy armchair against the wall.

Luke sat down in his swivel chair. "So Carly hates you now," he
observed, spinning back and forth.

"I'm working on it."

"Don't work too hard. Abe's the better dude in every way, man.
So what do you need, amigo?"

Wilder couldn't help but smile. He'd forgotten how blunt Luke
could be. "I need you to hack a system for me, get some information."

"And you can't do it yourself because..." Luke turned his monitor on, and the welcome screen reflected back in his dark glasses.

"Because I'm not good enough. You could do it, though."

"Fair enough. And what intel do you want from Monroe Studios?"

Wilder narrowed his eyes. "I never said Monroe Studios."

Luke smiled. "I know. What do you want from them? They have
good security, NSA good. They must have spent a *fortune* on their
system. I can't get at most of it."

"You've tried?" Wilder asked, surprised.

Luke shrugged, sticking an earbud into one ear for his screen
reader. "I wanted to see what happens this season with the whole
who killed LeMarc storyline. Couldn't get at any spoilers, though.

Did find a few emails about you. You know, Carly would probably be more willing to forgive you if you told her why they canned you."

Luke started typing, and Wilder decided to forge ahead with his request.

"I need to know where she is."

"Grey?"

"Yeah. She's kept in an undisclosed location, and we were just plugged into her virtual world from the studio compound. I need to know where she actually, physically, is."

"No one knows," Luke said, still typing. "Rumors say her city is on an island, but they're wrong. It's underground out in farm country somewhere. For now."

This was news to Wilder. "You saw that when you hacked in?"

"Mm-hmm. Found something that talked about how much Vitamin D they're giving her to make up for the lack of real sunlight."

"But you don't know where exactly?"

"Nope. There's farmland everywhere."

"Can you find out a more specific location?"

"Nope."

Wilder groaned in frustration. "It's going to take me years to figure out where they have her hidden. And who knows what they'll throw at her in the meantime?"

"You don't have years," Luke said. He stopped typing, swiveling back toward Wilder. "They're moving her to another country at the end of this season, where it's cheaper to film and your mother's law firm can't hound them about silly things like civil rights. They've already built the set, but I couldn't find where it is. Like I said, their cyber-security is insane, and they're careful to keep their secrets secret. If you want to find her and tell her the truth so you can have your happy fairytale ending, you have to do it fast."

Wilder pulled at his hair, frustrated. He was the one who'd messed up the plan to get Grey out. He had to fix this.

"What if you were at the studio?" Wilder asked. "Could you get inside their system then?"

Luke shrugged. "Maybe, but I don't care enough about spoilers and I don't care enough about you. Sorry, but I've probed enough to know that these guys are not messing around. Monroe Studios is just a television studio, but there's some scary stuff going on there, man."

Wilder cared enough. "Do you think I could do it? Am I good enough if I'm on site?"

"Maybe. You're better than you think you are, but I don't know. Even on site, it will be hard."

Luke didn't have much more advice to give him, but as he was leaving, Wilder tried Carly one more time. She'd left Abe's lap to investigate the plate of muffins.

"Abe's a good guy," he said, coming up behind her.

"Well, now that I have your approval, I'm good to go," she said, whirling around to face him.

"Are you ever going to forgive me for leaving?"

Carly took a bite out of her muffin and shook her head. "Nope."

Wilder took the bus home. As he made his way down the aisle, he ignored the blatant staring of people who recognized him. He didn't look like his virtual avatar on the show, but Monroe Studios loved using him in commercials and media tours, and he had an army of social media followers.

He dropped into one of the threadbare seats closer to the back, dumping his bag next to him.

Rubbing his face with both hands, he suddenly heard Grey's voice speaking behind him. The person behind him must be watching the show on his phone or tablet. Why wasn't he using his headphones? People were starting to turn back to look at Wilder, thinking it was him who was playing out the scene, and he could feel his face turning red.

Despite himself, however, he couldn't help but lean back against his seat to hear better.

"What did you just say?" Grey's voice asked.

"It's Shakespeare," LeMarc's voice answered, a few notes deeper than Wilder's own. He smiled to himself. This was the first time he'd met Grey, though she'd known LeMarc before. Their families had been nemeses forever.

He remembered the thrill of that first meeting. Grey had been just as witty and beautiful as she'd always seemed from the television screen, not giving him an ounce. He'd quoted some sappy Shakespeare line at her, and she wasn't having it.

"I know it's *Romeo and Juliet*, I'm not an idiot," she'd answered back. "But I fail to see how some cheesy line about torches is applicable in this situation."

"Two foolish youths of rival families, meeting by chance one evening? I thought *Romeo and Juliet* was appropriate."

It was nighttime, one of Grey's runs down by the river, and LeMarc "stumbled" across her on his evening jog. It was the perfect setting for a romantic night: fireflies buzzing drowsily, the sweet perfume of honeysuckle and lilac hanging in the air, the steady lapping of the river meeting the bank.

Of course, Grey hadn't been in the mood for romance.

"Not a book with a happy ending. I'm pretty sure it has a higher body count than most of my action novels." Her brown hair was tied in a knot at the nape of her neck, with a few strands pulling loose in a way that knotted Wilder's stomach.

"That's my kind of romance," he joked, and when she laughed, he knew he'd done it, wiggled his way in.

"Are you walking down here alone?" he asked. "Weren't you kidnapped last year or something?"

Her next words struck him right to the heart, and Wilder closed his eyes as he heard it playing from behind him on the bus.

"I'm always alone," she said quietly.

Wilder had known exactly what to say.

"Not anymore."

He'd thought she'd fall right into his arms. He'd thought they would connect over their shared loneliness, and she'd never be alone again.

Instead, she rolled her eyes and told him he was the most ridiculous flirt she'd ever met, his parents were straight-up evil, and she still hadn't forgotten that he'd bullied her in the fifth grade. Then she gave him her number.

Wilder smiled at the memory. He missed her so much.

The video behind him switched to a commercial for the show's upcoming premiere. The whole season was going to be centered around this "What happened the night of LeMarc's death" storyline. As if Grey's life weren't horrible enough. The last season had ended with her waking up bloody and confused, just in time to get the news that her secret boyfriend, Collin LeMarc, had been murdered.

Pulling out his phone, Wilder shot off a text to Carly. *I'm sorry I never texted while I was gone. I missed you every day.*

After a moment, he sent another one. *You're my best friend, Car.*

He was almost home when his cell chimed with her response. *I don't have a best friend anymore.*

How was it that he had thousands of adoring fans, but the people who knew him best despised him?

The apartments where his father lived were girded with fire escapes. They were in a posh part of town his father couldn't afford, and each balcony was laced with decorative lights or stuffed with a jungle of potted plants and vegetables. Wilder slowly climbed the escape, keeping his face down low to avoid being noticed.

He slipped in easily, landing as softly as possible on his bedroom floor. He didn't want to alert his dad that he was home. He wasn't in the mood to deal with Theodore Blue tonight.

Creeping to the door, Wilder put his ear against it to listen for the tinny sound of the TV.

When he had first gotten back from his time on *The Real Life*, knocking on the door like a stranger, he'd been astonished at his father's sappy grin and bear hug.

"It's good to see you, kid." His dad had grabbed his duffel and pulled him onto the couch. "Tell me about being a TV star."

Wilder had gotten about five minutes in before his dad had asked him about the money. When he found out it was in a fund Wilder couldn't get to until he turned eighteen next year...

Wilder shuddered at the memory. He'd inherited his father's shiny charm, but there was something darker beneath his dad's polished haircut and polo shirt.

Listening at the door, Wilder couldn't hear any movement. Relieved, he sank onto his bed, curling into himself like he'd been punched in the stomach. What a terrible, awful day.

He rolled over and pulled his cell out of his pocket. There was another text, this time from the studio: *You have not posted anything to social media in six days. Your contract is very specific, Mr. Blue.*

According to his contract, Wilder had to keep up an active social media presence for a full year after he left the show. The text was right, too: the contract was specific, identifying how often, on which platforms, and even how many shirtless pics he needed to post. Mussing up his hair, he pulled his shirt off and snapped a photo.

It's only 5:00, but I'm ready for bed. What should I dream about? he posted. Let his fangirls have fun with that.

Unable to stop himself, he pulled up the video of LeMarc and Grey the bus rider had been watching earlier.

"I'm always alone," Grey said, looking out over the water. The camera, hidden on a nearby lamppost, had caught the glint of moonlight in her eyes.

As the LeMarc on the screen gave his answer, his gaze never leaving Grey's face, Wilder said his answer aloud as well.

"Me too, Grey," he whispered. "Me too."

MAJOR SCOOP: Photos of
Yusuf and Grey in the rain
<u>CLICK HERE</u> to see!

MondullahOTP

They look sooooo good
together!

GREYWATCH

Grey

4

The mountains of trauma Grey had encountered in her life had taught her one important thing: Ice cream can fix anything.

"Okay, I'll give it to you. That boy is *fine*," Ellie said, glancing through the front window toward the ice cream counter, where Yusuf was serving a little girl. Grey, Ellie, and Kamilla had selected a seat out on the sun-soaked patio, where they had a clear view of Yusuf but he couldn't hear their gossip.

It was a gorgeous day, with a slight breeze ushering in the scent of freshly mown grass. Even in her gray woolen uniform, Grey could feel the occasional whisper of wind tickling the hair on the back of her neck.

"Yusuf is a really nice guy," Grey said noncommittally.

Kamilla snorted. "Nice? A boy looks like that, Grey, and you don't worry about his personality."

After observing the electricity between Grey and Yusuf during Chem class, Ellie had called an emergency ice cream meeting after school, and Kamilla had invited herself along. Ellie had squealed at the promised reconciliation between her two best friends, but Grey wasn't so sure. United dread in the face of an anonymous terrorizer wasn't exactly the foundation for a solid relationship.

But Ellie was clueless about the texts, so Grey prepped herself for an hour of needling about Martha's Cones' dreamy new hire. They'd all been surprised to see Yusuf with a part-time job; his father was CEO of Starlight Mobile, and they were richer than a three-layer chocolate cake.

Grey considered him through the window as she absently licked the dripping trails of mint chocolate chip heading toward her hand. Yusuf was nice, and gorgeous in a way that made her stomach queasy. But feeling like this about a guy so soon after losing LeMarc made her feel queasy in a whole different way.

Yusuf caught her eye in the window and made a face, and Grey laughed, her face warming.

Ellie rolled her eyes. "That was embarrassing. You deserve it, though, for gawking. Ew. Even the word *gawking* is gross."

Kamilla wiped at her face with a napkin. "Yusuf doesn't seem to mind, though. I don't get why you don't just ask him out. You're clearly into each other."

Grey widened her eyes at her meaningfully. Kamilla of all people should know *exactly* why Grey wasn't making a move on Yusuf.

The wind picked up suddenly, and Ellie yelped as their napkins flew off the table. Grey hopped up to grab them, trying to balance her massive cone so it didn't splat on the ground.

She returned to her seat and tucked the napkins under the metal dispenser. "I've got more important things to worry about than boys."

"Like how you're going to explain your student council abdication to your mother?"

Ellie leaned forward, her eyes sparking. "Ooo, yes, drama! What will Astrid Monroe do when her perfect daughter has a breakdown in front of the whole school?"

"It wasn't a *breakdown*, and it was in front of like, twelve people."

Ellie swiped away Grey's defense with a wave of her hand. "Irregardless, you can't—"

"Regardless," Kamilla interrupted. "Irregardless isn't a word."

Ellie's side-eye game was unmatched. "*Regardless*, I for one am *more* than excited that this little student council spat has brought my two best friends back together. I wasn't looking forward to playing referee between you two all senior year."

Kamilla grinned. "I'm sure Astrid wouldn't mind your tantrum at today's meeting so much if she knew the heir of Starlight Mobile was crushing on you."

Grey let out an angry breath. "Kamilla, can I talk to you in private for a moment?"

Ellie's eyes widened. "You two aren't going to fight again, are you? I *just* said I don't want to be in the middle anymore."

"Now?" Grey said, standing. She knew there was an edge to her voice, and she fought to calm her rising frustration. What was wrong with her? She usually had more control.

Kamilla shrugged and stood, and the two girls walked several paces away, tossing their ice cream into the bin. Kamilla led her to an isolated spot near the corner of the building while Ellie stared after them.

As soon as they stopped, Grey folded her arms. "What are you doing? Why are you pushing this Yusuf thing? LeMarc died just a few months ago."

Kamilla shrugged. "Yusuf seems like a good guy. Maybe he can help you get over LeMarc."

"*Get over him*?" Grey couldn't even believe what she was hearing. Her throat felt swollen, like she'd swallowed a Lego. "I can't... That's not even... How can you say that? Did you get over Danny that fast?"

"Of course not. I loved your brother. Breaking his heart, breaking *my own* heart, was the hardest thing I've ever done."

Kamilla had been in *love* with Danny? And Grey had missed all the clues, right under her nose. She'd been so distracted by LeMarc, she'd stopped paying attention.

"But," Kamilla continued, "the last thing he said to me is that he wanted me to be happy. I know LeMarc would say the same thing to you, if he were able."

Tears sprung up in Grey's eyes, pools of frustration and anger—and guilt. "Whoever's sending these texts clearly doesn't think so."

Kamilla jutted out her chin. "Whoever is sending these texts is a monster. So let's prove them wrong. Let's figure out who really killed Collin LeMarc."

"You think we should solve his murder?"

It wouldn't bring him back, Grey knew that, but maybe if she could put together the broken pieces of what happened that night, she could start putting together the broken pieces of herself. "How would we do that?"

"We could start with whoever is sending these texts. Clearly they know something about what happened that night."

Grey pulled out her phone and pulled up *Lucy from Algebra*. The last text glared at her from the screen: *You have until the Christmas gala to tell the truth, or I won't be the only corpse in this town.*

She began typing, her thumbs tracing across the screen.

"What are you doing?"

"Texting back," Grey said through gritted teeth just as she clicked *send*.

This wasn't a plea for more information like her previous texts, or a scared denial of a truth she couldn't remember. It was a promise.

I didn't kill you, but I'm going to find out who did.

Kamilla leaned over the phone, reading the text. A grim smile spread across her face. "That's more like it. Do we tell Ellie?"

They looked over at Ellie, who was watching them both. The wind had picked up away from the shelter of the building, and it was whipping Ellie's long hair into a blonde plume.

"No," Grey said. "We don't. I don't want her to get caught up in this."

"Agreed."

They made their way back over to Ellie, and as soon as they left the shelter of the restaurant's wall, the wind hit them like a hurricane blast.

"What is with this wind?" Kamilla asked as they sat back down at the table.

The sky was growing dark, too, thick with clouds that hadn't existed minutes ago.

Grey eyed the dramatic sky. "I guess summer finally gave up the fight."

"You two are friends still, right?" Ellie asked, her face tight.

Kamilla shrugged. "More or less."

"So it's official! The glamour girls are back!"

Kamilla and Grey both groaned at the old nickname, but Ellie just smiled.

A few drops of rain plopped onto Grey's arm.

"Is it raining?" she called out, her words catching on the wind. "Seriously?"

She pulled out her phone to search for the weather forecast.

Ellie shrugged, seemingly as confused as Grey. It *never* rained here. It was undeniable, however. The rate of drops was increasing, leaving dark dots like chicken pox all over the patio cement. "Let's go inside to wait it out."

As Grey began towards the door of the restaurant, however, a flash of lightning lit up the sky like a flashbulb and the deluge started. A great crack of thunder pealed through the air a few seconds later, like the sky was ripping apart. The rain was sudden and unrelenting, sheets of it pouring down like a waterfall.

Cars driving by switched on their headlights, their underutilized windshield wipers jerking back and forth furiously.

Ellie shrieked as lightning struck the lamppost nearest them, the great boom of thunder sounding simultaneously. The bulb exploded like a firework.

As cold water sluiced down Grey's neck, she was suddenly thankful for the pleated skirt and knee socks St. John's Prep School forced its students to wear. She could count the number of times it had rained in Heringford on one finger.

Kamilla grabbed Grey's arm, ready to pull her into the ice cream shop. But a flash from Grey's phone caught her eye, a text from LeMarc's number, and she hesitated a few feet away from the doorway.

It was a response to the message she'd sent. The messenger had never responded before.

You don't remember what you did? Let me remind you.

A picture appeared underneath it, a photograph of LeMarc's body. His usually lively green eyes were staring, his face chalk-white and dribbled with blood.

The picture hit her like a hurricane, a wild assault of wind and clamor. Grey choked, sick rushing up her throat. She whirled around to find Kamilla, but her friend was already inside next to Ellie, shooting her an incredulous look from the other side of the glass.

Come inside, she mouthed, gesturing at Grey.

Grey shook her head and turned away, breathing hard. The rain poured down, but no amount of water could wash away the thick, heavy scent of blood in her nostrils, the tiny ripples of evil crawling over her skin.

Hands suddenly grabbed her from behind. She screamed, elbowing her assailant.

"Ah, Grey, that hurt."

She spun back around. Yusuf was standing there in the rain, his hair pasted to his forehead in a shiny black mat. He was rubbing his ribs with his other hand, giving her a rueful expression. Though it was Yusuf's face, all she saw was LeMarc, crumpled and waxy and *gone*.

She put a hand on Yusuf's shoulder to keep herself from sliding to her knees. "I'm so sorry. I didn't realize it was you."

"Clearly." Yusuf put his hand over hers where she was touching his shoulder. "Are you okay? The expression on your face, when you looked back at us in the shop, it was so *devastated*. I wanted to make sure you were all right."

The feel of his hand on hers felt like the only thing keeping her standing, and suddenly she couldn't keep the tears in. "I'm sorry," she repeated. "I'm just…"

She trailed off, her words dissolving into a puddle at her feet. Tears tracked down her cheeks.

Yusuf wrapped his arms around her, and she pressed her face against his shoulder. "LeMarc is dead," she said, her voice muffled.

"Yeah." His voice broke on the word.

Grey knew Kamilla and Ellie were watching from the ice cream parlor, but for the first time she didn't care what people thought. Yusuf's arms around her made her feel safe for the first time since LeMarc's death.

"I miss him."

He squeezed her tighter. "So do I."

She remained in his arms for a moment longer, relishing the warmth that spread through her. And then she pulled back out of his arms. "I'm sorry," she said for a third time. "I don't usually fall apart like this."

He smiled sadly, the rain running down his face in rivulets. "Maybe you should."

She bit her lip, glancing down at his lime green apron. "Quite the first day of work for you, huh?"

His smile widened into a more genuine one. "My dad said I needed to get a job to 'learn the value of money and the importance of hard work.' I thought it was going to be miserable, but I'm realizing there are some advantages."

His eyes twinkled as he looked at her.

"Oh?" she choked out.

He held her gaze for a moment, and she felt a flip in her stomach, jarring in her grief. "Mm-hmm."

Her cheeks warmed.

"I'm talking about the free ice cream, of course," Yusuf laughed.

A battle raged in her mind: She was experiencing all the sensations of nervous excitement—the butterflies in the stomach, sweaty palms, and blushing cheeks—but it was like an image superimposed on her grief. Her mind was still frozen with sadness, even while Yusuf's words slid down easily.

Her body was trying to push her towards healing while her mind still clung to the pain. But she didn't really *feel* it. Not in a way that mattered.

"So, as much as I love standing here getting drenched, can I entice you inside with another cone?"

Grey nodded. "Make it a mint chocolate chip and you're on."

❧

The rain cleared up quickly, so after another half hour Grey headed home to face her mother's anger. Her uniform was sopping, making her car smell like wet, moldy wool. The whole ride home, she practiced her speech trying to articulate why she quit the student council to her mother, desperate to think about something other than the photo on her phone. Or her commitment to Kamilla to track down a violent killer. Or whatever that flip of her stomach had meant when she was talking to Yusuf.

Ugh. Clearly the distraction wasn't helping. Her mother would be furious, but the words and phrases that might temper her anger were proving to be slippery. By the time Grey reached the marbled grand entrance of the house, she still didn't know what she was going to say.

As she entered, she heard music playing from upstairs. "Mom, is that you?" she called out, heading toward the noise. Sharon, their new housekeeper, often listened to music while she worked, but she had her Pilates class this afternoon.

The Monroe home was a behemoth of marble and gold and creamy lush carpets, an ostentatious display of wealth. As she headed back to the staircase through the main living room, she ducked around a grand piano and giant portraits of each family member.

As always, she paused to run a few fingers over Danny's.

"Mom?

When she got to her mother's room, the music was playing from behind the closed door. She was just raising her hand to knock when she was startled by a tall man with a mop of red hair. He opened the door, his flaming hair incongruent against the dusty roses of her mother's bedroom.

"Oh," Grey said, her face warming.

The man was her mother's usual type: young, muscular, and smarmy. A redhead was new. Usually her mom liked dark-haired men. Her mom's flavor of the week this week had blue eyes, brighter than she'd ever seen. The grin he gave her now made her skin crawl.

"You must be Grey," the man said over the music. "Astrid, you never told me your daughter was so beautiful."

The music turned off, and then Grey's mother appeared in a cloud of perfume and white silk. *The picture of a perfect housewife,* Grey thought, giving her mother the evil eye.

"Grey, Henry and I were just discussing the upcoming gala," her mother said.

Grey gave Henry another once-over. His hair was standing straight up. "Right."

"See you soon," he called out to Grey as her mother walked him down the stairs.

"Unbelievable," Grey said to the empty hallway.

She found her mother alone in the kitchen a few minutes later, pouring a glass of wine. "Seriously, Mom?" she asked, grabbing a juice from the fridge and perching herself on a hand-carved stool at the island. "He can't have been older than twenty. And what about Dad?"

"Twenty-seven, actually," her mother answered. "Though I don't see what Henry's age has to do with anything. Oscar knows perfectly well that Henry is helping me prepare for the gala this December. And what did you do to your hair? It's all limp and windblown."

Grey sighed. Of course her mother would comment on her hair. "It got wet in the rain."

Her mother looked out the window dubiously. The sun was streaming through like rays from heaven. "The rain, sweetheart?"

"Yeah, the rain. As in the freak storm that showed up out of nowhere to drop a river onto Main Street while I was at the ice cream parlor. It was crazy."

Her mother rolled her eyes. "Your ability to turn a common rainstorm into Homer's epic is astounding."

"But seriously, Mom, I wish you'd take dad's feelings into consideration sometimes. Any time. One time, even, would be nice."

Astrid flipped her blown-out hair over one shoulder and sipped her wine, leaning against the counter. "My little Grey goose. Always so serious. But I'd rather talk about the call I got from Tracy Emerson today about you resigning as student body president."

Grey grimaced. "Right. That. Well, I've been feeling a little over-whelmed lately, and I thought I could do with one less thing on my plate."

"Do you want to know what *I* find overwhelming? That my daughter lost her mind in the middle of school and started yelling at the son of Randolph Milkins."

"You literally got into a catfight with a woman at her *son's funeral*."

"The Milkins are on the board of your father's company. They're some of our biggest investors. We can't afford to lose their support."

"So to be clear, you don't care that I lost it, you just care who I lost it in front of."

"That's not what I said."

"That's exactly what you said."

Grey's mother set down her wine glass. "Fine. Why are you over-whelmed?"

Grey froze. "What?"

"You said you were overwhelmed, and then you whined about me not caring, so this is me caring. Why are you overwhelmed?"

Grey played with her juice bottle, shifting uncomfortably on her stool. "There's just a lot of stuff going on for me right now."

"Such as..."

"Well, I've been having some memory issues, I guess. There's a pocket of time... Have you ever blacked out time before?"

Grey's mother snorted, pouring another glass of wine. "Honey, that's a normal Tuesday for me."

"Mom, I'm serious."

Her mom let out a sigh. "How are your sessions with Dr. Hawks going?"

"I'm not crazy."

"The new school year must be stressful, right? And what happened this morning at your student council meeting adds pressure as well."

"I don't need *fixing*."

"Of course not. But here's what's going to happen. Your principal said even though you can't simply un-resign as president after this morning's outburst, he will allow for a reelection. So you'll get started on your campaign, and I'll call Deborah and see if we can't squeeze in an additional session this week."

Grey wanted to scream. "Fine. I will do an extra therapy session and I'll even go through an entire new election for the student body president job I already won if you promise not to bring the redhead around anymore."

Her mother took another sip. "We'll see."

At Grey's frown, she added, "I said *we'll see*, Grey, not no. Stop frowning so much. You're going to give yourself wrinkles."

Wilder

5

The next week passed in a blur. Wilder skipped class the whole week. He wasn't ready to go back to his normal life, and somehow the muted despair of Washington High School didn't hold much appeal. He was able to intercept the attendance calls to his father, so the consequences of his truancy hadn't hit yet.

On Friday night, Wilder took a bus across town. After what Carly had said, it was high time he visited his little sister, Lana.

He climbed the back way up to his mom's apartment using the fire escape and peered through the window. His sister was on the couch, but no sign of Angie, the usual sitter.

He tried the window, dismayed to find it unlocked. It made his life easier, but it worried him that his mom and sister were living alone and not taking basic security precautions.

The window slid open without a sound. Wilder slipped through, landing like a cat on the plush carpet. With barely a whisper of noise, he crept toward his sister.

Lana was illuminated blue and yellow in the light of a tablet screen, clutching a pillow and wrapped up like a little croissant in a blue fleece blanket. She flinched, and Wilder's gaze followed hers to the movie flashing across the tablet, a horror flick way too scary for a seven-year-old. Even as he watched, a woman was cut clean in two by a chainsaw-wielding murderer. And that was using the term "clean" lightly.

"I can hear you, you know," Lana said. Wilder started. His sister wasn't as absorbed in the horror film as he had thought.

"No, you can't," he argued, snatching the tablet out of his sister's hand from behind the couch. "I'm a ninja. I'm trained in the art of moving like a shadow, silent in the darkness."

Lana snorted. "Silent as night, maybe," she said, jumping from the couch to wrap her arms around him.

Silent as night. His mother used to say that to him when he was a child, laughing at the chorus of crickets and the cars that sped too quickly past their house late in the evening. Just like him, the nighttime couldn't seem to turn down the noise when it was supposed to.

Wilder hugged his sister as hard as he could. He'd missed her so much. "Where's Angie?"

"She had to leave at eight," Lana answered. "She stayed for a while after and tried calling Mom, but she never got an answer so she went home." She leaned back to look up at him. "Why didn't you come earlier?"

"I had to lay low at the studio headquarters in the dorms until the premiere. The studio wanted to make sure I didn't spill any secrets."

Any more secrets, he corrected silently.

"You've been back two weeks, though," Lana insisted. "I saw you on TV."

"I'm sorry I've been gone so long, but I missed you so, so much."

"Never disappear and become famous again, okay?"

Wilder held out his pinky, and she hooked hers into his. "Pinky promise."

"It's pinky *swear*," she corrected. "You're so dumb sometimes."

Shaking his head, Wilder stood back up, looking around. The apartment hadn't changed much since he'd left. Same mocha color on the walls, same clean, modern style of furniture. The apartment was small, but nice, and he couldn't help but compare it in his head to the one he shared with his dad.

"So anything exciting happen while I was gone?" he called out, wandering into the kitchen to peek into the fridge. He grabbed a pear and bit into it. Juice squirted out, dousing his fingers in sugary syrup.

"Mom made an office," Lana answered.

Wilder wrinkled his brow in confusion. "Here in the apartment?"

Lana nodded. "Yup! It's your old room."

"Oh." Wilder set the pear down on the counter, no longer hungry.

He shouldn't be upset. He was the one who'd asked to live with his dad in the first place. He'd needed to, to audition for the show. They never would have cast the son of their leading opposition if they didn't think he hated her.

Wilder plopped down on the couch next to Lana, tugging on her blanket. She curled up into him, wrapping the fleece to encompass him, too. He grabbed her tablet away before she could press play again.

"Can I have my movie back?" she asked, her muffled voice rising from the folds of the blanket.

"No. It's too scary for me," he said, yawning. "Let's watch something else."

"We can watch Grey!" Lana said, her head popping up out of the blankets.

Wilder raised his eyebrows. "Mom lets you watch that show?" he asked, knowing the answer already.

Lana smirked. "I'm big enough that I can watch whatever I want. And it was the only way I could see you."

Wilder kissed the top of his sister's head. "I'm never going to leave again."

"Until Mom gets home, at least."

When had she gotten to be so smart?

As the familiar intro music began to play, Wilder settled back on the sofa. The season premiere had started with the most over-the-top funeral smackdown Wilder could have imagined, footage from last spring, and then jumped to the first day of school. He felt a lurch in his stomach as he remembered the way Grey had looked at this Yusuf guy during the ice cream shop scene, like he was Apollo carting around the sun.

Wilder had watched a few of the actor's interviews, and he seemed like a jerk in real life.

Tonight's episode started off in the office of Grey's therapist, Deborah Hawks. The show runners had probably hoped, when they first introduced Dr. Hawks, that Grey would open up and the viewers would get a glimpse into her thoughts and fears, but that hadn't happened at all. Instead, Hawks had become the show's subtle antagonist, facing off against Grey in an intellectual and emotional battle. Dr. Hawks would push, and Grey would dance blithely away. Dr. Hawks would pull, and Grey would spin out of reach of her questions and assertions.

"You've missed your last few appointments," Dr. Hawks said, adjusting her glasses. "And your mom mentioned blackouts? Maybe we should start with your ordeal in student council. Tell me what happened."

Grey smiled, and even Wilder, who knew her so well, felt it looked genuine. She was good. "Yes, of course!" Grey said. "Thank you so much for your advice on seizing the opportunities this school year provided. It gave me the courage to really reflect on my future and not spend my attention and energy on activities that don't stir my passions. Your counsel gave me the courage to leave behind the familiar and explore the unknown."

Deborah Hawks choked out a laugh. "You're saying it's my fault you resigned as student body president?"

Grey didn't flinch. "I'll be sure to let my mother know to thank you, Dr. Hawks."

Hawks wisely decided to change the subject. "And how about boys? Any prospects there?"

This was the real reason for the scene, of course, and Wilder knew all of the show's viewers were waiting to see what Grey would say about Yusuf. He was in three of her classes, and the show had been pushing hard in the press about his potential as Grey's next love interest.

"We don't have to watch this if you don't want to," Lana said as Grey took a moment to consider the question.

Wilder didn't answer, just watched as Grey said, "You never know. There's a guy who's piqued my interest, I guess. And as I said before, maybe it's time for me to explore the unknown."

Wilder paused the video and pushed off from the couch, sending Lana rolling backwards. He paced back and forth a few times, trying to burn off the frustration. With an opener like that, this episode would definitely be all about Yusuf and his ridiculously perfect hair, and he didn't think he could handle watching him *pique Grey's interest* for the next fifty minutes.

"Please don't break my tablet," Lana said, and Wilder realized he had the thing in a death grip.

"I'm sorry. I just wasn't expecting her to fall in love with another guy so quickly."

He handed the device back to his sister, and she studied the screen, the little smile on Grey's paused face.

"She's not in love with him," Lana said.

"Oh, and you're a seven-year-old expert in love, now?" Wilder asked, dropping back down onto the couch.

Lana crossed her arms. "I've got a boyfriend, which is more than you have. Johnny Mink and I got married yesterday at recess."

"Poor kid. Give him my condolences."

Lana wriggled into him again, wrapping her arms around him. "If you love Grey so much, why don't you just find her and ask her to marry you? She'd say yes, I think."

He missed being a first-grader. Everything was so simple, so easy.

"Can I tell you a secret?" Wilder whispered. Lana nodded eagerly. "I'm too young to marry Grey, but I am going to find her. I'm going to visit her and tell her that I love her and that her world isn't real, and then I'm going to find her in real life and carry her off into the sunset. Just like in the movies."

Lana giggled. "Are you going to kiss her again? You guys kissed *a lot*."

The next few minutes were exactly what he expected: way too much of this new guy.

The only surprise was a new housekeeper, which set Wilder's mind whirring. Grey's housekeeper was the only cast regular who was real on set, cleaning and cooking in person.

Which meant the *old* housekeeper, Victoria Price, knew where the complex was.

Wilder excused himself, saying he needed to go to the bathroom. Instead, he crept towards his old bedroom, now his mom's office.

Walking down the hall to his old bedroom, Wilder couldn't help but notice that all of the family photos in the hallway with him in them had been taken down.

His bedroom looked completely different. The walls were the same color, navy blue, but the posters and sports trophies and bed were gone. In their place, bookshelves full of law books and philosophy texts lined the back wall. A giant desk sat in the corner where his bed used to be, stacked with papers and folders. There was even a nook with a bronze lamp and a plush leather chair for the late nights he knew his mother was spending, poring over case law and theories of morality.

His mother had spent years fighting against Monroe Studios, collecting information. Maybe she had info on the housekeeper. His mom had to have *something* in her files that would help him find Grey. Most of her work would be at the law office, but she'd kept plenty of files at home even before she had a whole office to house them.

The desk drawer didn't have anything good, just a few folders. He flipped through some binders in the bookcase, but didn't see anything useful, so he turned to the filing cabinet in the corner. It was locked, but Wilder knew his mom always kept keys to things under plants so she wouldn't lose them.

Sure enough, the orchid on top of the filing cabinet was hiding the key.

He flipped through the hanging folders, looking for something useful. Suddenly, a folder name caught his eye.

"There you are," he muttered to himself, pulling out the folder labeled *Victoria Price* and thumbing through it.

There wasn't any contact information for Victoria in the file, but Wilder found the name and address of someone with the same last name, Lillian Price.

"Gotcha," he whispered. He wanted to take a picture to remember it, but the company had bought him this phone, and he wasn't sure how much access they had to his photos. Instead, he grabbed a post-it and pen from his mother's desk and wrote out the address by hand.

Wilder had just barely settled back into the couch next to Lana when he heard a key in the lock.

"Mom's home!" Lana called, clearing *The Real Life* from the tablet screen. Wilder tried to run for the window, but he wasn't fast enough. He was only halfway through when he heard his mother's voice behind him.

"Wilder," she said sternly, placing her bag and keys on the counter. "What are you doing here?"

He swore and climbed out of the window, pulling his long legs back inside the apartment. "I wanted to see Lana. And you should be glad I did, or your seven-year-old daughter would have been home alone at nine o'clock in the evening. She said Angie left an hour ago."

"I got caught up at the office."

"Well, I know you work hard protecting Grey, but there's another little girl here who might like to see her mother occasionally."

"I do not need a parenting lecture from my teenage son. I happened to be working on an abuse case tonight. A ten-year-old boy. What I do is important."

"And Lana isn't?"

Her jaw tightened. "Why don't we go talk in my office?" She looked pointedly at Lana, who was staring up at them with big eyes.

When they entered the room, Wilder's mom sat down at her desk while he hovered by the door. She was tall, just like him, with thick dark hair, different from Wilder and Lana's blonde. Wilder had her eyes, though, the irises so blue people thought he wore colored contacts. Right now hers were fixed on him, and he'd never felt smaller. LeMarc's death might have happened on a TV show, but Wilder had the feeling his mother wished she could make fiction into reality.

"So, I'm back," he said.

His mother's jaw tightened.

"I guess I owe you an apology."

"Do you?" Her voice was so thin, it cut him like a wire.

"I probably could have given you some warning when I auditioned for the show," he admitted. Or when he'd gotten callbacks, all six rounds. Or when he'd been cast. Or when he'd started the press tour. There were a lot of times that he probably should have called his mother.

There was a long pause, and when his mother spoke again, he gained a new-found compassion for all of the criminals who had ever been cross-examined by her. "I'm curious. Do you know how I found out that my son was cast as the star of the show I've been fighting against for its entire existence?"

"No."

"I was at the office," she continued, still sitting in her chair, drumming her hands against a book on her desk, "right in the middle of explaining to my boss that these lawsuits we keep bringing against Monroe Studios are a worthy use of my Pro Bono hours because that studio is full of snakes and demons. And he kindly informed me that my son was, in fact, one of those snakes and demons. He'd seen you on TV that morning. I was... taken aback, you might say."

"That must have been an uncomfortable situation," Wilder said carefully, digging into the carpet with his toe.

His mother's face remained stone cold. "Why are you here, Wilder?"

He swallowed. Now was his chance to tell his mother the truth about why he'd signed up for the show. Why he'd lied. But he had a question to ask her first. "I thought, maybe, now that I'm back..."

He almost lost his courage halfway through, but when his mother remained silent, he continued. "I was thinking maybe I could move back in with you. Things are a little strained at Dad's place," he said quickly, powering through it.

His mother stood up, walking to the front of her desk and leaning back against it. Slowly. Deliberately. She was in full-on lawyer mode now.

"Tell me, Wilder, did you or did you not run off to live with your degenerate father without so much as a word of explanation or warning?"

"Yes, but—"

"And then did you audition for the very show I've been fighting against, for no apparent reason other than to spite me?"

"It wasn't to spite you," Wilder interjected. "I had a good reason."

His mother continued as though she hadn't heard him. "And now you're back, and you want to move in? Do you feel like there will be *less* strain here than with your father?"

Wilder took a few steps closer so he was just in front of her. "Mom, you're acting like I killed somebody or something. I was an *actor*. It's just a TV show."

It was the wrong thing to say.

She grabbed some papers off of her desk in her fist. "Just a TV show? Do you want to know what I've been researching this week?" She waved the papers in his face. "When Grey was just three years old, before the show began, we believe the studio used fear conditioning on her. They hooked that little girl up to a machine that stimulated the fear sensors in her brain and showed her pictures about travel. They terrified her over and over again, just so she wouldn't ever ask to leave. You know what else that's called, Wilder?"

Wilder shook his head mutely, feeling the tears prick at his eyes. *Oh, Grey*, he thought.

His mother continued, practically spitting in his face. "The other word for fear conditioning is torture. They *tortured* a little girl. These people, Wilder, they're evil. And you... you're their leading man."

Wilder tucked his hands under his elbows to stop himself from throwing them over his ears. He felt like an innocent man on trial, standing mute while his accusers spit out a litany of lies from the stand. He couldn't seem to form the words to defend himself. "I never... You don't understand, I was trying to help her. You know I'm not like that. I never tortured Grey. I was going to—"

"You never tortured her?" his mother interrupted, scoffing. "You *seduced* her, Wilder. LeMarc isn't real, but Grey's feelings were.

They might have manipulated some brain functions to mimic the physical sensations of a crush at first, but it was much more than that by the end. You made her fall in love with a mirage, a bit of augmented reality. And then she had to deal with the murder of the boy she loved and the trauma of not remembering what happened. That's psychological torture, clear as day."

"I didn't know they were going to kill me off," Wilder said in a small voice, but that wasn't true. He'd known they'd never let him live, not after what he did. He'd never thought that they'd kill LeMarc, though. Just recast him, find someone new to pick up where he left off. Grey would never have known.

"I had a plan," he insisted.

Wilder's mother rubbed her face with her hands. She looked so tired, Wilder thought, so sad. Just like Grey. "I have spent over a decade watching the studio throw trauma after trauma at this girl to boost ratings. A friend in a coma. A brother missing in action. For goodness' sake, she was *kidnapped* last year by her half-brother. I have spent all that time watching and fighting and *losing*."

And it was just going to get worse. After that first episode, what if they convinced Grey she'd really killed LeMarc? Who was the studio planning to make into the villain?

His mother shook her head, then delivered the final blow. "I don't want to hear your explanations or your excuses. I think it's best that you continue staying with your father. Moreover, I don't think you should come to visit anymore. At least for now."

Wilder felt the flush rising on his neck, the anger surging. "I'm not going to stop visiting Lana. She's my sister. You might not want to see me, but she does."

"Just get out, Wilder."

"No!" Lana cried, streaming into the room. She wrapped her arms around him, and he pulled her in for the hug.

"Lana, go to your room," their mother said. "It's time for bed."

Lana buried her face in Wilder's shirt. "No," she said, voice muffled.

Wilder rolled his eyes when his mother turned to him expectantly. "What if I visit once a week, while you're at work? I would be gone by the time you get back. You wouldn't need to see me or even think about me."

"Lana, go to your room!" his mom commanded. Lana threw her a look of pure venom and ran down the hallway, slamming the door to her room behind her.

Wilder and his mom glared at each other. "Just give me a chance to—"

"I don't want to hear it."

"Fine," he said, shrugging and walking to the door. "I'm leaving." If she didn't want him here, he didn't need her, either.

Just as he was about to leave, she called out his name again.

"What?"

"I've gotten five calls from Washington High this week. One for each day that you missed class. I better not get one on Monday."

"Whatever," he said, slamming the door behind him just like his sister had. He had completely forgotten that they would call *both* parents every time he skipped, not just his dad.

As soon as Wilder got home, he watched the rest of the episode. He knew he shouldn't, but he couldn't help himself. Yusuf carried Grey's books to class in two scenes, sat at her table at lunch every day, and convinced her to put up a fight against Todd Milkins to save her spot as student body president.

When he brushed her hair behind her ear by her locker, Wilder threw his phone against the room and it hit the wall with a dull thud.

After a moment, his bedroom door burst open and his dad slammed through it, bloodshot eyes tracking straight to the phone.

"I'm sorry," Wilder said quickly. "My phone slipped out of my hand. I didn't mean to wake you."

His dad walked over to where the phone was lying on the floor, and in a deliberate lunge, he smashed his heel against it. He smashed his foot down onto the phone again and again until it was a mangled wreck on the floor.

Then without a word he returned to his room.

It could have been worse, Wilder thought as he picked up the remains of his phone from the floor.

He pulled out his computer to watch the last few minutes of the episode, but he couldn't bring himself to do it. Somehow, what had seemed like a compulsion earlier now felt like the last thing in the world he wanted to do.

Instead, he looked for information on Victoria and Lillian Price online. There was nothing, not even an embarrassing old Facebook account. The studio must have scrubbed everything.

Frustrated, he spent a few hours watching videos on how to pick locks and break through security systems. It was more important than ever that he find Grey, and in order to do that he needed access to the studio's computers.

He was going to break into Monroe Studios.

Wilder snuck out of the house in the early hours of the morning. He could hear his father's snores through the wall, but he still tiptoed, holding his breath until he was out in the open air.

The night was wrapped around the neighborhood like a pillow, smothering it until all that remained was an eerie corpse, silent as the dead. The night owl bus service only ran on the hour, so he had to wait almost a half hour at the deserted bus stop.

He waited until he'd gotten off the bus and walked to the compound's fence to make the call. Monroe Studios was a cluster of buildings huddled on the outskirts of town, a little village unto itself. The main studio was the largest building, where the actors dove into their avatars and the editors culled through hours and hours of footage each week to splice together each episode. It also included the executive offices and legal. The building was shaped like a glass shard sticking up from the ground.

To the right of the main studio were the dorms where most of the actors lived, along with some of the technicians. One of the sacrifices young actors made to work on the show was privacy; each actor got their own room and bathroom, but the studio had the right to enter any room they wished. It was also where tutors worked with all the teenagers on the show. Wilder's tutor had been Fritz Barker, who also played an English teacher on the show. Though his character was a jerk who'd had a brief fling with Grey's mom, Fritz was actually pretty cool, and a good teacher besides.

To the left of the main building was the commons, which included the cafeteria and a mailroom. The best part was the games center, with a movie theater and bowling alley and arcade. Everything a teenage actor needed to forget he was trapped within a chain-linked fence.

The other buildings included offices for psychologists, a tiny medical center, the marketing team, and several more departments. In this darkness, the buildings looked like massive foothills, sprawled across the grounds. The main studio jutted up like a jagged mountain, warning away intruders.

Because of the strong backlash to Grey's show, the studio had an armed guard and video surveillance at the main gate. The main studio also had one of the best security systems money could buy. As much as Wilder wanted to put his breaking and entering skills to the test, he knew he couldn't get in without someone on the inside. He just hoped Reggie Meyers wouldn't still be upset about his last screw-up. He'd waited until it was do-or-die time so Reggie wouldn't have time to go into his usual over-thinking mode and second-guess helping him.

Now the trick was to get him to agree to help him in the first place.

With his cell phone busted, Wilder pulled up his laptop to contact Reggie through video chat. He moved to a portion of the fence lined with bushes and crouched down on the ground, hoping the foliage would provide cover if anyone walked by. As the line rang, he held his breath, worried that Reg might not even pick up.

Reggie picked up on the third ring. His face filled Wilder's screen: rotund, hairy, and skeptical. He had a Red Bull in hand, and Wilder smiled as he thought of the evenings and nights he'd spent in Monroe Studios while Reggie chugged Red Bull after Red Bull, ranting about government conspiracies.

Reggie glared at him through the camera. "Well if it isn't Mr. Blue, paragon of discretion. Got any more secrets to blab?"

The smile fell from Wilder's face. Maybe Reg was still a *little* upset about his last screw-up.

The bulk of Reggie's responsibilities was as a developer, improving his advanced tech that allowed Monroe Studios to create avatars that reacted to the actors' brain waves in real time. His occasional temper tantrums and ravings about working as a cog in the system were overlooked due to his virtual genius.

While almost the entire team of developers worked a 9 to 5, Reggie chose to work the night shift at Monroe Studios, alone in his corner room stuffed with action figures and comic book memorabilia. Wilder was pretty sure it was *because* the rest of the programmers worked during the day that Reg worked overnights.

Since he preferred working at night so he didn't have to encounter "suits with heads attached," he also manned the tapes. Grey usually slept like the dead, but if she did wake up in the middle of the night, Reg had the skills to animate an avatar without its actor, at least enough to have them groggily tell her to go back to sleep. That way, Grey wouldn't think her parents were dead when they wouldn't wake up.

"I guess we haven't talked since I left the show," Wilder said.

"Since you left? You mean since you were canned." Reggie took a long gulp from his drink. Wilder could hear the swallow over the line. "Maybe you should have thought for two seconds before you opened your big mouth, Loverboy."

Wilder didn't respond; there was nothing to say. He'd had a plan, a good plan, to get her out. And even though Reg had refused to help and wouldn't give him access to his computer, Wilder knew he'd been cheering for him to win. Reggie was well-compensated for his work with the studio, but he chafed against the corporate machine.

Wilder was sure, if he'd been able to hold out for just a few more weeks, he would have convinced Reggie to help him save Grey.

But that was then, and this was now. Reggie had picked up the phone, but his face showed that he wasn't exactly in a listening mood.

"Reg, hear me out," he began, but he immediately interrupted him.

"You're planning something, aren't you? You seriously think I'm going to help you now, when you've proven to have absolutely no self-control?"

"I just need to get inside the gates."

"What?" Reggie cried, laughing in disbelief. "Do you have any idea how close I was to being fired when you pulled your little stunt? If the studio execs found out that I knew what you were planning... They would have sued me for so much my grandchildren would be eating dust for breakfast."

Wilder wanted to punch through his computer screen. "I get that I messed up. Just get me through the gates, Reggie."

"To do what? Why do you need to get into the studio so badly?"

"I have a plan."

"I've heard that before," Reggie said, throwing his Red Bull can into a garbage bin off-screen. "I need more than that if I'm going to risk my job here."

"Don't you want a chance to fight the system?" Wilder pleaded. "For someone who talks about standing up to *the man* so often, you sure are willing to do whatever corporate asks."

"So I'm a sellout. I need details, kid."

Wilder sighed before rattling off his arguments. "Fine. I'm going to try again. The same plan as before: go in at night, tell her the truth. You know that Mark and Jacob never do their rounds; they're playing cards in the break room for sure. They'll never see me on the security cameras, and if I can convince her..." His voice faded away as he saw the skeptical look on Reggie's face. "Look, I know it's risky. But I have to see her."

"That's the hormones talking. Aren't you famous now? You can get any girl you want."

"They're not interchangeable, you know."

Reggie rubbed his face with one hand. "What good is it if she knows the truth? Don't you think she's happier not knowing that her whole life is a lie? Are you doing this for you or for her?"

"I'm going to find her, Reggie. I'm going to figure out where they're keeping her. She's not going to be living a lie forever. It would be much easier if you just told me where she is. I know you can get access to that info."

He'd made the appeal a thousand times, but he might as well make it a thousand and one.

Reggie at least had the decency to look ashamed. "No go. I like you Wilder, and you know I agree that this show is an immoral, rotten mess, but I like the freedom I have here, and I don't want to rock the boat. I don't know where the Heringford set is located, and I'm not going to go digging it up. And if I let you in tonight, and *he* finds out, I'm in serious trouble."

Wilder sagged in disappointment. It felt like gravity was stronger than usual: He couldn't seem to keep his body from sinking right into the ground until the earth swallowed him up.

"But."

Wilder perked up.

"If I happen to need security to check something strange on the monitors at the moment someone breaks in, well, that's not my fault, is it? I don't want to get fired, but after all these years I've grown fond of Grey, and I'm a sucker for young love. Besides, I get a kick out of screwing over the idiots who run this place."

Wilder was dizzy with relief. "Thank you, thank you, thank you."

"Give me five minutes, and then head to the front gates. Should be clear for you. There'll be a glitch in the security camera if anyone thinks to check."

"You're the best, Reggie," Wilder said, giddy with excitement.

I'm going to see her, he realized. *I'm really going to be able to talk to her.*

After signing off of the video chat, Wilder bounced up and down on his heels, waiting for the five minutes to pass. He made it to three before he headed toward the gate.

Reggie was true to his word. Whatever reason he'd come up with to summon the night gate security guards, it worked. Wilder didn't have a working pass card anymore to open the doors, but it was easy enough to climb up and jump the rattling fence.

He landed hard, tweaking his ankle, but no alarms went off. Silent as a shadow, he crept across the moonlit yard toward the studio.

Once inside, Wilder snuck through the hallways like a ghost, keeping his ears open for the sound of guards or late-night workers turning the corner ahead. Though thriving during the day, the studios were almost deserted after hours.

While on the show, Wilder had visited Reggie often at night. Even an amateur hacker like him knew what an honor it was to observe someone with Reg's skills.

When he arrived at the massive lab where the virtual reality machines were, Reggie was already waiting for him. "I can't believe I let you in," he said, stuffing a handful of Cheetos into his mouth.

"I could set this up, if you wanted. I do know my way around a computer."

"Nice try, kid. I'm not giving you access to the studio's servers."

Looking around at the massive lab, Wilder thought back to his first time entering the room. He'd gotten a private tour of the facilities by the company's CEO. The studio had invested a lot of hope in Wilder's ability to win Grey over, and when things were going well they treated him like a VIP. The huge space, the size of a small airplane hangar, was sleek and modern, white and silver like the inside of a millennium snow globe. On one wall were countless screens, all showing different camera angles. As Grey moved through her world, the scenes on the screen shifted to follow her movements.

On the other side of the room was a massive wall of machinery, two floors high, as intimidating as it was awe-inspiring. The AI that Reggie had developed, nicknamed Bruno, was some of the most advanced tech on the planet, and Wilder remembered how small he'd felt the first time he'd seen it. A frail human, dwarfed by the future.

He'd learned all about Bruno that day, its ability to read the signals from the actors' brains, the surges of electricity firing through their nervous systems. It used those signals to animate the actors' pre-created avatars. Reggie was a genius.

Bruno didn't just create virtual people in Grey's world, either. Most of the objects and items that filled Heringford weren't real. Her schoolbooks, her cell phone, her bedding, even the grass that lined the sidewalks on her way to school were all created by Bruno. There were some objects, of course, that had to be real. The studio couldn't feed her virtual food. Most furniture was real as well, along with her clothes and makeup, her car, and her bike. Everyone else's cars were real, too, though they were all self-driving.

The most incredible, and perhaps terrifying, power Bruno the AI had was to control and manipulate everything Grey felt, saw, smelled, tasted... It fed her sensory information constantly, and as she interacted with virtual objects in her world, Bruno calculated and adjusted, making sure the objects responded appropriately.

Though Grey wasn't in any way virtual, Bruno interacted with her brain waves through a node she didn't know was on her forehead. It was easy enough for the AI to protect itself. If Grey looked into a mirror, Bruno made it so she didn't see the node. If she brushed a hand over her forehead, the AI tricked her into believing all she felt was smooth skin, not the rough edge of the metal node.

Bruno's ability to process information at lightning speeds also allowed Grey to interact with virtual people in normal ways: hugging, handshakes, even kissing. If she were to throw a punch, Bruno's influence would stop her arm just as it hit the avatar's face, her fist crashing against thin air as if it were a solid object. And Grey would be left with bruised, painful knuckles for her efforts.

Wilder had been nervous during their first kiss: How good was Bruno, really? Would her face pass right through his? Would she be able to feel that something was wrong, that all she was kissing was a phantom made of air and lies?

He shouldn't have worried. Through the genius of Bruno's technology, her lips had moved against his in a way that sent a jolt of electricity through him—and that lightning between them, he was confident, had been real.

According to Reggie, there had been a lot of trial and error the first few years: virtual people walking through walls, Grey's hand passing right through objects, and Bruno sending her scents or tactile sensations at strange times. Luckily, after the first year or two Reg had smoothed out the kinks, and she'd forgotten about the odd happenings of her earliest years on the show.

"Reg, you know how we're not supposed to touch Grey's food?" Wilder asked, running his hand along the casing on one of the actor pods near Reggie's chair in front of the screens.

They called them pods, but they were really more like high-tech beds rigged up to connect with Bruno. There were four dozen of them spread across the expansive room. There was an additional lab a floor down that had an additional two hundred pods for large crowd scenes or school assemblies.

When diving into Grey's world as LeMarc, a technician had hooked him up. There was a headset he had to wear, which had a node that connected to his forehead, and a cuff he wrapped around his arm. It was surprisingly simple for such an amazing piece of technology.

He again thought back to the first time he'd done this. When they'd told him about the pods, he had envisioned a futuristic space pod, full of all kinds of gadgets and blinking lights. He'd almost been disappointed.

Now it worked in his favor, though. He could do it himself.

"Yeah," Reggie answered, typing something in. "The food's real and you're not, so you can't move it. Now *that's* an interesting problem. Most of my work is just improving the overall visual and graphics, but as a side project I'm trying to figure out a way around the food issue. There has to be a way to make virtual avatars able to influence real objects on set."

"But the Monroe's housekeeper makes her meals and does her laundry."

"She's real. There are a few workers who live on set, including her. You already know this."

"But Victoria Price has been replaced, right? I saw the new housekeeper on yesterday's episode. Grey's old housekeeper would know where she is, right?"

Reggie scratched his bulging stomach, still typing away on the computer where he was setting up the video loops. "You think Victoria's going to tell you Heringford's location? Do you have any idea how much they're paying her to keep her mouth shut? I'm sure she signed a nondisclosure agreement."

"So did I."

"But she's not an idiot."

Wilder leaned forward on the pod. "How long would it take you to get me her phone number?"

"You are full of requests tonight, aren't you? That's going to be a hard pass for me. I'm already regretting doing this, and you haven't even gone in yet. Speaking of, you ever going to get on that pod?"

Wilder wanted to ask more questions, but the pull to see Grey was stronger. He kicked his shoes off and climbed up onto the pod.

"Do you have it all set up?" he asked Reggie, lying down.

"You're good to go once you're plugged in. You'll be wearing a dragon onesie."

Wilder sat back up. "You wouldn't."

Reggie laughed. "I absolutely would, but I didn't this time. LeMarc's going to show up in jeans and tee. The green one she likes him in. Like I said, sucker for young love."

Wilder laid back once more, closing his eyes. It was cold in the lab, like always, but he felt warm all over. Anticipation spread through his blood like a drug.

When he opened his eyes again, he was in her bedroom. There was a thin light seeping in through the window, illuminating her face.

There she was. His heart skipped at the sight of her.

Grey's hair still looked damp from the shower. Wilder loved that she wore a ratty, oversized T-shirt and sweat capris to bed. Even when LeMarc was still alive, sneaking into her bedroom in the morning to kiss her awake, she'd never switched to girly pajamas. Thinking a frilly tank would look better on camera, the studio had assigned the actor playing Astrid to take her shopping for new PJs. They'd bought three sets, and those three sets had stayed nicely folded in Grey's bedroom drawer while she continued to wear the old ones.

Wilder took a seat at her desk by the window.

This was it.

"Grey," he called out softly. She didn't stir, so he said it again, this time a little more loudly.

After a moment, she opened her eyes.

50shadesofGreyMonroe

Is anybody else kind of worried about Grey? She looks so sad. Like, I get it's a show, but please just let our queen have ONE SHRED OF HAPPINESS without ripping it away!

ohdannygirl

I have been SAYING this! It's good to see Yusuf make her laugh again.

ishipgreymarc

Honestly, I don't think it's

GREYWATCH

Grey

6

There was a shape in the shadows that night. The moment Grey woke, she sensed him there, felt the air bending around him like a ripple in a still lake.

It was her name that had awoken her, just like on the mornings when LeMarc had snuck in with the sunrise, his eyes dancing with mischief and desire. Grey sat up, rubbing her tired eyes, and peered into the shadowed corners of the room.

There he was.

LeMarc was sitting in her desk chair, beautiful and impossible. The curve of his jaw, the cut of his torso under his thin T-shirt, the slow smile spreading across his face, it was as familiar as breathing. He looked so real, like she could reach out and touch him, fall into him until she drowned out the pain of losing him. Her eyes filled with tears.

He immediately moved toward her when he saw her crying, crawling onto her bed and kneeling before her. He pressed his hand to her cheek, wiping her tears away with his thumb. She could feel his hand there, the roughness of his skin and the warmth of his fingers against her cheek. Her soul ached for it to be real.

"Don't cry," he said, pressing his forehead to hers. "You've given up enough tears for me."

"I really am crazy, aren't I?" Grey placed a hand on his chest, gripping his shirt. "You feel so real."

LeMarc closed his eyes, just an inch away from her own. "I'm not a hallucination, Grey. I'm not a dream."

"I didn't realize my mind could conjure you up like this," she whispered. "The whole of you... love and grief and memory."

She smelled the musk of his cologne, felt his fingertips as they grazed her waist. Her mind had captured every detail of the boy she loved and built this shimmering effigy to soothe her anguish.

"You aren't imagining me here," he said. Even his voice was perfectly conjured, the baritone rumble that set her skin on fire. "Grey, it's me."

"LeMarc is dead," she choked out, pushing away the flash of the picture in her phone, the staring eyes and chalky skin.

LeMarc shook his head slightly, his forehead still pressed against hers. "You saw what they wanted you to see. They killed my avatar to stop me from telling you the truth."

"Avatar? What is that?"

"Do you remember what I told you that night, before they knocked you out? What I whispered?"

"You said that my life was a lie. That no one I knew was real, including you."

He smiled. "Not exactly sweet nothings, but at least it's the truth."

"That must be what you are, my mind searching for an explanation for what he said. My brain has conjured you up to process what happened, to allow myself to move on from all the questions LeMarc left with his death. To heal."

It was a more digestible explanation than the one she couldn't push away, that she had simply lost her mind. Was she truly mad? Was that the explanation for all of the strange things that had been happening? What if in a crazy haze she'd done something unthinkable to LeMarc? Perhaps she shouldn't be so flippant about her sessions with Dr. Hawks.

LeMarc pulled away, frustrated. "I'm not real, but it's not because you're imagining me. I'm an actor, Grey. LeMarc was just a role I was playing. Think of your life as one big play. Everyone you know is pretending. None of it is real."

So she should add paranoia to the list of symptoms.

LeMarc took her hand, his perfect face achingly earnest. "My real name is Wilder Blue," he continued. His hand felt warm, *alive*, in hers. "I might not have been completely honest about who I am, but I love you, Grey. I don't want you to live in this invisible cage any longer."

When he was alive, LeMarc had never told her he loved her. He'd felt the same way she had, she was sure, but he'd never said it out loud. Too afraid to say it herself, she'd waited until it was too late. She could hardly see through the tears that sprang up in her eyes. Now this beautiful mirage was here, and dream or not, she was going to tell him how she felt.

"I loved you, too," she said.

LeMarc gave a wry grin. "I've wanted you to say that so many times, but I never imagined it in past tense. Grey, I'm right here."

She wanted this, so badly. She wanted him, the taste of his lips and the low rumble of his voice as they talked through the night. There was danger here, slipping through his words and the touch of his skin against hers.

She knew better than to fall in love with a ghost.

"I can't do this," she said, lying back down on her bed. "I can't indulge in these kinds of fantasies about you. You aren't real."

LeMarc laid down next to her, propping his head up on his arm. She turned her head to look up at him.

"You aren't going to believe me, are you?" he said. "What can I do to prove that it's me? I'm not dead. I was fired from playing LeMarc, and I've come back to tell you the truth."

Grey reached out to touch his face. There was nothing he could say. She'd washed his blood off of her shaking hands. But as much as she knew he wasn't real, she didn't want him to leave.

One night. She would give herself one night to swim in this fantasy. A few more hours with the ghost who owned her dreams.

He leaned toward her, his eyes questioning, and she closed the gap between them. Her bedroom fell away as they kissed, the night swelling in a silent symphony, and all she could think was that she must be dead, too. His lonely soul had come to shepherd her into the stars of eternity.

Right there, she made her decision. If she'd fallen into madness, if the smell of his cologne and his lips on hers were the progeny of a broken mind, she prayed to drown in the madness forever.

She was going to hold onto the ghost of Collin LeMarc for as long as she could.

"Will you stay with me?" she asked. "Until I wake up?"

"Until you fall asleep, you mean," LeMarc said, laughing under his breath.

"Right. Until I wake up or fall asleep, whichever happens first."

Sitting up, LeMarc pushed his back up against her bed's headboard. "I'll be here." From his seated position, he brushed her damp hair behind her ear.

Yusuf did that, too, and Grey pushed away the guilt she felt rise in her. She wasn't sure if she felt it for flirting with Yusuf or for loving this afterimage of LeMarc.

"I've missed you so much," she whispered, staring at the ceiling. "I can't breathe without you here."

"I've missed you, too."

"Are you coming back? Will I see you again?"

"I'll be back, Grey," he said, the same fire in his eyes that had kept her warm while he was alive. "I'm never going to give up on you. I promise."

The day after LeMarc's visit, Grey was sprawled with Yusuf and Ellie on the school greens under a spreading elm, soaking in the sun before afternoon classes. The rain had washed summer away, but Grey was grateful for the cool breeze blowing through her stuffy school uniform.

"So that means *A* equals…"

Yusuf trailed off, leaving Ellie to answer the question. He was her emergency tutor for the moment.

When Ellie had gotten back her Algebra test that morning and immediately burst into tears, Grey had asked Yusuf to help her friend out during lunch. He was a member of the Mathletes, a fact which had docked him points in Ellie's world but now was coming in handy.

Ellie scrunched up her face in concentration. "*A* equals five?"

Grey winced and laid back on their picnic blanket, taking a bite of her sandwich. *A* equaled 396. No wonder Ellie had failed the test.

Yusuf glanced at Grey for a moment, as if his eyes couldn't help themselves from drifting in her direction, and then began patiently re-explaining the equation to Ellie.

Grey watched him as he leaned over the notebook he was scribbling something in. His dark hair fell in a curl over his forehead. Even while tutoring, his handwriting was neat and clear, unlike LeMarc's wild scribble.

She closed her eyes, letting the sun color the darkness red behind her lids. She wished she had time for a nap; she wasn't used to waking up in the middle of the night. Whether a dream or a fantasy, LeMarc's appearance had left her drained.

"No, you have to carry the negative sign through," Yusuf was saying. "Negativity should be an easy one for you."

Ellie sighed loudly. "You're funny, Mr. Mathlete, but you'd whine, too, if you had to spend your lunch break doing the thing you hate most in the world."

Grey knew Ellie hated feeling dumb, but Yusuf could really help her. He'd already shown a surprising amount of patience toward the grumpiest pupil in history.

LeMarc hadn't had much patience for school. He'd been smart, but if Grey was being honest, Yusuf was a far better student. He was more cautious, more observant, and more thoughtful. Easily better looking.

And according to her hallucination of LeMarc, he wasn't any more real.

After promising to come back, the hallucination had tried a few more times to convince her that everyone in her life was an actor, projected into her world like a moving photograph. Somehow her sick mind had taken Ellie's stray comment about TV commercials and created a whole conspiracy theory, wrapping it in specter form.

She opened her eyes again, looking up at Yusuf. He looked solid enough, laughing as Ellie made a rude comment about where he could stuff his exponents.

But every time Grey let herself start to think about Yusuf, it jolted her out of her own life, like she was just a spectator watching, judging the girl so quick to let a boy carry her books when her heart was buried in the cemetery east of town.

A few minutes before the end of lunch, Ellie raced off, claiming she needed to stop at the office before class.

"Sure. You're not just trying to get out of more math time," Yusuf called out as she left.

She ignored him.

"What are you thinking about?" Yusuf asked Grey after Ellie had disappeared into the school building. "You have a strange expression on your face, lying there."

She shrugged. "I had a weird dream last night, and I can't stop thinking about it."

Yusuf perked up. "Ooo, tell me about it and I'll interpret it for you."

"You're a dream interpreter now?"

"My cousin had a dream about elephants this summer, and I told her it meant she was going to make the basketball team this year. She did."

Grey laughed. "Doesn't your cousin play for Hilton Prep varsity? She's amazing. Does she even have to re-try out each year?"

"C'mon, just tell me about your dream."

Grey let out a gusty breath. This was easier when she was laying down and didn't have to look at him. "I dreamed of someone coming to save me."

It was true, but well out of reach of the tender deceased-secret-boyfriend topic.

"To save you from what?"

"From my life, I guess. From everything that isn't real about it."

Yusuf let out an awkward laugh. "Your life is plenty real."

Grey looked up at the leaves above her, considering. She wasn't so sure. Maybe her subconscious *was* trying to tell her something. "Is it, though? Sometimes I wonder if Grey Monroe is just a construct of who other people want me to be. The only people that I've ever been able to be myself around were Danny and..." She almost choked on the name.

"LeMarc?" Yusuf suggested gently.

LeMarc. What did it say about her, that in the first dream she had about him, he was coming in on a white horse to save her? "For once, I'd like to feel like the main character in my own life, you know? Instead of the girl awful stuff happens to."

Yusuf leaned over her, blocking out the sun. "Grey, you have no idea. You're the star of the show."

She wrinkled her nose. "Okay, enough of the self-pity. So what's your interpretation of my dream? I'm whiny and ungrateful?"

"Nope. I think it means you're going to be swept off your feet by a dark-haired man sometime soon." Wiggling his eyebrows comically, he stood up and stashed his notebook back into his bag.

"Need a lift?" he asked, holding out both hands. Grey reached out to grab them, but he snatched his back quickly.

"I... uh... I just realized I tweaked my shoulder in gym, so I probably shouldn't help you up."

"Okay, no problem."

She brushed the grass from her skirt, and Yusuf handed her her books. "Ugh, French class," she groaned. "Monsieur Dupont's third period said he's doing a pop quiz today. I should have studied during lunch."

She became keenly aware, suddenly, that Yusuf hadn't taken a step back after handing her her books. He was standing very close.

"You know, I thought changing schools was the worst thing that had ever happened to me," he said. "I was furious when my parents pulled me out of the place where all of my friends were and dropped me into a new school with slightly better test scores. But I'm really glad to be at St. John's."

He leaned forward, closing in the space between them.

"Me too," Grey said, taking a step back. "When I said earlier that I could only talk about things with a few people... You're included in that, too, now. I already feel like I've know you for years. You're a good friend."

"Someone you trust?" he asked, raising his eyebrows.

He'd taken her friendzoning in stride, she noticed, dodging around it with unexpected deftness.

"Of course."

"Actually, Grey, this might seem like it's coming from out of the blue, but there's something I need to ask you." The expression on his face was oddly serious. She swallowed, hard. Her palms were sweaty all of a sudden.

"You're not going to propose or something, are you?"

He shook his head. "No, this is about a few days ago, during that rainstorm. When you decided not to come into the ice cream parlor at first, it was after you'd looked at your phone. Some sort of message."

"You know, I think we should really get to class—"

Grey turned to leave, but Yusuf grabbed her arm. "What was it that scared you so badly?" he asked gently. "Is someone threatening you? You can trust me, Grey."

Grey bit her lip.

Trust him.

This wasn't a matter of trust. Bringing Yusuf in would only endanger him, and she wasn't going to do that, not when she couldn't remember what had happened to LeMarc. The person sending texts from LeMarc and Danny's phones could easily target Yusuf, too, and Grey was no closer to finding out who sent them than she'd been at the funeral. She'd tried his "Find my Friend" app, but it had been disabled, and the company required a password to reveal the location over the phone.

Grey sucked in a breath as the realization hit: She couldn't track his phone, not without a password, but the heir to the Starlight Mobile empire might be able to.

Yusuf was watching her closely. "What? It looks like you just realized something."

"If I give you a cell number, can you determine the location of the phone?"

Yusuf raised an eyebrow. "I'm not really involved in the tech side of things, but I know a few guys who work for my dad. I can check, at least."

Grey pulled him in for a hug, which seemed to take him by surprise. There was far too much elbow involved. "Thank you, thank you, thank you."

Yusuf pulled back, a slight smile on his face. "I was hoping to impress you with something *other* than my rich father's connections, but I'll take it for now, I suppose. Is this number I'm tracking down the one who sent the message that scared you so badly?"

Grey nodded. "I can't tell you much, but it's important. It has to do with LeMarc's murder."

"You're trying to find out who killed him, aren't you?"

She nodded again.

"Then I'm going to help. You get me that number, and I'll get you an address. And then I'm going with you to check it out. You're not alone, Grey. Together, we're going to take this guy down."

Wilder

7

Monday morning, Wilder woke up with a headache and a sense of dread. It was 6:15. Time to get ready for school.

Groaning, he rolled over to shut his alarm off. It had been two days since he'd seen Grey, but he still hadn't caught up on the missed sleep. If he just stayed in bed, he wouldn't have to go to school. He wouldn't have to face Carly's icy glares, or the fawning giggles of freshman girls who watched the show. He could dream of Grey all day. He closed his eyes as he thought back to the way she'd looked at him when she told him she loved him. He was already itching to go back to see her again.

He would have to face his mother if he skipped again, though, and that realization propelled him out of bed and into the shower.

His dad was at the kitchen island on his laptop when Wilder walked through the living room toward the door. It was the first time he'd seen him since the night he'd destroyed Wilder's phone.

"Sorry about your phone," his dad said, not taking his eyes of the screen. "I'm quitting, you know. Drinking, that is. Can't think straight when I've had a few."

Wilder grabbed his backpack from the floor in front of the couch. "Yeah, cool," he said before escaping out the front door.

The city bus dropped him off a full fifteen minutes before the first bell rang. He plodded up the front steps to the school with his head ducked down, trying to avoid anyone's gaze. With his navy hoodie and grim expression, he fit right in with the steely gray of early morning.

Nevertheless, as soon as he entered the school he heard the whispers stalking him down the hallway.

In stark contrast to Grey's uptown prep school, Washington High was a pit of linoleum and hormones. The hallways were scarred with dents and holes from decades of abuse, and the sickly green of the lockers didn't help the air of desperation. Even the students were less polished than the glossy avatars of Grey's world. As they stared at him now, whispering behind their hands, he tried to pretend that they were just as fake as LeMarc had been.

After picking up his schedule and locker info from the office, Wilder shuffled to the V wing in the far corner of the school to try out his combo.

Leaning against his locker was Mia Thompson, red-lipped and smoldering. He had no idea how she'd found out which locker was his, or how long she'd been posing there, but he had to admit, the effect was dazzling. She was wearing a black dress that hugged her abundant curves, her curly hair tumbling loose down her back.

Wilder had dated Mia for a few months in junior high, much to Carly's horror. Mia was wild and sumptuous, smart but uninterested, exactly the type of girl preteen Wilder had thought he wanted. Exactly the opposite of Grey and her earnest solemnity.

"Mia, what are you doing?" he asked, unable to stop himself from grinning at her shameless posing.

She twirled a lock of hair on her finger.

"I'm here to welcome you back," she answered in her low voice. "I want to be the first to get an autograph from *the* Wilder Blue."

He should have figured that his former flame would take a new interest in him now that he carried a bit of fame on his shoulders. Rolling his eyes, Wilder reached around her to start working on his locker combo. She ran a finger down his outstretched arm. "I missed you while you were gone."

"Seriously, you look great, but no thanks. I'm not thirteen anymore."

"Neither am I."

Wilder wasn't expecting the kiss, or he would have pulled away. He *should* have pulled away as soon as it started. But as Mia pulled in closer, her fingers gripping his arm, his mind shut down and his body took over.

Mia laughed against his lips, pushing him back against the locker.

When a throat cleared just a foot away, Wilder jumped back, hitting his head against the locker.

Abe, Carly's boyfriend, was standing in front of them, a few books in his arms. "Sorry to interrupt, but I need to get into my locker before school starts."

Wilder's brain switched back on, and he knew his face was stained as red as Mia's lips as he realized what he'd just done in the middle of the school hallway.

Mia gave Wilder a kiss on the cheek. "See ya," she said as she sashayed away.

As soon as she was gone, Abe whirled around, laughing, and punched Wilder on the shoulder. "Dude! I did not know you and Mia were a thing!"

Wilder sighed, turning back to his locker combo. "We're not." The last thing he needed was a rumor about him and Mia. "In fact, if you could not mention anything to Carly, I'd really appreciate it."

Abe considered for a moment. "If asked, I won't lie. But I won't bring it up if she doesn't."

"Thanks," Wilder said, finally getting his locker open.

If Abe weren't such a nice guy, Wilder would hate him. He was far too perfect, tall and dark-skinned with a 4.0 and great athletic record. But he was also kind and honest, and that could go a long way in Wilder's book.

Abe opened his locker, too, and traded a few books. "She's just hurt, you know. I'm sure you guys will work it out."

"I know," Wilder answered, shutting his locker. He didn't have any books to put in it yet. "But it would be a little easier to navigate this new local celebrity thing if I had my best friend to beat off the hordes of women."

Abe snorted. "Didn't look like you were so eager to beat off that particular woman, but I hear you. I'll put in a good word."

"Thanks, Abe," Wilder called as he walked away.

The rest of Wilder's morning was a blur of ducking stares and trying to stay awake in class. Missing the first week, he'd hoped to skip right past the introductions, but it was a mixed bag whether teachers forced him to introduce himself. He'd gone to Washington High for two years before the show, so the students all knew him, but his English teacher made a big deal about having a TV star in class.

His Economics teacher, on the other hand, made a point of announcing loudly at the start of class that he shouldn't be anticipating any special treatment.

The real problem was the lunch block. Wilder had been eating lunch with the same group since sixth grade. Most of his friends were welcoming him back as the same old Wilder, just like Abe, but Carly was a different story altogether. His only morning class with her was math, and she'd pointedly ignored his pleading looks the whole period.

"Still hate me?" he'd asked her as she left. She was wearing a ripped black t-shirt over a white tank today, an edgy look for someone dating Mr. Perfect.

"Asked and answered," she'd replied, pushing out the door.

Now, standing at the cafeteria entrance with a protein shake in hand, Wilder could see her snuggled up against Abe at their usual table, laughing at something Tanya, the pink-haired freshman from Luke's basement, had said. He wondered what would happen if he just walked over and sat down as though he weren't nervous about it at all.

Josh Tank, a member of Wilder's usual lunch crew, pulled up beside him. "Hey, Wilder! Long time no see. When you didn't show up the first week, rumor had it you'd transferred, but I'm glad you're back. You coming to sit with us?"

Wilder, apparently, was no longer a part of the *us*.

"Uh, yeah. Maybe."

"Thought you might want to sit next to Mia," Josh responded. "The pic she posted of you guys is all over school."

"The pic she posted?" Wilder repeated dumbly.

"Yeah, of you two kissing. She put it up this morning."

"Uh, you know what?" Wilder stammered, caught off-guard. "I just realized I have to do some catch-up work in the library today."

He backed up, waving goodbye to Josh.

Red-faced, he headed down the hallway. How had he not noticed that she'd taken a picture? Why hadn't Abe warned him? Carly was going to be livid. There was no way she would let him sit at their lunch table now, and this was just another piece of evidence to convince her that the Wilder she'd been best friends with was gone.

He didn't actually want to go to the library, so he headed to the H wing and the hollow under the stairs there. It was a favorite spot for couples dodging hall monitors, but today it was deserted except for old wrappers and an empty pop bottle.

He sunk to the ground, defeated, and then pulled out his laptop to check his email. His phone was still busted.

There was an email there from Reg, titled, *This email will delete any trace of itself two minutes after opening.*

Wilder snorted to himself, shaking his head. Reg was such a drama queen. But then he clicked on the email and started reading, and all traces of humor drained away.

Reggie had taken care of almost everything to cover their tracks from the visit. He'd distracted the guards, scrubbed the tapes, and removed any record of Wilder's trip into the virtual realm from the computers.

There was just one thing he'd forgotten to do. The node attached to Grey's forehead fed her sensory information, kept her connected to her augmented world, but it also recorded biometric data to make sure she stayed healthy. The sensor had recorded her wide awake that night, while the tapes showed her fast asleep.

Luckily, Reggie hadn't yet left for the morning when it was discovered, so he volunteered to investigate why the sensor had stopped reading accurately. But that was it. Reggie wasn't going to help him make any more visits and risk his job.

Wilder had barely finished reading when the email vanished, the screen returning to his inbox. Knowing Reg's skills, it probably was completely gone from the web, though everyone always said nothing could really ever be deleted online.

Wilder shut his laptop screen and shoved the whole thing back in his bag.

He really should have stayed in bed this morning.

The address Wilder had stolen from his mother for Lillian Price led to one of those recently-built homes with too many rooms and no personality, an overpriced box. He wiped his palms on his jeans as he approached. Lillian was the key to finding Victoria, and Victoria was the key to finding Grey.

Hopefully Lillian was a fan.

He rang the doorbell once. If he could just get her to sit down and talk, he was sure he could convince her to help. After all, he was Wilder Blue.

The woman who came to the door was probably in her forties, around the same age as Victoria. *Sister*, Wilder thought to himself. While Victoria was curvy and lush, however, Lillian was all bones and skin and weariness.

When she saw him, her eyes narrowed in confusion.

He pasted on his brightest smile, sticking out his hand to brace the door and make sure she couldn't close it on him. "Hi, my name is—"

"Wilder Blue," she finished.

Wilder nodded. "You're a fan of the show."

Lillian put a hand on her waist. "I wouldn't watch that disgusting show if it were Moses's brazen serpent."

"Oh."

"But I also don't live under a rock. What do you want from me? Did Monroe Studios send you?"

"No, of course not. I'm not here to bother you. I just... I was wondering if you could tell me where to find Victoria."

Lillian's jaw tightened. "I've been wondering that myself, actually. Maybe you should ask Monroe. I don't know where my sister is, and if I did, I wouldn't give the address away to a teenage boy."

Ask Monroe. She was talking about Ansel Monroe, Grey's father. The head of Monroe Studios. He was one of the wealthiest—and evilest—men in the world.

"What do you mean, ask Monroe?" Wilder pressed. "Victoria doesn't work for him anymore, right?"

Lillian sighed, a long, tired exhale as if she were a deflating balloon. "Fine. You can come inside."

She opened the door to let him in, gesturing to a high-backed chair in her front parlor.

"You know, you remind me of him," she said. "Same confidence. Like a battering ram with a hundred-watt smile."

"Who?"

"Ansel Monroe." She took a seat on the loveseat across from him. "I wondered how you managed to get the role, with a mother like yours, but now that I've met you it makes more sense."

The furniture in the room was expensive, with gold details and ornate carvings, but it was all far too much for the parlor. Lillian was clearly eager to show off her money but unsure how.

"I'm nothing like him. I want to help Grey, and all he does is use her."

Lillian scoffed. "She's not the only one. I wish my sister would never have gotten involved with that narcissist."

"Wait. When you say *involved*, do you mean...?"

She nodded. "Victoria was *so excited* to get this gig. She was almost ready to give up on acting. That's why she'd moved back home. And it started off so well. She had money to burn, even bought me this house. She was just the housekeeper, but after that hit-and-run storyline about her TV brother a few years ago, she was made a series regular. And she was getting offers for bigger roles. People loved her."

"But she turned those other offers down?"

"She did. I didn't realize it at the time, but she had personal reasons to stay on the show. There's a reason they replaced even Victoria's avatar, not just her as an actress. Apparently when Ansel Monroe cuts ties, he doesn't want a reminder of the past."

"So the romance ended, and she left the show. But she hasn't made contact with you to tell you where she is now?"

"She did." Lillian stood up and walked heavily over to a bureau against the side wall, a rococo-style monstrosity with an explosion of curlicues. She opened a small drawer and pulled out a postcard, bringing it to Wilder before sitting back in her chair.

With one long look at Lillian, Wilder flipped the card over to look at it. On one side was a picture of Machu Picchu, its peak wrapped in wispy clouds.

On the other side was a handwritten note: *Dear Lillian, Fell in love at the airport and eloped. We're going to travel the world together. I know this must come as a shock, but please be happy for me. Love you always, Victoria.*

He gritted his teeth. "So talking to her is a dead end. She's off with some guy in Peru."

Lillian shook her head. "My sister isn't in Peru."

"Fine. Maybe they're not still there, but she's somewhere *not here*. Somewhere out of reach."

She scowled. "You don't understand. My sister didn't elope with some stranger. They matched the handwriting well, but this is *not* the note my sister would write to tell me she'd run off to be married. And she definitely wouldn't sign it *Victoria*. That was her stage name. She grew up as Amanda Price, and that was what I always called her. Mandy. She would have addressed it to *Lil*, too, not *Lillian*. I don't think she's ever called me that before."

"So what... You think there's foul play going on?"

Lillian's hands gripped the arms of her chair so hard, her knuckles were white and smooth. "I wouldn't put it past a man who sells his own daughter to the world every week. Would you?"

"Monroe's corrupt, yes, but you actually think he hurt Victoria somehow?"

Lillian stood abruptly, snatching the postcard out of his hand. "With all my heart. The police refuse to open an investigation, and only sensationalist clickbait sites are even touching the story, but I know something happened to my sister."

Wilder stood as well, his mind whirring. "And if I can prove it, Monroe goes to prison. They'd shut down the show."

Reggie might not let Wilder back in to convince Grey, but maybe he didn't have to. The key to freeing Grey could be uncovering this secret Monroe was trying to bury.

Now all Wilder needed was the right kind of shovel.

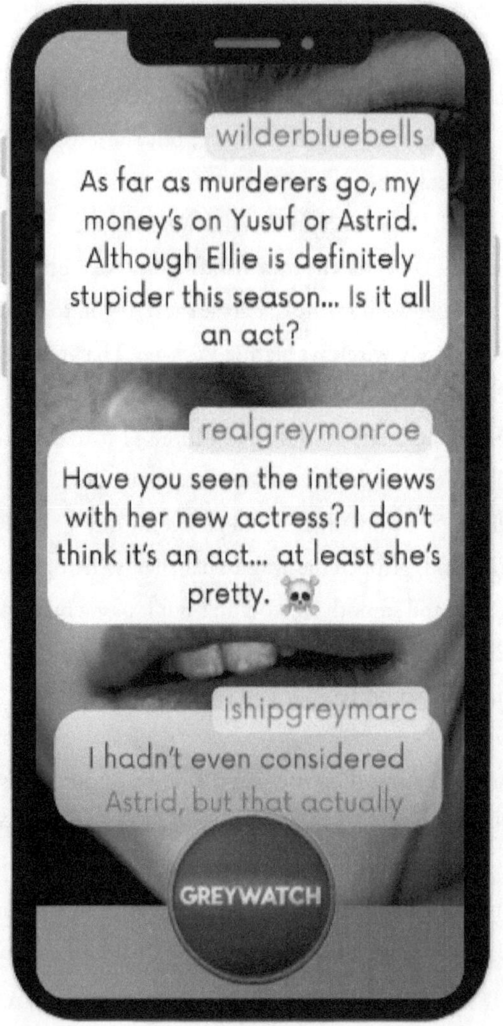
wilderbluebells
As far as murderers go, my money's on Yusuf or Astrid. Although Ellie is definitely stupider this season... Is it all an act?
realgreymonroe
Have you seen the interviews with her new actress? I don't think it's an act... at least she's pretty.
ishipgreymarc
I hadn't even considered Astrid, but that actually
GREYWATCH

Grey

8

The last thing Grey needed in her life right now was a carnival. Walking onto the fairgrounds just south of town and seeing the Ferris wheel looming above her, she was tempted to turn around, head home, and spend the evening escaping into a good book.

It had been weeks, and Yusuf still hadn't been able to find out anything about LeMarc's cell phone. She might have to start figuring out another way to chase down LeMarc's killer.

Although maybe if Yusuf put the same amount of energy into finding the location as he had into her re-election campaign, LeMarc's killer would already be behind bars. In a relatively short amount of time, Yusuf had managed to launch a campaign that would rival most presidential elections, not just a challenge for student body president.

Most schools would have just held a pep rally, or better yet a boring old assembly, to announce the winner of the hotly-debated second race for school president. From the looks of this place, St. John's had invited the entire Cirque-du-soleil. Booths crowded the fairgrounds, shouting for attention with giant stuffed animals, syrupy music, and a blast of colors that would make Crayola proud. A few rides were already half-loaded with students, even though Grey was ten minutes early. In just a few hours, she'd know if she was still student body president.

The centerpiece of the carnival, of course, was the soaring Ferris wheel, its carriages dangling like shining apples on a tree.

Grey would have lost courage and turned around if she hadn't seen Yusuf, Ellie, Kamilla, and their friend Adam Torres messing around near the cotton-candy machine.

Yusuf spotted her first, smiling brightly and waving like a maniac. He was wearing a burnt orange tee today, a color that would make Grey look like she was dying but brought out the warmth in his skin tone.

She didn't push away the swoop in her stomach at the sight of him. Maybe a night with friends would help take her mind off LeMarc.

As she approached the group, Ellie linked her arm through hers. "You ready to wipe the floor with Todd Milkins in this fake election?" she asked. "He's such a joke. Boy can't even kiss."

"You would know," Adam said, earning him a punch in the arm from Ellie. Adam had been one of Ellie's first boyfriends, back in the hormone-drenched summers of junior high.

"Kissing ability is definitely my top requirement for student government," Yusuf said. "No pucker, no power."

Ellie and Kamilla both gave Grey looks heavy with meaning, which she ignored. Thankfully, Yusuf didn't seem to notice.

Adam was a bit less subtle. "Well, Grey, if you want a testimonial, I'm sure our boy Abdullah over here would be more than willing to take one for the team and kiss you."

He clapped Yusuf on the back.

Grey was sure she was seven shades of red. "The dumb thing is I don't even care about being student body president, and somehow I'm still nervous about the results."

Yusuf put his hands on her shoulders, looking into her eyes. "Repeat after me," he demanded. "I am Grey Monroe."

"Are you serious?" she asked, laughing.

"I am Grey Monroe," he repeated. "Just say it."

"I am Grey Monroe."

"I am going to rule the world someday, and my first step in world domination is student body president at St. John's Preparatory Academy."

"That should have been my campaign slogan. I think you failed me as PR manager."

"You're amazing, and you're an excellent president, and Todd Milkins' head is way too big for his body."

"Amen!" Kamilla added. "Though I still think I would have been the better choice."

"The announcement isn't for another hour or two," Adam interjected. "You guys want to ride the Zipper?"

"I'm in!" Yusuf said, and the two guys set off to get in line.

Ellie held Grey back, keeping their walk at a crawl, and Kamilla slowed her steps to match them.

"So Yusuf," Ellie said.

Grey just shrugged.

"Are you kidding me?" Ellie said, her voice high and plaintive. "How are you two not a thing yet? You're already at obnoxious levels of cute, and you're not even dating."

"I don't know if I'm ready yet," Grey admitted, watching Yusuf and Adam shoving each other in line.

"Well, get ready. If I'm getting impatient, so is he, and tonight is the perfect opportunity. You guys could go to the gala together! He was saying earlier that his mom's making him go."

Grey looked to Kamilla, her thoughts going to the texter's threats, but she just rolled her eyes, her long lashes flickering. "Have you guys ordered dresses yet?"

Grey shook her head. "It's ages away. Besides, I would never pick a dress design or fabric without you guys."

"Good answer," Ellie said. "The theme is Versailles, you know. The perfect setting for a romantic night. The French are known for *amour*."

They were approaching the guys now, who were chatting with the clump of freshmen in front of them in line. "It's going to be amazing."

"What's going to be amazing?" Yusuf asked, overhearing Ellie's last line.

"Grey was just talking about the gala in December. It's going to be a magical night," Kamilla explained.

Yusuf grinned at Grey. "I'm glad you're going. Maybe we could drive together."

"We could go as a group," Adam suggested.

Ellie hit him from behind, and he let out a little yelp. "Nope. Just remembered that I'm going with a friend, so can't ride with you two. Shame."

"It's a date, then," Yusuf said with his broad smile, causing Grey's face to turn hot again.

When Kamilla defeated Grey an hour later in a best-out-five carnival games competition, Grey acknowledged her victory with a sincere smile. "I'll bring the tiara to school tomorrow," she promised, but Kamilla shook her head.

"Keep it for now. I might not be going against you for president this time, but I think defeating Todd is victory enough."

As the night wore on and the time for the presidency announcement neared, however, Grey got more and more nervous. It wasn't that she wanted to be class president; Yusuf had had to needle her into even standing up to Todd's challenge. But now that she'd tried for it, she hated the idea of failing. Failing publicly, too, right there for everyone to see.

Their heads would turn toward her when they announced Todd's name, and she wouldn't be able to shield herself from their judgment, their morbid curiosity, their pity...

"You okay in there?" Yusuf asked, tapping her forehead.

They were standing in line for the Ferris wheel, fifteen minutes to go until the big announcement. Ellie, Kamilla, and Adam had dissolved into a group of their friends.

"Yeah, I'm just freaking out about this class president thing. I shouldn't have let you talk me into campaigning."

"You deserve to be president. And it's better to try and fail than to give up before you've even started."

Their spot came up in line, and their conversation was interrupted as they boarded the gondola. Night was coming on fast, and the carnival had turned the Ferris wheel lights on. In addition to bright bulbs lining the wheel's spokes, the gondola was laced with lights as well, and Grey felt, for a moment, like she was entering an enchanted carriage.

Yusuf settled down next to her much closer than strictly necessary.

As the wheel swept them upwards, a breeze troubled Grey's hair, tickling her face. She was wearing a light summer dress, white and gauzy, and she shivered in the sudden cold.

"I'm not so good at the whole failing thing," Grey said, continuing their conversation. "I keep picturing everyone watching me as I lose, trying to read the emotions on my face."

"Then let's stay up here where no one can see you," Yusuf said, as though it were the most reasonable thing in the world. "Let's ride the Ferris wheel all night."

"You think I should miss the announcement?"

She shivered in the cold, and Yusuf scooted over so their legs were touching and wrapped an arm around her. He was so close, smelling of summer and spices, and Grey immediately felt warmer.

"We can hear it from here," he said softly. "I'll be the only one watching, and I promise there will be no judgment and no pity. I'll think of a really good joke to tell you, to distract you."

"Thank you." She leaned into his shoulder. "Are you okay staying up here with me?"

"There is nowhere I'd rather be."

He leaned forward, closing the distance between them, but at the last minute, Grey cleared her throat and turned away.

"Wow, everyone looks so small from up here," she said in a tight voice.

"Uh huh." Yusuf's voice was low and disappointed, but he didn't take his arm off her shoulder.

They were right at the Ferris wheel's zenith when with a shriek of grinding metal, the gondola dropped several feet and then jerked to a stop.

Grey whipped a hand up to the edge of their carriage to keep herself from pitching over the front as the whole gondola swung back and forth violently.

Yusuf did the same thing next to her, sliding out of his seat with a yelp.

"Okay, I wasn't expecting that," he said with a shaky laugh, patting himself all over as though to check for missing limbs before returning to the bench.

Careful not to sway the carriage, Grey peeked her head over to look at the wheel's operator below. He was inspecting the start/stop lever and scratching his head. A few other fairgrounds employees were snaking their way through the crowd of upturned faces towards him.

"You didn't sabotage the ride just so you don't have to be there when they announce your victory, did you?" Yusuf asked when she pulled back.

"No!"

"That was a joke, Grey."

He slid towards her and wrapped an arm around her waist, pulling her close.

When she raised an eyebrow at him, he grinned. "We need to anchor ourselves, in case the gondola starts moving again unexpectedly. The closer we sit, the safer we are."

Grey shook her head, fighting a smile. Her heart was beating fast from the quick drop, and maybe just a bit from the feel of Yusuf's hand on her waist. "Are you sure you're not the one who sabotaged the ride?"

"I plead the fifth."

When the announcement was made over the loudspeaker fifteen minutes later, she was still hanging at the top of the sky, wrapped in Yusuf's arms. The stars speckled the sky above them in a twinkling blur.

Grey was still student body president.

It was as though the ride had been waiting for it; before the announcer's voice finished, the Ferris wheel creaked back into motion. Students in a few of the nearby gondolas cheered.

Yusuf took her hand. "We'll be down soon. You want to get off and mingle with the commoners, O Great One?"

Grey shook her head. "Can we ride around again? This is really nice."

Yusuf smiled at her, wrapping his arm a little more tightly around her waist. "Yeah," he said. "It is."

It wasn't until later that night that Grey realized that with the motion of the Ferris wheel, she'd missed her phone buzzing. She had about a dozen texts congratulating her on her victory, but one message pulled her gaze. LeMarc.

When the bough breaks, the carriage will fall. Tempting, but I'm not ready for this to be over. Tonight was a warning, Grey. The gala is coming. And then I'm coming for you.

The next Monday, seated at a table in the corner of the buzzing cafeteria, Grey handed her phone to Kamilla to read the newest message from LeMarc's number.

Kamilla's dark eyes traveled back and forth across the screen for much longer than the time it took to read a few sentences. She was wearing glasses today, a fashion statement since she had perfect vision.

"Kam?" Grey checked.

Ellie was heading their way, brown lunch bag in hand, and Grey didn't want her asking questions about why Kamilla found Grey's phone so engrossing.

"I didn't get a message." Kamilla handed the phone back to Grey.

"Later," she whispered just as Ellie approached.

Ellie dropped her lunch onto the table with a dramatic flourish. "I just had the most amazing, out-of-body experience of my *life*. Liam Porter asked me to the gala. *Liam Porter*. And it's still two months away! I'm dead. Literally. Dead."

Grey shoved her phone into her pocket. "Cool."

Ellie narrowed her eyes at Grey. "Cool? That's all? For *Liam freaking Porter*? Are you kidding me?"

"I'm sorry. It will take some time to arrange the celebratory fireworks display."

"Mmm, and the parade's not going to be ready for at least a few hours," Kamilla chipped in.

Ellie rolled her bright blue eyes. "Whatever. He's the most gorgeous guy in school besides maybe Yusuf. And unlike Yusuf, Liam's into normal stuff and not Pithramamus and his theories or whatever."

"Pithramamus?"

"The triangle guy. But seriously, I am captain of the Grey/Yusuf ship, and I'm glad you two are finally a couple."

Kamilla put a hand under her chin, hiding a grin. Of course Grey's friends had drawn the wrong conclusion about Grey's trip around the Ferris Wheel with Yusuf, but he'd just wrapped his arms around her to keep her from flying out of the wheel when it broke down. To keep her warm in the cool night air. And she, of course, had only laid her head on his shoulder because she was grateful for his work on the campaign. It was a friendly gesture, nothing more.

Grey picked a carrot up from Ellie's bag and bit into it, trying for casual. "We're just friends."

Ellie let out a dramatic sigh. "Liar, liar, pants on fire."

Grey sat up straight, and Kamilla's head jerked towards Ellie, who was digging into her lunch bag and didn't seem to notice.

Liar, liar, pants on fire.

It had to be a coincidence. Ellie wasn't exactly an evil mastermind, and even if she were, she wouldn't taunt Grey to her face like that, surely.

Right?

But Kamilla's face was ashen, and Ellie knew them both so well... What if she'd seen Grey and LeMarc together this past summer? Kamilla and Danny?

How would she react to knowing both her friends were keeping secrets from her?

Grey stood up to leave, gathering up her food tray.

"I just got here," Ellie pouted. "You're not mad I called you a liar, are you? We have eyes, you know, and things were looking a little steamy on that Ferris wheel."

"I forgot I have a... math thing." Grey pulled at her woolen skirt. "Actually, Kamilla, could you come help? You and fractions... match made in heaven, right?"

Ellie threw up her hands. "Worst friends ever."

Grey shrugged. "You could come, too, you know. I just need some help with the... the fractions."

Ellie wrinkled her nose. "Ugh. Count me out."

They'd barely gotten out of the cafeteria when Grey felt a tug on her arm.

"Grey." Yusuf's hair was wavier than usual today, falling across his forehead in a curly tumble.

Kamilla, apparently, was immune to the allure of run-your-hands-through-it hair. "Sorry, Lover Boy, but we have important things to discuss."

She dragged Grey away, but Yusuf stumbled after them. "Important things relating to the mysterious texter?"

Kamilla steered Grey to the side of the hallway and stopped. "Seriously, Grey? You told him?"

"I..."

"She didn't just tell me, she *enlisted* me," Yusuf clarified. "And good thing she did, because I have a lead." Yusuf held up a scratch piece of paper, the corner of a sheet of notebook paper that had been ripped off. On it, an address was written in his perfect handwriting.

Kamilla snatched it out of his hand. "What's this address to?"

Yusuf leaned against the bank of lockers, looking around and lowering his voice. "According to my guy at the phone company, the phone that sent a text to Grey during that rainstorm has been in that location for weeks, only leaving once."

"Leaving where? When?"

"The carnival."

Grey shuddered. The texter had claimed that he'd been responsible for the Ferris wheel's malfunction. Had he been watching her that night?

"So where is this address?" Kamilla asked. "I don't know this street."

"It's on the edge of town," Yusuf answered. He kicked at the ground. "A cabin in the woods."

"Creepy."

"That's not the worst part," Yusuf said, his shoulders hunched. "It isn't just any cabin. It's where they found LeMarc's body. It's the cabin he was murdered in."

The cabin. She didn't remember it at all, just walking with LeMarc by the river and then her blood-covered bed, but that's where they'd found him. She hadn't even known there was a cabin out there.

Grey leaned one arm against the locker before her knees gave out, and Yusuf was right there, putting his arm around her.

But Grey didn't deserve a comforting arm. LeMarc's murderer was still out there, and she was holding important evidence that could help in the investigation. "I think it's time we told the police what's going on. Share the texts with them, send them to investigate the cabin."

Kamilla grimaced. "I want to catch this guy. I want him to pay. We should go ourselves, check it out."

"Are you insane? We find evidence that a brutal murderer is hanging out at the scene of the crime and you want to pay him a visit?"

Kamilla shrugged. "The police won't know how to fix this. They're completely inept."

"And we, as high school students, are much more capable." Grey looked over to Yusuf for support. "Tell her she's crazy."

Yusuf shrugged. "We wouldn't have to go in. We could just... look through the windows."

Grey's mouth dropped. "You're joking, right?"

Yusuf leaned in, hushing his voice to a whisper. "Grey, I didn't just get the location of the texter, I got the transcripts of the texts. This guy accused you of murder."

"I didn't kill LeMarc."

Yusuf's arm around her tightened. "I know. But maybe we should get some solid evidence to prove that before we turn you into the police's prime suspect."

"You honestly think I would put you two in danger just to save my own skin? Never."

Kamilla and Yusuf exchanged a weighty glance. How could they think this was a good idea?

"What if it *is* Ellie?" Kamilla blurted out. "She's the queen of drama, maybe she wanted to stir up some drama when she found out we'd been keeping secrets. Do you really want her to go to jail for sending a few texts? Think about this."

"I am the *only* one thinking about this. We're not going to some creepy cabin by ourselves. I don't get why you guys are pushing this."

"Grey, what if we just—"

"No." Grey cut off Kamilla before she could even finish her sentence. "We call the cops and tell them what's going on. We let them search the cabin and question whoever they find. Final answer."

She pulled out from under Yusuf's arm and plodded back to the lunch room. Her friends had gone mad, trying to play hero when clearly this was a task for professionals. This wasn't a storybook or comic book, this was real life. Grey was going to find justice for LeMarc, but not through some ill-conceived attempt at playing the hero.

Ellie was innocent, just like Grey was, and that would become clear as soon as Grey turned over her phone to law enforcement. The police would search the cabin again and find the clue they needed to solve the case. And then, finally, this horrible nightmare would be over.

Wilder

9

During his first several weeks back at school, Wilder kept messaging Reggie to get back into Grey's world, but all he got for his efforts was a series of increasingly frustrating GIFs of people saying "no." He looked up all the info he could about Victoria and her connection to Monroe, even trying his hand at hacking into the studio's servers, but that wasn't any more successful.

At the end of the third week, Wilder was invited to meet with a studio executive at Monroe Studios after school. At least the receptionist presented it like an invitation, but Wilder knew the meeting wasn't optional.

His palms grew sweaty as he thought of what this might mean. What if Reggie hadn't been as smooth in fixing the cover-up as they'd thought? What if the email had been traced?

But this could also be an opportunity. If Wilder wanted to find out what happened to Victoria Price, he was going to need to step it up. A few hacking attempts and some internet searches weren't going to prove something nefarious had happened to Grey's house-keeper.

So after seventh period, he pulled a baseball cap low over his eyes and hopped on a city bus.

After arriving at the studio, Wilder was escorted through the main gate by an uptight woman in a pantsuit and red lipstick. Wilder didn't recognize her; she must be new. He waved at Charlie, the gate security guard, who nodded his hat.

"Hey, Wilder," he called out. "Long time, no see."

Wilder followed the woman, who still hadn't introduced herself, through the studio hallways. For such an uptight company, the feel of the main studio was earthy and grounded. The hallways were adorned with wood paneling going halfway up like a seventies' den, with the top half crowded with photos of Grey, almost like family photos on a mantle piece.

Other than the state-of-the-art lab, everything was brown and gold and green, as though Monroe Studios was making a concerted effort to avoid appearing cold or corporate. This studio felt more homey than Wilder's real home did.

The woman dropped him off next to a few chairs stationed outside of the CEO's office. Wilder must be in big trouble, if he was seeing the big man himself.

"Wait here," the woman said, and then walked away, her shoes clicking loudly on the wooden floor.

After a few minutes, the door opened, and Wilder saw a familiar face. He smiled, ready to say hi, when he realized he didn't actually know its owner. He'd only seen that thick dark hair through his computer screen.

It was Yusuf Abdullah, Grey's new love interest on the show. He was a new character, so his avatar looked just like him.

"Yusuf," Wilder said in surprise.

Yusuf looked up and grinned. Wilder wanted to punch his smile right off of his perfect face. He was always smiling on the show, and it drove Wilder crazy. No one was that happy. He was surprised Grey didn't see right through this guy's act.

"It's Michael, actually. The studio wanted a more diverse name for the show. They're trying to battle that article that exploded last year, the one that said the show was too White."

Right. Michael Michigan. Dumb name.

Michael held out his hand for Wilder to shake. "You're Wilder Blue, right? Grey's ex?"

Wilder shook Michael's hand. The actor had an aggressive hand-shake, all power and force. "Yeah. Or LeMarc was, at least. My character."

Michael nodded. "So tell me, Blue, how did you do it? Grey was kissing you by the second date. My character has been Prince Charming for three weeks, and the girl's cold as a fish."

That's not what it looked like on the Ferris wheel last week. Wilder had watched the most recent episode with white knuckles.

"Her boyfriend just died," Wilder defended. "The studio's prob-ably pressuring you for more action, but don't forget that she's a real person. She needs time to grieve."

Michael shrugged. "Whatever. There isn't a shortage of hot, bored girls in the dorms. Tess, the actress who plays Ellie, is just *wow*. But I've got to admit, I'm curious. *A virtual kiss.* None of my friends have crossed *that* off of their list. And from last season, it looks like she's pretty good."

He paused, as though waiting for Wilder to confirm.

When he didn't, Michael continued, "You're right about the studio, though. I just met with Mr. Monroe, and he's mad I haven't gotten anywhere with her. I tried to sneak in a kiss the other day, and she turned at just the right moment, so it turned into a kiss on the cheek. I swear she did it on purpose."

Wilder nodded, ready to throw up.

"I don't want to lose my job. She's killing me here. Any tips on how to win her over?"

Wilder considered telling him that jumping off the nearest bridge was a great strategy for romance. "Maybe she senses you aren't being completely genuine with her."

Michael rolled his eyes. "Yeah right. She fell for you, didn't she? You were just as fake as I am. As *everyone* in her life is. She's never noticed. I'll figure it out. I will definitely get that kiss soon. Just building up more tension for the audience, right?"

"Well, good luck," Wilder said, meaning exactly the opposite.

After Michael left, Wilder sat fuming. It was awful enough watching Grey fall in love with someone else, but someone like *that*? Wilder was surprised Michael could walk without tripping over his ego.

Wait for me, Grey, he said silently, wishing there was some way for her to hear him. *I promise you, I'm coming back.*

Wilder's thoughts were interrupted by someone calling, "Come in, Mr. Blue," through the doorway.

Taking a deep breath, he opened the door.

The CEO's office was massive. Everything in the room was dipped in luxury; the furniture was ornately carved, the carpet lush, the ceiling coffered. A sitting area was complete with a bottle of some expensive alcohol on ice, which didn't seem to be a puddle of water. How often did someone come in to change it?

Two of the walls were made up of windows, but instead of looking out to the compound, they displayed virtual landscapes. As

Wilder watched, it shifted from a sunny meadow to a calming sandy beach.

The man himself was standing behind his desk. Ansel Monroe.

Grey's father. Her real father.

Wilder's mother had once called the CEO of Monroe Studios a man who ate souls for breakfast in hopes of finding one for himself. Looking at his perfect suit, his perfect hair, his perfect pocket square, and his dead eyes, a diet of tortured souls didn't seem as improbable as when his mother had first said it. A man who sold his daughter to the world every week, who tortured her for the entertainment of millions, was a brand of evil Wilder couldn't even fathom.

When Monroe wanted to be, he was magnetic, drawing all the energy in the room and wearing it like a shiny crown. When Wilder had met him that day he'd started at the studio, he'd been entranced by the man's charisma, all the parts of him Grey had inherited.

But it had been a long time since Wilder had seen Monroe smile.

Ironically, after a hallway of photographs of Grey, her father's office didn't have a single one.

Instead of saying anything, Ansel Monroe walked over to a bureau sitting against the wall, slid open a drawer, and pulled a stack of magazines out of it. He dropped them down on the desk in front of Wilder with a loud smack.

The one on top featured a clear shot of Wilder leaning against a locker, eyes closed and lips glued to Mia Thompson's. The cover read *Wilder's New Flame!* He'd avoided looking up the picture online, but here it sat, pointing at him like an accusing finger.

"I'm sorry," Wilder said. "I didn't realize she was taking a picture."

Ansel Monroe gestured at the seat in front of his desk. Wilder sat down on the edge of the padded chair. His hands were shaking. Ansel Monroe wasn't large, or strong-looking, or even very tall, but he was utterly terrifying.

Monroe remained standing.

"Actually, your indiscretion came at a good time," Monroe said. "Grey seems to like this Yusuf character, but LeMarc was so beloved, the public is still having a hard time accepting a new love interest for her. If Wilder Blue has a new girlfriend, maybe they'll be more likely to let you go. To let LeMarc go."

"Oh," Wilder said, feeling like he'd just been stabbed through the heart. "That's good. So why am I here?"

He wouldn't have been summoned here just for a *well done*.

"Take some more pictures with this girl. You got your replacement phone, right? Walks in the park, feeding the ducks, something cheesy and cute. Not something you've done with Grey. Make sure to get a few more kissing shots. If you arrange a time, we can even ensure there are paparazzi there to take photos."

Wilder choked on his own disbelief. "What? I'm not going to fake-date Mia Thompson just because you ask me to."

Monroe leaned forward on his desk. "This isn't a request, Wilder. You've already broken contract once already, and that same contract clearly states that we're in charge of your public image for a year after you leave the show. Unless you want me to sue you for more than your entire family tree back to Adam is worth, you'll take the pictures."

Having a lawyer mom who didn't hate me would come in handy right now, Wilder thought. But his mom would never back him now, not even against the hated Ansel Monroe.

"Fine. I'll go on a few dates with Mia. She'll love the publicity."

"Good." Monroe swept the magazines into the trash next to his desk.

Wilder tapped the edge of his chair, trying to figure out how to bring up Victoria. Monroe wouldn't bow to intimidation, and Wilder definitely didn't have anything to bribe him with. Perhaps if Wilder surprised him enough, he'd lose his cool and say something he didn't mean to.

Before Wilder could open his mouth, however, Monroe cleared his throat heavily. *Meaningfully.*

"What? Is there more than the fake dating thing?"

Monroe put his hands behind his back. "During your time on the show, you showed an unusual adeptness at persuasion."

"Persuasion?"

Monroe nodded. "You could get Grey to do what you wanted her to."

Wilder's stomach squirmed. It was too close to what his mother had said about him. "That's not true. I never manipulated her."

Monroe ignored the defense, considering Wilder thoughtfully. "What would you do to convince her to do something dangerous? Go somewhere risky without alerting the police?"

Wilder smiled grimly. "Grey's too smart for the plotline you've written, isn't she?"

"We want her to visit a cabin in the woods, but the actors playing her friends haven't been able to convince her to go. She called the police yesterday, tried to report the texts she's been getting."

"Tried?"

"No spoilers. Let's just say her report isn't going through. Watching Grey filing police reports isn't exciting content for our teen viewers."

The worst thing was, Wilder knew exactly how to do it. The studio was probably going about it the wrong way, trying to use the texts' accusations to pressure Grey into keeping it from the cops. She would never put others in danger to protect herself.

But she would go to protect people she cared about. To get her to that cabin, all they needed to do was make it seem like Yusuf or Kamilla, even Ellie, was abducted and brought to the cabin. Drop a classic *come alone and don't involve the police* note on her pillow, and nothing could keep her from going to help them.

Not that Wilder was going to tell Monroe any of that. "What on earth makes you think I would help you manipulate her?"

Monroe leveled a dead, robotic gaze towards him. "I'll shorten your contract by a month. One month fewer on the books at Monroe Studios, one month fewer where we control your image."

"You're that confident in this Yusuf character, that you think I'll be irrelevant by then?"

Monroe sighed. "Take it or leave it, Mr. Blue."

Wilder crossed his arms. If he *didn't* help Monroe, what kinds of horrors would he do to Grey to coerce her into some horrible plotline? But if he did, maybe Monroe would make her life horrible anyway. "What's going to be waiting for her at that cabin you want her visiting?"

Monroe shook his head. "No spoilers."

Wilder rolled his eyes. "I'm not going to help you manipulate her."

Monroe didn't move, not a twitch of his finger, but something in his presence tightened, sharpened, making him all the more menacing. "I'm getting her to that cabin, Blue. Even if she has to be dragged kicking and screaming. In fact, it's been a while since we had an abduction. Might be a nice callback to a previous plotpoint."

"Father of the year."

"I get results. And I get ratings."

Wilder shook his head. "You don't deserve her."

"Neither do you, *LeMarc*. If you aren't going to help, get out. "

Wilder stood, but hesitated before turning away. He still hadn't gotten anything on Victoria.

Here goes nothing.

"You want to know how to convince Grey? Tell me one thing, and I'll write the script myself."

"What one thing?"

"Where's Victoria Price?"

Ansel Monroe didn't get flustered. He didn't loosen his tie, run his fingers through his hair wildly, or take a few staggering steps back in dismay. But Wilder could see it in the way his cheek twitched, how he rubbed the pads of his fingertips together.

Ansel might not know where Victoria was, but he obviously knew she wasn't in Peru.

"Victoria is no longer engaged with Monroe Studios."

"And you personally? She's no longer *engaged* with you?"

Ansel's jaw twitched again. "Get out," he said calmly.

Wilder almost believed there wasn't a tsunami of rage storming behind those dead eyes.

"You sure you don't want me to stay so you can lie some more?"

"I said get out. Now."

Wilder turned to go.

Behind him, Ansel added, "And I expect more pictures with you and Ms. Thompson within the week."

Monroe didn't even call an escort for him to go back to the front door. He must really be rattled.

He knew something about Victoria, something dangerous. Was Lillian right after all? Had Monroe committed murder? If so, how? When?

Why?

Wilder walked down the wood-paneled hallway, trying to stop his hands from shaking from mingled fear and anger, but then his steps slowed. He came to a stop in front of a picture of Ansel and the Secretary of State.

Monroe hadn't called him an escort.

This was Wilder's chance, if he was brave enough to take it. He turned into another hallway and headed for the bathroom. It was only a little over an hour before the end of the business day, when Monroe would go home to the mansion he'd built on Grey's pain. Wilder could hide in a bathroom stall for that long, keep out of sight. The office didn't entirely shut down, but there were few enough people in the evenings that Wilder could sneak back to the CEO's office.

And then he was getting some answers.

Just to be safe, Wilder waited as long as he could stand. It was 6:30 by the time he slipped out of the bathroom stall. Only one person had come in while he was hiding, and whoever it was hadn't seemed to notice the scuffed-up sneakers in the stall at the end.

He urged himself not to creep, but to walk purposefully. If you just pretend you belong, most people don't second-guess it.

Fortunately, he didn't run into anyone on the way to Monroe's office. There were only two other offices in the hallway, and neither of them seemed to have light coming through the door, but it was hard to tell. After pressing his ear against Monroe's door and hearing nothing, he tried the door handle.

Locked, of course, but it'd been worth a shot. Wilder had watched a bunch of videos on picking locks the first time he'd planned to break in here, but he'd never actually had to do it before, and he didn't have any tools.

He pulled out his phone, the replacement that had arrived from the studio just the day before. *What can I use to pick a lock instead of a lock pick set?*

The results sprang up before him: paper clips could work as picks, and a common alternative to a tension wrench was the underwire of a bra. *Yeah, not going to work for me.*

Paper clips, though... He could check the other offices, see if one of the other execs had a bowl of paper clips on their desk.

The first office he checked was locked, but with the second one he struck gold: Not only was the office unlocked, but it belonged to Cassandra Evensworth, who happened to have a whole box of paper clips and a few stray bobby pins in her desk.

Now all he needed was something to create tension. His online search said a screwdriver or wrench would work, but those would be in the facilities area, and no doubt the janitorial staff was in and out of that place this time of night.

Confidence. The janitorial closet and offices were on the bottom floor, so Wilder took the elevator down, wiping his sweaty palms on his jeans the whole way down. *If you act like you have every right to be there, people will believe you do.*

One of the custodial workers had his cart halfway out of the closet when Wilder arrived.

He let out a deep breath and plastered on a smile. "Hi! I was hoping you could do me a favor."

The cleaner looked up. He was young, probably in his early twenties, with longish red hair and acne. Perfect. The younger he was, the more likely he was going to be to follow directions. "What fav—"

The young man trailed off, his eyes bugging out. "You're Wilder Blue."

Wilder nodded and ducked his head, as though embarrassed at the attention. "I was hoping you guys had a screwdriver down here. Flathead, preferably."

The cleaner nodded. "Yeah, no problem, man." He disappeared into the closet for a few moments, and emerged with a screwdriver in hand.

"Perfect," Wilder said. "Thanks. I'll bring this right back."

"Just leave it in the closet if I'm not here."

Back on the elevator, Wilder let out a long breath, his stomach squirming. That had been really easy. *Too* easy, right? Why was it that manipulating people was so easy for him? And why hadn't he ever noticed before his mother and Ansel Monroe pointed it out?

Like a battering ram with a 100-watt smile.

The hallway was still empty when the elevator dinged open on the eighth floor. This was the riskiest part, because if Wilder was caught picking the lock to Monroe's office, he'd be arrested for sure.

It took forever, but eventually Wilder felt the final pin go.

"Gotcha," he whispered, tiptoeing through the door.

The office was dark, the virtual windows making up two of the walls gray and opaque. Wilder didn't turn on the light.

For someone who kept such massive secrets, Monroe didn't seem too concerned about security. His filing cabinets weren't locked.

As he flicked through the files, Wilder was sorely tempted to read each word, but he forced himself to give them just a cursory glance: Right now, he was looking for evidence about Victoria, and if Monroe was guilty of murder, it was highly unlikely he was keeping paper evidence in his office at work.

If there was a clue here, it was on the computer.

After finishing his check of the files, Wilder sat down on Monroe's office chair and cracked his knuckles. Time to get to work.

Unfortunately, even Monroe wasn't arrogant enough not to have a computer password. This was going to take a while.

He'd only been working for a few minutes when music suddenly blasted through the room. His cell phone was ringing, and like an idiot, he hadn't silenced it.

Wilder cursed and scrambled in his pocket for the phone, pressing the button to silence it. It was Reggie calling.

Wilder answered with a quick swipe. "Hey, Reg. I'm glad you finally called back, but now is not really a good time."

"How come? I can't imagine Monroe is stupid enough to leave around whatever you're looking for in that office."

Wilder shot to his feet. There was no way a man like Ansel Monroe would have cameras in this room. "What office? I'm not in an office."

"Gotcha. So I don't have to worry about warning you that Ansel Monroe is heading back up now?"

"Oh crap."

"Yeah, I thought so. The office doesn't have cameras, but the hallway sure does. The balls on you, kid, to ask for a screwdriver like that. How security didn't see you, I have no idea. They must be playing cards again."

Reggie had been watching the whole time. He must have just gotten in--how'd he even know to look at the cameras?

"How long do I have?"

"About ten seconds."

Just at that moment, Wilder heard the *ding* of the elevator. He cursed again, looking around for a place to hide. Behind the desk was out of the question. He settled for behind the couch, even though its bottom was a good three inches above the floor. If someone looked at the perfect angle (like while seated at Monroe's desk), they could probably see him.

Wilder had barely ducked his head behind the couch when Ansel put his key in the door and jiggled it. Hopefully he wouldn't realize it was already unlocked.

"Come on in," Ansel said as he entered the room. He wasn't alone.

The light snapped on, and the two intruders came over to where Wilder was hidden. He forced himself to stay perfectly still. One sat down on the couch, just inches away on the other side of the sleek sofa, and Wilder put a hand over his mouth to silence his breathing. Could they not hear his thumping heartbeat? It was louder than Lana's piggyback-ride squeals right in his ear.

"What did you find out?" Wilder recognized Monroe's voice, and from the sound of it he wasn't the one on the couch.

"It seems he visited the sister a few weeks ago. She must have tipped him off to Ms. Price's disappearance."

Wilder squeezed his eyes tight, fairly certain he was the "he" in question. The couch-sitter was a man, but Wilder didn't recognize the nasally voice.

"Still no sign of her?"

The man on the couch shifted his weight. "No. But the security officer that day is still convinced Victoria Price never left the compound."

"Well, he's wrong. Wherever she is, alive or dead, she's not in Heringford. This is not our liability, right?"

"I'm not sure a judge would agree with you. You've intentionally covered up her disappearance, which is definitely unlawful. If you'd conducted a search or filed a missing persons report like I counseled, you wouldn't be in this position."

Wilder could hear a tinkling sound, like ice in a glass. Monroe was pouring himself a drink. "We're so close to moving locations, we can't afford an investigation to stall things. I want to move out of US jurisdiction as soon as possible after the finale airs, or we'll never get away with putting Grey in that kind of danger. What are my options, Redmaine? Should I just let the boy ask his questions, or should I go with an NDA? A Cease and Desist?"

Redmaine. This was Monroe's head lawyer, his mother's nemesis.

"He's a teenager, and a TV star at that. If it weren't for his mother, I would say do nothing. But we can assume that she's already prepping a case. Several, probably."

"I never should have hired him. But you should have seen his audition—kid had half the board in love with him after a few minutes. If only Grey had his charisma. Takes too much after her mother to be any sort of leading lady, and the viewers are getting sick of her caution."

Wilder's hands formed into fists at the attack on Grey, but Redmaine wisely remained quiet.

"It felt good, too, to stick it to that awful woman by hiring her son," Monroe continued. "But I digress. I *did* hire him, and now it's a problem."

"I can have a briefing on your options for handling this ready first thing tomorrow."

"Perfect. Nothing in writing, of course. I'll have Terri move my 8:30."

The men talked for a few minutes more, but Ansel clearly wasn't in the mood to chat. The office plunged into darkness again as they left and Monroe snapped off the light.

Wilder peeled himself from the ground, staggering because one of his feet had fallen asleep.

Monroe hadn't killed Victoria, but she was missing, and he hadn't reported it. According to what the lawyer had said, she'd entered Grey's world one morning and never left.

Had someone done something to her? If so, who? It clearly wasn't Monroe, unless he was lying to his lawyer.

But on his way back down the staircase to the building's exit, there was one thing pounding in Wilder's mind that drowned out the rest, the words Monroe had spoken with the scaly coolness of a serpent: *I want to be out of US jurisdiction as soon as possible after the finale airs, or we'll never get away with putting Grey in that kind of danger.*

Three of them struck him like a sledgehammer: Finale. Grey. *Danger.*

Grey

10

On Monday evening, Ellie showed up unexpectedly after dinner with a duffel bag over her shoulder. "You have plans tonight? It's been a while since we had a sleepover and just talked."

"And you dropped your phone in the toilet, so you couldn't text me?"

"You would have ignored a text."

Fair enough. Grey could pretend not to see a text, but it was a lot harder to pretend she didn't notice her friend standing right in front of her. Maybe Ellie still knew her better than she thought.

She opened the door further and let her in.

Grey swiped a bag of chips from the kitchen on their way upstairs. Ellie wouldn't touch them, but she was feeling the need for comfort food.

Up in the bedroom, they both sat cross-legged on her bed. "So, what boy is causing you grief?" Grey asked through a mouthful of chips, settling in to hear Ellie's latest guy drama. It would be a good distraction from obsessing over what the cops thought about the printout of texts from her cell she'd turned in as evidence.

Ellie shrugged. "I thought maybe we could talk about something other than guys tonight."

When she saw Grey's surprise, she added, "I don't know, I just feel like things have been different between us since I woke up from the coma. We don't really talk anymore."

Grey nodded. "What do you want to talk about?"

"Maybe we can start with you quitting the student council," Ellie suggested.

"I un-quit. There was a whole campaign, carnival, flyers, remember?"

"But I never asked you why you quit in the first place. And I should have. Because clearly whatever caused you to snap is still happening. You're so stressed all the time, and I get the feeling like you're keeping things from me. I miss my best friend, Grey."

"I've missed you, too," Grey admitted.

This was the old Ellie, the one she'd mourned after the coma.

With all the secrets she was keeping from her friend, she'd pulled away from El. She hadn't considered what a huge part she had played in their friendship turning into a shell of what it had been.

"I'm sorry I've been so stressed. I think some of my past trauma is starting to catch up with me. And there are... new stressors, too."

Ellie stretched out across the bed, head on her hand. "Such as..."

Grey swallowed. She didn't want to tell Ellie about the texts for her own protection, but maybe it would be nice to have someone to talk to about how broken she felt all the time. "Do you sometimes feel like if people knew the real you, the you no one gets to see, they'd turn the other way and run?"

"Don't be ridiculous. I've seen you without makeup, babe, and you're a little washed out, maybe, but you wouldn't send people *running*."

Grey shook her head. Obviously Ellie wasn't relating. But if she wanted a real relationship again, she needed to be vulnerable. "It's not a physical thing. It's deeper than that. Like, take student council. I just... I got overwhelmed by the return to school and the pressure to be as perfect as everyone thinks I am."

Ellie rolled her eyes. "Yeah, right. You can't help but be perfect. You just inhaled half a bag of chips in two minutes, and you won't gain any weight. No wonder Yusuf is into you."

"That's not what I mean."

"You could seriously have a boyfriend by the end of the week if you just realized how beautiful you are and flaunted it a little more."

Grey decided to try one more time. "I've been struggling a lot with this need to be perfect, though, and it doesn't have anything to do with boys liking me. All of the stuff that's happened to me, to us, doesn't it ever get to you? I feel like I'm trying to keep up this charade that everything's fine, but it's not. Even in therapy I can't stop pretending to be the golden girl, but I don't know how to move forward, and I'm second-guessing everything, and I genuinely might be going crazy. Does that even make sense?"

Ellie smiled kindly. "Of course it does. We all feel unsure and insecure in new relationships, even me. But that doesn't mean you shouldn't move forward. You are good enough for Yusuf, Grey. I think you'd be more settled if you ended this will they/won't they situation with him and just took the plunge. He's nice, cute, and smart, and I *know* you like him. Has he asked you out yet?"

Grey let out a disappointed breath. "No. No, he hasn't."

Two days after turning over a print-out of her phone messages to Officer Phillips at the police station, the night after Ellie stayed over, Grey still hadn't heard anything about the police's search for the mystery texter. She'd been expecting to at least be pulled in for questioning, if not arrested outright.

She'd made the right decision, though, no matter what Yusuf and Kamilla thought. Kamilla had almost had an aneurism when she learned Grey had spilled everything to the cops, but that was what *anyone* would do. *Should* do. Trained detectives were definitely preferable to random teenagers when it came to this kind of stuff.

And besides, no police had shown up at her door to arrest her for the murder of LeMarc, so Yusuf's fears had been unfounded.

Grey was sitting on her bed, typing up a history paper on her laptop, when her phone beeped.

She gritted her teeth. She used to love those notifications on her phone, when each buzz promised some cheeky message from LeMarc tempting her away from her homework. But now each one sent a trickle of fear through her heart.

Bracing herself, she grabbed her phone from the nightstand and checked.

The text wasn't from LeMarc's number, however.

Ms. Monroe, this is Officer Phillips with the Heringford PD. We've had a new break in the case, and we need your help. Please meet us at 1342 Applewood Lane ASAP.

Well, that didn't *sound* like they were planning on taking her into custody. Did that mean they believed the accusations from the mystery texter weren't true? Was that where her interrogation was going to take place?

Officer Phillips was a familiar name. He was one of the police officers who'd been tasked to investigate her kidnapping, and she'd recognized his giant mustache when she'd turned her text print-outs to him at the station.

A police car was parked on the curb in front of 1342 Applewood Lane as Grey pulled up, though Officer Phillips wasn't in it. She turned off her car and looked up at the house. The alarm bells went off in her head. Shouldn't a cop ask to meet in a public place? It was a modest home, but well-kept. Window boxes with bright pink flowers accented the blue siding, and an American flag fluttered in the light breeze. Something about the idyllic scene felt off, like a chord with one note a hair flat.

The door was ajar.

Maybe there was a reason Officer Phillips wanted to meet at a random house instead of in a public location. He could have found a clue there, maybe even LeMarc's phone. And perhaps the cops left the door open because they were waiting for her.

She pulled out her phone. *I'm here.*

After a few moments, she got a text back. *We're upstairs. Come on up.* The upstairs window curtain fluttered open, and Officer Phillips waved from behind the glass.

Despite this reassurance, Grey adjusted the keys in her hand to stick out between her fingers. With her other hand, she opened the car door and got out.

She hesitated for a moment on the doorstep. Why weren't they coming down to greet her? This all felt so strange. Her pulse quickened, as if warning her of danger.

But then she shook her head, laughing at herself. She'd been reading too many spy novels lately, apparently. The mystery texter wouldn't wait until she was practically in police custody to come after her. And if the police were going to arrest her or something, they would have just done it. They wouldn't have texted her to come to some random house.

She'd seen Officer Phillips from the window. There was nothing to be scared of here. She pushed through the door, dropping her car keys into her purse. The house was decorated in cheery yellow florals, with family pictures crowding the buffet near the entryway.

"Officer Phillips?" she called out.

She picked up a framed photo of a middle-aged man with a mustache and cop uniform, standing tall in front of an American flag. Officer Phillips.

Was this his own house? Why had he invited her here?

A muffled bang came from upstairs, sending her heart racing again. Should she leave, or should she climb the stairs? Common sense told her to call the police, but this *was* the police.

Something was definitely wrong. She could feel it, the sickly ripple of impending disaster under her skin.

Gritting her teeth, she crept up the stairs. "Officer Phillips?" she repeated, even louder this time. "Officer, is there something wrong?

She opened the first door to the left, peeking inside.

Slumped on the floor, face down, was Officer Phillips. He was perfectly still.

"No!" Grey threw herself onto her knees next to the prone officer, pulling out her cell phone and dialing 9-1-1.

She put it on speaker before leaning over to shake Officer Phillips.

The voice over the phone was far too perky for someone who spent his days listening to people's catastrophes. "9-1-1, what's your emergency?"

"Hello, there's a man here, passed out. I'm trying to rouse him, but he's not responding."

"Does he have a pulse?"

Grey pushed her shaking fingers against the officer's throat, searching for a pulse. She couldn't find one—was it because it wasn't there, or was it her trembling hands? Even through all the tragedy in her life, she'd never done this before.

"I... I don't think so. Should I do CPR?"

"If you're certified. We're sending an ambulance to your location now. Please stay on the line and let me know if anything changes."

Grey tried to think back to her CPR training in health class. Her certification wasn't expired, was it? She *definitely* knew the patient should be lying on his back. The first thing she had to do was roll him over.

Grabbing Officer Phillips's shoulders, she carefully pulled him around.

That's when she saw the blood.

His dark uniform, so blue it was almost black, had soaked up the majority of it, but the light brown carpet revealed a pool of darkening crimson. And the smell—how had she missed it before?—was thick and sharp. Unmistakable.

Grey swallowed, gasping for air. It had to be the mysterious texter, the enigma at the other end of the line.

He had never been more than a mystery, an incorporeal threat. But murder was real. It was messy and bloody and visceral. A *person* did this, a person who hated Grey.

She'd tried to do the right thing, the smart thing, and now someone was dead, just like LeMarc. And he hadn't just died. *Someone* did this. Someone killed him.

Her stomach heaved, and she pushed away from the body just in time to avoid throwing up all over it.

"Hello?" came the voice from the phone. "What was that noise?"

9-1-1, Grey realized. They were still on the line.

"He's... Someone... There's blood," she choked out. "It's everywhere."

"The ambulance will be there shortly."

Grey could already hear them arriving, the solemn wail of the ambulance growing louder every second.

The next few hours were a blur of sirens and questions and blood. After all the crises in her life, you'd think she'd be used to it by now, but it was all still as horrible and exhausting as ever. Apparently Officer Phillips hadn't told anyone else about the texts; no one asked her a single question about them.

By the time she got back to her room, she could barely walk. She closed the door against her parents' concerned faces and collapsed onto her bed, the tears already streaming from her eyes.

Her phone beeped, but she ignored it, pulling a pillow against her face to stifle the ugly sobs ripping through her.

All those smiling photos on the mantlepiece, the locked elbows and grins with missing teeth. Every photo taken from now on for the Phillips family would feel like something was missing, someone important standing just out of frame. Grey knew that feeling, the heaviness of empty spaces.

She needed Danny. She needed LeMarc. She needed *someone*.

She pulled out her phone to text Kamilla, but she paused at the sight of her painted nails.

She'd washed her hands ages ago, scrubbing the dried blood from between her fingers where it'd slipped when she pressed down on the wound. Somehow, though, she still saw it there. She *felt* it there.

She was going to pull up Kamilla's number when she saw she had another text. A text from LeMarc's number.

No, she thought, *I won't look*. But she couldn't stop herself from clicking on the notification.

The message was short, but it made her want to throw up all over again.

Now look what you made me do.

Wilder

11

Wilder was sitting at a table in Club Blanc, trying to ignore the heavy thumping of the music blasting through the twenty-one-and-under club, when his phone buzzed. With the pounding beat shaking the walls, he wouldn't have heard or felt it if it hadn't been in his hand. After a quick glance to make sure Mia was still distracted by the bulldozer she was dancing with, he swiped up to see it. It was a text coming in from Reggie.

No, the text read. Short and not at all sweet.

Wilder began typing away, his thumbs flying over the letters. *Come on*, he wrote. *I need you. I can't see her without your help. I promised her I would come back.*

It had been almost a month since he'd visited Grey, and he still hadn't returned. Reg was still refusing to help Wilder get back into her virtual world, and his rejections had only grown more gleeful since he'd caught Wilder breaking into Monroe's office. Apparently his weakness for young love only stretched so far.

Mia sidled up to Wilder, wrapping her arms around his neck. "You're on your phone again? You're the worst fake boyfriend ever," she said, pitching her voice so only he could hear her over the music.

Wilder pressed send and tucked his phone back into his back pocket. "Sorry. Just checking in with a friend. Want to go outside?" He gestured in case she couldn't hear him.

"First, a selfie!"

Wilder obliged, smiling as she snapped a photo of herself kissing his cheek. He blinked the flash out of his eyes.

Mia posted it immediately, and Wilder could see her caption: "Clubbing with the bf. #LovingLeMarc."

At least Grey couldn't see it. It was a bit unfair, that he could watch and overanalyze so many of her interactions with Yusuf, and she didn't know Mia existed.

As soon as Mia was done, he led her outside, their hands linked.

The air outside was cool compared to the cramped, stifling club. Mia, wearing a leather jacket over her skin-tight short black dress, should have been melting, but she looked cool and polished as ever. She leaned against the wall, pulling him in for a kiss. Her lips tasted like sweat and strawberries.

"There's no one out here," he said, pulling away. "No one watching."

Mia smiled wickedly. "I know, but you're fun to kiss. And I know *I'm* good at it."

Wilder considered her for a moment. He was glad he'd decided to be up front with Mia about the studio's request. She'd been excited, not offended like she should have been.

"You're really cool to do this. Not many girls would be okay with being the fake girlfriend. I promise, if I didn't have a contract with Monroe Studios, I would never use you like this."

Mia laughed. "We're using each other. Do you have any ideas how many followers I've gained? People across the country are talking about me right now. You're my ticket to fame, baby."

"Well, as long as you're happy, I'm happy."

The club's neon sign was on in the back alley, illuminating Mia's face in a pink glow as she took Wilder's hand. "What would you be doing tonight if you weren't out with me?" she asked, playing with his fingers.

Wilder shrugged. "I'd probably be at Luke's, trying to convince Carly I haven't turned into a terrible person."

And continuing to look for some kind of clue about Victoria Price, he added silently.

"She confronted me at school the other day," Mia said, as though she were discussing the weather.

Wilder pulled his hand away in surprise. "What?"

"Carly. She stormed up to me after English and warned me not to break your heart again. She said *again*. Were you really heartbroken after I dumped you in junior high? We dated for like, a month."

Wilder crossed his arms. "Don't make fun of me. Thirteen-year-old Wilder was devastated."

Mia tossed her wild curls back. "He was also a terrible kisser."

"Thanks," Wilder laughed, shoving her arm.

"You make up for it now. That Grey Monroe taught you a thing or two."

Wilder laughed again, but this time he had to force it out, keeping the corners of his lips pinned to his cheeks through sheer will.

Mia wasn't fooled. "You know, you were already in love with her back then. I thought it was just a celebrity crush at the time."

"With who?" Wilder asked, backing up a step. "Grey? I'm not in love with her. My character was."

"Mmm-hmm."

"I'm *not* in love with Grey."

"For an actor, you're a terrible liar."

Suddenly, the door from the club began to open. Faster than a flash, Mia pulled Wilder in by his jacket and began kissing him again. He had to put his hand on the wall to keep from crashing into her.

"I told you it was Wilder Blue!" a voice said from the doorway. A flash went off behind Wilder as the club-goer took a picture.

He pulled away slightly, but Mia held him fast with her coat jacket. "Contract," she murmured into his ear before kissing behind it.

He signed a few autographs, and he and Mia took a picture with the club-goers, a young couple who loved the show. They seemed okay with the fact that Wilder had a girlfriend that wasn't Grey. Monroe's strategy seemed to be working.

He practically had to drag Mia away from her adoring fans. "You must love this," Mia said as they turned the corner, holding hands.

She didn't understand him at all. It didn't even occur to her that someone wouldn't want their whole life posted on social media.

"Did Carly really tell you not to hurt me?" Wilder asked, instead of trying to explain it to her.

"Yeah, I think you might have a chance to rebuild that bridge."

There was a new bounce to Wilder's step, suddenly. Clearly Carly still cared.

He walked Mia home. She lived in a nice part of town, in a small but well-kept house. On the doorstep, he gave her a hug.

"I'm really not in love with Grey," he repeated, for good measure.

"Mmm-hmm. You know I have eyes, right?"

"It was my job to convince her LeMarc loved her."

Mia wrapped her arms around his neck. She was always touching him in some way, like she needed the physical connection to feel connected to him at all. "Can I give you some advice?"

"Sure."

"She's falling in love with someone else, Wilder. And her real location may be close, who knows, but she might as well be on the moon. To her, you're a memory. Move on. Find someone new."

He scoffed, feeling tired and bothered all of a sudden. Mia might have guessed at his feelings for Grey, but she didn't understand. "Like you know what love is. Grey's not the only one who's trapped in a digital world. You're not looking for anything real, just followers."

She rolled her eyes. "Real is overrated. Grey's happy in her fake world, and I don't blame her. The real world is awful; she's better off without it. She's better off without *you*."

"You have no idea what you're talking about," Wilder said, pulling away. "I should go."

"Whatever. Have a good night."

Wilder stormed away, hands in his jacket pockets. Light spilled onto the walkway in front of him as she opened the door. Once she closed it, everything was dark again.

As he walked home that night, he tried to block out Mia's words. She might be observant, to notice how he felt about Grey. But she had no idea. No idea at all. Grey wasn't happy. She might not be able to see the bars of her cage, but she could feel them, the iron structures keeping her world small.

As he walked, a dark plan started swirling in his mind. He might not be able to find Grey's location in the real world, but maybe he could get back to see her in the virtual world again. If he couldn't save her, maybe he could convince her to save herself.

He would only have to break about fifty laws, and one of the only friendships he had left, to do it.

Wilder's sister, Lana, had plenty to say about his new girlfriend when he called her on Monday. He put her on speakerphone while he typed on his computer. He was creating something she wouldn't approve of, and his stomach twisted like a sea serpent when he thought about how illegal it was, but it was his only way to see Grey.

"She's pretty," Lana was saying. "But her posts are dumb."

"Hey now," Wilder warned. "That's not nice. You don't even know her."

"Can I meet her?"

That was the last thing Wilder needed, for Lana to grow attached to his fake girlfriend.

"We'll see."

"That means no."

"I said *we'll see*, Lana. That means we'll see. I'd need to figure out how to keep Mom from finding out." He deleted a line of code. Not what he wanted. This was harder than he thought.

"Wilder?"

"Yeah, kiddo?"

There was a pause on the other line. "Does Daddy ever ask about me?"

Wilder stopped typing.

No, he thought. "Absolutely. All the time."

"Can you tell him I can do a cartwheel?"

Wilder closed his eyes. "Of course. I didn't know you can do that. He's going to be so proud! Just like me."

"Thanks!" she said, and then dove into a rambling story about the dog in the apartment next door.

And Mia thought he wasn't a good liar.

A few days later, Wilder got home from school to see his father slumped down onto the couch watching a football game. A bottle hung from his fist.

Warning lights flashed in front of Wilder's eyes, and for a moment he stood frozen in the doorway. His father should be at work. The only reasons he would get the day off would be if he took a sick day, or if...

"I was fired," his father grumbled. "My idiot manager blames me for everything that goes wrong. Barely more than a kid, and he's telling me what to do."

Tread carefully, Wilder thought.

"They didn't appreciate you," he offered. His father grunted in agreement.

Wilder began to sidle against the wall toward his bedroom. "You'll find another job."

His father's head swiveled toward him. His voice was sharp and cutting as he responded, not a hint of slurring. "I wouldn't have to if we had the Monroe money."

Wilder froze against the wall, petrified by his father's attention. He was used to this, the drunken anger and the stilted apology the next day, the half-hearted promises to stop drinking. But the gleam in his father's eye as he took another swig scared him.

Staggering to his feet, his father continued, "What's the amount you've got, sitting in your bank account useless? Fifty thousand? A hundred thousand?"

He closed the space between them, his bottle still in hand.

Ted had Wilder and Lana's eyes, or they had his, rather, but his were bloodshot and ringed with dark shadows. His breath reeked of bourbon.

Searching his father's face, Wilder couldn't find the man his mother must have fallen in love with. He couldn't imagine him being young and romantic.

They were the same height, now, he realized. He'd used to think that the top of his father's head reached the sky.

"Lana wanted me to tell you she can do a cartwheel now," Wilder said, eyeing his father's hand. The glass bottle still hung from it. "I told her you were going to be proud of her."

When his father didn't speak for a moment, Wilder looked up and met his eyes. The emotions he saw there were more familiar than he'd like to admit. Shame. Guilt.

Anger.

"Do you think she'd be proud of you right now?" he said slowly, his heart beating a scattered rhythm.

He should have kept his eyes on the bottle. Fast as a blink, his father cracked it against Wilder's face. It didn't break, but it caught him right at the bend in his brow, knocking him back into the wall.

His vision went dark for a moment, and he slid to the ground, clutching his face.

By the time he sat up and looked around, feeling drunk and confused, his father was gone.

Wilder dreamed of the sea that night, a still, calm ocean glassy in the moonlight. The only tiny ripples were made by his boat, a canoe this time, slowly drifting toward the horizon. The water reflected the face of eternity like a mirror, a thousand tiny specks of starlight.

He could feel her next to him, sharing this moment of peace.

He'd always dreamed of the sea, but it wasn't until he went on the show that Grey was there, too. She never spoke, and in the dream he never looked at her directly, but she was *there*, a presence of light and warmth next to him in his narrow canoe.

When he awoke, he was all alone.

He didn't have the will or the courage to go to school that day. His head was throbbing, and he was still feeling a little dizzy. His face had swollen almost immediately after his father had hit him, and overnight a mottled bruise had formed over the right side of his forehead.

He rolled out of bed around two or three in the afternoon and stood in front of the bathroom mirror, wincing as he gingerly pressed his finger to the bruise. His father could make a living room feel like a prison cell, but he rarely hit him, and never on the face.

He wished he were still friends with Carly, so he could have her help him with cover-up for his photos. The studio would be furious if he posted one with his eye busted up like this.

Suddenly, he heard a thump from his father's room.

His eyes went wide in the mirror before he even registered the surprise. His father was still home.

Wilder didn't want to find out if he was still angry.

He ran back to his room and grabbed his wallet and keys. Throwing on some shoes before rushing out the door, still in the gym shorts and tee he'd slept in, he ran down the apartment corridor and raced down the stairs. He didn't stop until he was out in the fresh air.

The day was overcast, the scent of rain heavy on the air, and Wilder immediately shivered in the late October chill. He should have grabbed his sweatshirt before running out, at least.

The bus was blessedly empty except for an oblivious old driver with a handlebar mustache. The man didn't recognize Wilder, and didn't bother to ask what a banged-up teenager was doing boarding the bus in the early afternoon on a Tuesday.

He got off as close as he could to April Street. It was another mile to Luke's house, and again he chided himself for leaving without a hoodie. Leaves crinkled beneath his feet as he walked, but most were still clinging to the branches, pretending they didn't notice how cold the nights were getting. The whole street was bright with the colors of autumn. Wilder breathed in the scent of fall, something he didn't experience often downtown.

When he got to Luke's, he ducked down into the basement to check whether his friend was working on his computer. It was empty, just flickering lights in the darkness. Wilder collapsed onto one of the ragged couches, letting out a long sigh.

He'd really been hoping Luke was here.

Maybe he was. Maybe he was right above Wilder right now, lying on a couch just like this one. Wilder had never been upstairs before, but it was worth a shot.

He heaved himself up again and trudged up the rickety steps, circling back around the house to the front door. The hanging baskets were gone this late in the year. There was a Halloween windsock in their place, painted as a ghost. Orange and purple lights were wrapped around the porch pillars, and a Jack-o-lantern sneered at Wilder's approach.

Wilder had never been through Luke's front door before. None of the basement crew had. Without giving himself time to second-guess it, he rang the doorbell.

He could hear it echo through the house, and a few seconds later, he could hear little footsteps pattering toward the door.

The little girl who opened the door looked like a miniature Luke, with sandy hair and a wide, friendly face. She was probably three or four, with big hazel eyes. Luke always wore his sunglasses, so Wilder wasn't sure if it was a family trait.

He smiled at her, and she smiled back. "Hi," he said through the screen door. "Is your big brother home?"

She just cocked her head at him, like a lost puppy. Just at that moment, however, Luke peeked his head around the door. "Is that Wilder's voice I hear?" he asked, picking up the little girl in his arms. He didn't have his white cane; he must not need it in such familiar territory.

"Yeah. Sorry, I know I don't usually come to the front door, but I was wondering if you have time to talk."

"Sure." Luke opened the screen door. "The front door thing isn't a rule, you know. You guys are welcome to visit me at the top half of my house, too."

Wilder walked inside. Luke led him into a parlor, where a large front window let in lots of light. Someone had pulled the curtains aside. Luke gestured at one of two blue armchairs positioned in front of a massive fireplace and set the girl into the other one.

"No, Daddy," she whimpered, holding her hands out to be picked up again.

"Daddy?"

Luke shrugged, picking the girl up again and dropping a big kiss onto the top of her head. "Yeah, Daddy. Maggie killed any college plans, but I wouldn't have it any other way, you know?"

Wilder nodded, stunned. He'd assumed Luke hadn't gone to college because he'd chosen it, not because he'd been a teenage dad. After a moment, he realized Luke couldn't see his nod and verbalized, "Yeah."

"Not that I'm encouraging you to follow in my footsteps," Luke said. He sat down in the chair, perching Maggie on his lap. Wilder sat down in the other one. "Watch out with Mia, man. I love my daughter, but life would have been easier if I'd had her five years later."

"The mom?"

Luke shook his head.

"Sorry."

"I'm over it. So what do you want to talk to me about? Something tells me it's not dating advice."

Wilder pulled his laptop out of his bag. "I've been working on a project that I think I've figured out, mostly, but I hit a little bit of a roadblock."

Luke nodded. His daughter began pulling on his ear. "Sure. I can take a look."

"Thanks. I've never done ransomware before, and I—"

"Ransomware?" Luke interrupted. "Are you kidding me?"

"I know it sounds bad," Wilder conceded, opening his laptop to boot it up. "But I'm not stealing money or anything. I just need some leverage to convince a friend to help me out with something."

"Wilder, that is all kinds of illegal, not to mention stupid. You might be famous, but they'll still throw your—" He paused, head tilted towards his daughter. "Your bottom in jail if you're caught."

"Luke, I have to do this. It's my only way to see Grey again."

Luke let out a frustrated groan. "That's what this is for? You're using it to blackmail someone into helping you get into the studio? To illegally hack Grey's augmented reality? No way. I'm not helping you with this, and I can't let you risk it. She's just a girl, Wilder. She's great, yes, and I know you're in love with her, but this is the wrong way to go about fixing this problem."

"Fine. Don't help me," Wilder answered, slamming his laptop shut and shoving it back into his bag. "Like I said, I think I have it figured out without—"

He cut off, seeing a familiar car pull up.

"What?" Luke asked. "Did you stop talking because you realized what an idiot you are, or is it the car that I just heard parking on my street?"

"It's Carly," Wilder said, watching her pull her bag out of the car. Abe wasn't with her.

Luke sighed, standing up and placing Maggie back on his hip in one smooth motion. "Maybe she can talk some sense into you," he said, heading for the door. He navigated his home with such ease, sometimes Wilder forgot he couldn't see where he was going.

"Luke, please don't talk to her about this. If I knew you were going to turn into such a narc, I wouldn't have told you anything."

"Sometimes you forget I'm not seventeen. And sometimes I forget you are."

"What's that supposed to mean?" Wilder asked, but Luke opened the door and didn't answer.

"Hey Carly! I'm up here," Luke called out. Through the window, Wilder could see her stop in surprise and head toward the house.

"Hi, Maggie!" she said as she entered, shucking her shoes at the door and giving the little girl a hug.

Wilder looked down at his own feet. Was he supposed to take his shoes off? He never did in the basement.

"You knew he had a kid?"

"Some people are concerned with others instead of just themselves," Luke answered for her.

As Luke led her into the parlor, Carly stopped dead in her tracks. It took Wilder a moment to realize why. He'd forgotten about the bruises.

"What happened to your face?"

"What's wrong with his face?" Luke asked, setting Maggie down and heading to the dining room to grab another chair.

Instead of answering, she folded her arms, waiting for Wilder's response.

"I... got into a fight."

"Is this why you weren't in school today? How did you really get that black eye?"

"It's none of your business how I got it."

Carly ignored the chair Luke had brought in. "Of course it is. You're my friend."

"You've been treating me like a leper since I got back," he said, exasperated. "You *explicitly* said that we weren't friends anymore."

"That's before your dad gave you a black eye!"

Luke's eyebrows flew up. "Wait, your dad hit you? Seriously? That's messed up, Wilder."

"It's also completely untrue," Wilder lied, standing up from his chair. "I'm used to tabloids making up stories, but I thought you were too good for that, Carly."

She wasn't buying it. That was the trouble with people who knew you better than their own reflection. They didn't need words to tell them things; they could read everything on your face. "Look me in the eyes, then, and tell me your dad didn't do that to you."

"Why do you even care? I thought you'd be happy someone punched me."

She threw up her hands. "Okay, I give up. I can't be mad at you anymore. I'm just crazy worried. With Mia, and now your dad, and I know you aren't talking to your mom..."

"Stay out of my life." Wilder grabbed his bag and stormed toward the front door, turning back at the last second. "It's better without you in it."

Walking down the front path, knowing Carly was watching him leave, he fought back the urge to turn back and make a rude gesture at her.

Maybe there was something broken inside of him. This was what he *wanted*. He wanted Carly to forgive him, for her to finally want to be his friend again, and now that she did it made him so angry he wanted to punch his fist right through Luke's front door.

He sought refuge at Mia's that evening, setting up camp on her couch. He didn't want to go back to his dad's, and there was nowhere else to go. He was surprised Mia's parents would let her boyfriend stay the night, even on the couch, but her father worked nights, and her mom was a fan of the show.

His fake girlfriend didn't seem overly concerned about his injuries. In fact, she posted a pic of the black eye with the caption, "My bf took a punch defending my honor today #KnightInShiningAr-mor."

After a few minutes looking at her phone, she laughed. "Your fans are protective of your face," she said. "You should really be paying me as your publicist."

They watched a chick flick that Wilder could have lived without, but at least it wasn't Grey. He didn't want to watch her right now, not if it wasn't for real. He didn't need Luke to use his ransomware. Luke was the one who'd said he was better than he thought he was.

Mia fell asleep halfway through the movie, head on his lap, and he shook her awake once the credits started rolling. She yawned prettily and mumbled something about her evening skin care routine.

When she got up to head back to her room, Wilder stopped her by grabbing her hand. "Hey, I never said sorry about the other night," he said. "We left things in a weird spot."

Mia smiled her crooked grin. "Wow, a boy who apologizes. You better be careful, Wilder Blue, or I'll fall in love with you for real. Grey's a lucky girl. I hope she knows how much LeMarc loved her."

Wilder laid back down on the couch. It was too short for him.

She will, he thought. *She will*.

Grey

12

G rey told herself she was calling Kamilla for comfort after finding Officer Phillips's body. And she'd thought she was, truly. But when Kamilla announced that it was time to check out that cabin and stop this psychopath once and for all, Grey said yes without hesitation.

No one else was going to die because of her. She was going to find out who did this to LeMarc and Officer Phillips.

And she was doing it tonight.

However, when midnight came around and a car pulled up at her curb, headlights off and motor idling quietly, it wasn't Kamilla's. It was Yusuf's.

A streetlight was out, blanketing the car and its occupants in darkness, but Kamilla's face was illuminated by her cell phone as she sat in the back seat.

"Are you crazy?" Grey asked her friend as she climbed into the front seat. "Why did you call Yusuf? How could you get him caught up in this?"

Yusuf was dressed in a striped polo and jeans, looking more like he was heading for the country club with daddy's golf buddies than to a creepy cabin in the woods.

Kamilla shrugged. "You're the one who invited him into this craziness. I just filled him in on the details."

"And invited him to come!"

"I invited myself," Yusuf said, slowly pulling away from the curb and driving down the deserted street. "LeMarc was my friend, too, remember?"

"I've gotten enough people killed today, ok? The police officer I went to..."

Her voice cracked.

"So it wasn't a heart attack, then, like they're saying?"

Grey shook her head, wiping away a tear. "This is not a game, and it's not some fun adventure. We could die tonight."

Yusuf shook his head. "This guy doesn't seem to want you dead. If he managed to kill a police officer with only a day of planning, getting rid of you wouldn't be a problem. He's had months to make a move, and he hasn't."

That's not quite true. He'd had a chance at the Ferris wheel, and he hadn't taken it. He was waiting for the winter gala, for some reason.

"Could be a she," Kamilla pitched in. "But it's a valid question. What *do* they want?"

"They're clearly not trying to scare me into confessing. The text said to tell the truth, but they killed the police officer I reported the texts to."

"So if the texter doesn't want you arrested for murder and they don't want you dead, what do they want?"

"To torture me? Draw out my terror before they eventually kill me?"

Yusuf turned onto a dirt road. The cabin was right at the outskirts of town, and Grey felt the usual flutter of fear in her chest as they pulled away from the well-lit roads of Heringford. The trees cast crooked shadows all around, reaching arms that grazed the car with scratching fingers.

Her phobia was flaring up. *We're not leaving town*, she repeated to herself. *We're not leaving town.*

Yusuf turned on the car's headlights. "If we're trying to figure out their motivation, there's one question we haven't asked."

"And what's that?"

Yusuf pointed his thumb behind him, where Kamilla was sitting in the backseat. "Her."

"I'm not a question, Abdullah."

"Yes, you are actually. Grey was with LeMarc when she blanked out that night, and she woke up with blood all over her. She was clearly there in the cabin with him when he died."

"I didn't kill him," Grey said, her voice catching on the words.

"I know. I believe you. But even if you don't remember it, you were there. That's the reason you're getting the texts. So why is Kamilla?" He looked at Kamilla in the rearview mirror. "You weren't there at the cabin that night, right?"

"Definitely not."

"And you're not missing time?" Grey asked, turning around to look at her friend.

Yusuf was right. Why Kamilla? And why were the texts coming from Danny's phone? She'd been so focused on her own guilt, she hadn't considered what the texter wanted from Kamilla.

Kamilla shook her head. "I don't know why this guy is texting me."

"Has he sent you any more texts the past few weeks?"

Her eyes darted to the side. "More texts?"

"Yeah. He keeps texting me."

"No, no more texts," Kamilla said, but her eyes trained on her feet.

Was she lying? If so, what was in those texts that she wasn't willing to share? It couldn't be worse than an accusation of murder.

She turned back to Yusuf to ask about tracking Danny's phone, too, but the words died on her tongue. Yusuf was looking in the rearview mirror at Kamilla while the car turned slightly left at a swerve in the winding road.

But his hands never moved.

The car took the turn without him. The steering wheel had skimmed under his fingers, following the road's twisted path through the trees, but he hadn't moved his hands at all.

Grey gasped.

Yusuf turned towards her. "What? Did you realize something?"

She looked into those chocolate eyes, and for just a moment she had the oddest feeling, like she didn't know the person behind them at all.

"No, I just thought I saw... I don't know."

He searched her face, and the concern and warmth there was so *Yusuf* it knocked her back into herself. He really cared about her.

"Really, I'm fine. I'm just worried."

Kamilla reached a hand forward and placed it on her shoulder. "We're coming up to the house now. We'll sneak in, find the cell phone, and bring it home. In and out."

Yusuf killed the lights again, and less than a minute later they were pulling up to the side of the road. About a quarter mile ahead, Grey could see the silhouette of a building through the trees.

The house didn't have any lights on. She could barely see it through the trees, but she could feel its presence, almost as though it exhaled frosty breath into the nighttime air.

"This is madness," she murmured, gnawing on her lower lip. "What are we doing?"

After shutting off the engine, Yusuf turned towards her and took her hand in his. "If you say we aren't doing this, then we aren't doing this. But this person won't stop unless someone stops them."

She thought of Danny, seeming so grown up in his military uniform, looking at her as though he already knew it would be the last time. She thought of LeMarc down at the riverbank, whispering in her ear.

"I've already lost so much. I can't lose anybody else."

"You told me you felt like you weren't the star of your own life, that you were just waiting for someone to save you. So don't wait anymore. Be the hero, Grey."

"I'm not sure I know how."

"Of course you do," said Kamilla from the back. "You were born for this."

Grey let out a long breath. "Okay, I'm ready."

Yusuf nodded. "The two of us can go in while Kamilla waits in the car. If we're not back in fifteen minutes, drive back home and call the police."

She expected Kamilla to argue, wanting to come with them or at least extend the time, but she nodded. "You guys got this."

Their footprints sounded loud as gunshots in the brisk autumn air as they crept towards the cabin. It didn't usually get cold here, definitely not enough for the leaves to fall, but Grey was glad she'd put on a thick cable-knit sweater before leaving the house. It was freezing out here, and she couldn't tell if the way she was shaking was because of the chill in the air or because she was terrified.

They slowed their pace as she got closer to the cabin, Yusuf holding out his hand to signal for them to approach at a crawl. His cell phone company contacts had said LeMarc's phone almost never left the cabin. So either the texter hid the cell phone here when he wasn't using it, or the perpetrator himself was in the cabin right now.

Even though Grey knew she'd been here the night of LeMarc's death, no bells of recognition went off. She had no recollection of this place.

Close up, Grey could see the signs of neglect all over the derelict cabin: planks missing from the front porch, a broken pane in one of the windows, and weeds climbing so high they grazed the windowsills. Grey nudged Yusuf's shoulder and nodded towards the broken window. They'd have to be especially quiet, if there wasn't even any glass between them and the interior of the cabin.

Splitting from Yusuf, she crept up to a different window, peering inside. It was too dark to see; she could barely make out the shapes of furniture within. There seemed to be dark patches that looked like doorways, so there were probably multiple rooms.

"Do you think he's inside?" she whispered.

Grey was too focused on the window, covering her eyes with her hands, to hear someone approaching from behind. She had no warning when a hand snaked out of the darkness and covered her mouth, muting any attempts at a scream.

As soon as the hand closed over her mouth, Grey's elbow shot back into her attacker's stomach. The arms around her were strong, and from their position it was clear her assailant had the height advantage.

She was rewarded with a soft grunt, and she used the attacker's surprise to try to wrench herself from the man's grip. He hadn't been as surprised as she'd hoped, though; his arms squeezed even tighter.

"Grey, stop," came Yusuf's voice in her ear, so soft she could barely hear it.

What?

She stopped fighting, and he let go, uncovering her mouth.

Grey whirled around. *No, the killer isn't Yusuf. It can't be him.*

As soon as she opened her mouth to ask what on earth he was doing, however, he quickly covered it with his hand again, bringing his other hand up to place a single finger to his lips.

Quiet.

What was going on? Grey did her best to communicate the question with her wide eyes, but Yusuf kept his hand clamped over her mouth. He used his head to gesture at the trees behind him.

Grey was glad his hand was there, then, to cover up her gasp. Two bright eyes flashed at them from less than twenty feet back, circles of light. She couldn't see well, but it looked like some sort of canine, either a dog or a wolf. The eyes moved back and forth as the animal prowled through the trees, constantly moving but keeping its distance.

After a moment, Grey realized the prowling was accompanied by a familiar tinkling noise, the sound of a dog collar jingling.

Yusuf leaned towards her with a whisper. "On the count of three, we run back to the car."

As though it could hear and understand him, the dog stalked over to cut off the path between them and the car. It let out a low, savage growl that rumbled like thunder.

"What do we do?"

Yusuf gestured towards the front door of the cabin with his head. Was he mad?

"What if the texter is in there?"

"Maybe the dog will get tired of growling and leave."

As soon as he finished, the dog let out a glut of barking and sprinted towards them.

Yusuf grabbed Grey's arm and shoved her roughly towards the cabin. They stumbled together through the door, closing it a second before the dog slammed into it.

They stood with their backs against the door of the cabin, breathing hard. On the other side, the dog was barking himself into a frenzy. It would be a while before they could leave.

But a far greater danger might be on this side of the door, hiding in the shadows.

The cabin looked empty. Yusuf flipped on a light, and a wood-hewn front room sprang into view, complete with a worn leather couch draped with woven blankets, a hearty fireplace with a wooden mantle, and a tiny kitchen and dining area. A door in the back opened to a bedroom that also looked unoccupied. A second door was closed.

Grey hastened to the fireplace and picked up a poker. "You get the bedroom, and I'll check the bathroom."

Yusuf crossed his arms, looking impressed. "Is it bad that I find you wielding a fireplace poker like a sword really attractive?"

"There could literally be a murderer hiding in this house with us."

Yusuf shook himself. "Yup, yup, yup. Focusing."

He grabbed another rod from the fireplace kit and headed to the bedroom.

Grey's hands were so clammy, she could barely open the bathroom door. *One, two, three!* On instinct, she let out a warrior cry as she pushed through the door, fireplace poker aloft.

The only occupants were a sad-looking shower and rose-pink porcelain sink.

"No one in the bedroom, either," Yusuf said from behind her.

Grey let out a long breath. The texter wasn't here. Had he left the phone behind?

"Do you recognize anything in this place? Anything seem familiar? You were here that night."

Grey scanned the room, but it seemed completely foreign to her. She didn't remember ever having been in *any* cabin, let alone this one in particular. She didn't see any signs of violence, either. Where had LeMarc been, when they shot him? Was there a lot of blood? Had they had to change out the rug? The questions buzzed through her mind like snatches of song through radio static.

"Do you have your phone?" Yusuf asked, derailing her morbid train of thought. "We should text Kamilla and let her know we're ok, have her keep a lookout for the mystery texter returning."

Grey pulled her cell from her pocket with shaking hands. She was about to pull up Kamilla's texts when the screen lit up. It was from LeMarc's number, but it wasn't a text.

It was a phone call.

Yusuf's dark hair fell over his forehead in its signature curl as he looked down at the phone.

"Speakerphone," he urged.

Grey nodded, her hands shaking with nerves. Before she could chicken out, she answered the call.

The voice on the other end of the line was distorted, filtered through some sort of machine. "Grey Monroe. We speak at last."

"What do you want?"

"I apologize I'm not much of a host. I didn't realize I'd have house guests tonight, or I would have laid out some cheese and crackers."

Grey closed her eyes, trying to calm her racing heart. He knew they were there.

"Who are you? Why are you torturing Grey like this?" Yusuf cut in.

The voice laughed. "The why comes later. All you need to know is the when. The winter gala is only weeks away. Are you ready?"

"Ready for what? What are you planning?"

"You know, Grey, I never congratulated you on your recent election. Student body president. Quite the accomplishment."

Grey and Yusuf looked at each other in confusion at the sudden shift in conversation, but didn't answer.

"Do you enjoy your position of power?" the voice asked, soft and sibilant. "Does it make you feel like you have control over something? You must feel so powerless. Your brother gone. Your love murdered. And the awful thing is, you're still utterly helpless.

There's nothing you can do about anything that's happening. Does that make you angry, Grey?"

The air in the cabin was tight, like a rubber band ready to snap. Grey wasn't sure how far he could push her before she would either shatter or explode, and she didn't know herself well enough to know which would happen.

"I'm not angry. And I'm not afraid of you."

Another laugh. "You should be."

The caller hung up abruptly, leaving the dial tone playing over the speakerphone. It sounded like a flatlining heart rate monitor. *Time to call it.*

Yusuf kicked at one of the sofa legs in frustration. "You're not going to that gala. Pretend you're sick. I'll come over and stand guard."

"Um, have you met my mother? She'd wheel me in on a stretcher if she had to."

He threw up his hands. "I feel like we're just playing right into his creepy little plan. If we can't go to the cops, and we can't outsmart him, what do we do?"

"We should go before he comes back. Obviously the phone isn't here. He has it wherever he is."

"You're right." Yusuf picked up a huge gnawed bone from a braided wicker basket next to the door. "Hopefully his guard dog is easily distracted. I'll throw this the other direction, and then we make a run for the car."

"Let's do it."

Just as Yusuf was about to open the door, however, massive bone in hand, something metallic on the mantle caught Grey's eye. "Wait."

She walked over to the mantle and picked up a silver bracelet. It was 90's retro, a charm bracelet with little metal symbols hanging from it.

"Is it yours?"

Grey shook her head. "No."

"So another girl was here? Maybe the killer's a woman?"

Grey turned back to him, her stomach tossing like a salad. "Not just any woman. I know who this bracelet belongs to."

"Who?"

"It's how the killer knew we were here, how she's been following our every move. How she knew I was going to Officer Phillips."

"She?"

Grey clenched the bracelet in her fist. "I bought three of these in the fifth grade for me and my two best friends. Mine had a horse, because I was obsessed with Black Beauty. Ellie's had a dolphin. But the sunflower—this sunflower—went to Kamilla."

Yusuf's shoulders fell. "She said she wasn't here that night."

"She lied. And that means…"

She trailed off, but Yusuf finished for her. "It means Kamilla killed LeMarc."

Wilder

13

Wilder stared at his computer screen, watching the cursor blink. He'd gotten home only an hour earlier from a classmate's Halloween party, where he and Mia had gone as characters from some teen drama he didn't watch. Without changing out of the ripped jeans and letterman's jacket she'd made him wear, he'd immediately dived for his computer to finish off the program. And now he was done. It was ready. All he needed to do was press "send."

Ransomware was illegal, to be sure, and Reggie was a friend, even if their friendship was at times tenuous. If Wilder sent this, there would be no friendship left.

But Monroe's warning of Grey being in danger kept running through his head. He needed to see her, to convince her of what was real. If he couldn't prove Monroe was connected to Victoria's disappearance, it was the only way to help her.

Wilder pressed "send" and shut his laptop quickly, breathing fast. With shaking hands, he picked up the new phone the studio had purchased for him and found Reggie's name.

"What?" Reg said on picking up, clearly annoyed. "I'm working, kid. I'm way behind."

"Fine. Are you having a good Halloween?" he asked in a bright voice, hoping Reggie couldn't hear his voice shaking.

"No. I just finished saying I'm behind on work, how is that a good Halloween? And now I get a phone call from you, where you're going to beg me to sneak you in again and make it out like I'm the bad guy."

Wilder bit his lip. Now or never. "I didn't call to beg. I'm not trying to get back in to see her," he lied. "I am, however, still trying to figure out where she is, and I'm not giving up on that. I think I might have a lead. I sent you a link through email. Do you mind just looking at it?"

"Fine," Reggie grumbled.

Wilder held his breath as he waited for Reggie to open his email and click on the link.

A tsunami of curses flooded through the phone. "What is this? Are you kidding me right now, Wilder? You honestly think I can't work around this crap ransomware?"

Wilder could hear a flurry of typing on the other end of the line.

"I think it will take you time," Wilder responded. "And you can't be guaranteed to have it done by morning."

"I can't believe I just fell for that," Reggie exploded, throwing in a few expletives. "Like an eighty-year-old grandma! You're a devious little piece of trash, you know that?"

"Let me visit her, and I'll set your computer free."

"You're seriously going to pull this crap and then trust me to work Bruno for you?"

"You left me no choice."

There were a few moments of no sound from the other end of the line other than the clacking of keys.

"When you said you were into coding, I thought you'd taken some YouTube course," Reggie shouted. "Not that you created illegal ransomware to infect unsuspecting victims!"

"Reggie, you know I don't want to do this. Just let me see her, and I'll give you the decryption key."

"And what's stopping me from just calling the cops on your—Ugh, never mind. If you're cold enough to do this, you would rat me out in a second."

"I might have recorded our conversation the last time you broke me in," Wilder lied.

"I knew I *never* should have helped you in the first place. I can't believe I'm being extorted by a teenager."

"I'll be there in twenty minutes," Wilder said, already jumping out of bed to throw on a sweatshirt.

"Good. Then I can kill you in person."

By the time Wilder reached the studio, Reggie had calmed down a bit. He still threw a Red Bull can at Wilder as he walked in, but at least he was no longer threatening murder. "Apparently I'm not the only one who hates you. That bruise looks nasty. I hope the guy who gave it to you was wearing rings."

They weren't alone in the lab, Wilder realized. At the edge of the room stood a woman in her twenties that fit every stereotype of a programmer he could have thought of, from her frizzy brown hair to the tee that read, *<programmer joke> !False: It's funny because it's true.*

She met Wilder's eyes briefly and then looked quickly away, wrapping and unwrapping the hem of her tee around her pointer finger again and again.

"This is Brooke," Reggie said, nodding to the woman. "We were working on some Bruno code when I got your call. She's good with secrets."

"Uh, hi Brooke."

She held up a quick hand, still looking at the ground, and Wilder turned back to Reggie. "Is Bruno ready?"

"What do you mean? Bruno's always ready. It's covering up your manipulative, scheming tracks that I have to set up, and that's done. You get one hour with her to start. Every time you say something annoying, it drops ten minutes."

"Deal," Wilder said. "I'll take it."

"Fine. You got anything else you want to say to me?"

Wilder paused. "You'll get the decryption key once I'm back."

Reggie shook his head. "You're an idiot. Let's get this over with. Lie down."

Wilder lay down and wrapped the cuff around his upper arm. Who cared about his friendship with Reggie when he was about to see Grey?

Not me, he tried to convince himself silently.

"You ready?" Reggie asked abruptly.

"Yeah. Send me in."

The first thing Wilder noticed was the blinding pain ripping through his head. It felt like a rabid wolf was trapped behind his eyes, lashing out with claws bared. He cried out, gripping his head as though his hands could keep it together. It felt like it was about to split in two.

Reggie must be messing with his pain receptors.

Falling to his knees, Wilder begged, "Reggie, stop. Please, stop it." The pain subsided a bit, though his eyes were still streaming water and his head still pounded.

When he looked up, he could see Grey peering down at him, her worried face blurred through his watery eyes. "Are you okay?" she asked, voice small.

"Yeah, I'm fine." He tried to stand, but he swayed a bit, and Grey reached out an arm to steady him. "I might have made an enemy of the developer who controls my avatar."

"Is that why you're wearing that?"

Wilder looked down to see that he was in a pair of short neon orange track shorts, a Barbie tank top, and snowboots.

"Seriously, Reg?" he called out, but the outfit didn't shift to something normal. The pain in his head had died down, though, so maybe Reggie had made his point.

Grey reached for her lamp and switched it on. As the room sprang into warm focus, he drank in everything: the red crease the pillow had left on the side of her face, the damp spot on the pillowcase where she must have been drooling, the ragged fringes of her plaid pajama shorts.

He loved every imperfect bit of her, and all the perfect parts, too: her big blue eyes, long, smooth legs, and bemused smile.

"That outfit looks even more ridiculous with the light on."

"At least I look like LeMarc. He could have made me look like a creep, I guess. Made you think a murderer had crawled through your window."

Suddenly a line of text appeared in front of him, hovering in the air. It happened sometimes when the show's producers or director wanted an actor to say a particular line. They hadn't used it a lot with Wilder, but he noticed sometimes that Yusuf delivered some of his lines like he was reading them, and the actress who played Ellie needed a lot of help.

This time the words read, *Good idea. Next time.*

Awesome. Wilder hoped he wasn't going to have Reggie's commentary following him around the whole night. The next time line was hopeful, though. Maybe Reggie was still considering a next time.

Looking down at his clothes, however, Wilder doubted it.

"So you can look like anyone you want?" Grey asked. "You don't always look like you?"

Wilder shrugged, sitting down next to her on the bed. "I don't ever look like me. Not here, anyway. This is just my avatar's appearance. I'm actually a blonde in real life."

Grey made a face. Okay, so she wasn't into blondes. Wilder fought down disappointment. It had never occurred to him that she wouldn't be attracted to the way he looked in the real world.

"I'm actually three hundred pounds, too, with pock-marked skin and greasy hair, but it's good to know you were only dating me for my looks."

Grey shook her head. "I would have loved LeMarc no matter what he looked like. My hallucinations are definitely getting stranger, though. My slow descent into madness continues."

"You sure you weren't crazy before? You once admitted to me that you liked liverwurst."

Grey barked out a laugh. "That's something LeMarc would have said."

She traced a finger up his arm, and he shivered at her touch.

"I told you the last time, I'm not a fever dream. I've been thinking about it, and I've come up with some ways to convince you. I want to show you that I'm real. Let's go for a walk, and I'll tell you all about it."

Grey picked up her alarm clock. "It's midnight, ghost boy. Real people do this thing called sleep. And I'd rather not have anyone see me conversing with air."

"You don't really want to go to sleep," Wilder said, confident that it was the truth. "You know I won't be here when you wake up."

Grey leaned forward, wrapping her arms around him and resting her cheek against his shoulder. "Of course I don't want to sleep when you're here. But I don't want you to vanish when I close my eyes. I want you to be real. I want you to be here when I wake up, sneaking through my window like you used to."

"I can't," Wilder said into her hair. "You know I can't. But we have tonight. I have an hour, and then I have to go."

Letting go of him, she leaned back and brushed a curl away from his forehead. "Why did it take you so long to come back?"

"It's complicated. But, like I said, it gave me the chance to come up with some ways to convince you that I'm telling the truth."

"Right. The walk." She yawned, stretching her arms out and arching her back. "Fine. Let's go for a walk, and you can tell me your arguments. Just let me get dressed."

He nodded, and after a moment where neither of them moved she raised her eyebrows. "Without you in the room, preferably."

He walked into the hallway and closed the door behind him.

Nice try, floated green words in front of him.

"Shut up," Wilder murmured, leaning back against the textured hallway wallpaper. "You're the one who films every moment of her life. You have a camera on her right now."

Nope. It's turned off when she's changing. She's a minor. Minus 10 minutes for thinking I'm a creep.

After a few moments, the door opened and Grey came out, wearing a blue sweater that matched her eyes. She'd thrown her hair up into a bun on the top of her head.

"Where do you want to walk?" she asked, her voice lowered so as not to wake her non-existent mother and father.

"Maybe down by the river?"

Even in the dark hallway he could see her face blanche and her eyes widen, and he realized his mistake as she started shaking her head in horror.

"Right. That's the last place you saw me. Where your memory goes blank."

Grey leaned her forehead onto his shoulder again, and he could feel her shaking as he rubbed her shoulder. "I'm sorry," he whispered. "I wasn't thinking. I just thought it would be nice to go on a boat ride with one of Old Mitchell's rowboats he leaves tied up there."

The words appeared in front of him again. *Those boats aren't real. She'd fall right through. Try again.*

Grey pulled away, shaking her head. "No, I'm the one who's... Sorry, I'm just under a lot of stress right now."

"What about a drive?" Wilder suggested. "We could talk in your car, and if you're right and I'm not real, no one will see you talking to the air."

Nope. They'll notice the gas gauge is lower, Reggie spelled out, even as Grey answered, "My parents would hear the garage door."

"Maybe we could just sit in your car for today. No need to drive or walk anywhere," he revised.

"Okay. The car it is."

Grey took his hand and started leading him down the stairs, slow and silent. When they arrived in the garage, she turned the light on, and Wilder laughed out loud when he saw her car.

"What's so funny?"

Wilder shook his head. "Nothing, I'd just forgotten how nice your car is. I mean, this is a *Porsche*. I never got to ride in it as LeMarc, since we were still a secret."

Have I mentioned you're an idiot? Ten minutes off.

"I thought nothing in my world was real. Doesn't that include my car?" Grey retorted, heading for the left side of the car.

Wilder grabbed her hand to stop her, though, and pulled her back.

"You're not actually going to drive it. Sit next to me," he importuned, pulling her back to the passenger side. He opened the door to the backseat and slid in.

She crawled in after him, lying down across the seat to lay her head back in his lap, her knees bent. She was probably sending Bruno into overdrive, shifting her perceptions so she'd think her head was higher than it really was, changing the smooth texture of the car seat's fabric into his leg. She pulled the door closed with her foot.

"The car is real, actually. It needs to be, for it to move you from place to place. Besides, no amount of artificial intelligence could fake the feeling of sitting in a car this great. You aren't going to fall asleep if you're laying down, are you?"

She grinned up at him. "Maybe. What are you going to do to keep me awake?"

She looked enchanting, even with her hair in a messy bun and the stale garage light casting odd shadows on her face, but his time was limited, and he had some convincing to do.

"I'm going to tell you what to do to prove this world isn't real."

She raised an eyebrow. "Go on."

Wilder had thought this out, and he was confident that he could convince her, now and forever, that he was telling the truth. "Okay, Bruno is too good and the actors too well-trained for you to throw a punch or something like that, so my first test is to throw your food at someone. It has to be your food, not theirs. Your food is real, the people aren't."

"So if I throw a donut at my friend it will go right through her?"

"Probably not a donut. The junk food you eat is fake; your calorie intake is pretty closely controlled. But they also can't starve you, so the food that's prepped for you by your cook, that's real."

Grey sat up. "Wait, does that mean my housekeeper is real? If she cooks real food?"

Wilder nodded. He wanted desperately to bring up Victoria, look for clues, but Grey had enough on her plate without yet another person she loved being murdered. It gave him an idea for something to ask Reggie later, though.

"Well that's something, I guess. I would never throw food at someone, though. I could never be that cruel."

"Cruel?" Wilder hadn't ever seen anything on the show that would indicate that throwing food was cruel in Grey's world.

"Throwing food is one of the most offensive things you can do to someone. It's cruel. Unforgivable. I'm sick just thinking about it." She did look a little green, and the cadence she used as she explained how offensive it was, it sounded like a line she'd memorized from hearing it over and over again.

Wilder thought back to what his mother had been researching about how the studio might have tried fear conditioning on Grey. He closed his eyes, pushing away the thought. He didn't want to think of the ways they trained Grey to reject things that would reveal her world's secrets.

"Ok, the next one's easier: Ask somebody what their favorite TV show is. See their reaction. If they look confused and ask what a TV show is, you might be crazy. If they look surprised or flustered, then you know they know what it is and don't understand how you do."

Watch it, Reggie's text appeared. *If she starts asking those questions, they'll start looking into ways she could have found it out. That's another twenty minutes.*

Wilder felt his heart flutter in panic. How many minutes was that, now, out of the short hour he had?

"TV," Grey answered, narrowing her eyes. "Ellie mentioned it a few months ago, I think."

"That's because the actress who plays Ellie is an idiot," Wilder said.

Grey looked like she wanted to defend her friend, but she didn't say anything.

"You think I'm being a jerk?" he asked.

"No, I think you're my subconscious. I think *I'm* being a jerk, since I'm frustrated with Ellie's shallowness right now. Though if you're my subconscious trying to tell me something, I still haven't figured out what the Barbie tank represents."

Wilder looked down at his ridiculous outfit. He'd forgotten he was wearing it. "Reggie, please?" he pleaded.

Grey sat up straight when his clothes turned into a regular green tee and jeans. "What just..."

Words appeared before him in the air. *You're lucky Brooke is such a softie.*

Rolling his eyes, Wilder moved onto number three. It was his big sell. "The third one we can do right now, if you're brave enough. End this, once and for all."

"What is it?"

"Drive out of town. One town over, to LeMarc's old school."

She made a choked noise, and Wilder leaned forward, putting his arms around her waist.

"No way," she said, pushing back her flyaway hairs with a fluttering hand. "There's no way."

"I know you're afraid of travel. That's... There are reasons for that. But it's the fastest way to see that there's something wrong. Nothing exists one town over, Grey. This city is all there is to your world."

"I can't. I'm not just nervous about it, it's like my whole body rebels if I even think about driving out of here. I tried, once, to leave. I wanted to show myself that I was strong enough, so I asked Mom to take me to a store outside of the city limits. It almost killed me. It took me hours to stop sobbing."

That sounded like more than just fear conditioning. It sounded like the studio was manipulating Grey's fear centers. What a horrifying idea, that Bruno could go past manipulating her five senses to play with her emotions too, or at least the physical indications of a feeling like fear.

"I think if we do it tonight, it will be better," he guessed. "I'll be here with you this time. Come on, Grey. Even if I'm not real, even if I'm just your own psyche trying to tell you something, shouldn't you still *try*? Maybe what your brain is trying to tell you is that you need to conquer your fear. How can you defeat your mystery texter if you're afraid?"

"Driving out of city limits is not going to help me defeat him."

"No, but it will prove to you that you're brave enough to face anything," Wilder said, moving his hands to her cheeks, letting his thumbs graze her cheekbones. "Even a murderer. Even the fact that your life isn't real."

"Even losing the boy I love," Grey added in a faint voice, her eyes never leaving his. There was regret swimming there, and sadness.

Wilder tried to pretend he didn't see goodbye there, too.

"You haven't lost me. You'll never lose me," he pleaded. He kissed her, a rough, urgent kiss, but she pulled away.

"This is what my dreams have been trying to tell me, isn't it? This is why I'm seeing you. I'm suffocating with grief after losing you and Danny, and the only way my mind could teach me to be brave enough to move on is by having it be a message from you."

"That is... a really big leap, and not at all true," Wilder said frantically. This was going exactly the opposite of how he'd hoped. "I'm trying to convince you *not* to let me go. To hold off on falling for Yusuf just a little longer, long enough for me to get you out. Don't lose faith in me, Grey. I'm right here."

Time to go, kid.

"No, not yet," Wilder murmured. "I just need more time."

Grey put her hand against his cheek. "I would give anything for more time with you. But time was never on our side."

Wilder shut his eyes tight, willing himself to stay in Grey's world, to hold on just a little longer.

Even before he opened them, however, he knew he was back in the lab. The air temperature dropped, and the lights brightened behind his lids.

When he finally opened his eyes, Reggie was laying back in his computer chair, legs up on the table, considering him. Brooke stood next to him, picking at her elbow.

"That didn't quite go as planned," Wilder said as he sat up.

"There are worse endings for star-crossed lovers," Reggie said.

Wilder had thought talking to Grey again would make him feel better, but somehow he was even more empty than before. He unhooked himself from the pod and pulled a slip of paper from his pocket.

"Well, you held up your end of the deal, tank tops and headaches notwithstanding. Here's the key." He handed the paper over to Reggie.

Reggie shook it off. "I searched your bag and your pockets. Found that right away. I've been using my computer this whole time."

Wilder pulled the paper back, confused. "Why didn't you pull me out earlier, then?"

Instead of answering, Reggie took a swig from his Red Bull and swallowed. After a moment, he said, "Life is full of choices, Wilder. With the email you sent me, you made a choice. You made the wrong choice, and that makes it easier to make the wrong choice again the next time. I don't want to see you turn to the dark side."

Wilder closed his eyes and let out a breath.

"Reg, I'm sorry for what I did," he said finally.

"And *there's* the apology you should have given about an hour ago. You know, while you were under, I did some research on you, to see where you got good enough to create this tech, or who you got it from. This Luke guy seems quite the Fagin to your Artful Dodger."

Wilder clenched his jaw but didn't speak. He didn't know why there was online evidence that Luke had taught him his hacking skills, and he didn't like it.

"I don't know what that means, but sure. Reggie, can you do me a favor?"

Reggie burst out laughing. "You're kidding, right?"

"You know Victoria Price? Grey's original housekeeper?"

"Sure. You asked about her before."

"She's missing, and I'm pretty sure her dead body is somewhere in Grey's compound."

Brooke wrapped her t-shirt hem around her finger, a mindless habit. "That's horrible! I thought she moved to South America."

Reggie, on the other hand, was 100% suspicious. "Let me guess, you want me to tell you where the compound is so you can search for her."

"No. I want you to see if the nodule she has, the one that connects her to Bruno so she can see what Grey sees, is still in the compound. Does it have a tracker?"

Reggie leaned back on his rolling chair. "No, but given a little time I might be able to figure out her location from the signal it sends back." He let out a sigh. "I'm inclined to say no just because you're such an obnoxious little criminal."

Brooke cleared her throat. "I'll do it. I can check for her location."

Reggie rolled his eyes. "Softie."

Wilder tried not to look too excited.

"Thank you," he said to Brooke.

His meeting with Grey might have gone up in epic flames, but that didn't matter if he could find Victoria Price—and hopefully free Grey for good.

We got ZERO screen time between Danny and Kamilla, and now she might be LeMarc's killer?!?! GIVE US THE DAMILLA CONTENT WE DESERVE!!

realgreymonroe

Tried drawing a picture of them together lol

GREYWATCH

Grey

14

Kamilla had great table manners for a manipulative, lying murderer.

As she paused from her eating roasted lamb at the Monroe's dinner table to ask Yusuf about adjusting to a new school, Grey seethed quietly.

"I mean, you're obviously insanely lucky to have me and Grey as friends," she prompted, "but you had to have left some behind, too."

It reminded Grey of a book she'd read once about Jesse James, the infamous robber who'd ransacked trains, stagecoaches, and banks in post-Civil War America. James was as polite as he was dashing, and he'd read his Bible every night.

Somehow, that hadn't stopped him from stealing and killing his way up and down the Midwest.

Grey couldn't get the face of Officer Phillips out of her mind. With every lift of Kamilla's fork, her head reverberated with the image of his bloody body on that bedroom floor.

Could Kamilla really have done something like that? Could she really be behind everything?

Yusuf was playing his part flawlessly, matching Kamilla smile for smile, laugh for laugh. Responding to her question, he winked at Grey and said, "It was hard, but you guys more than make up for it."

Grey's mother had been ecstatic when she'd mentioned that she'd like to have Yusuf over for dinner instead of just Kamilla, even though she'd insisted he was just a friend. In Astrid Monroe's mind, the words "boy" and "friend" couldn't exist as distinct entities; they were inevitably fused together into a much more complicated whole.

Grey was glad for his steady presence at her side, however. It helped her stay calm. Not only was Kamilla plotting who-knew-what at the other end of the table, her mom had also invited her latest fling, Terrence, to dine with them. The man was needling Grey's dad, Oscar, at every opportunity. He was closer to Danny's age than her mother's, and his teeth were suspiciously white.

"Well, Oscar," Terrence said, "your wife sure is putting her whole heart and soul into planning for this gala. She's spent so much time on it, I'm surprised you remember what she looks like. And the money spent! You must dread this time of year."

Her mother laughed nervously, sensing the coming danger. Grey's father's eyes remained frowning even as he pulled his mouth into a smile. "Astrid has always been a magician when it comes to parties. I don't mind the expense."

Terrence's eyes sparkled over his glass. "No, it's good that you let her... have her fun," he said, emphasizing the last three words. No one at the table was under the illusion that he was still discussing parties. "A lesser man would keep her on a shorter leash."

"And only a lesser man would speak about women like they're pets," Grey interrupted, face flaming. "My mother doesn't wear a leash."

"Grey," Astrid scolded. "You know that's not what he meant."

Yusuf's warning hand on her knee kept her from immediately snapping back. When she looked over, she could read the message on his face plain as a newspaper headline.

Kamilla flashed her a sympathetic look, one she'd given a hundred times after Astrid said or did something outrageous, but it had never sent Grey spinning with anger the way it did now.

Choking back her rage, Grey put a smile on her face sweet enough to melt cement. "Of course not. I apologize."

Terrence laughed out loud. "No problem, Princess. I don't mind a little fire in the women around me. Makes life much more fun. Don't you agree, Oscar?"

Grey's father didn't respond, just sat in a miserable slump, pushing his asparagus around his plate.

By the time the dinner ended, Grey was ready to scream. Kamilla offered to help with the dishes, and instead of joining her, Grey quickly excused herself and Yusuf and pulled him onto the front porch. The sun was setting, the burning sky reflecting the simmering anger rushing through her.

"Wow," Yusuf said. "That was... wow."

He ran a hand through his thick hair. His dark eyes were melted gold in the sunset, reflecting the radiance of the sky. "How often does Kamilla come over for dinner?"

Grey took a seat on the top step, and Yusuf settled down next to her. "We weren't talking this summer, but before that it was once a week at least. More during the summer. She always liked Victoria's cooking, and our new housekeeper isn't bad, either."

"Can I ask a question that might make you angry?" Yusuf asked. Grey shrugged.

"Why doesn't your dad do something about your mom's boyfriends? I know I should have been focusing on Kamilla, but I felt really bad for him in there."

Grey thought back to the cold plastic chairs of the Heringford police station the night she was rescued from Paul, her kidnapper, wedged between her father and Danny as she tried not to think about anything at all.

"I'm sorry," her father had said, long legs jiggling up and down on the linoleum floor. "I'm so sorry, Grey."

"It's not your fault," Grey had answered, pulling the woolen blanket a cop had given her tighter around her shoulders.

"That's not entirely true."

Grey hadn't spoken to her father for months after finding out her abductor, Paul, was the result of an old affair of her father's, her half brother. She hadn't said a word to him until Danny was about to leave for basic training.

Now, leaning into Yusuf, Grey simply answered, "My father has his demons, just like everyone else. I think he's decided that inaction is the best way to avoid doing something you regret. His mistakes have come back to haunt him before."

"Huh," Yusuf said. "I guess."

LeMarc wouldn't have agreed with that, Grey thought. *He would have argued that regret blossoms from unspent opportunities, unspoken words, unfought battles.*

She thought back to her first nighttime vision of him, where he'd told her he loved her. Unspoken words.

She still hadn't seen him again after their conversation in the backseat of her Porsche. The phantom, the ghost, the specter of LeMarc hadn't returned. And here she was, sitting and waiting like a damsel in a tower. Waiting on LeMarc, waiting for Kamilla to escalate, waiting for something to make her *move*. Her father wasn't the only one who suffered from inaction.

"If it is Kamilla who's doing this, we need to know. We need evidence."

Grey stood and paced back and forth, her mind working it out like an algebra problem. "We need to return to the cabin. See if there's anything we missed."

Yusuf grinned. "Back to the detective duo. Yeah, that could be great. Really exciting."

Grey narrowed her eyes. "Exciting? Who are you, Jack Ryan?"

He threw her a perplexed look. "You've heard of Jack Ryan?"

"I don't only read Jane Austen novels, you know," she said, nudging his leg with her toe.

Yusuf's face cleared. "Right. I guess you've read the books." He leaned back on his arms, gazing up at her. How could he look so relaxed? She felt like every ounce of her was being slowly pulled in different directions by a thousand safety pins.

"You look so beautiful in the sunset," he said suddenly.

It was so unexpected, Grey actually laughed out loud. She wasn't wearing anything spectacular, just some shorts and and a baby-pink tee, and her hair was pulled back into a quick French braid, with a few stubborn strands around her face refusing, as usual, to stay put.

"No, I'm serious," he said, leaning forward. "You don't have any idea how beautiful you are, do you?"

If it had been LeMarc, she would have rolled her eyes and told him exactly how many kisses fake flattery would get him: zero. And then she would have kissed him anyway, and secretly savored the compliment all week. But with Yusuf, it left her feeling flustered, unsure how to navigate back to safe waters. She wanted that with him, someday, but not yet.

The ghost of LeMarc might be done with her, but she wasn't done with him yet.

Grey was saved from answering by the door opening. Kamilla, as though summoned by the mention of her name like a demon from the deep, sauntered onto the porch with a saavy grin. "Now, what could you two be talking about alone on the porch with such serious faces?"

"Just student body president stuff," Yusuf lied.

Grey nodded.

"Right." Kamilla leaned against the porch pillar. "You go ahead and whisper your sweet nothings. If it weren't for the horrifying death threats from a mysterious texter, I'd be excited for the gala coming up and the prospect of your first date."

"We're going as friends," Grey said quickly.

Yusuf raised his eyebrows. "We are?"

Kamilla grinned. "Ok, I don't even care about the mystery texter. I'm *living* for this drama. And El is going crazy about it, too. If the two of you aren't a couple after this thing, I think she's going to explode."

Grey forced herself not to react. If Kamilla was the mystery texter, how could she stand here and talk about the gala so soon after calling in that threat?

"Maybe I shouldn't go," Grey said, trying to keep her voice level.

"You have to. Remember the last time you went off the mystery texter's script? He killed a police officer. What if you skipping out on the gala puts someone in danger? Someone like your mom?"

Grey met Kamilla's eyes. Was that a threat? Did Kamilla know what Grey and Yusuf suspected?

They'd tried to act unsuspicious when they'd returned to the car the night before, filling in Kamilla about the phone call and resisting the urge to shake her down until they found the phone. After finding the bracelet, Grey and Yusuf had decided not to confront Kamilla, but to keep an eye on her until they got confirmation that she really was the texter.

"Nothing's going to happen to Grey's mom," Yusuf said.

"Coming to the gala is the only way to guarantee the killer's focus remains on Grey and not on her family."

"And what about you? You've received the texts, too." Grey studied her friend's face. "Are you worried?"

Kamilla crossed her arms, meeting Grey's gaze. "As long as we go to the gala like we're supposed to, I'm confident everything will turn out the way it should."

Grey gritted her teeth. *The way it should.*

"I'm going to win this," Grey said, dropping the pretense. "I'm going to find justice for LeMarc."

Kamilla smiled. "That's the spirit."

Usually the Big-Ben chime of the doorbell was a happy noise, but from the first note, Grey knew something horrible was going to be on the other side of the door.

It was the day after her tense dinner with Yusuf and Kamilla. Grey had noticed the shiny black car pull up in front of the house from her bedroom window, had watched as a woman in sharp military dress climbed out and peered up at the house. The woman walked like a soldier, each step precise and deliberate. Each time her foot came down, Grey felt it like a blow to the chest.

She raced down the stairs, calling to her dad as she charged toward the door.

No, no, no, she thought.

She made it to the door first, whipping it open. The soldier raised her eyes to meet Grey's, and her gaze carried the confirmation.

Grey's world collapsed. All of the perfect houses on the street began to dissolve, spinning away into clouds of dust and smoke. The walls around her began to crack and crumble, the piano breaking to pieces in a clatter of notes, the door handle melting beneath her hand like a chocolate bar on a hot summer day.

And then the world jumped back into focus, everything around her in its place, and Grey realized it was her who had collapsed, unwound, crumbled. Dissolved entirely.

She felt her father come up behind her and put his hand on her shoulder. She closed her eyes, focusing all of her attention on that human connection. For once, she wished that the ghost of LeMarc was right, and nothing around her was real, that this woman with a face creased with sadness wasn't standing before her, preparing to say words that didn't need to be said.

This felt like a dream, a horrible nightmare, bubbling to the surface of her consciousness and escaping into reality.

"Mr. Monroe?" the woman asked.

Grey's father was breathing in harsh, uneven gasps. "Is this about Danny?"

The woman nodded once, a curt, efficient nod. "Mr. Monroe, I deeply regret to inform you that Private Daniel Monroe…"

Now it was the woman's words that were dissolving into a river of pain and grief. Only a few made it through, cresting the waves like flotsam in a choppy sea. *Killed in Action.*

Grey streamed up the stairs to her room, ignoring her father's calls, and threw herself onto her bed, sobbing.

For so long, she'd thought it would be better to know what had happened. She'd thought that the gnawing mystery of it was the hardest part, that the thousands of violent death scenarios that had played out in her mind like toxic nightmares were worse than knowing the truth. She'd thought hope was more painful than despair.

She'd been wrong.

Danny was dead, and there was no chance of finding out that he'd been trapped in some putrid prison, searching for escape, or that he had been hit on the head and gotten amnesia, that he was living out this great life in a completely different country.

After about twenty minutes, a gentle knock came at her door.

"Grey?" her father called. "Is it all right if I come in?"

"Yes," Grey answered, voice muffled by her bedsheets

Her father entered and walked to her bed, sitting on the edge of it. Grey kept her head buried in her pillow, but he began softly stroking her braided hair, and that started her crying all over again.

When her father spoke, his voice sounded foggy, like morning mist. "Captain Cooper said he died saving five of his fellow soldiers, including her. He sacrificed himself so they could escape the POW camp they were being held in."

She pictured her brother, face dirt-streaked and thin, jumping on a grenade, shouting for his friends to run. It was so easy to picture, Danny being the hero. He'd always been her hero.

What was she supposed to do, now that he was really gone?

"That doesn't make it okay."

"Nothing makes it okay," he said, his voice breathy as he spoke through his tears. "But he was a real hero. I hope that when faced with the same choice, I would risk my life to save others like he did."

"Me, too," Grey agreed into her pillowcase.

"I'm going to go call your mother. She hasn't heard the news yet."

Grey finally raised her head from her pillow, propping herself up onto her elbows. "She'll be upset that planning for a funeral will interfere with planning the gala," she spat out.

"Your mother loved Danny. Just like she loves you."

He groaned as he pushed himself off the bed. "Oh, I feel old today. Every part of me aches, especially my heart. Every year, I get more aches and pains. Never get old, Grey."

"Like Danny?" she asked, before she could stop herself.

Her father's face fell into a horrified, grotesque mask of emotion. "That's not what I—"

"I know," she said, mortified at her own words. "I'm sorry."

Her dad leaned over and gave her a tight hug. "We'll get through this, princess. We always do."

The moment the door closed, Grey dissolved into sobs again. Eventually, her tears dried up and she laid in bed, lonely and silent, until she finally fell asleep.

"Grey." Grey shifted, only half awake, and looked toward the source of the voice, silhouetted against the window.

"LeMarc?" she asked, rubbing her eyes. She glanced at the clock. 12:30 in the morning.

LeMarc stayed at his place by the window, but as her eyes adjusted she could make out that it was him.

"What's wrong?" she asked, sitting up in bed. She reached for the light. When it snapped on, she gasped in horror. LeMarc was wearing an LA Dodger's sweatshirt, ripped in the elbows.

It was the exact same sweatshirt Paul had been wearing the night he'd crept into her room, his eyes wild and hands shaking. He'd pressed a knife against her throat, and she would never be able to forget the sound of his voice as he told her to stay quiet. She'd been trapped in his basement for a whole week before being rescued.

"Wha... Where did you get that sweatshirt?" she asked, instinctively drawing back, farther away from him. "Why are you wearing that?"

LeMarc took one slow step toward her. His eyes were red and strained, underlined by dark smudges, and his mouth drew a long, grim line. "Am I real?" he asked in a hollow voice.

"I don't... I don't know," she responded, a flutter of fear in her voice. Why was he acting like this?

He took another step forward. His hand curled into a fist. "Am I real?" he repeated, more forcefully this time.

"LeMarc, what's going on? I don't understand," Grey said, pulling her blanket up around her.

Another step. And another.

"I want you to be real," she said, voice shaking.

Suddenly, he jumped forward in a fury, kneeling on the bed and shouting the same words in her face over and over: "Am I real? Am I real? Am I real?" His spittle flew at her, his face twisted in anger.

Grey covered her face, trying to stop the tears. "Stop! Stop it!"

But he was like a savage dog, snapping and growling in her face, repeating his question with increasing frenzy.

And then suddenly, he stopped dead still, his mouth just inches from her ear, and whispered, "Your life isn't real, Grey. No one in your life is real. Including me."

Grey woke to an empty room.

It had happened again.

For the last few weeks, she'd been having horrible nightmares about LeMarc's ghost visiting, angry, attacking her, hating her. This new, horrible LeMarc felt just as real at first as those nights she'd had him back, those precious hours where she'd seen that smile again, but these nightmares left her gasping, heart pumping with fear.

Her racing heart soon calmed, though, slowed by the inertia of sorrow.

There had been so many nights of raging storms these past few weeks, her grief rough and brutal and visceral. But tonight, grief came softly.

She wondered if Danny would visit her someday, like LeMarc did. The thought made her want to curl up and dissolve into tears again. She closed her eyes, unwilling to let the tears overwhelm her again. She was so tired of crying. If the ghost of LeMarc were right, and none of this were real, it wouldn't be so hard. Life would be easier, if she were living her life on a stage. Endings would be happy, tragedy only a stepping-stool to something better. She wouldn't have to be so afraid.

She was tired of being afraid, too. Tired of crying and tired of trembling.

Quietly, she got out of bed and walked to her closet. She pulled down a sweater, grabbed the pair of jeans she'd been wearing that day, and slid them on.

She wasn't going to be afraid any longer.

She went down into the garage and climbed into her car. As she pressed the button to open the garage door, she felt it, the rush of paralyzing fear that always hit her at the thought of leaving. This time, she found the strength to shove it down, to move past it. Hands shaking violently on the keys, she turned them in the ignition and placed her hands on the steering wheel.

With one more flash of fear, she pressed on the gas and began to drive.

"I can do this," she said to herself. "LeMarc knew that I could do this."

She got all the way to the edge of town before the fear really hit. It came like a crashing wave, strong as grief, strong as love, all-consuming and terrible. She cried out, but she wouldn't do it, wouldn't let it stop her. She was going to keep her foot on the gas pedal, no matter how much it wanted to move to the brake.

"I can do this," she said, over and over as the tears started to fall. "I can do this."

Her head began to pound, and her hands were shaking so violently she was scared she would lose control over the car. Her tears were coming faster now, making it hard to see, so much so that when a single raindrop fell, she didn't even see it.

The storm came on suddenly, like the crack of a whip splitting the heavens right in two and releasing a wild torrent of rain. It pounded against the windshield, and the wind howled like a pack of wolves descending on her from the dark clouds. Lightning streaked across the sky, and the thunder growled its angry response.

Grey could barely see. She slowed the car, but didn't stop. Her headlights barely cut through the sheets of pouring rain, so she kept her eyes trained on the vanishing yellow and white lines painted onto the road. The wind was coming even harder now, and she could feel it pushing the car as she kept her hands firmly on the steering wheel.

The world lit up like daylight as lightning struck just a foot in front of the car. Grey screamed and swerved, the car slipping on the slick roads. It went right over the curb and onto the grass. She slammed on her brakes and the car skidded to a stop halfway down into the ditch.

Grey sat in her now immobile car, her chest moving up and down as she gasped for air. The rain still lashed against the windows. Her hands were still on the steering wheel, her foot smashed down on the brake with all the force she could muster.

As she sat, the wind screaming around her, her mind caught up with the rapid-fire events of the last minute and she realized what had happened.

What was she thinking? She was following instructions from a hallucination now, putting herself in real danger because why? Because she couldn't admit to herself that LeMarc was really gone? That Danny was?

She'd been right to be afraid. It was like the whole universe was trying to tell her to go home, stay home, never leave.

After about ten minutes, the wild rain lessened, and the lightning flashed far on the horizon. The storm disappeared as quickly as it came.

Even though her car, thankfully, pulled out of the ditch with little trouble, it took a long time for Grey's hands to stop shaking enough for her to drive back home.

Wilder

15

A few weeks after he visited Grey, Wilder woke up to a text from his mom: *Just spoke to Carly. CALL ME IMMEDIATELY.*

Wilder's fingers tightened around the phone, and he had to hold himself back from chucking it across the room. Carly must have finally told her about Wilder's bruises.

When he got to school, he scanned the blacktop, looking for her oversized green army coat. She usually hung outside with Abe and their friends until the bell rang.

Finally he spotted Carly lounging at a picnic table by the science wing. Under her unzipped coat she was wearing a t-shirt for a screamo band he knew she didn't like. As he approached, she rolled her eyes at him, crossing her arms across her chest and looking pointedly away.

His hands were shaking and his heart was pounding in anger as he walked up to her. A few of their friends sitting with her greeted him, but he ignored them.

"What is the matter with you?" he half-yelled at Carly. "How dare you go telling my mom stories? You have no idea what is going on with my life. You've made sure of it, actually. So stop sticking your nose in now."

Carly stood to face off against him, keeping her volume much lower than his. "I'm not an idiot, Wilder. I'm not going to let your dad hit you and not say anything."

It hadn't snowed yet, but her breath was visible in the fall chill as she spoke.

"You don't know anything. You just guessed my dad was the one who did this."

She shrugged, crossing her arms. "Fine. Look me in the eye and tell me it really was some random mystery opponent and not him, and I'll tell your mom I was wrong."

Wilder let out a frustrated growl. Carly would smell his lie as easily as microwaved fish. "I don't have to prove anything to you."

She smirked. "That's what I thought."

"Uh, guys?" Abe said, leaning between them. "Perhaps this is a private conversation that might be better to have later on, after school?"

He nodded behind him, and when Wilder turned around, he saw that Kyle Ostvig had a phone in his hand, and he was holding it up like he was filming.

Wilder clenched his fists, trying to calm down.

"Just leave me alone," he spat at Carly.

He whirled around and stormed into the building.

Later that morning, Wilder knew the exact moment the video dropped on social media. It happened during math class, in the middle of work time. Kyle must have captured enough on his cell to get the general gist of it, because suddenly everyone was looking down at their phones, letting their gazes slide up to him, and then looking away and clearing their throats when they saw him looking back. The teacher, working with a student up front, didn't even see.

He squared his jaw and tried to refocus on the math problems on the page in front of him, but he read the same problem three or four times without processing it at all. He focused on keeping his breathing steady and not looking back at Carly, who sat in the back corner.

The whispers buzzed around him until the teacher called out, "No talking, guys. These are due at the end of the period, so focus."

When the bell rang at the end of the period, he'd only answered one of the problems. He crumpled up his worksheet and threw it into the garbage on his way out.

Carly caught him before he got too far down the hall. "Wilder, come on," she pleaded, grabbing at his arm to slow him down. "I'm sorry."

What an odd reversal of roles, that she'd spent months ignoring his apologies, and now she was the one pleading for forgiveness.

"I don't want to get into this in the middle of the school hallway. I'm sure the events of this morning are already trending."

"Tonight, then. Come over for dinner, and let me apologize. I'll help you do damage control. You know you're going to forgive me. You always do."

Wilder spotted Mia at her locker up ahead, and veered away from Carly without responding. He needed Mia right now, uncomplicated Mia who didn't demand anything from him but fame.

"Hey, babe," he said, leaning up against the locker next to him. Carly sent him one last worried look, but she continued down the hallway without him.

Mia had on a tight white halter and a short skirt today, her hair thrown all to one side. The side of her long neck was exposed, and he kissed her bare shoulder.

In response, she threw him a look dark enough to blot out the sun.

"What?" he asked defensively. "Why are you looking at me like that?"

In response, Mia held her phone up and began reading from the screen. "'You lied to protect his abusive father... What a trash girlfriend.'"

Wilder opened his mouth to respond, but Mia held up a finger to stop him. "Oh, don't worry, there's more: 'LeMarc deserves better, you—' I'm not actually going to read what they called me, since we're in school, but I'm sure you can imagine."

Mia slammed her locker shut. "And this one, *this* one is my favorite. This girl wrote, 'Please just die. Jump in front of a train or something. You don't deserve to live.' I'm *so* happy she said 'please.' Never forget to be polite when you tell someone to off themselves, right?"

"This is going to blow over," Wilder said, trying to put an arm around her waist. She shoved it away. "People suck. People online suck more. But they also have short memories."

She lowered her voice, so the people pretending not to stare at them from their lockers couldn't hear. "You never even thought, when you asked me to post about your bruises, what blowback might hit me. This is my reputation we're talking about here. How could you do this to me?"

"We can fix this. We'll figure out something to post. Let me come over tonight and we'll work on it."

He grabbed her hand and kissed her knuckles, but she pulled away, her red-stained lips quirking up into a skeptical smirk.

"You don't care about me, you just need a place to crash tonight. Well, get another fake girlfriend. I'm done."

She flipped her hair in his face as she wheeled around, leaving him leaning against the locker alone.

Wilder was surprised at how hurt he felt. Mia might be a fake girlfriend, but she was a real friend, and he didn't have many of those left. *Any* of those left, really.

She was right, too. He didn't have a place to stay tonight. Maybe Luke would let him sleep on one of the basement couches.

Wilder tried to make it through the rest of the school day, but it was useless. He hid out in the back of the library for the last few periods, watching mindless videos on his laptop. The forest of bookshelves provided cover from the librarians at the front, and he pulled his sweatshirt hood up over his headphones to discourage any other students from bothering him.

He lingered at his library hide-away until 5:00, when all of the after-school study groups had ended and the library was closing, and then he made his way out of the school building.

The cold November air hit his face as he pushed open the doors, and he stuffed his hands into his jacket pockets. It hadn't snowed yet, but the sky had the dead, gray quality of winter, and it was getting colder every day.

He headed to the old wooden bench across the street. The 830, the city bus that he took to Luke's, stopped there at 5:20 on week-days, so it wouldn't be a long wait even in the cold.

He didn't get onto the 830, though. Before it arrived, the uptown bus pulled up, the 815. He climbed on, pulling his hood down as he huddled in his seat.

He didn't need Luke right now, a scratchy couch and thin blanket. He needed someone else.

He got off a few blocks away from his destination, and he pulled his jacket closer around him as he walked down the familiar street. The temperature was dropping with the sun.

He stopped at a small brick house with a bright green door and walked up the steps. The blue light of the television was shining through the window, even with the curtains closed.

He rang the bell and waited. After only a few seconds, the door opened.

Carly was in a Pokemon t-shirt and shorts, and she had a cup of hot chocolate in her hands.

Wilder crossed his arms, leaning against the door jamb. "This doesn't mean I forgive you," he said in a flat voice.

"You lasted..." She pulled out a phone and made a show of checking the time. "Ten hours. You literally only lasted ten hours, lightweight. I can hold onto a grudge for *years*, if I'm really committed. I *still* hate Mia, and it wasn't even me she dumped. "

Wilder let out the kind of laugh where he didn't open his mouth, just let a few puffs of air from his nostrils. "Yeah, I didn't really plan on giving up this easily, but I didn't have anywhere else to crash tonight."

She stepped forward to wrap him in a one-armed hug, careful not to dump hot cocoa on him.

"So you really don't hate me anymore?" he asked as they pulled apart.

She took a sip of her drink. "Not right now. Don't do anything to annoy me and we're good." She opened the door wider to let him pass.

Abe was sitting on the couch with a remote in hand. The screen was paused on a still from a new action movie.

"Hey man," Wilder said, giving him an awkward wave.

"I'm sorry to hear about this stuff with your dad," Abe said. Instead of denying it and starting an argument with Carly, Wilder just nodded.

"Have you seen him at all today?" Carly asked as she settled, cross-legged, on the couch next to Abe. Wilder dropped down into the Lopez's lazy-boy.

"Naw. He sent a text a while ago that was pretty livid, but I haven't gone home."

Wilder had gotten several texts that afternoon, but he'd only read three: one from his father, telling him if he came home he'd be a dead man; one from the studio, politely requesting his presence the next morning; and one from Reggie, heavily implying that this was karma for the ransomware incident. Not exactly warm regards.

He'd gotten about fifty from his mother, and several calls, but hadn't read or answered any of them.

"Mom is cooking some of that cardboard pizza you love tonight, so things are looking up. Maybe your *whole* life isn't falling apart."

He threw a pillow at her, and she swore in Spanish when some of her cocoa spilled on her lap.

Abe restarted the movie, and Wilder settled back into the chair. After a while, he lost interest in the movie and pulled out his phone. He spent a few minutes looking for spoilers on the GreyWatch app, but there was no information about tomorrow's show.

A text notification popped up on his screen, and he was about to swipe it away when he saw the name: Ben Emerson. On the show, he'd been known as Danny Monroe.

Heard the gossip about your dad. Couldn't have happened to a nicer guy.

Yeah, Ben still hated him.

"You look like you're about to break your phone in two," Carly's voice cut in, pulling him back into the living room. She was cuddled into Abe, but her eyes were on him, reflecting the flashing light of the movie.

"Danny from the show sent me a text," Wilder explained. "It's dumb and petty."

Carly sat up and put her palms flat on the couch. "You know Ben Emerson?" Her voice was weird and breathy. "I thought he'd left the show before you went on!"

"We did press together a few times," Wilder explained. "And he hates me. From the moment we met, he's despised me for literally no reason."

"Do you think you could introduce me?" Behind her, Abe shook his head and rolled his eyes.

"I *just* said he hates me."

"But he knows you. It's a start."

What was this? Tough, no-nonsense Carly was a fangirl?

"He still lives close, did you know? He's going to school at the U."

"If you start listing off his address, I'm going to be very disappointed."

"Me, too," Abe echoed.

Carly wasn't the first girl who'd been ensnared by Danny Monroe. When Ben decided to leave the show to attend college and they'd put out a casting call for his replacement, the outcry from fans was so intense that they decided to send Danny to war instead of keeping the avatar going with a different actor.

Ben had played Danny from the very beginning, one of the few actors who'd lasted the whole series. He'd been three years old when the show began, and had grown up on the world's TV screens. His character's MIA status was the studio's signal that they were keeping the door open for him to come back.

Wilder looked at the text again, considering. "Ben was on the show for a long time," he said slowly, thinking. "Do you think he's ever been on set? To Grey's actual world?"

Carly shrugged. "Maybe. I think they did a special there, in the early years, but he would have been young."

Young, maybe, but at least he might remember how long the trip was to get there. Wilder felt a thrill of excitement. After months of getting nowhere looking for Victoria, here was a new lead.

"Do you two want to meet him? We could go tomorrow night. It's only a few hours drive."

Carly narrowed her eyes. "The whole country is talking about you right now. Is this really the time for a public outing? Why are you all the sudden so eager to visit someone who hates you?"

Wilder shrugged, trying to look casual. "It's a way for me to make it up to you for leaving like I did. Introducing you to your celebrity crush."

"I'm cool with it as long as Carly isn't allowed to touch him," Abe said.

Carly's eyes were still slitted, her arms crossed. "You're a terrible liar, and I hate being manipulated, but I *really* want to meet Danny, so I'll let it slide this time without drilling you about why you want to go."

Wilder laid back into the lazy-boy. Reggie might never let him back in to see Grey as LeMarc, but if he could find her, find her for real, he wouldn't need to. She could meet the real him, Wilder Blue.

Hopefully she could learn to love blondes.

Mrs. Lopez let Wilder sleep on their couch that night as long as he promised to call his mother in the morning. He agreed, but then set his alarm early enough that he would be gone before he was forced to follow through, taking the early bus to school instead of waiting for Abe to pick up him and Carly.

A half hour or so before school started, Mia texted him and asked him to meet her by the front of the school.

When he arrived, she pulled him in for a sizzling kiss.

He pulled back, eyebrows raised.

"I thought you hated me?" he asked, keeping his voice low so no surrounding students could hear. "I ruined your reputation by selfishly being punched in the face by my own father?"

"And then I realized that dumping you in your time of need would make me look even worse."

"Ah, I see." Wilder stuck his hands in his pockets and kicking at the ground. "I haven't posted anything on social media yet. You want me to say your strength and grace have been the life raft that's helped me stay afloat through this terrible time?"

"Yes, please." Looking over his shoulder, she added, "Don't look now, but Carly's ready to boil water over there."

Wilder did look, just in time to see Carly steaming their way, Abe trailing behind her.

"Carly and I made up last night," he informed Mia.

He'd filled Carly in that his relationship with Mia was fueled by PR, but obviously his best friend was still adjusting to the idea.

"What's the deal?" Carly asked Wilder when she reached them. "I thought she'd real-dumped you from your fake relationship yesterday."

"Wow, Carly, why don't you shout that a little louder?"

Mia linked her arm through his, kissing him on the cheek. "This power couple is back on track." In a sultry voice, she added, "Which reminds me, Wilder, where are you taking me tonight?"

Carly grimaced. "Sorry, but the three of us have plans already. Real ones."

Wilder rolled his eyes. "We're going to visit Ben Emerson at his dorm," he told Mia. Carly glared at him, but he still added, "Wanna come?"

Mia's smug smile reminded him so much of a cat, he almost expected her to start purring. It matched the cat-eye makeup she was sporting today. "I'd love to," she said, more to Carly than to him.

"The more the merrier," Abe said cheerily, and Carly elbowed him in the stomach.

Even though Wilder still got more side-eye at school that day than a clown at a wedding, he found himself able to shrug off the looks easily. Having Carly back made a big difference, even though she gave him a firm talking-to about sneaking out of the house instead of calling his mom like he'd promised.

During lunch, Wilder texted Ben to see if he was free for a visit. Ben texted back immediately: *Can't. Party tonight.*

Wilder responded, *I like parties. Address?*

He wasn't really expecting a response, but to his surprise, Ben actually texted an address back.

With how much Ben hated him, there was a 50% chance that it would lead to a retirement center instead of a hot college party, but if there were even slight odds that Ben knew where Grey's set was located, it was worth the drive.

Wilder had made no progress in finding Victoria Price or getting back in to convince Grey her world wasn't real, and the midseason finale gala was fast approaching.

ladybluebell

I can't believe the gala is finally here!!!

realgreymonroe

I can't believe they've managed to keep her dress a secret—seriously, people, NO set photos?

ishipgreymarc

LeMarc would have looked amazing in a tux.... *sigh*

ladybluebell

He looked amazing at the

GREYWATCH

Grey

16

Grey shot up from sleep, her sweat-soaked hair clinging to her forehead as she gasped for breath. Her room was still dark, no whisp of LeMarc's voice on the air.

A nightmare. It was just another nightmare, the same one she'd had over and over again in the weeks since his last visit. Always the same, but she never remembered that until she woke up. She was always just as terrified as the first time.

Grey curled up into her blanket, checking the clock. 4:00 AM.

The phantom LeMarc's words echoed through her mind, the same words he'd said the night he'd died. No one in her life was real. Including him.

It was the gala tomorrow. Today, actually. She needed to be alert to tackle whatever Kamilla was planning, and she was going to be exhausted if she didn't get back to sleep, but she turned on the light and padded over to her closet. She dug around for a box high up on the shelf, stuffed beneath a stack of clothes she'd outgrown.

Bringing it back to her bed, she sat cross-legged and pulled her blanket around her.

The nightmares had been bad enough before, but after losing Danny, they felt even worse. She wished she were little again, when Danny would sneak into her room and they would giggle the night away. Her brother had always kept the monsters at bay.

She opened the box. On top lay a locket LeMarc had given her, broken but treasured. Underneath was a jumble of pictures, notes, and mementos she'd stashed away like a squirrel during winter, saving them to indulge in when her heart grew cold.

She pulled out a selfie she'd printed off of her and LeMarc. He was making a face at the camera, and she was smiling up at him. He'd just commented that if they wanted to keep their relationship secret, photographic evidence was not the way to go. She'd taken the picture anyway.

"It was real," she said to the photograph of LeMarc. "We were real."

Carefully, she put the picture and the locket back into the box and returned them to the closet. Tomorrow, she'd be a princess at the ball, and it would be a different prince at her side.

She wished he felt as real as the ghost who still haunted her dreams.

Grey walked through the event center doors and into the gilded past. The room was transformed into Versailles, glittering with mirrors and luxury. A shower of pendants hung from the center dome on invisible strings, drops of suspended gold.

Ghosts of French courtiers danced in measured steps, faces alabaster with powder and dresses sewn with jewels and lace, mingling with the costumed crowd.

Grey could see her mother across the room, white wig piled high with tumbling ringlets. She was standing with Grey's father, surveying the assembled elite over her empty champagne flute. Her father, decked in a gleaming brocade tunic and his own wig, looked pained as Astrid turned and muttered something to him. No doubt Grey's mother was disparaging the attire of a guest, or gossiping about one of her "dear friends."

When Grey had suggested canceling the gala after the news of Danny's death, her mother was horrified at the idea. "Danny would have wanted dancing," she'd said, and then she'd started whining about how the catering company had asked to replace the gold napkins they'd requested with white.

Despite the danger hidden in the corners of the room, the dreaded final culmination of the mystery texter's plan, she had to agree with Astrid: Danny would have wanted dancing. He would have cavorted across the ballroom raucously with whatever poor soul he'd convinced to be his date, laughing at his mother's disapproving face.

She tried to keep her breathing steady and deep through the corset her mother had forced her to wear.

Despite the discomfort, she had to admit the dress was stunning. When she'd put it on for the final time and turned toward the mirror in the dressmaker's shop, it had taken her a few moments to find her words. Layers of shimmering gold formed a double skirt draped over a panier, sumptuously adorned with ribbons and glass beads. The bodice was a rich gold as well, with off-the-shoulder sleeves that exposed her gold-dusted collarbone.

Despite tonight's theme, she'd convinced her mother to let her go without a wig. Two hours at the hair salon had provided her with a high cascade of dark, shiny curls, one hanging down perfectly to brush her neck and lay across her clavicle. Her makeup was heavier than she'd ever worn it, gold brushed onto her cheeks and layered onto her eyelids, lashes long and dark around her blue eyes. The sparkle didn't match the pale powdered faces around her, but she loved it so much she didn't care.

She caught her mother's eye, and Astrid smirked in satisfaction at Grey's final look.

Ellie ran up to her, squealing. "You look incredible! Yusuf's going to *die* when he sees you. Tonight is definitely going to be the night——He's kissing you for sure, you nun. Did you bring breath mints?"

Ellie was in a ruffled pale pink gown and an impeccably styled wig complete with an ostrich feather. Grey had seen the dress during several of the fittings, but she hadn't ever seen the whole look together.

"You look amazing. Liam's a lucky guy," she responded, looking around for Ellie's escort. Liam Porter had followed through on being Ellie's arm candy for the ball, though his current absence didn't bode well for him lasting the week.

"Have you seen Kamilla?"

"I'm right here," came a voice from behind them.

Kamilla was in a dark blue gown, the rich jewel tone gorgeous against her copper skin. "Tonight will be one to remember, that's for sure."

Grey looked around for Yusuf, eyes skimming over tipsy guests. Suddenly, as though choreographed, the dancers and party guests parted, and there he was. His gaze met hers from across the room.

As he took her in, his lips curled up and he tipped his head in a formal little bow.

He was drenched in gold just like her, with velvet breeches and a heavily-embroidered coat. His waistcoat was a slightly darker gold, with a ruffled lace collar tucked into it. He'd also escaped the wig, but he carried a feather-decked hat.

She put all her effort into looking graceful as she made her way toward him. He headed toward her as well, and they met in the middle. He bowed again, kissing her hand, and she attempted a curtsey.

"You are breathtaking," he said in an awed voice.

"You don't look so bad yourself. What a coincidence that we both wore gold."

He laughed. "That's one word for it. Your mother sent very specific instructions, actually."

Grey glanced at her mother, whose smile was even more smug than before, if possible.

"So what's the plan?" Yusuf asked as the next song began. "Just stay here until Kamilla makes her move?"

"There is no plan. Kamilla knows what happened that night, and there has to be a reason she's been doing all of this. Something I don't remember. She's the only one who can tell me the truth about LeMarc. I don't need justice anymore, I just need to *know*. I need the truth."

Yusuf flashed a worried look in her direction. "But is knowing the truth worth whatever fresh torture she has for you? Is it worth your life?"

"I'll be fine, Yusuf. I know Kamilla. She isn't going to kill me."

"Tell that to Officer Phillips."

"We just need to act normal, figure out what she wants."

"Does normal include dancing?" Yusuf asked, holding out his hand.

"I'm not exactly a dancer, and I don't know if I have the breath for it. There's an actual corset under here."

"Swoon all you like. I'll just pretend it's for me."

Yusuf took her hand and led her to the dance floor. He wrapped an arm around her waist and took her hand with his other arm.

And suddenly, they were dancing. The glittering lights, the music, the firm hand at her waist, it was all as intoxicating as champagne. Grey felt her tight muscles loosening as they swept across the marble floor, and she wasn't sure the lightheadedness was solely from lack of air.

This is what she needed after the pain of Danny's death and the nightmares of LeMarc. She needed to be reminded of what was right in front of her, of what she had left.

Over his shoulder, she could see that Liam had found Ellie, and they were twirling away to the eight-piece orchestra. Kamilla was nowhere to be seen.

Yusuf was an amazing dancer. "I know tonight could be terrible," he said a few dances in, "and we might be dead before the ball is over, but in this moment, I'd rather be here with you than anywhere in the world."

After another hour, she noticed Kamilla in the doorway, her blue gown draped around her like a queen. She was staring at Grey and Yusuf on the dance floor.

When she saw that Grey had noticed, she gestured for her to follow and then turned away into the nighttime darkness, disappearing as quickly as she'd appeared.

Grey was so distracted she tripped over her own dress, stumbling mid-dance. Yusuf caught her. "Are you all right? You look like you've seen a ghost."

"I'm suddenly a little light-headed. I might step out for just a moment, get some fresh air."

Yusuf looked behind him, trying to see what had spooked her. "We should stay together," he said, face scrunched in confusion. "Kamilla could be planning something right now."

She is. But I just lost my brother, and I'm not going to lose you, too.
"I'll be fine." Grey said quickly. "I just need some air."

He dropped his arms, obviously torn. They were standing in the middle of the dance floor still, immobile in the midst of swirling pairs of dancers.

"I'll be right back," she promised.

He nodded. Leaving him alone on the dance floor, she fled out the side door and into the night.

She emerged outside just in time to see Kamilla disappear into the event center's gardens. The moon was out tonight, casting everything in a silver blue as Grey set off to follow.

Kamilla was nowhere to be found at the garden entrance. Looking back at the building, Grey ventured further into the gardens. She found Kamilla amongst the roses, perched on a bench in the middle of a spiral of sleeping flowers. Grey sat next to her, wincing as her corset pinched even tighter.

Kamilla's skin was perfect in this low light, smooth and silky as the ocean on a wind-free day. In her blue gown she looked like a glittering jewel, royal as Marie Antoinette. She looked up at Grey with worry in her dark eyes.

"I got another text."

Grey gritted her teeth together. She didn't want to hear any more lies. "Did you?"

"This one scared me, Grey."

What was she playing at? "You weren't scared by the death threats or creepy cabin or murdered police officer?"

"Of course I was, but... just read it."

She held out her phone, and with a sigh Grey took it. She was tired of the act, but playing along was probably the safest option. Kamilla still didn't know Grey knew.

She read the text. *You look beautiful in blue. See you soon.*

"The texter is at the ball, Grey. He knows what color I'm wearing."

Grey tightened her jaw. How could Kamilla sit there and lie to her like that? "You sure this is a threat and not a reminder of your pre-planned rendezvous?"

Kamilla leaned back, her long neck twisting. "What are you talking about?"

"Like the one you had in that cabin the night LeMarc died. When you left your bracelet behind."

Grey pulled Kamilla's bracelet from a pocket hidden in her skirts. Kamilla's eyes widened.

"I wasn't in that cabin. I don't know why you're saying these things."

From her purse, she pulled the old tarnished tiara they passed between them. "Victory to you. Honestly, it would be impressive if it weren't so cruel. You've been in league with the texter all along! It might even be you."

Kamilla pushed away the tiara. "I can't believe you would accuse me of working with this guy. He's been texting me, too."

"And because of that I ignored the obvious. That you're the only one who could possibly know enough to pull this off."

Kamilla pushed off the bench, her blue dress flowing behind her like a cape. The silk fabric rippled like water. "This is ridiculous."

"The only thing that's ridiculous is how long it took for me to figure this out. So what's your endgame, Kamilla? What is it you want? You want me to suffer? You want me dead?"

Suddenly, both of their phones beeped at the same time. Grey let out a growl and clicked on hers. It shone blue, an artificial star.

The east hallway. 11:00. Don't tell the boy, and don't be late.

Kamilla held her phone towards Grey. "Do you believe me now? We both just got the same text."

Grey shook her head. "So you have a partner. What do you *want* from me?"

Kamilla let out a frustrated yell. "I'm not behind this! I don't know how my bracelet got there. Maybe they're framing me, like they accused you."

"Well, I guess we'll see at 11:00, won't we?" Grey said, crossing her arms.

Kamilla rolled her eyes. "Fine. I guess we will." She fled out of the garden, leaving Grey alone on the cold stone bench.

Only a few minutes later, Yusuf rounded the corner.

"There you are! Are you okay?"

It took all of Grey's willpower to close off her face from the emotions surging through her. "Fine. Just needed some air."

Yusuf sat down next to her, the exact spot where Kamilla had been moments before. "What's going on, Grey?"

He looked like a prince out of time here amidst the roses, like a storybook come to life. His skin was dark against gold, his eyes almost black in the low light. "I'm sorry. I just got overwhelmed and needed a moment."

Yusuf bit his lip, looking into her eyes. "I'm sorry. I should have realized how difficult tonight would be for you."

"It's okay," she said. "I'm having a nice time, I really am."

"Me, too," he said, smiling shyly. "Even with everything going on. Every time I'm with you, it's a nice time."

He reached out and took her hand, his fingertips gentle against her skin. "Have I mentioned how beautiful you look tonight?"

Shivers ran up her spine at the way he was looking at her, like if the world were to explode around them he wouldn't even notice.

He leaned forward, and it should have been perfect, the scent of roses on the air and the moon shining and her heart racing. But it was too much like that night by the river, and far too different from that night, too. Everything was blurring together, the past and present and future.

At the last second she pulled back, ever so slightly.

It was enough, though, for Yusuf to stop moving forward, hanging there in a frozen, cruel moment of realization. He let out a breath and leaned back, shaking his head.

"Let's go dance the night away," Grey said gently, placing her hand on his knee. "I feel like Belle in this dress, and I'm not going to waste it."

"Does that make me the Beast?" he asked sadly, but he stood and held out his hand nonetheless, ever the gentleman.

"I'm sorry," she whispered, but he either didn't hear her or he didn't choose to respond.

For the next few hours, Grey tried to pretend there were no gruesome texts, no ghost of a beautiful dead boy haunting her dreams, only Yusuf's hand at the small of her back and the shimmering ballroom. She attempted with everything she had to step into the dream, fall into the fantasy of the night, just let go and dance with the boy who was *real*, *here*, *now*.

It didn't work. She pretended for Yusuf, but she could see in his eyes that he didn't believe her fake smiles. She hated herself for breaking his heart before she'd even had a chance to give him hers.

At fifteen minutes to eleven, she excused herself to use the restroom and headed to the east hallway. She tried to clear her mind of what awaited her tonight, but she couldn't stop the onslaught of terrifying images. Every scary book she'd ever read, every terrifying tale told around a campfire came flooding back.

There was no sign of Kamilla, but there was a broom closet at the side of the hallway. Looking up and down the hallway, Grey opened the door and pushed herself inside.

It was much smaller than she'd expected, though she didn't know why she'd thought a broom closet would have space. It was dark, too, but she wasn't sure if she should turn on the light in case someone could see it from the hallway.

She struggled with her massive skirts, trying to push them aside in the tiny space and position herself to press her ear against the door.

Without warning, the door snapped open, and Grey would have let out a scream if a hand hadn't covered her mouth and pushed her back against the wall. Her eyes fluttered closed in relief as she realized it was only a very annoyed Yusuf.

He pulled the door closed behind him, pulling on a dusty string above them to turn on the single, uncovered light bulb. "Detective duos don't work very well if one partner doesn't know what the other one is doing," he chided, removing his hand, but Grey shushed him.

"I'm sorry, but be quiet now. The texter will be in the hallway at 11:00."

"Quiet! I'm not the one who almost screamed. How do you know the texter will be here?"

She made a shushing noise. "I got a text. Kamilla got it, too. She's still pretending not to know what's going on."

"You spoke with her alone? Grey, I told you, you need to—"

She put her hand over his mouth. "And I told you, you need to be quiet."

They stood close together, inches apart, pushed together by the tiny closet and her broad skirts filling most of the space. The space where her hand touched his skin tingled, and she hastily removed it.

"We should turn the light out," she said, looking away to break the tension, and he reached up to pull on the string again, plunging them both into darkness. Light still crept in from the hallway, enough that she could just make out his face.

Yusuf stood still, seemingly transfixed. He was breathing slowly, his eyes locked on hers. "I don't know what we're doing in here, but honestly I take one look at you and I forget everything," he said softly. "Why won't you kiss me, Grey? What are you so afraid of?"

The look in his eyes drew her in like quicksand. She swallowed, knowing if she let herself be pulled in, she might never resurface.

Made brave by the shadows, she reached out to touch his face, tracing her thumb across his jaw. His skin was smooth under her touch, and as she let one finger trace across his lips, she felt them turn up into a slow smile.

He leaned toward her to whisper in her ear. As he moved forward, her hand dropped to rest on his chest.

"I've never felt about anyone the way I feel about you," he said in a low rumble that sent a shiver through her.

Suddenly, she was ambushed by a memory, another voice in the darkness, another boy, another smile. She closed her eyes, sickened by the flash of memory and desire.

"Grey? Are you all right?" Yusuf's hushed voice asked.

She opened her eyes to see his face hanging in front of her, full of concern. Her hand still rested on his chest, and she could feel his heartbeat, steady and alive under her fingers.

Here was the same choice she'd faced in the garden, twice in one night. Wish for the past she couldn't let go of, or reach for the future that terrified her. It was a second chance to take a step forward, instead of always sliding back. She thought of LeMarc's ghost, his urgent question.

Am I real?

As much as she hated it, as hard as it was to admit to herself, she knew the answer.

"I don't want to chase after ghosts anymore," she whispered, making her decision. "I want something real."

She craned up to meet his lips, and he responded immediately, wrapping his arms around her and leaning her back against the closet wall. His lips were soft but urgent, and as they kissed she finally let go of the girl she'd been since LeMarc died. She was ready to move forward, to fall again, to let in someone new.

He pulled back, his eyes searching hers. "I've been wanting to do that for *so* long."

"Did it live up to expectations?" she asked, voice breathy.

"Exceeded. Definitely exceeded."

Suddenly she heard voices in the hallway.

"Do you have your phone on you?"

Yusuf nodded, pulling it out of his pocket.

She reached over and pushed the button on the side to turn it on, and the screen illuminated with the time: 11:00 PM.

She put a finger to her lips, and this time, Yusuf obeyed.

As the voices grew closer, Grey was able to identify them. It was Ellie and Liam, giggling loudly. "You are so bad!" Ellie was saying, clearly in full-on flirt mode.

"Do you think it's them?" Yusuf asked in a whisper.

He was answered, however, with a bunch of loud, sloppy kissing noises and a high giggle from Ellie. Grey put her hand over her mouth to keep from laughing. Apparently the gala's French theme extended to Ellie's kissing techniques, too.

Yusuf's phone went off suddenly, a loud electronic chirp.

"What was that?" Ellie asked from the hallway. Grey widened her eyes at him as he stumbled to silence his phone.

"The ghosts of French royals who had their heads chopped off?" Liam asked.

"You're such a weirdo," Ellie said. "But we should get back to the ball. There's less than an hour of dancing left."

Their laughter faded away in the direction of the ballroom.

"That was close," Grey said.

"Actually, I think Ellie would be thrilled to find us hidden away in a closet like this. It would make her whole night."

"You're not wrong. Who was the text from? Are your parents wondering where you disappeared to?" Grey asked, nodding towards his phone.

Yusuf squinted down at it, reaching up to pull the string that turned on the light. As soon as the closet lit up in its orange glow, Grey realized just how close she and Yusuf were standing, and her cheeks reddened. Yusuf was distracted, however, by his phone.

"It's an email, actually. No message, just an audio file."

"Audio? Like a voice note?"

He looked up, a haunted look on his face. "It's from LeMarc."

She twisted in the crowded closet so she could see the phone clearly, holding onto Yusuf to keep from falling over.

Yusuf pressed play, and the audio started with just one word.

"Grey."

Grey let out a surprised gasp. It was LeMarc's voice, clear and sharp as if he were standing in front of her.

"It's LeMarc," Yusuf whispered. Grey nodded, hungry for more. Just the one syllable from his lips, him saying her name, shot a lightning bolt through her whole frame.

The voice continued. "You don't want to kill me. Please don't do this."

"Is he..." Grey began, her heart thumping. "Is he still talking to me? Is this a recording of that night?"

Yusuf didn't meet her eyes.

LeMarc's voice still sent her spinning, even though it was uttering such horrible, awful things. "Please, I'm begging you. Please just put the knife down."

His words rose, speeding up, more urgent with every breath. "You don't want to do this. You don't—No, please stop—Don't! Please, I—No!"

The words cut off with a horrible gurgling noise.

Grey put a hand over her mouth, tears streaming down her face. It wasn't real. She'd heard wrong. This couldn't be happening.

Yusuf swallowed hard, staring at the cell phone. He looked at a loss for words.

While he stared, the phone let out another chirp. He pulled up the text, and Grey leaned over the phone to read alongside him.

Puts a damper on the detective duo, doesn't it? Perfect, perfect Grey. Class president, straight-A student... Murderer. I hope you've gotten used to keeping secrets, Yusuf, because this is one you need to keep. Tell anyone about what's in this file, and Kamilla dies.

They barely had time to finish reading before the final text came in: a picture of Kamilla, gagged and tied up with tears streaming down her cheek.

You have until the gala to tell the truth, and then I'm coming for you. This is what he'd meant. All along, this is what he'd been planning.

"We were so wrong. Kamilla didn't have anything to do with this. With any of it. All along, it was..." Grey cut off, unable to say the words.

It was me. She was the one who'd killed LeMarc.

Why? How?

"What do we do now?" she asked quietly.

Yusuf clicked off his phone and put it in his pocket. He still hadn't met her eyes. "We keep the secret. We never speak of it again. And we pray the police can find Kamilla before it's too late."

He swallowed, and Grey could see the panicked haze in his eyes. "Yusuf—"

"Don't," he interrupted, holding out a hand. He was leaning away from her, putting as much space between them as possible in the cramped closet. "I won't show this to anyone for Kamilla's sake, but I don't want anything else to do with this. With you."

He reached for the door handle and jerked it open, tumbling out into the hallway over her massive skirts.

"You're a murderer. I never want to speak to you again."

Wilder

17

Wilder, Mia, Carly, and Abe were still a block away from Ben's party when Wilder confirmed that Ben had led him true; he could hear the thumping bass and see the cars parked along the curb long before the house came into view through the inky darkness.

"You know, this will be my first college party," Abe said from the driver's seat. "I'm a little nervous." With as tall as he was, however, there was no way anyone would guess he was a high schooler unless he told them.

"You'll fit right in. College boys are almost as dumb as high school ones," Mia said, pulling at a split end. She'd worn her eye makeup dark and smoky tonight, and under her coat Wilder could see she was wearing something shiny and slinky.

They had to park a block over and walk to the house. Mia was teetering on tall, spiky heels, so Wilder gallantly offered her his arm. Carly and Abe walked in front of them, hands intertwined.

"I can't believe I'm going to be meeting Danny Monroe!" Carly said, turning back to Wilder. "We're officially even."

Abe scratched his head with the hand not holding Carly's. "So how worried should I be?" he asked, and they all laughed.

The frat house was smoky and crowded, the tang of sweat and alcohol on the air. Mia slid off her coat, handing it to Wilder to hold, and whispered, "Save a dance for me," into his ear before disappearing into the throng of people.

A few people recognized Wilder as he made his way through the dancing crowd looking for Ben, and he nodded at their slurred greetings. Carly trailed right behind him, looking uncomfortable as she clung tightly to Abe's hand.

When they got to the kitchen, he tried asking a few people if they'd seen Ben. Most weren't sure, but one girl shouted that she thought she'd seen him out back. He waved his thanks and walked with Abe and Carly out to the back lawn.

The night was cold, which meant the backyard was almost empty, but the bite of the air felt good after the packed frat house.

"Where did Mia go?" Carly asked when they were outside.

"Probably to get something to drink. She'll find us."

Ben was sitting on a lawn chair in the middle of the yard with just a sweatshirt and jeans on, bottle hanging from his hand and a few empty ones on the ground next to him.

"He looks drunk," Abe commented.

"He doesn't have a reputation as a partier," Carly said, "But yeah, he looks really drunk."

Wilder led them to stand before Ben. When the actor saw him, he took another swig from his bottle. "Well, if it isn't Wilder Blue. That really is some shiner, huh?" After two weeks Wilder's bruise had faded from black and purple to a mottled purple and yellow, but it was still visible even in the dark, apparently.

"Hey, Ben. This is my friend Carly and her boyfriend Abe. Carly's a big fan."

Abe waved, and Carly fluttered her lashes and did some sort of strange curtsy maneuver.

"I loved you on the show, Danny. I completely understand you wanting to have a normal college experience, but maybe they can bring you back for cameos or something."

"You didn't see tonight's episode?" Ben said, a glint in his eye. "I'm officially dead. KIA."

"They killed off Danny?" Wilder said, shocked. "Right in the middle of the season like that?"

Ben snorted out a laugh. "Of course. Monroe doesn't care what it might do to Grey, just how audiences will react. But at least I went down a hero. Saved a bunch of soldiers before eating it."

Ben leaned forward in his chair. The more he talked, the more his words were slurring together. "What are you doing here, Wilder? Just tell me what you want."

"Are you okay? It's below freezing, and you're not wearing a coat. You're out here all alone."

Ben took another drink from his bottle. "You mean this isn't the normal college experience? Getting drunk and contemplating the abyss? Screw you, Wilder. You didn't come here to check up on me. What do you want?"

Wilder bit his lip. Carly and Abe were watching him, too, waiting for his response.

"Have you been in contact with Victoria Price?"

Ben scrunched up his face. "Vic? No, I haven't heard from her in weeks. That's seriously what you wanted to ask me?"

Wilder grimaced. He might as well go for it. "Do you know where the set is? Where they're keeping her?"

Ben started laughing, wildly, uproariously. "You want to know where she is? You want to ride in on your white horse and save her, is that it?"

Wilder was dead serious when he answered, "Yes. I want to save her."

At that moment, the back door opened and Mia slipped out, red cup in her hand. Her silver dress glittered as she slunk over to them. When she arrived, she wrapped an arm around Wilder's waist. "Well. Danny Monroe. We should totally take a selfie. Fans will go wild."

Wilder winced, and Ben laughed again. He held his bottle into the air. "A toast to us, Wilder, the two men loved by Grey Monroe. The two men she told her secrets to, she shared her world with. The two men who destroyed her."

Wilder felt the accusation like fire, lapping at his heart, eating up his resolve. "I didn't destroy her."

"Not for lack of trying." Ben's bitter smile was back. "I do know where Grey is, as a matter of fact, but I would rather die than tell someone like you. I spent my whole life pretending to be her brother, her protector, and in truth I did more harm than good. But this time, I'm going to protect her for real. Stay away from her, Blue. Give up now, before you actually find her and ruin her life again."

After that, there wasn't much more to be said. Wilder didn't even ask the others if they were ready to leave, just handed Mia her coat and began walking back to the car. They followed him, wordless.

Once they got back into the car, Wilder slammed his hand against the door handle in frustration. He was more angry at himself than at Ben, furious that the accusations slung at him tonight might actually be true.

"I'm sorry, Carly," he said to the back of her head. "You drove all this way to meet him and got about a second before things fell apart. I told you he hated me."

Carly turned back from the passenger seat as Abe pulled onto the road. "Ah, he's overrated anyway. Who cares about Danny Monroe?"

"He's right, though. I mean, Mia, you said it too. Grey's better off without me."

Mia pulled her curly hair into a bun, procuring a ponytail holder from her coat pocket to secure it. "Maybe. But I don't think anyone can argue that what the two of you had wasn't real, even if she's never seen your real face. You obviously still love her. And I watch the show. She loves you, too. Enough that she's dragging her feet about literally the hottest man ever to walk this earth."

"Preach, sister," Carly said in a strange moment of solidarity with Mia. "Michael Michigan's smile is a gift we mere mortals don't deserve."

Abe let out a sigh and shook his head, flipping on his turn signal for a left turn.

"So let's do this," Carly said. "We can figure this out together."

"I'm in," Abe said. "If only because I have a new, sudden hatred for Michael Michigan and want to see him defeated."

"Me, too," Mia said. "If you dump me in favor of Grey, that's a book deal right there."

"You guys want to help me rescue Grey?"

Carly groaned. "Can we not frame it as the man riding in and rescuing the maiden in a tower? We'll help you find her, and then we'll tell her you're an idiot and give her the opportunity to save herself."

For the rest of the ride home, Wilder filled them in about his efforts thus far to find Grey. Carly was appropriately horrified that he would create ransomware and use it on a friend, but it felt good to finally let people in on his plans. None of them had any ideas about finding more about Victoria except waiting for Reggie's news, but Carly heavily implied that a conversation with his mother might help and was already overdue.

That night on Carly's couch, Wilder felt hope dripping into his bloodstream like an IV. For the first time in a long time, he wasn't alone to figure all of this out. He had a team backing him up. It felt really good.

As if triggered by his moment of hope, his phone pinged with a call from Reggie.

Confused, Wilder took the call, sitting up. "Reg, what's up? It's after midnight."

Reggie's voice came through the line, husky and muffled. Wilder could almost smell the Cheetos through the phone. "You ever heard of the golden rule, Wilder?"

"What?" he asked, half-certain this was a dream. "Like, do unto others?"

"Yes. The inverse is also true. Don't do unto others things you wouldn't want done unto you."

"Has your Red Bull fermented? What are you talking about?" Wilder asked, trying to keep his voice down. The Lopezes were already asleep.

"You blackmail someone, extort someone, and they might just turn around and do it to you."

Wilder felt a cold sense of dread creeping up from his toes to his head. "Are you saying you're going to blackmail me?"

Reggie chuckled. "That's exactly what I'm saying. Here's the deal. I've programmed a horrible nightmare into Grey's system. She's been seeing you every night, but you're angry, unstable, and terrifying."

"What?" Wilder cried. "How could you do that? Grey hasn't done anything!"

"I'll stop torturing her if you do me a favor."

Wilder ran his hand through his hair. Do unto others. "What do you want me to do?" he asked, terrified of the answer.

"My sister's ex is a psycho. She left him last year, but now he's suing for custody. She's made a few mistakes, and he thinks he can steal her kids away."

"That's... horrible. But what do you want me to do about it? I don't see how I can help."

Reggie cleared his throat. "You can't. You're useless. But your mother... She's the best, and that's what my sister needs right now. I could hire her, but I could never do it without the studio knowing. Spending my paycheck to support their greatest opposition... I'm guessing Monroe wouldn't approve."

Wilder wrapped his blanket around him, thinking. "She's still your sister. Wouldn't they suspect you of helping?"

"I wouldn't be paying for it, so I could claim it was a coincidence. Your mother volunteers her services, without pay, or poor little Grey keeps waking up screaming."

"My mom hates me, Reg. And how am I supposed to get her to work for free without telling her why?"

"That's your problem."

"Have you at least found anything on Victoria?"

Reggie sighed. "Yeah, I have. There's a spot in the woods where she might be, close to the cabin Grey and her friends just visited. You get me your mom's help, and I'll give you the location, too. Two favors for the price of one."

"Three favors. You get me into seeing Grey again, and it's a deal."

"You're pushing it, Blue."

"Those are my terms."

Reggie grunted. "Fine. Call me tomorrow to let me know what your mom says."

With that, he hung up.

Wilder kept the phone at his ear for a few moments, hearing the dial tone's flat accusation. He'd been willing to pay the consequences of his ransomware. But he hadn't expected Grey to have to pay them.

Wilder threw down his phone and put his head in his hands. Ben was right, every step he made was just another sledgehammer, breaking Grey's world into pieces.

Well, this time he was going to fix it. He had no idea what he could possibly tell her, but the next morning, Wilder was finally going to call his mother.

Wilder knocked on the door to his mother's apartment, hoping she'd decided to go into work on a Saturday. Carly was standing behind him. Since she was the one who'd convinced him to do this in person instead of over the phone, she had to be there for impact, too.

That morning, he'd finally had his meeting with Monroe Studios about all the negative press surrounding his dad, where one of Ansel Monroe's slick-haired execs had talked at him about the company brand. Mostly, the message was *make this go away*. As always, his visit to the studio headquarters had left him antsy and frustrated.

Wilder was about to knock again when Lana opened the door and immediately gave him a tight hug around the middle. When she pulled away, she asked, "Did Daddy really punch you? Everyone's saying he's an alcoholic."

Wilder stammered, unsure how to answer, but Carly saved him with a chipper, "Hi, Lana! Long time no see!"

"Carly!" Lana shouted, running past Wilder to wrap her arms around Carly's waist. "I missed you! I like you so much more than Mia!"

"You've never met Mia," Wilder pointed out, turning to watch the hug.

Carly held up a hand. "No, she's right, Mia's terrible."

"Wilder?"

Wilder spun around to see his mother in the doorway. She was wearing jeans today, casual for her, but she'd paired it with a suit jacket. It was the first time he'd ever seen her look unsure.

"Mom! Hi."

It was like the wifi to his brain had shut down, and the next words he was supposed to say weren't loading. The four of them stood suspended for a moment in an awkward tableau, unsure of what came next.

"Lana, why don't we go and play in your room?" Carly finally said.

"Can Wilder come?"

"I think he's got some stuff he needs to talk to your mom about, actually," she responded, taking Lana's hand and guiding her past Wilder and his mom towards Lana's room.

"Why don't you come on in," his mom said to him. "Do you want some food?"

Wilder stepped across the doorway, and she gestured at the kitchen table. He took a seat in his usual chair. "No, I'm good. I ate at Carly's."

"Of course. Her mother called me when you first arrived to let me know you were safe."

"Yeah," Wilder answered, picking at the edge of the table. "It was cool of them to let me crash there."

His mom perched onto a chair across from him. When she was sitting down, all he could see was the jacket she was wearing, not the jeans, and he felt like he'd suddenly taken the witness stand. His mother's looks could peel the skin off a potato. Right now, he was pretty sure her gaze was stripping the thoughts right out of his brain so she could examine them one by one.

"You could have stayed here. We've just had calls and visits from press, no one hiding in the bushes. I tried calling and texting, but you didn't pick up."

"I figured you wouldn't want me here. You made that pretty clear the last time I visited," Wilder said, an edge creeping into his voice. He was here because he needed her, but being in this apartment just reminded him of how angry he was with her.

It was his fault, he knew. He'd chosen to live with his father, out of the blue, and refused to let her visit. No explanations, just complete radio silence. But that didn't make him any less angry.

In fact, he was pretty sure his guilt was just ramping him up more.

"That's not fair," his mother defended. "You said things were strained, but you never said his drinking had gotten so bad. That he was hurting you."

Wilder burst up from his seat and started pacing back and forth. "I said things were bad with him! I *asked* you if I could come home, and you said no. You work with kids every day in bad situations, and you couldn't figure it out?"

He'd had a vague plan, when he'd come here, to deny everything, to pretend that Carly had gotten it wrong. Now he was just trying not to cry.

"How long has it been going on?"

Wilder sat back down at the table. "It was okay at first. I knew things wouldn't be easy with him, but I wanted to get on the show. I *had* to save her. And I knew that wasn't going to happen unless I cut things off with you, so I moved in with Dad. He tried those first few months, he really did. But then with having to take care of me money got tight, and he started drinking more..."

"Why didn't you come to me?" his mom asked, leaning forward. "Why didn't you tell me what was going on? This is what I *do*, Wilder. I protect kids who need protection. How could you not ask for my help?"

"I thought I could handle it. I thought it was worth it, to save Grey. But I've just made things a thousand times worse for her."

She paused, considering. "I don't even know if that's true. Despite all the venom I shot at you about seducing her, you might be one of the few people in her life that actually cared about her."

"That's not what I meant when I said I'd made things worse. I've made an even bigger mistake, and now it's hurting her. That's why I'm here. I need your help."

"What do you mean? What did you do?"

Wilder explained to his mother what he'd done, going all the way back to the reason he'd been kicked off the show and what he'd done since. The only thing he left out was the part where he'd riffled through her files. Baby steps.

When he got to Reggie's deal, her face hardened into lawyer mode. "Let's see how eager he is to torture a teenage girl when I bend those skills he wants so badly to suing his pants off," she said, aflame with fury.

"You can't go after him legally. If you take him to court for blackmail and it comes out what I've been doing, the breaking and entering and ransomware and all of it, Monroe Studios will throw every lawyer they have at us."

"I've been fighting those idiots for years," she said dismissively, still fired up.

"And you've been *losing* for years. If I go to Juvie, that's it. There's nothing more that I can do to save her."

"It isn't your job to save her. It's *my* job. And now that I know they're planning to move her, we can take legal action against that as well. And I can appeal for a search at the compound for Victoria Price's body. You've provided new avenues for this fight."

"A fight that could take years. Reg said if you help his sister, he'll let me in to visit her again," Wilder insisted. "Give me one more shot at this, Mom. I *know* I can convince her of the truth. Or I can go with Grey to find the body and get you real evidence to push through your appeal for a search of the compound without Monroe being able to cover it up first. The legal option isn't working fast enough."

"So I'm supposed to aid and abet my son in his life of crime?" his mother answered, voice dry as tinder.

"I love her, Mom," he said, leaving his heart on the kitchen table. "I loved her before I joined the show, and every second I've spent with her I've fallen harder. I *have* to try. I can do this. I can convince her."

His mother let out a deep breath, studying his face. He knew how much she loved the rule of law, how much she believed in the legal system's ability to protect freedom and justice. She'd built her whole life on that trust. He bit his lip, willing her to bend the rules, just this once.

"Let me take a look at the case," she said finally, and Wilder sagged with relief. "If this woman actually deserves these kids, and that's a big if, I will help her. I'm not going to sacrifice these children to help Grey, but I'm also not going to turn away from a family in need."

"Perfect. That's amazing. Thank you, thank you, thank you."

"I have some other requirements, too," his mother added.

"Anything."

She counted off her conditions on her fingers. "One, you move back home. The Lopezes have been great, but obviously you need more supervision. No more sneaking out at night and making malware in your spare time. Two, you keep me apprised of any actions you take, and I have veto power. If Reggie's letting you in, you're not technically trespassing, but I'll be able to know if you're crossing the line. Three, I speak to this Reggie character myself and let him know exactly what I think of this stunt. And fourth, you break things off with the fake girlfriend as soon as everything settles down. She might be okay with it, but you've manipulated two teenage girls too many at this point, in my opinion."

"Done, all of it," Wilder agreed. "I'll call Reggie tonight. And I'll break things off with Mia as soon as we figure out what to do next. We'll make it look like I cheated, so she gets her book deal."

"She sounds like a gem," his mother said dryly.

"I'll pick up my stuff from Carly's this afternoon. A bunch of it is still at Dad's, but I don't really want to go there."

"I'll stop by," his mother said, a hard smile on her face. "I'd love to have a few words with Ted."

Wilder headed into Lana's room to tell her the news. "Looks like I'm here to stay," he said, and she immediately started dancing around the room and cheering.

Carly was wearing a candy necklace, sitting at Lana's tea set in a chair much too small for her. "Your mom's taking the case?"

Wilder nodded, grinning. "As long as Reggie's sister isn't a psycho, she's taking the case."

"Then welcome home, Wilder. Let's go save your girl."

Grey

18

Throughout the rest of December and for the entire month of January, it seemed like the world held its breath, the calm before the storm. The police investigation into Kamilla's disappearance petered out to nothing, and there were no more texts—not even when Grey sent message after message, trying to bait the kidnapper into revealing something, anything, that could lead her to Kamilla.

Ellie came over almost every night, teary and scared, and Grey found herself lying to her over and over again, wrapping every truth and half-truth in a shroud of secrecy and lies. The worst thing that she could do would be to drag Ellie into this mess and get her into trouble, just like Kamilla.

Just like LeMarc.

Yusuf didn't send the audio to anyone, just like he said he wouldn't, but he hadn't spoken a word to her since he'd called her a murderer. When she passed him in the hallway his gaze would slip past her, his shoulders stiffening for just a moment before he called out a greeting to a friend, relaxed and cheerful as ever.

She had no idea how long it would take for him to break down and send the file to the police, but he would eventually. He might have feelings for her, but he was too honorable to hold onto a poisonous secret like that for long.

Honestly, she yearned for that, for it all to be over. Anything would be better than these sleepless nights knowing that the boy she loved was dead and her best friend was suffering who-knew-what because of her.

Lying in bed two nights before Valentine's Day, Grey couldn't help but wonder if her dad was right that it was better to do nothing than to make a mistake. If she hadn't snuck around with LeMarc, he'd still be alive today.

She'd been so weighed down all year with all the things that had broken her, her *trauma*, and now she knew the truth: She was the one who broke things. It was all her fault.

The only benefit of her guilt-driven insomnia was that when Grey did sleep, she was too exhausted to have any more nightmares about LeMarc. The grasping, beseeching phantom had vanished into the night, and he'd taken the ghost she yearned for with it.

She knew she didn't deserve to miss him, but she couldn't help herself. There was a part of her heart that would always remain empty and echoing, and she still tripped into that hole in the dark, quiet hours each night before falling asleep. In the silence of her shadowed bedroom, she even wished for the twisted version of him, the one who'd left her gasping in fear. The nightmares were awful, but for those few moments before the twist, he was real again.

But if there was anything Grey was good at, it was pretending. She couldn't control the way her heart raced with panic and guilt whenever she thought of LeMarc's face, or the gaping hollow in her center that grew with each dragging day. But she could control putting on her makeup each morning, enough concealer to cover up the dark circles from those nights of silent madness. She could control the smile she faked during student council and science class and track practice.

She couldn't lose that control. It was the only thing she had left.

How differently she'd felt as the holiday had approached last year. She and LeMarc had unknowingly gotten each other copies of Romeo and Juliet for Valentine's Day. His face had lit up in surprise when he'd opened it, and he'd howled with laughter as he handed hers over, urging her to open it. Even after Danny was declared MIA, LeMarc had always been able to make her laugh.

LeMarc had spent hours telling her made-up story after made-up story about where Danny was, how brave he was as he made his way home to them. She'd been scared, but there was hope there, too. She'd still believed that Danny was too good, too important to die.

Now, there was just this cold sense of emptiness when she thought of her brother, and the thought of LeMarc made her want to scream.

I killed him.

Even after a month and a half, the words felt foreign in her mind, a language she was learning but still couldn't fully comprehend.

Ugh. She just wanted to fall asleep. Forever, if possible. She turned over to face away from the window, flipping her pillow to the other side.

"Grey?" said a gentle voice behind her.

She shot up, heart thumping. She blinked a few times to make sure the figure standing before her wasn't a trick of a tired, grieving mind, but LeMarc looked solid as ever, his hair a bit ruffled and a wide smile on his face.

She knew from the first moment that it was *him*, not the nightmare but *her* LeMarc. He looked as thrilled to see her as she was to see him.

"I know, you miss the neon orange booty shorts," he said, swaggering to her bedside. "I miss them, too."

Grey wrapped her arms around him and pulled him down onto her bed. He laughed at her exuberance as he went down.

"You're here! I thought I'd lost you, that my mind was punishing me for what I saw on Yusuf's phone. What I did."

He made a face at Yusuf's name. "Excuse me for not mourning your relationship with Yusuf. His real name is Michael, by the way, and his ego's as big as his hair."

Grey reached over and turned on the light. He was still laying down on the bed next to her, looking up at her with his usual adorably devilish expression.

She brushed the hair back from his face, running her fingers through it. It felt so good to touch him. "I don't want to talk about Yusuf. I just... I need you. Everything has fallen apart, and it's all my fault. I needed you so badly, and now you're here."

"I'm sorry for the nightmares," he said, propping his head on one hand. "Reg was upset with me, and he took it out on you. One good thing came out of it, though. Because he feels guilty about torturing you, he's made us a picnic."

"My friend is missing, maybe dead, and now I know that I'm the one who killed you. I'm not exactly in the mood for a romantic picnic. I just want you here, to tell you I'm sorry, so sorry. I never meant to hurt you. I still don't remember anything from that night. I have no idea what happened. Why I did this."

LeMarc held up his hand. "Stop. You didn't kill me, Grey. No one did. I'm right here. And if you don't think you deserve a picnic, it probably means you really need one."

He hopped off of the bed and held out his hand, bowing in an exaggerated gesture. "Allow me to escort you to Hickman Park, Madame."

She took his hand, and it felt warm and rough and real. Was she really crazy? Did it matter? Maybe this was her mind's way of dealing with her own actions. Maybe all along, her subconscious had known what she'd done, and was trying to reconcile the truth with what she could handle.

If LeMarc wasn't dead, she'd never killed him. The memories she was suppressing had never happened.

"One night. I'll let myself pretend for one night that I never killed you."

LeMarc smiled. "I'll take it."

On their way to the park they walked down Main Street, holding hands and walking right down the middle of the road. The streetlamps lined their way, not another soul in sight.

"We should come up with a way for you to know if it's really me, so Reggie can't trick you with fake LeMarcs anymore," LeMarc suggested as they neared the park.

"It wasn't exactly difficult to figure out that he wasn't you. And you aren't any more real than the nightmare version of you was."

"Still. Reg could trick you with something more subtle. We should come up with some sort of sign."

"Like a password?"

He shook his head. "Nah, Reggie can hear what I say, even if I whisper it. You've got a camera in your eye, and an audio piece in the node on your forehead."

"I do not!" Grey exclaimed. She reached up regardless, feeling her forehead. There was nothing there. Just another weird paranoid delusion.

"He couldn't fake a kiss," LeMarc said just as they arrived at the park.

There was a giant picnic blanket laid out in the middle of the soccer field. The lights were on, illuminating the field in a misty glow. She could just make out the desserts and treats laid out on the blanket.

She began to walk toward it, but he pulled her back with their linked hands, twisting her to face him.

She smiled, reading what he wanted in his eyes. She leaned in for the kiss, and the lights above them seemed to swell, turning the world around them into a blaze of light.

As he pulled away, he squeezed her hand. "*That* is how you'll know it's me."

"I love you," she blurted, trapped by the moment. "I know this is just my mind processing my guilt, and eventually I'll have to accept the truth of what I did, but for right now, you're more real to me than anything else. With the loss of Danny, too—" her voice broke, and she rested her forehead against his. She wanted this, no matter how dangerous this fantasy was. "I don't know how to say goodbye."

"Then don't. Come have a midnight picnic with me. You danced with Yusuf all night, now it's my turn for a dance."

She nodded, and they began to walk again, hands still entwined, toward the picnic blanket.

"Oh, and Grey?" LeMarc said as they walked.

"Yes?"

She saw the moment in pictures, photographs that she'd carry in her memory forever. The lights illuminating the mist around them. Their hands, melded together. And LeMarc, dark hair and the scar she'd forgotten she loved, looking back at her with a promise in his eyes. "In case you didn't know, I love you, too."

She spent two hours of bliss with LeMarc, laughing about his awful attempt at a British accent and arguing about whether or not raspberries should be called redberries to fit the blueberry/blackberry pattern. She cried to him about Danny and told him how horrified and confused she was at the audio file Yusuf had received.

And even though she knew it was fake, those moments felt more real than anything she'd ever experienced.

Grey was halfway through a rambling story about one of Danny's childhood escapades when she realized LeMarc wasn't listening. He was staring at a half-eaten pie with a somber expression. Staring *through* it, really.

She reached over and brushed back his hair from his forehead, startling him.

"I was listening," he blurted.

At a skeptical look from her, he grinned guiltily. "I was not listening. Sorry."

"You've just sat through all my fears and griefs. Tell me what's worrying you."

He's not real, she reminded herself. But maybe hearing her hallucination's worries would give her insight into her own.

He leaned back on both arms, digging at the heel of one shoe with the toe of the other. "I have something I want you to do for me, but I would give anything not to have to ask it of you. You've been through so much lately, and the midseason break is ending in less than a month. Things are going to get bad for you again, and I don't want to add to it."

"I would consider one of my best friends being missing *bad* already. I wasn't expecting my hallucination to ask me favors, but go ahead."

"I'm not a—" He cut off. "Fine. I'll just ask you, and then if you do it you'll know this world isn't real, that *I'm* real."

He sat up and crossed his legs elementary-reading-carpet style. "Someone died in this city. Someone real, from the outside world. I need to find the body, but it's in a remote part of the woods, somewhere right on the edge of the compound. Past the cabin you went to with Yusuf and Kamilla. The scenery has been built out, so you can see it, but there aren't any cameras out there now. We can't check to see if the body's there. If we go now, you'll be able to see the body, and the camera in your eye could record evidence that something's out there."

She had no idea why her subconscious wanted her to drive out all the way to the edge of town, but she would have said yes to anything LeMarc asked. Even this LeMarc, the one who lived in the empty spaces of her heart and mind.

"I thought there were no real people in my world. No one except my housekeeper."

LeMarc looked up at her sadly, laying his hands over hers.

She gasped. "My housekeeper. You think Victoria's body is out there. But... she's not dead. She just quit."

He shook his head. "I'm so sorry, Grey. I know you loved her."

"I know I've been hallucinating, but this is another level of insanity. Have I completely detached from reality?"

LeMarc grasped her hands tighter. "There is *nothing* wrong with you. And if you go out there, get this evidence, we can get you out of here. We can prove it. This is how it ends, Grey. This is how it all ends."

"And then what? What happens after the end of the world?"

"I don't know what happens. But I know we'll be together."

Grey nodded. "Then let's go end it."

Wilder

19

Grey was quiet on the ride out to the woods. Too quiet.

Wilder knew she didn't believe they were really going to find Victoria's body out there, and he didn't even want to imagine how devastated she would be when she realized this wasn't a hallucination. It seemed cruel to push her into this so soon after she'd lost Danny and while she was reeling from that fake audio file they'd shown her.

But wasn't it more cruel to leave her trapped in a fake world, where everyone she knew was lying to her? She didn't need more merciful lies, she needed the truth.

He reached across the parking brake and took her hand that wasn't on the wheel, winning a slight smile on her face.

He turned towards her and leaned his head back against the seat, drinking in the sight of her. She hadn't gotten her makeup off completely, and some of her mascara had smeared under one eye. Her hair was up in a sleep-tossed ponytail, and her eyes were red from the late hour. And still she was the most breathtaking girl he'd ever seen.

She rolled her eyes at him. "Stop staring, weirdo."

He grinned. "Just savoring the moment."

She held up their joined hands. "I know what you mean. I know this is madness, but I don't want to be sane if it means I can't have this anymore."

She dropped his hand. "I wish more than anything you were real. I wish I could ask you what happened that night."

Wilder grimaced. "You don't think it's suspicious? You don't have a violent bone in your body, but you brutally murder the boy you love with no warning and wake up the next day, totally fine again? And who would record audio for something like that instead of, I don't know... stopping you?"

Grey's jaw tightened. Wilder could kick himself. He knew she was barely keeping it together, and prodding at her wounds with his questions wasn't helping.

Suddenly, in front of his eyes, Reggie projected a map. They were getting close. "Half a mile more, and then we'll park. We'll need to walk through the woods a short way."

She pulled to the side of the road and leaned over to grab a flashlight from the glove compartment, but she didn't get out right away. "The last time I was in these woods at night, there was a dog."

"Something tells me it's not the dog you're afraid of."

She closed her eyes, shaking her head. "What am I doing here?"

"I'm right here next to you. You can do this."

"*Can* doesn't mean *should*," she responded, but she opened the car door and got out.

He and Grey held hands as they entered the forest, while her other hand held the flashlight. The trees stood like pillars of smoke, more felt than seen. It was a cool night, with a slight breeze, but under the canopy the air was still. Twigs and leaves crackled under their feet, but there was no other sound.

"Reg, any chance you could give us some frog or cricket noises?" Wilder said aloud. "This silence is freaking me out."

A Britney Spears song sounded like a blaring siren through the night.

Grey yanked her hand away from his, whipping her head around with panicked eyes.

Wilder laughed. "I guess he's playing it for you, too. At least it's better than that eerie quiet."

Her answering look was clear: *hardly*.

Reg turned down the music and provided some typical night-time sounds. Every once in a while, he would flash the map up for Wilder as they walked. They were getting close. He squinted ahead, looking for any sign of Victoria.

As soon as Grey neared the body, Bruno would process the image coming in from her cameras and he would see it too. Bruno was stunningly fast, but there was still a delay. For a split second, Grey would be alone in her shock and grief.

He took her hand again.

Even though he had the map, Grey saw Victoria's body before he did. She gasped and stumbled towards the shadowy figure slumped on the ground, her flashlight beam bobbing up and down. Wilder rushed after her, grabbing her as she fell to her knees before the corpse.

He hadn't considered what an extended amount of time would do to an undiscovered body. If he hadn't known it was Victoria, he wouldn't have been able to identify the half-decayed corpse.

Grey turned away, emptying her stomach in the grass.

Wilder held her ponytail back, trying to avoid looking at Victoria's shriveled, yellowed skin as he took in the rest of the scene. It was hard to see without Grey's flashlight, but he could see she was wearing a silk blue dress, much too fancy for a walk in the woods.

The body was resting on a faded red picnic blanket. Two wineglasses were there, one in her shriveled hand and one on the blanket next to her, along with a bottle of something. It wasn't a wine bottle. Maybe a cleaning product? He couldn't see the label from here.

After Grey finished, she stood, wiping her mouth. She was holding onto his hand like it was the only thing keeping her from blasting away, her nails digging in.

"We can go," he offered, but she shook her head.

"I want to know what happened."

Wilder recognized the stubborn set of her jaw. "If you're up for it, I'm with you. That bottle on the picnic blanket, can you pick it up?"

It took her a moment, but she managed to shine a light at the picnic blanket. He winced at the insects skittering away from the sudden light.

Grey reached down and plucked up the bottle.

Bleach.

Grey rolled the bottle in her hands. "She must have drunk it. She killed herself."

"Still think you're crazy?" Wilder asked.

She shrugged helplessly. "Either this is real, or my mind is truly broken."

"This is real, Grey. I'm sorry, but it's real."

They didn't stay for long. Now that Grey's camera had captured the body, Wilder had what he needed. They were silent on the ride back, both stunned by the gruesome scene they'd witnessed.

Back in Grey's bedroom, Wilder wrapped an arm around her waist. "I'm sorry, Grey. I shouldn't have asked you to do this. You were already on the verge of breaking, and I'm worried I've pushed you over."

She stared past him as she climbed into bed, her eyes haunted. "I think I broke a long time ago, LeMarc. I'm just sorry you were the one to pay the price."

Wilder sat up in the pod but didn't get out at first. He needed a moment.

It was odd, but in all his planning to find Victoria, he hadn't considered the fact that he'd never seen a dead body before. He should have prepared for it, somehow. It wasn't like he hadn't known what they were going to find, and he'd never given it a second thought. But then again, maybe there wasn't a way to prepare for something like that.

"You ok?" Reggie asked. He was on his usual swivel chair, Brooke standing behind him. According to Reg, she'd been a big help in finding Victoria's body the past few weeks.

"I don't think so."

Reggie suddenly grew very interested in his laptop. He was definitely better with programs than people.

Brooke, however, came over and placed a hand on Wilder's shoulder, light as a bird. "That must have been so hard. But this proves you were right."

Wilder swung his legs over so they were dangling off the edge of the pod. The metal edges were freezing in the air-conditioned room.

Brooke was right. Now that a body had been found, there would have to be an investigation. They might even have to shut down the whole production.

"We have to get this footage to the police."

Reggie's eyebrows flew up. "You mean the footage of you illegally entering Grey's world? That footage?"

"Reg, I know you could get into trouble for helping me, but—"

"No buts. I could get *arrested* for this, Wilder, and you know Monroe's legal team will ensure *he* won't be. You have no evidence that the studio knew something had happened to Victoria, or even that Ansel was involved with Victoria in the first place. And do you really want to drag this poor woman's family into the media circus that would result? Their loved one's suicide talked about in every nail salon and grocery store in the country?"

"But what if it wasn't suicide? What if there was foul play? Would you really stand in the way of finding justice for her?"

Brooke shook her head. "There was no one else in the compound. It's sad, but the only explanation is that she went by herself out to the woods with the intention of taking her life. She'd just had her heart broken."

"But... but she had two wine glasses."

Brooke shoved her glasses further up her nose. "What?"

"Why use a wine glass to drink bleach? And why bring a spare? Come on. Victoria didn't drive out there, she walked. She walked *miles*, presumably so she wouldn't be found for a long time. So why wear a nice dress? Why set up the picnic at all?"

Reggie scratched his scraggly beard. "You're looking for logic from someone who was suicidal? And you're missing what I'm saying. Even if an invisible, untraceable assassin snuck into the compound and dressed her up all nice before shoving poison down her throat, it doesn't change anything. I'm not giving you this footage, Wilder. And I've already given Grey a warning not to tell anyone from her end. I'll figure out how to account for the missing gas in her car."

"Well, can we at least turn over the data you collected that told you where the body was?"

Reggie shook his head. "I'm not going to make myself an enemy of Monroe Studios in a futile attempt to get Grey out or, even more unlikely, actually hold Monroe accountable for something. That's not how the world works, Wilder."

"Reg, *please*."

"No. You had your chance to convince her, and you failed. I'll still let you in to see her as part of our deal, but you say anything about any of this, try to convince her to tell someone, and I'm pulling you right out." He slammed his laptop closed. "And now I feel like the bad guy again, even though I have risked *everything* over and over again for your stupid junior high crush. Brooke, make sure he gets out without any pit stops, please. I'll blitz the cameras."

He picked up the computer and headed towards the door.

Wilder jumped off the pod, but didn't follow him, just shouted after him. "For the record, I'm definitely not in junior high, so you're wrong on multiple levels!"

Reggie just flipped him off and disappeared through the back doors towards the tech burrow.

Brooke scrunched up her face, arms crossed across her body. "Reggie's just worried. I don't think, when he first let you go in for a quick romantic meeting with Grey, that he predicted it would spiral into dead bodies and police investigations."

"I know he's risked a lot. I just got my hopes up."

"Good," she said firmly.

Wilder looked up at her, and for the first time she met his eyes.

"Your hopes should be up. When you find real love, like you and Grey, it's worth fighting for."

Wilder leaned back against his pod, crossing his arms. "I didn't have you pegged for a romantic."

She looked down at the ground with a slight smile, a dusting of pink on her cheeks. "I spend hours looking at screens, watching fake people say fake things to create fake drama. It was nice, seeing you with Grey. You have your flaws, but you were real. And you're going to get her out of there, I know you will."

"Even without that footage?"

"Even without that footage. Just don't lose hope."

It seemed a tall order, holding onto hope when it slid so easily through every crack in the sidewalk, but Wilder clung to the word as Brooke escorted him out. *Hope.*

He *would* figure out a way to lead the police to Victoria's body without implicating Reggie. He was getting Grey out of there, and he was going to do it before she was put in any danger.

Like Brooke had said, when you found love as real as his and Grey's, it was worth fighting for.

Grey

20

G rey didn't tell anyone about Victoria's body.

If she were braver, she would have. She *should* have. But if the police drove out there and found nothing, it would confirm, once and for all, that she was crazy.

Grief could give you visions of your former love in the lonely hours of the night, a few sparkling hours of relief, but it didn't create elaborate conspiracy theories and conjure up corpses in the woods.

The only explanation was that she had lost her mind, and if she really had, no one could know.

It was there in the message she'd suddenly seen floating before her in the air, like the messages her vision of LeMarc said he got occasionally from his friend Reggie in the "real world." During the picnic she'd had with him, he'd mentioned that Reggie kept bugging him with pictures of his mom every time he leaned in to kiss her.

Add this to your list of secrets, Grey. If you tell anyone about your hallucinations, they'll know you've gone mad.

You can't let them find out.

She could barely admit it to herself. Because if she *was* crazy, it was a perfect explanation for what had happened to LeMarc. She'd killed him in a fit of insanity, and then blacked it out of her memory. The missing motive wasn't a motive at all, just a broken mind and a shattered love song.

So she didn't seek for answers, didn't report her nighttime venture. She kept it wrapped up in the shadows of her heart, tucked in next to her fear for Kamilla and her grief over Danny. In her sessions with Dr. Hawks, while the therapist prodded and poked her about her friend's disappearance and her brother's death, she didn't even allow herself to think it.

As the February days slipped through her fingers and March grew ever closer, Grey kept thinking about her hallucination's promise that things were about to get bad again. As if her best friend being abducted, maybe dead, weren't already bad enough.

It was the story of her life every year, the clockwork of tragedy: the school year brought a new onslaught of drama, then a period of calm at the beginning of the new year, and then March began and all hell broke loose. She'd never thought about it before dream-LeMarc pointed it out, but once he did, it was obvious. Her life had a rhythm, a pace to it.

Like the seasons of one of those TV shows he always talks about.

Grey set that thought aside. She didn't have to indulge the madness. There was only so far into the rabbit hole she could go before she'd never find her way out of Wonderland.

Day after day, week after week, no news came on Kamilla. The whole PD was looking for her, pulling in Kamilla's friends for questioning. Grey stumbled through it the best she could, lies upon lies.

The texter had been clear that if she said anything to the police, he'd kill Kamilla.

She could only wait and pray, hoping Kamilla was still alive. Still fighting.

On the first Monday afternoon of March, Yusuf texted Grey to meet him at the ice cream shop during his break.

When she arrived at the shop, she could see him through the window, serving out a double scoop. He wore his green apron well over his jeans and tee, converse high-tops on his feet.

She thought back to the first time she'd seen him here. She'd gotten another text that day, a picture of LeMarc. A photograph that had changed everything.

At quarter past, when he emerged from the shop for his break, he was still wearing the apron. He carried two cones in his hands, cherry for him and mint chocolate chip for her. Her favorite.

When he arrived at her table, he presented her with the cone. "Nothing better than a good cone."

He took a seat across from her.

She nodded. "When I was a kid, I wanted to live in a place where it snowed. All the pictures and books made white winters seem so magical. But then my mother told me you can't eat ice cream in the snow because it's too cold, and that killed any desire I had to vacation in Norway."

It was time to stop pretending she didn't notice the homicidal elephant in the room. "I still don't remember anything, Yusuf. Nothing that could be at all useful in figuring out who took Kamilla. I don't know who else was in the cabin that night."

Yusuf pursed his lips. "There might be a reason you don't remember."

"What do you mean?"

"I showed the phone to a friend—" He held up a hand at her objection. "A trusted friend, Grey. I wouldn't put Kamilla at risk. This friend is good with digital files, and I was hoping he could see if there was any audio in the background, any clues in the noise that could give us a lead."

"And what did he find?"

Yusuf let out a long breath. "He found the rest of the audio clip."

She narrowed her eyes in confusion.

Yusuf held his cone out to her. "Hold this."

She took it, unsure of what was happening. What did he mean, the *rest* of the clip?

Yusuf pulled his cell phone out of his pocket.

No, Grey realized, he pulled *LeMarc's* cell phone out of his pocket. "Apparently, the sound bite was edited. Cropped. I have no idea what kind of magic my friend had to do, but he got the whole thing. And it's… just listen, Grey."

She handed him both cones and picked up the phone. The play button was the shape of a knife.

Tears clouded her eyes. "I can't do this. I can't listen to this again."

She held out the phone for him to take back, but he pushed it away. "Just listen."

With shaking fingers, Grey pressed *play*.

The clip started earlier than the original had; the extra time must be tagged onto the beginning.

"Please don't do this," LeMarc's voice pleaded, his voice breathy and terrified. "Please."

Grey could feel the tears streaming down her face, and almost handed the phone back again, but stopped as LeMarc spoke further.

"Think about Grey," he said slowly.

Grey looked up at Yusuf in shock as LeMarc continued onto the part of the clip she'd already heard: "You don't want to kill me. Please don't do this."

Grey stopped the audio, throwing the phone down on the table. She could barely speak through her tears.

"He cut the audio clip to make it sound like he was talking *to* me, not *about* me. He said *Think about Grey*. The texter started the clip at my name, but it wasn't me. I didn't kill him."

Yusuf picked up the phone, avoiding her eyes. "I am so sorry. I can't believe I thought you were capable of this."

Grey wiped her running nose with her sleeve. "I believed it, too."

"But you understand what this means, right? He told the killer to think about *you*. About how LeMarc's murder would impact you. He felt that would be enough to stop him."

Which meant the killer was someone LeMarc thought would care about her feelings. Someone who loved her.

"Who?"

Yusuf shrugged, handing her back her ice cream cone. "I don't know, but this is a lead. And if you can find it in yourself to forgive me, I would really like to be the detective duo again. I miss you, Grey. I can't believe I finally got you to kiss me and then I immediately messed it up."

Grey took the proffered cone, and Yusuf took the opportunity to put his hand over hers. "You're not alone anymore, Grey. We're going to find who took Kamilla. We're going to solve this."

She hadn't killed LeMarc. The weight of guilt had been crushing her, and now she felt so light she thought she might just be able to fly. She might be crazy, but she wasn't homicidal.

Even with the reprieve, though, she wasn't completely sin-free in this. She was still the one who'd brought LeMarc into her life, and someone she cared about had killed him. Had they killed him because of her? Because she loved him?

She'd started this mess, that night on the river when LeMarc had become her Romeo and their star-crossed love had begun.

And she was going to be the one to finish it.

⚜

That Saturday morning, Grey was awoken by someone banging on the front door downstairs and ringing the doorbell repeatedly.

She padded down the stairs as the banging on the door continued, PJ's still on and hair in a messy bun. Her parents had left already for a brunch with some out-of-town friends.

"I'm coming!" she called out as she trudged to the door, wiping the sleep out of her eyes. "Calm down," she added in a mutter. It might be past eight already, but it was a Saturday, for goodness' sake.

Ellie was on the other side of the door, and as soon as she opened it, she pulled her into a hug.

"What?" Grey said, laughing as she let her go. "What was that for?"

"You haven't been answering your phone all morning."

"I was sleeping, and my cell was on silent," she answered. She'd left it up on her nightstand. "Why were you calling? Is it Kamilla?"

"It wasn't just me," she said, her face breaking into a grin brilliant as sunshine. "Your parents have been calling all morning, too. They called me when they couldn't get a hold of you."

Grey pulled Ellie inside, closing the door behind her. "Your words should make me nervous, but you seem really happy."

"I have some news," she answered, still looking like he'd won the lottery. "It's good news, Grey. Really, really good news."

"Then go ahead and tell me, instead of building it up like this."

Ellie took her hands in his. "Your brother, Danny. His captain said that he died getting his fellow soldiers out of the place they were being held, right? She saw him get shot?"

"Yeah," Grey said, deflated. She didn't understand. Ellie still looked like she was singing rainbows, even as she talked about Danny's death. She'd thought maybe they'd found Kamilla.

"She was right about one thing. She saw him get shot and go down. But she was wrong, too."

"Wrong about what?" Even though she didn't know what he was going to say, the tears already forming in her eyes, like her body knew something she didn't.

"The shot didn't kill him. Danny wasn't killed that day. He's alive. And he's not a POW anymore, either. He's back in the States, and he's okay."

Grey grabbed onto Ellie's arms to keep herself upright. "He's alive?" she asked, her throat tight.

Ellie nodded. "Your parents are with him now, and they're headed home. They'll be here soon."

Unable to hold it together, Grey collapsed into full-on sobs. It was the best kind of tears, ridding her body of all of the pain and grief that had built up there over the past weeks.

"I'm going to see Danny," she said, hardly convinced that what she was saying was true.

"They should be here any minute."

With sudden urgency, she let go of Ellie and raced upstairs to get her phone. El was right behind her.

Throwing herself across her bed, she grabbed the phone from her nightstand. Fifteen missed calls, and over two dozen texts.

She dialed her mom's cell, holding her breath. Ellie joined her on the bed, and Grey tried to ignore the fact that she lay in almost the exact same place LeMarc's ghost had.

The phone only rang once, and it wasn't her mother who answered.

Danny's voice sounded tired, but it was definitely him. "Look who finally woke up."

"It's really you." She put her hand over her mouth, trying to keep him from hearing her cry.

"The one and only. I'd love to chat over the phone, but this would probably be better face-to-face. We're pulling into the driveway now."

She actually screamed, startling Ellie next to her.

"He's here! He's here!" The whole world around her had a funny bubbly quality, like the edges were fizzing away.

It was strange: Everything with LeMarc felt so real, even though it was a dream, and yet this was real life, and she wanted to pinch herself.

She ran down the stairs. Ellie didn't follow her completely this time, stopping at the top of the stairs, letting the Monroe family have this moment.

By the time she opened the door, Danny was right behind it. His smile was as bright as the golden buttons on his uniform. He was taller than she remembered, dark blonde hair partially covered by his hat, perched crookedly. His arm was in a sling, but Grey threw herself into him anyways, wrapping her arms around his neck and burying her face in his shoulder.

She took a deep breath in, smelling the wool of his uniform and the tang of his aftershave. It wasn't until she heard him say, "It's okay, Grey, I'm home," that she realized how hard she was crying.

They were blocking the doorway, but her parents waited until they pulled apart, standing behind their children with their arms around each other. For a second, the four of them were a family again, a unit bonded by love and blood.

That night they ate dinner as a family, and everything was good and right again. Danny somehow managed to come out of the horrors of war with a hundred hilarious stories, and he had his father laughing so hard she had to pat him on the back, hard, several times to keep him from choking.

Yusuf stopped by a little after dinner.

"And who's this?" Danny asked when he opened the door.

Grey rolled her eyes, coming up behind him. "Uh, that's Yusuf. My... friend."

Danny was his usual cheery self, making a joke about how the military had trained him on all sorts of guns, but for just a split second, he gave Grey a sad glance she couldn't interpret.

It was over so quickly, she wasn't sure if she'd really seen it at all.

Later that night, Danny crept into Grey's room like he had when she was a little girl and laid next to her on top of her covers. He still had the sling on, but he'd changed into a tee and pajama pants.

"Was it really awful?" she asked, her voice quiet to keep their parents from hearing.

He stared up at the ceiling. "Yeah. It was."

"But you're home now. And a hero."

Danny laid his hands on his stomach, studying the ceiling as she studied him. His blonde hair was shorter than she was used to, a military cut. "I'm not a hero, Grey."

"Of course you are. You saved all of those soldiers."

He closed his eyes for just a moment, and then finally turned to her, a fake smile on his face. "Okay, you win. I'm incredibly brave, and heroic, and not bad-looking at that."

"You are a hero," she repeated. "You're my hero."

His smile faltered just a bit, but he nodded. "I'm sorry I left you. I'm sorry I hurt you, that you had to go through losing me like that. I just thought... I thought I was doing the right thing."

"I understand," Grey said. "I understood when you left."

He turned back to staring at the ceiling again. Grey wondered what the ceiling had looked like in the underground cell they'd kept them in, whether he'd been able to see anything at all in the darkness.

"Do you really like Yusuf?" she asked.

He rolled his eyes. "You're not old enough to have a boyfriend. But I like him. He's a good fit for you."

Grey knew her brother far too well to buy his light, carefree tone. Of course he wouldn't like seeing her with Yusuf. He still saw her as a little girl. She smiled to herself as she thought about how he would have reacted to her dating a LeMarc, their family's sworn enemy.

LeMarc would have gotten a punch to the face, not a handshake.

She hesitated for a moment. "Did you... Do you have your cell phone still?"

Danny shook his head. "I don't have any of my stuff. The military sent it home after I was missing for a while, but Mom said you never got it."

So who intercepted it? Could Astrid be lying?

Her mother couldn't be the texter, though. She'd been in the car when Grey had received the first texts.

"I'm glad you're home."

He smiled at her, and this time it was a real one. "I missed you, Grey. I'm glad to be home, too."

Grey waited two whole weeks to tell Danny that she knew about him and Kamilla. She was just happy to have him back, and with him there they felt like a real family again.

But she saw his face when he heard about her kidnapping, noticed the way he stared off with a pained expression when he didn't think anyone was watching.

He deserved to know.

Danny was filling out job applications at the kitchen table when she got home from school that day, pencil in his mouth even though he was typing on his laptop. He spat out the pencil when he saw her enter so he could talk. "Do you think resurrection would go under "skills" or "experience"?

Grey pulled open the fridge to grab the chocolate milk. "Is it a repeat thing? If you can do it on command, it's a skill. If you just did it the once, I'd go with experience." She pulled a glass out of the cupboard and poured herself a full glass. "Want some?"

Danny shook his head, running his fingers through his hair. "This is way more stressful than I thought."

Grey sat across from him, sipping her milk. "Speaking of stressful situations, I have a hypothetical for you."

"Weird segue, but color me intrigued. Is this like a school bully type of hypothetical, or a surprise-half-brother kidnapping type of thing? With your luck, it could go either way."

Grey wrapped her hands around her glass. "Let's say that hypothetically, I found out that two people I cared about had been together and hadn't told me."

Danny's face fell, but she pressed on. "And then something bad happened to one of them. To both of them, actually. And I'm heartbroken that they didn't trust me enough to tell me, but mostly I just love both of them, and I'm scared for the one who's in trouble, and I think it might be my fault she's even in trouble in the first place."

Grey's voice broke, and her eyes filled. "What would I do?"

Danny closed his laptop screen, clearing his throat. "How did you find out? "

She sighed, playing with the hem of her school uniform skirt. "Kamilla received some scary texts from your phone."

Danny's eyes widened. "From *my* phone? I haven't texted her since she dumped me, before I left. I don't even have my phone."

"I know. I got texts too, from someone else's phone. The person who's sending them is the person who took Kamilla."

Danny grabbed her hand. "Grey, this is way over your head. Why haven't you gone to the cops? These texts could be evidence."

"I know, I know. But I went to the cops before, and one of them was killed. I don't want to be the reason Kamilla dies. The texter was clear. No cops, or he'll kill her."

His hand tightened around hers. "They've murdered a cop? Grey, you have to—"

He cut off suddenly, and his eyes lost focus.

"Have to what?"

Danny's jaw tightened, and his eyes snapped back into focus.

"What just happened?" Grey asked.

"How have your appointments been going with Dr. Hawks?" Danny asked. "Have you told her about these... theories?"

Grey sat back, crossing her arms. "They're not theories, Danny. I wouldn't make this up."

Danny crossed his arms, too, mirroring her. He wouldn't meet her eyes. "Listen to yourself, Grey. I know you've had a hard year, but this is ludicrous. I didn't send any texts."

"I know you didn't, you don't have your phone. But you did believe me a minute ago, and then you changed your mind, just like that. What happened?"

Danny's words sounded tight, like he was still clenching his teeth as he talked. "I'm sorry, but you're on your own on this one. I'm out."

He stood up from his chair, grabbing his laptop. "Put my glass in the sink for me, will you?"

"Danny," Grey said to his back as he walked away. "Danny!"

He ignored her, disappearing through the doorway.

Stunned, Grey picked up the glasses and put them in the dishwasher. She put her hands on the edge of the sink, leaning in as she tried to figure out what had just happened.

It was almost as if someone had spoken to him right in the middle of the conversation, telling him what to do.

Maybe like there were words floating in front of him, telling him to pretend she was crazy. Just like she'd seen after she'd found Victoria's body.

She closed her eyes, teetering between paranoia and revelation. "This world is real," she whispered to herself. "My world is real."

LeMarc visited again the first week in April, claiming that his long absence was due to Danny's PTSD nightmare "scenes" pulling more night staff into the studio. Danny had woken her up screaming almost every night since his return.

She watched LeMarc from across the room, trying to soak in the sight of him this last time.

"It doesn't matter what you do to find the kidnapper, as long as you do something," LeMarc said, picking up her English notebook from her desk and flipping through. "They'll make it work. They finally figured out that audiences would rather see you as the hero than the victim. No Danny coming to your rescue this time." He held up her English notebook with a raised eyebrow. "This is quite the poem you wrote. *My angel stole the flames of Hell to ignite the fire in his eyes.* Is this about me, or has Yusuf actually gained a personality?"

She jumped off of her bed and grabbed the notebook from him. "That's personal," she said. "I needed an outlet. It's not like I can tell Yusuf or Danny about you."

LeMarc snorted. "Yeah, that wouldn't turn out well for me. The studio would flip, and I'm guessing they wouldn't let me visit you from jail."

She placed the notebook back on her desk and took his hands in hers. His lips turned up immediately, his thumbs tracing circles on her hands. Here in the low light, he looked like an angel, bending down to earth with the fires of the underworld smoldering in his eyes.

"It's like this connection I have to you is the last bit of your fire left here on Earth," she said softly.

He moved even closer to her, their braided fingers tightening around each other, feeling so solid and real it almost stopped her from saying what she knew she had to next.

"But the longer you're here, the harder it will be to say goodbye. This phantom of you I've conjured up, you're not the boy I loved. You're just the ghost of my own fears and desires."

"That's not true," he whispered, his face ashen. He took a step back but didn't let go of her hands.

"As much as I thought I knew LeMarc, I didn't, not really. There was so much about him that I never got to learn."

"Why are you all of a sudden saying these things?"

She pulled her hands away from his, turning away so she didn't have to see the wounds she was inflicting, even if he wasn't real. "Kamilla. My friend is in danger. I need to focus on the dangers right in front of me, and I can't when half of me is trying to figure out if they're just illusions. The things you say, they've started slipping into my life. My *real* life. Danny will say something, or Ellie, and I'll wonder if they're reading it off of words floating in the air."

She picked at the metal spiral of the notebook. "I thought I could keep you, that I could indulge in this fantasy and still have my real life, but I can't. I'm slipping further, and this might be the last chance I have before I lose myself completely."

"You don't mean that."

She turned back to him, and he looked just as broken as she felt. Maybe she was already lost.

"Grey, *I* am your real life. What we feel for each other can't be faked."

"You said I needed to be a hero. *This* is the hardest thing I've had to do, harder than facing any mystery murderer could ever be. *This* is the moment I need to be brave."

She knew she couldn't kiss him and hold her resolve, but she put a hand on his chest. "Goodbye, LeMarc."

She turned around and climbed back into bed, pulling the covers up over her head despite his protests.

The hallucination lasted for another hour or two, pleading and begging her to change her mind. She pressed her hands against her ears and squeezed her eyes shut to fight the tears, but she stayed strong. She never pulled the covers back down.

Eventually, the phantom's pleading stopped. She felt his hand on her shoulder through the blanket.

"I love you," he said quietly. "I will never give up on you." The weight disappeared from her shoulder.

She pulled the covers back down from over her head, sitting up.

She was alone, no one there to fill up the emptiness of her darkened room.

Over the next few days, Grey felt like someone had wrung her out, every joint and muscle aching. It wasn't until Danny had disappeared that she'd realized sadness could actually cause physical pain, make you hurt in so many ways.

Danny noticed, or at least she thought he did. He was being exceptionally kind, urging her and Yusuf to go bowling with him or join him on trips to the bookstore for hot chocolate and book chats.

When he woke her early on a Tuesday morning to go for a run, she threw a pillow at him and muttered that she wasn't sure why she'd been so excited about the return of a sadistic monster.

"Five minutes to get dressed. I'll be warming up outside," he said in response, throwing the pillow back at her.

"I hate you!" she called out drowsily, but ten minutes later, she was trudging down the front porch steps in a pair of black running leggings and a track jacket.

"Good morning," Danny said, finishing up his ankle rolls. He'd just lost the sling the day before.

"Did I mention I hate you?"

It was still dark outside, but the half-hearted kind of darkness that preceded sunrise. They ran for a few minutes in silence. Danny was much faster than she was, but he held back, letting her determine the pace.

She had to admit, it felt nice to stretch out her limbs, and the cold spring morning air felt energizing against her face.

"You've gotten faster," he said finally.

"Longer legs," she responded, breathless from the exercise.

"It's weird. I left a kid sister behind, but you aren't a kid anymore."

"Terrifying, right?"

He grunted his agreement.

"So what's up?" he asked finally. "You've seemed really down this week."

"A maniac texter has been torturing me for months and is probably holding my friend captive in his house of horrors, and my brother doesn't believe me."

There was no response, just his steady breathing beside her, the sound of their feet smacking the pavement.

"And..." she started, but then faltered.

She was used to telling Danny everything, but admitting she'd been seeing LeMarc's ghost would just confirm to him that she was losing it. She'd been clinging onto the secret since his reappearance, clutching it so tightly her fingers were sore.

"And what?" They turned the corner around the elementary school.

"Never mind," she said, picking up the pace to a flat-out sprint. They couldn't talk if they couldn't breathe.

She ran about a hundred feet before realizing he wasn't beside her. He'd stopped, crossing his arms and watching her. She jogged back to him.

"What?"

"Swings. Now." He gestured to the elementary school playground. She sighed gustily but followed him to the swings and dropped down into the swing next to him.

"And what?"

Grey dug her toes into the little rocks that they used to line the playground, pushing them into a pile. "Do you remember Collin LeMarc? The guy who used to pick on me in elementary school?"

Danny nodded. "I heard about what happened to him. It's awful. He was so young."

"He wasn't just a random kid," she said, stomping on the pile of little rocks to flatten it. "He was... We were..."

"You were friends?"

"He wasn't just my friend. He was my everything. I loved him."

"Wow," Danny said, almost sounding impressed. "A LeMarc."

"And his ghost has been visiting me at night."

Danny's head shot up. "What?"

She closed her eyes. "I know it's not real, but it *feels* so real, and I miss him so much..." She felt the tears forming as she spoke, her throat restricting. "The... ghost or hallucination or whatever it is... keeps telling me I'm the star of this thing called a TV show, a story in moving pictures, and that the whole world is watching everything I do. I know it's just my subconscious, my paranoia, telling me that my world isn't real, but he feels more real to me than my life does, sometimes. And it felt so good to have him back."

Danny looked like he'd been suckerpunched. "Wow," he said again.

Grey shook her head. "It's not what you're thinking. I'm not crazy. I know he's a dream. It's just hard to let him go." When Danny didn't respond, she hurried to reassure him. "And I've stopped it. I told him I didn't want him to come back. That I'm moving on, learning to heal. I know it's the right thing, but I miss him. Even the ghost of him."

After a few more moments of silence, she urged, "Say something."

Danny swallowed, holding onto the swing chains with white knuckles. "Am I the first person you've told about this?"

She nodded. "Yeah, I'm not about to tell Dr. Hawks. She'd have me committed. I'm *not* crazy."

Danny closed his eyes for a second, and then cleared his throat and jumped out of the swing. "Of course you're not. You're grieving. I'm so sorry for your loss, Grey. I'm sorry I wasn't here for you this summer, when you were going through this. Mom and Dad never said anything."

Grey winced, getting up from the swing. "They didn't know. Can you imagine what Astrid would have said if I'd brought a LeMarc home? Our sworn enemy?"

Danny shook his head. "A secret boyfriend. You really are a teenager."

"You won't tell anyone, right?" Grey asked as they starting running again. "About LeMarc, or about the hallucinations?"

"I would never betray you," Danny said, his voice low and miserable. "Your secret's safe with me."

When Grey got back from the run and walked into her room to grab clothes for a shower, LeMarc was sitting on her bed.

It was odd to see him in the sunlight, thin as it was this early in the morning. Her curtains were open, and the light was dusted onto his skin and hair, setting him aglow. He'd never come during the day before, her phantom of the darkness, and she felt a pain through her chest as he sat there, smiling up at her. He was wearing his green shirt today, the one that made his eyes pop and added depth of color to the dark brown of his curls and brows.

"You're not real," she whispered.

He'd been seventeen when he'd died, but the sadness on his face as he responded was ancient, weighed down with the burden of eternity. "No, I'm not," he said slowly, his gaze never leaving her face.

She felt a release, a give, somewhere inside of her. The part of her that manifested itself as LeMarc was finally ready to move on.

"I need to give you up. I told you the other night, I'm not going to try to hold onto something I've already lost. Not anymore."

"I know," he said, getting up off of the bed and walking slowly to her. "I just came back to say goodbye. This is the last time you'll see me."

She took a deep breath, her sweat-soaked jacket making her shiver. She put a hand to his face, cupping his jaw. The hallucination hadn't shaved, and she could feel the roughness under her fingers. "You're going to be happy with Yusuf," LeMarc said, his voice a whisper. "You know it's right, you just have to stop overthinking it."

She nodded.

"And you're brave enough to stand up to this villain. You're the bravest girl I know."

Wrapping her arms around his neck, she pulled him toward her for one final, desperate kiss, clinging to the last breath of a fantasy.

As he pulled away, LeMarc's mouth pulled up into a smile. "Goodbye, Grey," he said.

He vanished, leaving her arms hanging in the air, encircling nothing.

She swallowed, her heart racing, and sat down hard on her bedspread. This should have given her peace, the ending to her star-crossed love story.

But LeMarc had told her the way to identify if Reggie was trying to fool her, to know if it was truly him. He'd told her to kiss him. The studio could fake the flecks of gold in his green eyes, the way the sunlight hit his hair, even his crooked smile, but they couldn't fake a kiss.

That hadn't been LeMarc.

Wilder

21

Wilder stuffed his hands in his jacket pockets, searching for Carly's blue hoodie on the blacktop. Whatever monster decided they should have a fire drill in this weather deserved the worst kind of torture. There was a spring cold snap going on, and some of the teachers were having their students do jumping jacks just to stay warm. He was pretty sure Carly had Higgins for first period, but he couldn't see her through the flapping arms of Mr. Hernandez's freshmen.

"Ugh, it's freezing out here," Mia said from behind him, circling to his front and shoving her arms into his jacket. "I wasn't allowed to stop at my locker to grab my coat."

He wrapped his jacket around her as much as he could, savoring her body heat.

"Maybe you shouldn't have picked the miniskirt today. I thought we were supposed to stay with our classes. You have Whitaker, don't you? W's are at the other end of the field."

Mia rolled her eyes. "You always take the rules so literally."

"Not really. Do you see Carly?" he asked, craning his neck to try to spot her again. "Luke called, said he had some news for me about Grey. I thought she might want to go with me."

The studio had texted, too, but Wilder was significantly less interested in that invitation.

Mia nodded. "Carly will be excited to hear. She's so intense about everything she does, I think she's more eager to help Grey than you are."

"No one is more eager than I am. And who are you to be calling someone *else* intense?" he added, just as his phone started ringing.

"It's Reggie," he said in surprise, swiping his phone to take the call. Mia grunted as his movements pulled his jacket away from her.

"Reg, what's up? I'm at school."

Reggie's voice was thick with panic. "She told them. Grey talked to her brother about you visiting, and now the studio knows."

"What?"

Just then, the all-clear signal went out. The crowd of students began shuffling toward the door.

Mia raised a questioning brow.

"I got a text from them this morning, asking me to come in. What did she tell him? Was it enough for them to know it was really me?"

"Definitely enough. The idiot girl told him LeMarc's ghost said she was on a TV show. Brooke called to warn me. I'm boarding a plane in a few minutes."

Wilder swore. "Don't you think fleeing the country is a bit of an overreaction?"

Despite Reggie's fear, they weren't facing a terrorist organization, just a studio that made a TV show.

Carly came up, rubbing her arms to keep herself warm. "What's going on? Wilder looks like he just wet himself."

"Someone's fleeing the country, I think?" Mia said, pulling her arms out of his jacket.

Wilder shushed them and turned away, his mind racing. "What do I do? How do I fix this?"

"You three! Time to go in!" a teacher called from the other side of the blacktop, waving them in. The mob of students funneling into the school doors was shrinking quickly.

"I don't know," Reggie said on the other side of the line. "But I'll tell you this: Monroe Studios makes millions off *The Real Life*. They're not going to shrug this off. Listen, I gotta go, but watch out for yourself, Wilder. Adios."

"Reggie!" he said, but the only response was a dial tone.

Carly and Mia were both still huddled around him, despite the teacher calling again from the doorway. "Was that call about what I think it was about?"

"The studio knows," he confirmed. "Grey told her brother I've been visiting, and they heard it all. I have to go talk to my mom and figure out what to do."

"You can't go home! That's what they'll expect you to do."

"This is a TV studio, not the mafia," Wilder said, shoving his phone in his jacket pocket. "I'll be fine."

"Not so sure about that," Carly muttered.

"At least let me take your phone," Mia said. "It's the studio's, right? They can ping it to see where you are. Maybe they'll think you're still at school. You take mine. "

The teacher was now heading in their direction, clearly angry. "Okay, I'm leaving. Sorry you have to deal with that," he said, nodding at the teacher.

"We got this. Go," Mia urged.

He heard his name being shouted as he peeled off running toward the parking lot, but he knew the teacher wasn't going to chase after him, and at this point he wasn't worried about his attendance record.

With Carly's words echoing in his ears, he decided to go home and call his mom's work from there. He felt exposed, like he was in some sort of spy movie, and he wanted to get somewhere safe. A dark thought snuck through his defenses, reminding him of something Luke had said to him when he'd first gotten back: *Monroe Studios is just a television studio, but there's some scary stuff going on there, man.* Wilder hadn't paid much attention at the time, but he wasn't eager to find out what Luke had meant by that.

Luckily, Wilder's mom left her work number on a small cork board by the fridge for those nights when she worked late and needed a sitter. As soon as he got home, he used Mia's phone to dial her office. An intern picked up, and when Wilder asked for his mom, she answered, "I'm sorry, but she's in court for the next few hours. I'll let her know to call you when she's out."

Wilder hung up the phone, tempted to slam it against the counter in frustration. He wished he could call Luke, but he didn't have his number memorized and Mia wouldn't have it in her phone. He pulled out his laptop and sat down at the kitchen island, opening the screen to check if Luke was on.

Nope. He pulled up a search, entering in different variations on *breaking and entering, trespassing, sabotage,* and any other crimes they might try to throw at him. Since he was a minor, maybe he would get away with probation or juvie and not a full-on jail sentence. Maybe he'd get a judge who was a hopeless romantic, or a fan of the show.

It wasn't long before Wilder regretted leaving school. After only a half hour, he was stir-crazy and had devolved into trying to decide what his most likely prison nickname would be.

He turned on the TV, but then an advertisement for the live season finale of *The Real Life* the next day came on and he snapped it off. Instead, he changed into shorts and a tee and began doing his evening workout behind the couch, hoping push-ups would distract him from the fact that everything he'd worked toward was falling apart, that he'd failed.

He hadn't convinced Grey that he was real. This wasn't a fantasy book, and his love for her wasn't strong enough to break her virtual and mental chains.

As usual, he'd just made things worse.

He was four sets of sit-ups in when someone knocked on the door. Wilder scrambled up, hoping Mia or Carly had sent Luke over, or that his mom had gotten his message and sent someone to check on him.

When he opened the door, two mountain-sized men stood in front of the door, grim and menacing. One was big-featured and hairy, with a full beard and curly hair pulled into a ponytail. His arm was the size of Wilder's whole torso. The other was colorless, with white-blonde hair cut short, sharp features, and flat blue eyes. They both wore dark suits, and the hairy one had big golden studs in his ears.

Wilder thought back to what he'd said to Carly, that Monroe Studios wasn't the mafia. The two pro wrestlers at his door made him second-guess his conclusion. These men were so cartoonishly brutish he wondered for a split second if maybe he was the one living in the virtual world, and they were avatars designed to intimidate him. "I'm sorry, we're not interested in any products or religion or anything."

The hairy man chortled. "We're not here to sell you something. We're your drivers."

"I don't need drivers. I'm not going anywhere."

"Mr. Monroe requests your presence," the blonde one said. "Immediately." His voice was lower than Wilder would have expected, a rolling bass.

"I think I need to call my mom," Wilder stalled, easing the door closed. "If you'll excuse me for just a—" He cut off as a massive, hairy hand grabbed the door, keeping it open.

"Mr. Blue," the pale man said, his deep voice vibrating down to Wilder's bones, "I don't think you understand. This meeting is mandatory. And we'll only ask nicely once."

"This is illegal," Wilder said, his voice thin and crinkly as an autumn leaf. "This is kidnapping."

The hairy man grinned, showing off a gold tooth, but the pale man remained emotionless. "We've been paid for worse. Just this morning, for example, we received instructions for what to do to a little girl named Lana if her brother didn't—"

"Fine," Wilder said quickly, interrupting the threat before he had to imagine these men hurting Lana. "I'll talk to Ansel. Just leave my sister alone."

"Look at us, coming to an agreement," the man said as Wilder stepped out of the apartment and the hairy one shoved him down the hallway. "And I thought we weren't going to get along."

The two gorillas were silent the whole ride over. Wilder watched out the car window as the city sped by, wishing he'd never auditioned for the show in the first place. All he'd brought Grey was sadness and doubt, and soon they would take her far away and she would live her happy life with Yusuf, just out of reach on the other side of the TV screen.

When they arrived at the studio and passed through the gate, the hairy one opened his door, a warning in his eyes. Wilder had thought they would drag him to Ansel, gripping his arm with their sausage fingers, but they left him free to walk. Squeezed between the two men, he felt like a doomed prisoner making his way to the execution chamber.

Hairy and Pale-face came into the office with him. The CEO of Monroe Studios, Grey's father and his former boss, stood gazing out at the fake scenery of his office walls. Right now, the screens were projecting lush mountain valley, awash with the dramatic glow of sunset.

Even monsters can appreciate beauty, Wilder thought, an image of Victoria flashing before his eyes. They just didn't care if it was real. One of Ansel's men gestured to the same seat Wilder had sat in when Ansel had told him to fake-date Mia. He took the chair, trying not to look terrified.

"I didn't think you had it in you," Ansel said casually, still looking out at the fake view. He stood with his hands behind his back, which was ramrod straight. And then he turned around, and Wilder saw the rage boiling in his eyes.

"Never underestimate the power of love."

Ansel scoffed. He didn't know what love was, Wilder realized. He'd never loved anything in his life.

"As soon as Grey revealed your scheme, we sent another actor in, playing LeMarc, to convince her he wasn't real," Ansel explained. "He did a great job. Very convincing. But something was off."

"Grey knew it wasn't me?"

"Grey has never met you," Ansel spat out, leaning his hands on his desk. He looked tight all over, like he was flexing all of his muscles at once under his expensive suit. "You think she would still feel anything for her precious LeMarc if she knew he was a pathetic liar whose own father hates him? But she knew there was something different about the avatar."

Wilder's heart swelled. She'd known it wasn't him. Ansel might not be willing to admit it, but Grey *knew* him. "How do you know she didn't buy it?"

Ansel crossed his arms. Behind him, the screens on two of his walls shifted to a view of a lake, lapping waves glittering with white. "She told Danny she could tell the difference when LeMarc kissed her. Benjamin Emerson's return has proven to be an inspired development this season. I don't know what the childish spat was about that made him run off for the college life, but I'm glad it's over. Grey still thinks LeMarc is a hallucination, but she's terribly confused. And we can't have her that way moving into our finale tomorrow, can we? It's airing live."

"So what do you want from me?"

"Convince her."

Wilder laughed, trying to stand. A heavy hand on his shoulder shoved him back down. "I would rather die than help you lie to her for longer."

"That can be arranged," Ansel said drily. "But something tells me you'll come around to my side."

He pressed a button on his desk, and suddenly the screens behind him shifted again. This time, the view wasn't mimicking what would be seen through a window.

On one panel, Wilder saw his mother at her desk at work, reading through a file. From the angle and the glare on the footage, it looked like the camera was positioned outside of her office window.

On another panel, Wilder could see Lana playing on her school's jungle gym with some friends, laughing as she attempted the monkey bars.

"You can't just threaten people and get away with it."

Ansel sat down at his desk, hands resting on the wooden armrests. With the high-backed chair and flawless suit, he looked like a monarch passing judgment. "Watch me."

Wilder couldn't keep his eyes from drifting to the footage of his mother and Lana. His mother was running a hand through her hair, looking stressed as she stood up and walked out of the frame. A few seconds later she returned, a new file in her hand.

"So I go into Grey's world, convince her I'm not real, and you leave my family alone?"

Ansel nodded. "She doesn't believe you're real anyway. This way, you actually get to say goodbye."

Wilder swallowed. "Fine. I'll do it."

Monroe didn't give Wilder any time to prepare or plan, leading him straight to the lab. Unlike during his nighttime visits with Reggie, the lab was full of people, technicians and developers and even Ben Emerson watching Grey on the screen. He must have just come out from a scene in her world and decided to stay.

When Ansel walked in, everyone got quiet, halting their conversations and movement and averting their gazes. Ansel strolled over to the pods, his two goons propelling Wilder behind him.

Ben narrowed his eyes when he saw Wilder. "What's he doing here?"

"Fixing his mistake," Ansel responded. "Right, Mr. Blue?"

Wilder nodded, gritting his teeth. He couldn't take his eyes off Grey on the screen. She was at the riverbank, the place he'd first met her. The last place she'd seen him. He didn't know what it meant that she was there now.

"Let's get this over with," Ansel said. "Hook him up."

Wilder laid down on the pod, and a technician carefully placed the cuff on him, the headset with the neural node. Her hands were cold.

"Oh, and Mr. Blue?" Ansel said quietly, just as Wilder closed his eyes. "You say anything out of line, anything to tip her off, and..." he paused. "Your sister really is a happy little girl, isn't she?"

Wilder opened his eyes, and he wasn't in the lab anymore. He was upright, and the sun was shining, and there she was.

She sat facing the river, her knees up and her arms wrapped around them. Her shoulders weren't shaking, but Wilder could tell she was crying.

He tried to capture the picture in his mind, what it felt like to be there to see her in real color instead of through a screen. He thought of the words she'd said to him the last time he'd seen her, when she'd ripped his heart out and left it bleeding on the floor. *I thought I could keep you.* He'd thought he could keep her, too. Despite everything, he'd thought he would win, that he'd find a way.

She didn't look back as he walked up behind her, didn't glance over as he sat down next to her, leaning back on his hands. She wiped her hand over her face; he'd been right about the crying.

"I'm tired of saying goodbye to you," she said.

"You didn't actually think that was me, did you?"

Now she did look over, studying his face. "It wasn't?"

He shook his head.

"I knew it. So you *are* real? That's what you're going with now?"

Wilder took a deep breath. "I am real."

Grey's men were likely poised in front of the computer, ready to pull him out.

"But I'm dead, Grey. You know I'm dead."

"I don't understand." A slight breeze blew strands of her long, straight hair into her face, and he pushed them back.

"I'm not a hallucination, I'm a ghost." The lie tasted bad in his mouth, like cigarette ash and stale bread. Her eyes grew wide. "I got a chance to come back, to help you get over losing me," he continued. "And I couldn't. I was selfish. I didn't *want* you to get over me. I didn't want to let go of what we had."

Wilder bit his lip, hard, trying to keep himself from crying. "I just want you to be happy, Grey. And holding onto you like this, sabotaging all of your attempts to heal, it's just making you hurt."

He couldn't stop the tears, now, and Grey reached over to brush away one that ran down his cheek. "I don't want to hurt you anymore," he said through the tears.

At least he had ended with the truth. She deserved, for once in her life, not to be lied to.

She fell into him, their lips meeting like long-lost lovers. He wrapped an arm around her, pulling her closer as they kissed.

He'd known no one could reproduce the spell that was woven every time their lips met. He didn't believe in ghosts, but he believed in magic. He believed in her. This was the last time he would kiss her, and he wished he could make it last forever.

"LeMarc," she breathed against his lips. "I will always love you. I should have said it when you were still alive."

"I love you, too. And that's why, after all the goodbyes, this is the last one."

She nodded, taking his hand and kissing it.

A sudden glow began to materialize around them, growing brighter, and Wilder realized it was coming from him. That was some fast work from the programmers, especially without Reggie there.

He held a hand in front of his face, and the light grew until he could no longer look directly at it. He closed his eyes against the brightness.

He heard her, just before he was pulled out, her voice full of awe and sadness. "Goodbye, LeMarc. Goodbye for the last time."

When he opened his eyes in the lab and sat up, he could see Grey on the screen, alone by the riverbank, sobbing into her arms.

Ben Emerson looked away from the screen for just a moment, giving Wilder an indecipherable look.

"Well, Mr. Blue," Ansel said. "That was quite the performance. You might have a future as an actor after all."

"I played your stupid game. I broke her heart for you. Now will you leave my family alone?"

Ansel smiled, and his smile was far more terrifying than his anger. "Your family's safe," he promised. "But we'll be keeping an eye on you, Mr. Blue."

"Whatever." Wilder headed towards the door, an escort right beside him.

"Oh, and Blue?" Monroe called out.

Wilder turned around, crossing his arms. "What?"

"I took the liberty of deleting the footage of you and Grey in the woods that night. When you found the... dog... who'd accidentally ingested bleach. Cleared up the body, too. Such unpleasant business, but I assure you, it's been taken care of. No one is ever going to hear about that dog again."

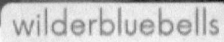

wilderbluebells

Ben Emerson's return to this show = *chef's kiss*

ohdannygirl

AMEN! I missed Danny so much!

realgreymonroe

Kamilla better get unkidnapped soon! I want to see them together!!!

wilderbluebells

You don't think it would be

GREYWATCH

Grey

22

The drive to the texter's cabin was much less frightening with the sunshine lighting up the trees along the road and Danny's country music blasting over the radio, but Grey still gripped her seatbelt with white knuckles.

Tired of feeling useless to help Kamilla, she and Danny had decided to go to the cabin where LeMarc was murdered to look for more clues.

As they neared the cabin, however, Grey realized she'd overlooked one thing. "I forgot about the guard dog. It came after me and Yusuf when we were here the last time."

Danny shrugged, keeping his hands on the wheel. "I'm good with dogs. We had a few bomb dogs with our unit, and they were wild about me."

"Dog whisperer. Yet another skill to add to your resume."

Knowing Danny, she half-expected him to start barking to prove his skills, but he didn't even crack a smile. He must be just as nervous as she was.

"You really care about her, don't you?" Grey asked, looking out the window at the trees flashing past.

In her periphery she saw Danny glance at her, but she kept her body turned away, hanging her hand out the window to catch the air currents.

"Of course I do. I love her. Enough to keep it a secret from you, which nearly killed me."

"So how long were you and Kamilla together? How did it start?"

He cleared his throat. "I guess it started on our birthday, just before your junior year."

Danny's birthday was August 31st and Kamilla's was September 1st. The two of them always joked about the fact they were almost exactly a year apart but two years in school.

Grey twisted around to look at him. "Before junior year even started? You were together for almost a *year*?"

"Not *together* together, but that was when I first started seeing her as more than just my little sister's friend. She brought me cookies and made some dumb joke about me being an old man. You and Ellie were at a soccer tournament at the high school, and Kamilla and I somehow ended up going bowling to celebrate. It wasn't a date, but it just... made sense."

Grey put a hand on his shoulder. In the sunlight, his pupils had constricted and his eyes looked like two pools of gleaming blue. "We're going to find her, Danny. I promise."

Soon the cabin came into view. Without the forgiving shade of night, it was even clearer how neglected the building was. The walls, the roof, even the battered mailbox with its door half-hanging off and a bird nest perched inside it, were all in desperate need of repair.

When they parked, Grey scanned the trees for the dog. She didn't see him, but he must be there somewhere. She and Danny climbed out of the car.

Danny squinted at the cabin, shading his eyes from the sun. "Did you guys check out the cellar when you were here before?"

"The what?"

Grey hadn't even noticed it at first, but Danny was right: there was a cellar entrance at the far end of the cabin, its door handles wrapped with a heavy chain and lock.

Danny pulled his keys back out of his pocket. "Do you mind pulling the crowbar out of my trunk? Should be with the spare tire."

He tossed the keys to Grey, and she snatched them out of the air. "Sure, no problem."

She pressed the button on the fob to unlock the trunk and leaned down to pull it open.

Without warning, Danny jolted upright, his whole body tensing as though something horrible had just occurred to him.

"Wait, Grey, don't open the–"

It was too late, however. She'd already pulled open the trunk and seen what was inside.

She scrunched up her nose. "Dog food? But you don't have a..."

She trailed off, her stomach and her throat colliding in a sour lump. Danny didn't have a dog.

But these cabin walls, the ones that had stood witness to her worst nightmare, they were guarded by a growling, snapping dog.

In the audio file, LeMarc had been speaking to someone who knew Grey. Who loved her.

No.

She looked back over her shoulder at Danny.

Just at that moment, a dog streaked out of the trees towards them, barking like mad. Grey hadn't been able to tell the breed that night, but now she could see it was a rottweiler, a flash of black and brown approaching at full speed.

Grey recoiled in fear, but the dog didn't even glance at her. He rushed up to Danny, barking happily, and Danny crouched down to scratch his head. The rottweiler's tongue lolled out.

"Good boy, Charlie."

Grey pressed herself against the car, heart racing. This was Danny's dog. Which meant the cabin was his, too. And that meant...

Grey couldn't even think the words.

"Were you living here at the cabin the whole time?"

"Grey, I can explain."

"You weren't ever MIA, were you? Never a prisoner of war?"

Danny shook his head. "Dishonorable discharge. I was the one who sent the letter about my MIA status. And later, I paid an actress to inform you I was dead."

"I can't even..." Grey trailed off. Words couldn't capture the hurricane of questions whirling through her mind. "*Why?*"

He stood, talking over Charlie's eager barking. "I couldn't face you and Mom and Dad. And I couldn't bear to have Kamilla find out."

"And what about LeMarc? Officer Phillips?"

Danny closed his eyes suddenly, shaking his head. "No, I'm not going to do that."

"Do what?" Grey asked, taking a few more steps towards the door.

Danny opened his eyes. "Sorry, I just—"

He grimaced, letting out a low growl. "No!"

"Danny, you're scaring me."

But he wasn't listening. He put both hands over his eyes. "I'm not going to hit her! You're going to have to find some other way to end the scene."

Grey's blood ran chill. Danny wasn't talking to her, which meant he was hearing voices in his head, and it sounded like those voices wanted blood.

She was only a few steps away from the car door. She lunged for it, reaching for the handle with grasping fingers.

But something was wrong. The blood was rushing to her head, and her legs were starting to shake. She stumbled, missing the door handle with her outstretched hand. Blackness was creeping in at the corners of her vision.

"I'm going to pass out," she said. Her voice sounded tinny in her ears.

"Grey!" Danny's voice called from somewhere very far away.

And then everything went dark.

Wilder

23

Instead of going home, Wilder went directly to Luke's place. It was the first time he'd been here since he'd told the hacker about the ransomware.

He knocked on the front door a few times, but when there was no response he headed down to the basement. Luke was ensconced away in his dark computer room in the back. No one else was there, and Wilder shook his head in wonder when he heard Luke's screenreader jabbering at 4x speed.

He could barely understand it, but Luke obviously could; his hands flew over the keyboard, paused as he listened, and then continued on.

"Which one of the cretins are you?" he called out as Wilder entered the room, leaning against the doorway. Luke paused his screenreader, plunging the room into sudden silence.

"It's Wilder."

"I wasn't sure you'd come after your last visit. Your argument with Carly was better than Jersey Shore reruns."

"We're friends again, actually."

"I know. Carly actually tells me things."

"Right."

"Things like the fact that you found a legit dead body in the woods around Grey's home, but can't turn the footage over because it would reveal all the stuff you've been up to with the super-genius that I can't believe you're friends with and I'm not, Reggie Myers."

"You know, Reg seems impressed by your skills."

"Reggie Meyers knows who I am?" Luke asked, leaning forward in his chair.

"Yeah, though I don't think he approves of what you've been teaching me. I might have gone ahead and used the ransomware you told me not to."

Luke rubbed his eyes under his glasses. "Yeah, Carly told me that, too."

Wilder crossed his arms, hesitant to say what he was thinking. But he forged ahead regardless. "And just out of curiosity, asking you to create a worm to kill Bruno would be just as bad as the ransomware thing, right?"

Luke shook his head. "I thought I caught you at Anakin, but you might be too far down the path to the Dark Side to be saved."

"I don't want to kill him, really, just put him to sleep. Shut him down—temporarily."

"Long enough for Grey to see how much of her world isn't real," Luke filled in.

"I'm getting a little desperate," Wilder admitted.

"I think you hit desperate a while ago, Vader. But before you go nuclear on the most amazing piece of tech ever created, maybe

I should tell you why I asked you to come." Luke was suddenly solemn, his dark lenses reflecting the blue light from his computer screen. "Have a seat."

Wilder sat down on the raggedy armchair. "So why'd you ask me to come?"

"Well, I knew turning in the footage of you finding the body would get Reggie in trouble, but I got to thinking, what about the footage of the initial suicide? Victoria had a camera in her nodule."

One of the springs in the chair was digging into Wilder's back, so he shifted to get more comfortable. "Of course, but I asked Reggie about that before I even entered Grey's world. Victoria had the power to turn off the camera, the whole nodule, if she wanted, and she turned it off before she killed herself. That's why it took so long to determine the location of the body. Reg checked for footage first thing, and he couldn't find anything."

"Well, then, Reggie was lying his face off."

Luke turned back to his computer and started typing, pulling up window after window. "I was able to use your ransomware to open a backdoor into the system. There were definitely files from Victoria's nodule, and someone went in and intentionally deleted them. It seems Reggie Myers isn't as good as he thought, though, because I found them again."

He pulled up one last window, a video file. The still showed a picnic blanket spread out beneath a forest of plastic trees. This was Grey's world without Bruno's assistance, and it was from Victoria's perspective; there was even a bottle of bleach in her hand.

Wilder pushed himself off of the chair, ignoring its miserable groan. "I cannot tell you how much I *don't* want to watch this woman die."

"There's an additional layer on top of this video file that I want to show you. It's what was being projected into Victoria's world, what she was seeing due to Bruno."

"So adding moss and leaves to the trees?"

Luke shrugged. "I can't tell you anything about trees, but I could hear the audio when I played it before, and well... Just watch."

He typed a line of code into one of the open windows, and a new video popped up. These trees looked more real, painted with moss and rough bark, and the sunlight shone through in an evening slant.

There was also a new figure in the picture with her.

"Is that..."

"The big man himself, Ansel Monroe? I couldn't place the voice at first, but it sure sounds like him."

"Look at her hand."

Instead of bleach, there was a bottle of wine clasped in her long fingers. She'd thought she was drinking wine.

"Dude, I'm blind, remember?"

Wilder realized he was pointing at the screen, and hastily dropped his finger. "Just play the video."

"One little TV role, and you become a total diva," Luke muttered before pressing play.

Victoria's voice was low and sultry as it played through Luke's speaker. *Ansel, you shouldn't have come. This is all being recorded. Anyone from the studio could see if they were looking.*

The virtual Ansel smiled, running a hand over Victoria's cheek. *Let them see. This past week without you has been the worst of my life. I made a mistake, my love. I never should have given you up.*

"Barf," Wilder muttered, but Luke shushed him.

I missed you too, more than you could possibly imagine. You've never come to the compound like this before, but living in this empty world with Grey, it's like I can hear your echo in every room. I can see you in her face, sometimes, and it hurts so badly I can barely breathe.

This Ansel might be fake, but Wilder still wanted to punch him in his virtual face. The scene was a digitized dream, but Victoria's pain had been real.

As though in response to Wilder's thoughts, Ansel smirked. *Pour yourself some wine, angelface.*

You don't want any?

I brought it just for you.

The wine made a sloshing noise as it poured out into the glass. Was that the real noise the poison had made, or was that fabricated, too?

The liquid was red as blood, reflecting the light. It looked so real.

Luke pressed pause. "I'm guessing you can imagine what happens next. The noises are... unpleasant."

"Luke, this is..." Wilder trailed off, unable to find a description strong enough to announce just how he was feeling. Reggie was the one who'd helped him get to Grey, risking everything for Wilder to be able to convince her. How could he do this?

"We need to get this to the police. Reggie left town this morning. He won't be easy to find."

"I'll send it in. Victoria was a TV star. The cops will put everything towards finding this guy."

"Why would he do this?"

Luke shrugged. "I don't know, but this evidence is pretty damning."

Wilder dove towards the door. "Get this footage to the police, okay?"

"What are you going to do?"

Wilder didn't stop, just called behind him. "I'm going to get Grey out of there."

Grey out of there."

"Pick up the phone, Ben," Wilder muttered, jiggling his leg up and down on the ripped, plastic bus seat. Mia didn't have Ben's number, of course, but Wilder had risked texting his own number to get it from her. People were staring and whispering, but he didn't care. There was a little less than an hour before the finale started.

Wilder had called his mother first thing and told her to drive to her sister's place in South Dakota for a few days. If this worked, Monroe would be coming after them.

Wilder's phone beeped with a text. *What do you want, Blue? I'm already at the studio prepping for the finale.*

I need five minutes. Please, Ben.

Wilder could see that Ben was typing, but it felt like a thousand years before the next message popped up. *You live close to the studio, right? Send me your address. I'll be there soon.*

Wilder sat back in the bus seat, staring at his phone in confusion. He hadn't expected Ben to even answer, let alone leave the studio compound an hour before the live season finale.

What game was he playing?

It didn't matter. Whatever was motivating Ben to meet with Wilder, he would take it. Luke had been right; Wilder was desperate, and Ben was his last chance.

By the time Wilder got to his mother's place, Ben was already there, leaning against the front door with crossed arms. The good thing about acting virtually is you didn't need a stop at the makeup trailer; Ben was clad in sweats and a burgundy tee.

"The studio let you leave this close to air time?" Wilder asked.

Ben shrugged. "I didn't exactly stop for permission. I'm not in the first part of the episode. Not until Grey gets to the carnival grounds."

"Still. Thanks for coming. Why did you ask to meet in person instead of just answering my text?"

Ben nodded towards the door, and Wilder pulled out the house key and let them both in, leading Ben to the living room. For some reason he was nervous, his hands shaking and sweaty.

Ben walked around the room with his hands in the pockets of his sweats, studying the place.

He stopped at a picture of Wilder and Lana on the bookshelf. "Sister?"

Wilder nodded.

"I have a sister, too," he said softly.

"I thought you were an only child."

Ben kicked at the couch gently as he spoke. "I've been on *The Real Life of Grey Monroe* since I was six. It's all I know. And I was *so desperate* to get out. I hated lying to Grey. I hated that everything about my family was fake. Because they *were* my family, you know. I spent way more time with Astrid and Oscar and Grey than with my real parents. It wasn't until I quit and left for college that I realized it wasn't fake after all."

"The show?"

"No, of course the show's fake. But Grey and I being brother and sister, our friendship, it was real. She's the closest thing to family I have, and I abandoned her. Every week I would watch her being lied to by that scumbag Michigan, and finally I decided to go back to the show. She needed someone who really cared about her to protect her. But I never thought they would do *this*. When you came to that party, I'd just found out what they were doing with my character. I was... Well, I guess I wasn't handling the guilt very well."

Wilder looked at the TV, its screen blank and glassy. He knew Grey wasn't really inside, but still. It made for a tiny cage.

Wilder just hadn't ever thought about the fact Grey wasn't the only one trapped in it.

"What exactly do you feel guilty about? What is it the studio is doing?"

Ben flashed him a crooked smile so devoid of mirth it could have been a sob. "It's not what they did, it's what *I* did. I killed you."

Wilder took a step back. "Uh..."

Ben shook his head. "No, not *me*, you idiot. Danny. Danny killed LeMarc."

Wilder slumped down onto a chair, knocking his elbow on its wooden arm. "They're making *Danny* the mystery texter?"

Ben shrugged. "The audience has watched me grow up. Even with the PTSD nightmares and odd, unexplained disappearance, it's surprising how few fan theories actually point to me as the killer. Quite the plot twist."

"But you aren't okay with this, are you? That's why you answered my text, why you came to talk to me. You want to save her, too."

"I came to you because I know you're willing to risk anything to save her, and I'm planning to add some reality to this season finale," Ben said, gesturing at the TV. "Live, for the whole world to see."

"You know where the compound is. You want to go get her?"

Ben shook his head. "We don't have time to get there. If we want to get to Grey, we have to do it virtually."

Wilder swallowed down his pang of disappointment. He wanted to *see* Grey with his real eyes, convince her in person. Visiting her virtually hadn't worked, no matter how many times he'd tried it.

But it was their only chance. He stood, hands curling into fists. "I think I could handle one more cameo as Collin LeMarc."

"Good, because it's time to go," Ben said, looking at his watch. "We have a half hour until the show starts. Let's go save my sister."

As they tumbled down the stairs to the street, Ben pushed a few buttons on his cell and brought it to his ear. "Hey, we're heading out. We'll be right down."

When they got down to street level, Ben looked around. "He's been circling the block."

It was a sunny day, for once; spring seemed to be fighting its way back from winter's chokehold. The air was still brisk, so Wilder pulled on the Monroe Studios hoodie he'd grabbed on his way out of the apartment.

Just then, a shiny black limo pulled around the corner. "You have got to be kidding me. I thought you snuck out?"

Ben grinned. "I thought the shaded windows might be helpful for getting out unseen."

"There are SUVs with shaded windows," Wilder said as the limo pulled up and the two of them climbed inside.

Ben immediately sprawled across the sideways bench, putting his legs up and leaning back on a few pillows someone had thrown in.

Wilder pulled out his phone. "I'm going to text some friends to meet us at the studio as backup."

"This isn't a team sport," Ben said. "There's a very good chance we'll end the night in handcuffs."

"My mom's a lawyer. And I trust these guys. They know the whole sordid tale. It's the friends I brought to the party."

Ben's eyebrows shot up. "You're going to invite your *girlfriend* to this?"

Wilder wrinkled his nose. "Fake girlfriend. PR stunt. They wanted the viewers to switch their allegiance to Yusuf."

Ben let out a humorless laugh. "Wow. Daddy Ansel's a piece of work, isn't he?"

I'm going in, Wilder texted to Abe, Carly, and Mia. *If you want to come, meet me a block west of the studio. I'll be in the limo. Good chance of getting arrested at the end of this.*

Carly lived even closer to the studio than his mother, so she might be able to make it there quickly, but he wasn't sure about Abe or Mia. Mia lived farther from the studio than his mother did, and he didn't know where Abe's house was.

His phone beeped two seconds later. *Limo? Sexy.*

Wilder wasn't sure if that meant Mia was coming or not.

Carly's text came in a few seconds later. *We're on our way.*

When they pulled up a block west of the studio, Abe's car was already there. When Carly had said they were on their way, she must have really meant it. Abe was sipping from a Caribou Coffee cup, so maybe they'd already been on the road. Wilder was surprised to see Mia get out of the car with them.

Abe and Carly looked around in wonder as they climbed into the limo. Wilder had ridden several to premieres and parties when he was on the show, but this had to be their first time. It was probably Mia's, too, but she was maintaining her cool exterior.

"Hi, Benjamin," Mia said with an added husk to her voice. She slid into the same bench he was on, causing him to have to sit up hastily.

Carly threw Mia a nasty look.

"Were you guys hanging out?" Wilder asked, looking between Mia and Carly. "How did you get here so fast?"

"Luke called me to tell me you were about to do something stupid. We were meeting to come up with a plan," Carly said as the limo started moving, "but after like five minutes Mia wanted to drive to get a strawberry frap. Girl's got the endurance of a four-year-old."

"I'm sitting right next to you."

Carly grinned wolfishly. "I know."

Ben gave Wilder a worried look.

"It's going to be hard enough explaining *you* when we get in the building. What are we going to say about them?"

"Maybe you guys should stay in the car," Wilder said.

They all started talking at once. "Okay, okay," he said, throwing up his hands. "You win. If they ask, you're friends of Ben's."

"We're going through the gate," Ben said as the car slowed and then crawled to a stop. "Everybody quiet."

They sat in tense silence, watching through the tinted glass as the guard on duty spoke briefly to the driver. After a few moments, he waved them through. Wilder let out a deep breath.

"Easy peasy," Abe said.

The limo pulled them right up to the front entrance, where another guard was posted at the door. "It's Rich," Ben said just before they exited the limo. "He's one of the OG guards, been here since I was a little kid. I can talk us through."

"He hates me," Wilder said. He'd once been caught sneaking a six-pack in for Reggie, and Rich thought he was a trouble-maker.

Reflecting on the past year, he was probably right.

"Seems to be a common thing for you," Carly said pointedly. Ben winked at her, grinning, and she turned a deep shade of red. Abe rolled his eyes.

Rich was tall and dark, with a broad face that wasn't very good at hiding a smile. He whistled as the limo drove away. "Now *that* is how you arrive in style, Benji."

"It's Ben, now," Ben said.

"Mmm-hmm. I know, Benji."

He jerked his head in Wilder's direction. "What's he doing here?"

Ben shrugged. "Monroe wants LeMarc's spirit to show up during the finale, give some sort of speech about how he knows she can do it, that she's a hero. It's dumb, but the viewers will eat it up. They've kept it quiet, but Monroe asked me to pick him up on the way in."

Rich narrowed his eyes at Wilder, taking in his Monroe Studios sweatshirt and tousled hair. Wilder jutted out his chin, trying not to look like a little boy who'd been caught with his hand in the cookie jar.

But suddenly, the guard's face softened. "Kids should get protection from their fathers," he said finally. "They shouldn't need to be protected from them."

Wilder's hand slid up to his eye. The bruising had faded months ago, but he still dropped his gaze at Rich's words, pulling his chin back in. "I thought you hated me."

Rich nodded. "Nothing personal. I'm a bit protective of our Grey."

"And now that I'm off the show you can like me again?"

Rich shook his head. "No, now that I've met that Michael Michigan, I see you in a bit more flattering light."

"Amen," said Ben. "We really gotta get in there, though. We're so late. The show is starting in like a minute."

Rich waved them in without even asking about the extra guests. Thank goodness he hadn't recognized Mia.

A few people gave them surprised looks as they saw Wilder walk past, but they were only stopped once as they made their way to the lab, by a sweaty-looking man in a business suit.

As soon as he saw Ben, he looked so relieved his eyes welled up. "Where have you been? They have someone hooked up to be Danny in your place already. Grey is already on her way to the carnival grounds, and you haven't signed the release yet."

He held out a leather folder.

"The release?"

"Yeah, they're going to try to get Grey to climb the Ferris Wheel before they blow it up, and there's a risk to her, so you have to sign this release in case things go bad. It's just saying you won't sue for emotional trauma from watching your TV sister die."

Ben winced as he took the leather folder from the man. "Just that."

Inside, there were some official-looking documents. As Ben signed, the lawyer looked Wilder up and down suspiciously.

"I don't need to sign one if I'm just doing a guest spot, right?" Wilder asked quickly. "Monroe never mentioned it when he asked me to come in."

The lawyer shook his head. "I haven't been given any instructions to that end. I can call up and ask."

"We're so late already," Ben butted in, eyes wide. "And it would take time for you to find another release form. We really need to go."

The man shrugged. "All I know is I needed to get your signature or I'd be fired, and I got your signature."

As they walked past him, Wilder could visibly see Ben let out a long breath.

"I thought you were both supposed to be good actors," Carly whispered.

Wilder elbowed her in the side. "Ssh. We might actually get away with this."

"Just wait until we get to the lab," Ben said, nodding hello to someone as they passed. Wilder knew a lot of people here, but Ben seemed to know *everyone.* He'd grown up on this show, and they obviously all loved him. "You know the plan, right?"

"Yeah. Pretend Monroe asked for me, try to get hooked in, take my last shot at convincing Grey."

"What are you going to do if Monroe is in the room?" Mia asked.

"I'll say I asked him to come, since I know he loves Grey," Ben said. "And pretend I'm oblivious to the fact that he can't keep his mouth shut."

"Wilder, you got this," Abe said, clapping a hand on his shoulder.

Wilder smiled back at him nervously. "I'm glad you came. If it comes down to punching, you take the lead."

As they reached the fork that branched off from the studio to the offices where the programmers and developers worked, however, Wilder slowed to a stop.

They would have all their best developers here at the compound for this finale.

Including Brooke.

"Wait," he called to the others, who were already ten feet ahead.

"What are you doing, Blue? The show has already started."

Wilder held up a hand to shush Ben. "Ansel Monroe said I was good at manipulating people. Persuading them to do what I want."

Carly shrugged. "That's what we're counting on, right? You'll only have a minute or two to do your thing before Monroe shuts you down."

"I've been in to see Grey several times, though, and I haven't been able to convince her that her world isn't real."

"This time you will," Abe said.

Wilder shook his head. "Grey can believe that she's hallucinating or seeing a ghost because that makes more sense to her than the idea that her whole world is fake. All the alternative explanations, no matter how absurd, seem reasonable in comparison."

"So what can you do to convince her?" Ben asked.

"The only thing that will convince her is the one thing that's even more unlikely than her whole world being a lie."

"Which is?"

Wilder put his hands on Ben's shoulders. "You."

Ben's eyes grew wide.

"You said Grey is your sister and you love her. We all know she feels the same about you. You grew up together. She *knows* you would never torture her like the mystery texter has been doing."

Ben shook his head. "I can't tell her I've been lying to her her whole life and then ask her to trust me."

"Yes, you can. And you'll have to do it without me."

"Why? Where are you going?" Mia asked.

Wilder looked down the hallway towards the tech offices. "To shut off Bruno."

The whole group looked at him like he was crazy.

"I don't think there's just a big red button for you to push."

Wilder bit his lip, a gesture he'd adopted from Grey. If Brooke found out what Reggie had done, how Bruno could be used for evil...

"I happen to know a programmer who I think will help. And if not..." He smiled. "I've been told I'm pretty persuasive."

He had a fleeting glance of Carly rolling her eyes to the moon and back before he sprinted away down the hall.

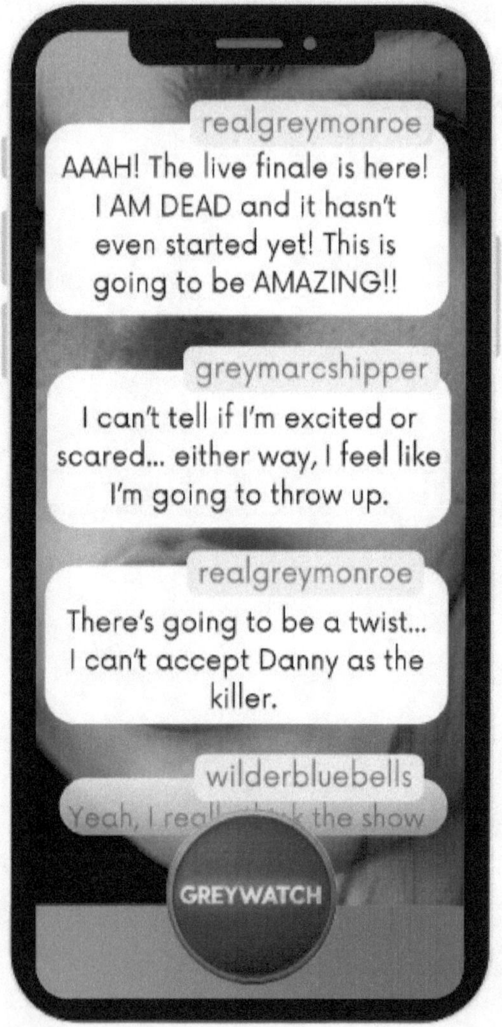
realgreymonroe
AAAH! The live finale is here! I AM DEAD and it hasn't even started yet! This is going to be AMAZING!!
greymarcshipper
I can't tell if I'm excited or scared... either way, I feel like I'm going to throw up.
realgreymonroe
There's going to be a twist... I can't accept Danny as the killer.
wilderbluebells
GREYWATCH

Grey

24

Grey woke up in her bed, her arm thrown over her face. Sunlight streamed into the room, the orange hue of late afternoon.

Ellie was perched on a chair with her feet up on the bed, frowning at a fresh spray tan.

She perked up when she noticed Grey stirring. "Good! You're finally awake. I need your opinion. Do you think I got my tan too dark? Yours looks more natural."

Grey sat up carefully, letting out a moan at her sore head. She was still wearing her green print dress. "Where's Danny?"

Ellie shrugged. "How should I know? I think he was the one who brought you home. He said you were dehydrated. Which is *terrible* for your complexion, by the way."

Grey threw the covers off, stumbling out of bed. "I have to find him."

She bolted to the door, and was surprised Ellie followed her downstairs and out the front door. "But you didn't say if you thought my tan was okay!"

Her mother was in the garage loading a suitcase into the back of her car.

"What is she doing?" Grey asked Ellie.

Ellie tugged on her crop top. "Right. No one should just leave the garage door open like that. Super tacky."

Grey rolled her eyes. "I meant the suitcase. Where's she going? And why is she doing that herself? I don't think my mom's lifted anything heavier than a martini for years."

Ellie snorted. "True. Maybe she's surprising you with a vacation?"

"I'm agoraphobic."

Ellie shrugged. "Maybe an in-town vacay. A spa day, maybe." She brightened up at the idea. "Oooh, I want to come, too. My toenails are in desperate need of a pedi before sandal season."

Grey ran over to the garage, ignoring her friend.

"Mom, what's going on?"

Astrid brushed some loose hair out of her face. Just the fact that she had loose hair in her face made Grey's chest restrict in fear. Her mother was always perfectly put together. "Oh good, you're looking better. I was thinking we could go on a little trip."

Grey ignored Ellie's *I told you so* look. "Mom, I don't leave town. You know that."

Astrid smiled her toothpaste-commercial smile. "I've already planned for that. Dr. Hawks provided some medication that will help you to sleep through the whole trip. When you wake up, we'll be in Cabo."

Now Grey was really scared. "Why is it so important for us to leave town today?" she asked, scared to hear the answer.

Astrid looked away, unwilling, or unable, to hold her daughter's gaze. "I'm just in need of a little trip. Your father and Danny are coming, too."

"I can't leave. Not right now," Grey insisted, her voice rising. "Not until you tell me why we're really leaving town."

"Grey, stop flipping out," Ellie said, putting a hand on her arm. "I know you hate travel, but you're going to be asleep the whole time. I'd kill to go to Cabo right now."

"No!" Grey shouted, shaking off Ellie's hand, all of her energy and fear directed toward her mother. "Mom, tell me the truth. What's happening today here in Heringford that's so bad we have to leave?"

Astrid's smile faltered. "I... I got a text today from a number I don't have in my phone."

No no no no no.

"What did it say?"

Astrid steepled her hands together as though she was praying. "The text was nonsense, Grey, but it said... It said I should say goodbye to you, because today would be the last time I could. I've tried calling Danny, but he's not picking up. I haven't been able to get a hold of him since he dropped you off."

"When was that?"

"You've been out for a full day. You must have really needed the sleep."

At that moment, Grey's phone beeped. Danny didn't even bother using LeMarc's phone. *Speak of the devil.*

It was a short text. *Fairgrounds. Come alone or she dies.*

Without hesitation, Grey turned and fled right past Ellie's confused face. Her mother called after her, but she jumped into her Porsche next to her mom's car, pulling her phone out of her pocket.

Yusuf picked up on the second ring. "Yusuf, carnival grounds... Kamilla...."

"Whoa, slow down," Yusuf said. "Let's try complete thoughts."

"My mother just got a text from Danny saying today is the day. And then he sent a text to me saying he has Kamilla at the fairgrounds. He said I should come alone."

"Fat chance. I'm meeting you there."

"He could kill her, Yusuf."

"He could kill *you*. I'll be there soon."

Yusuf was already parked at the curb near the fairgrounds when she arrived. It was the same place she'd found out she was student body president so many months ago. The Ferris wheel loomed large, a monster rising from the scattered booths and warehouses. The maze of colors was still and deserted as she pulled up behind Danny's car.

"This is it," she said.

Yusuf looked over to her, fear flashing in his dark eyes. "I guess it is."

They held hands as they headed down to their fate.

The booths were all closed up, their garish colors mocking Grey and Yusuf as they crept through the deserted fairgrounds. Grey pulled a ponytail holder out of her pocket, letting go of Yusuf's hand to put her hair up. She should have changed into workout clothes and tennis shoes. At least she wasn't wearing heels.

Suddenly, a noise sounded to their left. Grey jumped back, knocking into Yusuf. He grabbed her from behind to keep her from falling. The wind was picking up, blowing bits of garbage and debris around their feet.

"You stay here," he whispered. "I'll go ahead and check things out."

"No way," Grey argued. "We go together."

"I'm just going to look," Yusuf promised. "Stay here."

She watched as he headed toward the sound, giving her one last look as he turned the corner and disappeared.

The fear was stifling here. Unable to stand still with it writhing around inside of her, she walked over to the nearest booth. There had to be something she could use as a weapon in one of these things. She ripped the fabric to peek inside, sending up a silent apology to the carnival for the vandalism. It was empty.

The next booth had a large wooden stick leaning against the inside of the tent, probably used to hold up the canopy when the booth was in use. She grabbed it in her hands, feeling the heft of the rough staff under her fingers. It made her feel better to have a weapon in her hands, even if she didn't know how to use it.

Suddenly, from the direction Yusuf had headed, she heard a cry.

"Grey!" Yusuf's voice yelled out, striking her to the core. "Grey, run!"

She started running, but not away from his cries. Her feet pounded against the packed dirt of the fairgrounds, the sound of her own heartbeat beating a fast rhythm against her ears.

"Yusuf!" she called out.

She was answered with a pained cry. The wind rose around her suddenly, swelling as though it was trying to hold her back. The booths around her shook in the onslaught, flapping noisily. She grunted in frustration as her speed was cut down, willing herself to keep moving forward, to keep making progress toward Yusuf.

She fought through it, her face stinging with its bite. The wind made her eyes tear up, but she moved blindly toward the direction of his cry, hands tight on the staff, hoping it was strong enough, that she was strong enough.

And suddenly, she turned a corner and there they were. The wind threw bits of paper and dust sprinkling down around her.

Danny was wearing his old basketball hoodie, the one Grey had snuck into her room after his disappearance to hold onto at night.

He smiled when he saw her, a dead, empty smile. In that cold grin, she saw the reflection of her own mad grief, a mirror of her lonely, desperate nights and her broken days.

He was holding a knife to Yusuf's throat.

Yusuf's eyes widened in horror when he saw her. He began to struggle against Danny's grip, and Grey's stomach turned as she saw a thin red line of blood start dripping down his neck.

This is Danny, she told herself, clenching her fists, though her mind was reverberating with the image of Yusuf's bared throat. *You can talk him down.*

"Where's Kamilla?" she asked Danny, her voice shaky and quiet against the roaring wind.

His eyes flew up to the very top of the Ferris Wheel. Grey followed his gaze.

The wheel's metal beams and flaking paint seemed much less magical by the light of day, its gondolas creaky and outdated in their gaudy orange. In the very top one, which swayed back and forth in the wind, was Kamilla.

She was tied up, and even from here Grey could see the fear in her hunched posture. As soon as she realized Grey was looking up at her, she started jerking around, making the gondola swing back and forth even more wildly.

"She's safe for now," Danny called out.

The wind was starting to die down, now, to more of a teasing breeze, swooping down long and slow like a trapeze artist.

"How could you tie her up like that?" The words tore out of Grey like shredded wood, splintered and uneven. "I thought you loved her."

Danny's face wrinkled in frustration. "I did. I *do*. But she ripped my heart out. Because of *you*."

Grey shook her head. "I didn't even know you two were together when she broke it off."

"She didn't want to lose your friendship, so she ended it. And I knew, I just had to convince you... So I brought you both to the cabin. And I would have convinced you we belonged together if that *LeMarc* hadn't interfered. I didn't mean to kill him, Grey. I had no choice."

Danny's eyes were wide, his hand around the knife shaky. She wanted to scream at him for taking LeMarc away, throw things at him until he was black and blue, hit him so hard he couldn't breathe. But he still had the knife up close against Yusuf's carotid.

"Danny, of course you had no choice. Just put the knife down and let Yusuf go."

Danny continued as though he hadn't even heard her. "I drugged you both so you wouldn't remember. And I wasn't going to hurt anyone, the texts were just so you'd be afraid, and then I could come in and save you and you'd think I was good enough for her. She would love me again, if I saved her. And it would have worked, too, if another of your boyfriends hadn't gotten in the way."

Yusuf cried out as the knife dug into his throat, and Grey took a few steps forward, holding out her hands. "Danny, don't!"

But then something odd happened. Danny's face lost its angry distortion, and his grip slackened on the knife. He blinked a few times, as if adjusting to the light.

"Danny?"

All of a sudden, he pushed Yusuf away and threw the knife into the ground. Yusuf stumbled backwards, his mouth round with shock.

Danny rushed towards her, and Grey stumbled back with a cry.

He slowed as he reached her, and this time he was the one who put his hands out as though calming a bucking horse. "No, Grey, it's me. It's me, the real me. The real Danny. I'm not going to hurt you or Yusuf."

"What's going on?" Yusuf asked, squinting at Danny. "You're supposed to be... I thought you were trying to kill me."

Danny's eyes were still wide, his hands still shaking, but he looked like himself again, like the brother Grey loved. The strange, warped villain he'd been for those terrifying moments was gone.

"Grey. I don't have much time before they pull me out for saying this, but all those things LeMarc told you in his nighttime visits, that this is a television show and we're all actors, it's all true. This isn't actually happening. Kamilla is in no danger."

Yusuf cleared his throat. "He's clearly crazy, Grey. We should go. We should run."

Grey didn't even throw him a glance. Her whole vision was taken up by Danny, his tall frame wider from basic training, his rumpled and jeans.

Her brother.

"I don't understand."

All of a sudden, Yusuf let out a frantic scream. "Grey! It's a trick! He's got a detonator!"

He kept screaming, but his words were covered up by an echoing boom. It sounded like a thousand gunshots, and it was coming from the Ferris wheel.

Grey looked up in horror. As soon as the explosion went off, the Ferris wheel let out a loud metallic groan and began to list to one side, twisting up on itself. Echoing pops sounded as all the spokes of the wheel snapped and the metal frame heaved up again, bending and contorting like an acrobat. Once the metal had all snapped, the entire wheel fell to the left.

Grey screamed as it hit the ground in a jarring crash.

The sound was like a sonic boom, the kind of firework that you felt more than heard. Dirt flew up into a cloud at impact, and clots of mud sprayed down all the way over where they were standing.

Grey looked back at Danny in horror, but he was watching the gnarled mess of metal with the same look of shock and dismay.

She didn't see the detonator, but it must be visible from Yusuf's point of view.

He'd tricked her.

If she hadn't been distracted, this wouldn't have happened. Her madness, her paranoia, had finally come back to haunt her, and not in LeMarc form. She'd believed him, for those few cruel moments of hope, believed his lies about her hallucinations being real. She'd wanted to believe it, that her brother couldn't do those things.

But she was wrong. There was no surviving a crash like that. Kamilla was gone, and Danny was the one who'd killed her.

Wilder

25

Wilder ran down the hallway towards Brooke's workstation, praying she was there.

Most of the programmers, with the exception of Reggie and a few of the upper managers, worked in a maze of cubicles crowded into one large room. Despite the high ceilings and boxed-off desks, the place didn't feel as corporate as most offices did. The cubicles were dark wood, nicely carved, for a start, and the lighting came from hanging incandescent lights, not the stark white of fluorescents. It felt more like a college library than anything else, except for one wall taken up by massive screens projecting the show, just like in the lab.

When Wilder arrived, the room wasn't deserted by any means, but it wasn't as packed as he'd feared. A few people were working away at their stations, and a group of employees, mostly techs and developers, were huddled in front of the large screens, absorbed in the story unfolding.

On the screens, Grey was walking with Yusuf towards the fairgrounds, her hair whipping in the wind. The music followed a pounding, suspenseful beat with fast-paced strings ripping through the air in a frantic crescendo.

As the volume of the music swelled, the cameraman punched in close to her face. She looked terrified. Hopefully Ben could get plugged in in time.

One of the programmers Wilder remembered vaguely, Drew something, nodded at him as he approached. "Listen to that audio. You can barely hear them talking. Whoever decided to have the finale outside and live did *not* confer with the sound team first."

Brooke was watching too, but she stood off to the side of the other developers, her gray eyes flickering back and forth between different screens.

Wilder came up behind her and put a soft hand on her arm. "Brooke."

She jumped about a hundred feet into the air, and Wilder put up his hands. "Whoa, just me. Didn't mean to scare you."

"Wilder, what are you doing here? How did you even get in?"

Wilder looked around at the group. A few of them were watching him instead of the show. "Can we talk in private?"

Brooke narrowed her eyes at him. "We're right at the climax of the finale. Can't it wait? I haven't heard from Reggie, if that's what you're here for."

Wilder shook his head. "It's urgent, Brooke."

With another glance at the screen, Brooke nodded, relenting. "We can talk in Reggie's office."

Wilder had spent so much time in Reggie's office when he was on the show, but he still had to hold his breath for a moment at the smell of rancid barbecue chicken and sweat in there. Reggie had a tendency to microwave his midnight snacks and then forget about them—for a week or two. The poor janitorial staff did their best, but Reggie usually put up a "Do Not Disturb" sign since he worked evenings and didn't want to have to interact with real humans.

The show had always given him so much freedom, so many exceptions. The great Reggie Myers, mastermind behind the world's most sophisticated software, used by TV shows and militaries alike. And he'd always hated them, chafing under the miles of leash they gave him.

Was Victoria's murder a message to Monroe and the show runners? Or was it more personal? As far as Wilder knew, Reggie and Victoria had never met.

Just like Luke's workroom, the office was crammed with equipment and hardware. It was also packed with nerdy movie props and gear that were probably worth a fortune.

Brooke turned on a screen up on the wall, and the show popped up. Grey was running towards Yusuf's screams.

Brooke leaned up against Reggie's desk, but Wilder couldn't stand still; he paced back and forth in front of her, not meeting her eyes.

"So what's this about?"

"How long would it take for you to shut Bruno down?"

Brooke choked out a laugh. "Are you serious?"

"How long?"

Brooke didn't answer, but her gaze traveled to a case on the wall with a big red button behind glass. A post-it note with Reggie's scrawl read *DO NOT PUSH THIS BUTTON EVER EVER EVER UNDER PENALTY OF DEATH AND DISMEMBERMENT!!!*

Wilder walked over to it, and Brooke let out a little whine from her throat as he neared. He'd noticed it before, of course, but when he'd asked, Reggie told him the button was connected to the sprinkler systems and could destroy all his equipment and collectables.

"There is actually a big red button? A literal big red button? Reggie is the most ridiculous human…"

Brooke loped over to put herself between Wilder and the case, holding out her arms. "Reggie was worried about hacking, someone being able to do something horrible to Grey by using Bruno. So he made a failsafe. But pushing the button isn't enough. There are two steps: Reg presses the button, and then Ansel Monroe uses his thumbprint on his phone to approve it."

"So I push the button, and then I get Ansel to—"

"No way I'm letting you push that button. You've gone too far, Wilder. I'm sure security will be here any second."

"They might be a little busy. Ben's in on it, too. He's going to go in as Danny, and explain to Grey that her world isn't real. And then we're going to prove it. Shut it all down."

"If Reggie were here, he'd never let you do this. You can't just shut down Bruno."

"Even if it was used to murder Victoria Price?"

Brooke's face turned white, and she let her arms fall. "What?"

"Victoria's camera *was* on that night, and the video shows the truth: she thought she was drinking wine with Ansel. Her nodule was feeding her fake information, so she didn't know she was drinking poison."

Brooke took a step back, shaking her head. "That's… not…"

"Brooke, please. Let me press that button."

She wrapped the hem of her tee around her finger, biting her lip. "Okay, fine."

"Really?" Wilder could be persuasive, sure, but he hadn't been expecting her to capitulate that quickly.

"Let's do this. There's a metal rod behind you we can use to break the glass."

She nodded behind him, and he turned to find it, scanning the room's assortment of old equipment and nerd paraphernalia.

"Where is it? I don't see—"

Without warning, everything went dark.

Wilder must have only been out for a minute or so, because someone was knocking on the door to Reggie's office when his eyes fluttered open.

"Everything okay in there? Heard a bang."

It had been long enough for her to tie him up and gag him, though. Was he wearing handcuffs? It felt like metal around his wrists, hooking his arms behind his back to Reggie's desk. Cold and hard.

Brooke was seated at Reggie's computer just a few feet away, booting it up. When she saw him shifting around, she winced.

"I'm sorry, Wilder. I didn't want to do this," she whispered.

To the knocker, she called, "I'm fine! We definitely did *not* break Reggie's one-of-a-kind stormtrooper helmet!"

A loud guffaw sounded through the door. "Have fun explaining that when he gets back."

Wilder tried to shout out, but the gag muffled the noise into a gurgling moan, and there were no more knocks on the door.

"Reggie invested in some replica Mandalorian handcuffs," Brooke said. "I told him at the time they were a waste of money, but turns out I was wrong. They even light up."

Wilder tried to pull his wrists apart. Replicas had to be garbage at actually keeping someone detained, right? As he twisted and pulled, the sharp edge dug into his wrists painfully and it felt like his arm was going to wrench off, but the cuffs didn't break.

It hadn't been Reggie who'd killed Victoria. He must have asked Brooke to help him search through the initial footage instead of doing it himself, giving her the chance to delete the information for all but Luke's prying fingers.

Brooke signed into the computer and pulled up the Bruno interface. What was she doing? Wilder tried to yell again, producing a low moan.

"Be quiet!" Brooke hissed. "Just give me a minute to figure out what to do with you. Everyone out there saw us come in together, so it's not like I can kill you. And if security knows you're here, which they will soon if they don't already, they'll find you before I can get away. I need to make it look like an accident. Or do what I did with that scheming whore, Victoria. Make it look like you killed yourself."

She paused in her typing and turned fully towards him, leveling a terrifying glance at him just as cold and hard as the cuffs around his wrists. It was like holding his hand against ice, so biting it made him numb.

Brooke kept muttering, almost to herself, though her eyes didn't leave Wilder. It was so incongruent, her frumpy hair and $E=MC^2$ shirt against the terrifying look on her face. "Ben, on the other hand, I can easily get rid of. I just need to set up the pod to produce an electrical surge. It'll kill him, stop him from talking before he tells anyone what you discovered on that footage, and hopefully fry the system so they can't trace it back."

She turned back to the keyboard with a determined nod.

That's what she was doing in Bruno's interface. She was accessing the pod Ben was using, manipulating it to go haywire and electrocute him.

The horrible part was Ben didn't even know about the footage. Things had been moving so fast, Wilder hadn't told him what he suspected about Reggie.

He wriggled more wildly, making more sputtering noises. His phone was in his back pocket. If he could just shift a little to the left...

Brooke spoke without ceasing her typing this time. How long until she finished the commands to Ben's pod?

"I'm sorry, I truly am. I told you before, Wilder, I believed in you and Grey. I would have liked to help you save her. But I have a love story, too, and I need to fight for it. I'm not going to lose him."

Seeing the confusion on his face, she lifted her hands from the keyboard. Wilder swallowed a cheer, looking back at the screen. Ben seemed to be in the system, since Danny was no longer holding Yusuf at knifepoint. He was pleading with Grey, trying to convince her her world wasn't real.

Wilder had wanted Ben to be able to stay in the world as long as possible, but now he needed Monroe Studios to boot him out before Brooke could finish her plot.

His finger was almost hooked around the phone in his back pocket. *Keep her talking.*

Brooke crossed her legs, leaning back on Reggie's chair. "People think Ansel just got lucky, but he has a gift. Really, just such incredible vision. While everyone saw *The Real Life* as the greatest show ever made, he envisioned something bigger. Something better. And he saw that potential in me, too."

Wait. Was Monroe the other half of the love story she was so eager to fight for? Why would someone like Monroe, with his long parade of blonde leggy girlfriends, go for someone like Brooke?

On second thought, she *was* half his age with an unhealthy power dynamic between them. Maybe she was just his type.

Wilder finally caught hold of his phone and got it out of his back pocket, careful not to drop it with his bound hands. He used his thumbprint to open it behind his back. He'd texted under his desk without looking at his phone plenty of times, but he'd never tried it behind his back. How would he ever be able to pull up Carly or Mia's number without looking?

Brooke continued with a wistful sigh in her voice. "We loved each other so much, and we could have been together, but when I got pregnant..." Her voice cracked. "He was just surprised, he needed time. It was Victoria's fault. She got to him when he was still processing, seduced him and tricked him... Everything fell apart so quickly. Even when I lost the baby, he was still under her spell, it was all her fault. But that doesn't mean our love wasn't real. It *is* real. And when he realizes what I did for him, for *us*..." She leaned forward, pleading. "I told you, Wilder, love is worth fighting for. And our love is real."

Wilder could hear the real story flowing like an undercurrent flowing beneath her words, the tale of a handsome narcissist playing the field. How easy it must have been for someone like Ansel Monroe to prey upon an insecure young woman like Brooke.

If Wilder hadn't seen the footage of poor Victoria, if he hadn't discovered her body with Grey, he might have felt sorry for Brooke. He, of all people, understood making stupid decisions in the name of love. But he couldn't forget the sight of the housemaid's shriveled body, still clutching a wine glass. Brooke had planned her murder with a calculated precision.

Wilder used Brooke's distraction to jiggle the phone from his left hand to his right. Carly should be in his recent contacts... He just needed to press the right button. It was the second from the left at the bottom of his screen, right? Or maybe the third from the left?

Second from the left. He pressed the general area where he thought it should be, but he had no idea where the button to call or text was. Maybe somewhere in the middle? He pressed randomly around the screen, hoping to get lucky and open the texting app. But if he did, how would he know?

Ugh, this was hopeless.

They were both distracted by a loud bang from the screen. The Ferris Wheel on the show was imploding, crashing to the ground in a sweeping boom.

"I thought they were going to try to get Grey to climb it before bringing it down. If they'd have known it would just be Kamilla at the top, they wouldn't have had to put the time into setting up the whole stunt in the real world, putting in all kinds of safety features so Grey didn't die in the collapse. So much money wasted. Poor Ansel."

Poor Ansel? Grey was staring at the wreckage of the carnival ride with the same haunted look she'd had after they'd found Victoria's body. For all she knew, she'd just watched yet another friend die. Thank goodness she hadn't been on that thing. No wonder Monroe had worried about the legality of putting her in that kind of danger.

Brooke took a step back, taking in the spectacle of the Ferris wheel's destruction. The wreckage looked like a huge metal spider, its spindly legs twisting into the sky.

With that step back, she was in reach of Wilder's long legs.

Two things happened in quick succession then, almost simultaneously.

First, Wilder reached out his legs and clamped them around Brooke's tiny ankles, yanking backwards. She shouted and went down, smashing her head against the desk with a loud crunch and collapsing to the ground in a pile.

Second, the door behind him slammed open and Abe stormed into the office, looking back and forth between Wilder and Brooke with wide eyes.

He dropped down next to Brooke, checking for a pulse.

"Still alive," he declared.

Wilder shook his bound hands behind him, trying for a meaningful look with his eyes. *Untie me, you big, wonderful idiot!*

Abe knelt down and pulled off Wilder's gag, then started working at the cuffs around his hands.

Wilder coughed, relishing the ability to breathe again. "How did you know I needed help?"

"Carly said you called her and then immediately hung up. I figured you were in trouble, so I ran here as fast as I could."

"Thank goodness. But with you here, what's keeping them from unplugging Ben?" Wilder asked, glancing at the screen.

"Uh, have you met Carly? She has half the employees staging a revolution in there. Ben's a favorite amongst the crew, apparently. But there are some who want to save their jobs, and they're hooking up someone else to jump in as Danny once they get Ben unplugged... It's all kind of a mess."

He finally got the handcuffs off, and Wilder sprang up, shaking out his wrists.

He grabbed a stapler off Reggie's desk and smashed it against the glass encasement around Reggie's D-day button. It shattered with a splintering noise and a cascade of glass raindrops.

With a cry, he slammed his hand against the button.

He was kind of expecting a noise or something. Knowing Reggie, a wailing siren and red floodlight was not out of the question.

But even though Wilder smashed the button with all his might, nothing happened.

Abe looked up from where he was kneeling. "Was that supposed to do something? Because it looks like the show's still going on." He nodded at the TV, where Grey was pulling herself together, turning back towards Danny with a face like a thundercloud.

Wilder jiggled the mouse to wake up the screen Brooke had been typing on. A dialog box was open in the middle of the screen.

Emergency shutdown activated. Fingerprint approval needed to continue.

Wilder cursed. "Multi-factor authentication. I need to find Monroe."

"They were calling him to the lab to deal with the chaos when you called. Go. I'll deal with this"—He looked down at Brooke—"this random woman who I guess fits in somehow to what's going on? Or maybe just really hates you? I'm not sure, to be honest."

It was really nice to have friends again, people who had his back even in the craziest of situations.

Wilder ran for the door, where some of the other developers were peeking in to see what was going on. "Thank you!" he yelled back, pushing past the gathering crowd. "I'll send security!"

He sprinted towards the hallway, racing towards the last man he wanted to see but the only man he needed—Ansel Monroe.

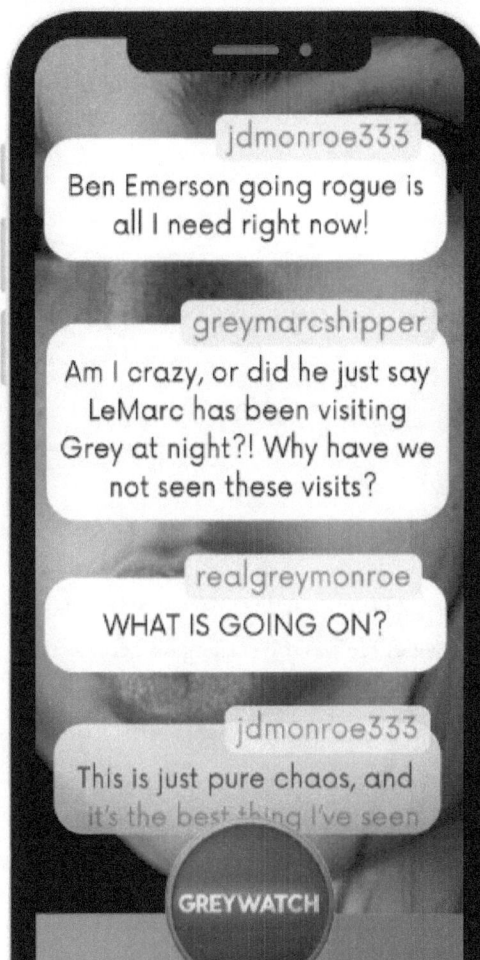

Grey

26

Grey gaped at Danny standing in front of her, his hair tousled by the wind. He was still shaking his head, as though they hadn't all just witnessed him murdering Kamilla.

Grief roared in her ears like a rushing waterfall. Kamilla was dead. Danny had killed her.

He'd tricked Grey into thinking he was the old Danny again, and then, when she let her guard down, he'd revealed he wasn't the old Danny at all. That brother she'd loved, it turned out he hadn't known him at all.

"You killed her."

Danny took a step towards her. "This isn't real, Grey. Kamilla's not dead. She was never even alive in the first place."

"Grey!" Yusuf called out.

She whipped her head around and let out a startled yell.

There was another Danny.

The second Danny had picked up the knife again, and Yusuf was back in Danny's grip. This time, the point of the knife was dribbling blood down his neck. He flashed her a pleading glance. "Grey, help!"

She took a step back, looking at the Danny right in front of her. He had his head turned back towards his doppelganger. "Wilder's friends must be keeping them from unplugging me, so a developer pulled up another avatar," he mumbled to himself.

"What are you... You aren't real. You killed her," Grey choked out. Danny whirled back towards her, shaking his head. "You killed Kamilla."

"No, Grey."

She backed up a few more steps. "I'm hallucinating again. The stress broke me, and I've completely snapped."

Danny shook his head, moving his hands to cup her face.

"Grey, listen to me," he said, his voice fierce. "That Danny is a piece of computer code. He isn't real. You *know* this world isn't real. You've known for a long time, and you just have to admit it to yourself."

"I can't," Grey whispered, tears falling down her face. She looked back at Yusuf, wincing as the blade cut in even deeper. "What if I'm wrong? What if I'm crazy?"

Danny was tearing up, too, brushing her hair back. A thousand memories hung in the air between them, scraped knees and night-time chats and strawberry ice cream cones with sprinkles.

"For years I've watched you grow up, and every season—every school year—I saw the distance between the real you and the person you show to the world grow. You try so hard to be perfect, to pretend that nothing's wrong. But LeMarc showed you a different path. He showed you that a broken authenticity is more beautiful than a perfect mask."

"In my case, *broken authenticity* is just a pretty way to say *totally insane*."

Danny shook his head, "You're not crazy, Grey. The girl you think you need to be, that girl who would take down her own brother and then spend the rest of her life pretending it didn't destroy her, she's no more real than this world is."

Grey let out a sob. "Who am I, if I'm not the girl everyone thinks I am? I don't even know what's real anymore."

Danny smiled. "Yes, you do. And you know exactly who you are. You're—"

Suddenly, he vanished.

His words cut off midstream, the roughness of his hands against her cheeks disappeared, and she was looking right through where he'd just stood.

She locked eyes with Yusuf, who was studying her, waiting for her next move.

"Ten seconds," the Danny with the knife said, "Before I slit his throat. I really do love you, Grey. It'll be a shame to mangle you. *Nine*."

"Grey, he's going to kill me," Yusuf called out.

"*Eight*," Danny said. "It reminds me of poor Ophelia, poor beautiful Ophelia. She lost her mind when she lost her love too, didn't she? *Seven*. Just a poor, broken soul who was never brave enough to be the heroine. The lost light they still write songs about."

He smiled. "*Six*."

And that was it. It was the smile that did it.

In all the years she'd loved her brother, she'd never seen his face twist like that. They could convince her that Danny had been shattered in war, destroyed by combat, but they would never convince her that he would look at her like that.

Even shattered, every broken shard of Danny's spirit would fight to protect her.

"*Five.*"

He would never smile at her pain.

"I'm not Ophelia," she said quietly. "I might be broken, but I'm not lost."

Danny's fingers tightened around the knife. "*Four.*"

"I'm scarred and I'm bruised, but I'm not crazy."

"*Three.*"

"And you're not real," she said, taking a step forward.

Danny's smile faltered. "Of course I am. *Two.*"

Grey shook her head, taking a few more steps forward. "No, you're not. None of this is real."

She walked forward until she stood just a few feet away.

Yusuf was looking at her in dismay. "This is real, Grey," he said, his voice so scared and tiny it pinged a shot of doubt through her heart. "We're about to die. You have to fight."

Danny shook his head. "There's no use fighting. I've already won. *One.*"

But his hand didn't move.

"This is a television show," she responded. She looked Danny right in the eye, and she could feel the power of her decision racing through her. "I'm the main character of a television show."

She saw the fear behind his eyes, and this time it was her who smiled.

"And I quit."

Wilder sprinted towards the lab, rubbing his red-rimmed wrists.

When he arrived at the lab, Ansel Monroe was looking down at Ben over his high cheekbones and sharp nose, sneering like Ben was a bug he was about to crush.

Ben sat in his pod with his chin high, doing his best impression of someone who wasn't terrified. Behind Ansel was a flock of producers, security guards, developers, and even a few cast members.

As soon as Wilder clambered in the room, Ansel's gaze popped up to him. "So you worked on this together. Congratulations, Mr. Blue and Mr. Emerson. You've just destroyed your lives."

Was his cell phone in his pocket? How could Wilder reach it?

"We might have just destroyed our lives, but we saved Grey's. In my book, that's worth it." He couldn't help it; his gaze fled to Grey on the screens. She looked so empty, drained down to the pulp.

Even though Ben was clearly awake, Danny was still on the screen, holding a knife to Yusuf's throat.

Wilder walked towards the CEO until he was standing next to Ben's pod. Ben swung his legs over the edge of his pod, cowering under Monroe's might.

Ansel pulled his shoulders back, straightening his back and building up his height. "Do you have any idea how powerful I am? How easy it will be for me to obliterate everything you love, everything you care about?"

"I love *Grey*," Wilder shot back. "I care about *Grey*." He paused for just a moment, tilting his head, and then asked, "Do you? Do you care about her at all?"

Ansel slapped him across the face, hard, and Wilder reeled back. "You're just a silly boy."

On the screen, Danny was counting down, his voice booming from the speakers. Behind Ansel and his entourage, Wilder could see the internal battle written on Grey's face on one of the close-up cameras. Another camera was shooting from a distance, and she looked so small standing there, a lone figure against the gnarled remains of the Ferris wheel.

"My dad uses fists," Wilder said, tossing his head back. "Definitely hurts more. A slap's a little weak, don't you think?"

Grey was walking now, walking forward toward Danny.

Ansel was storming like a thundercloud, ready to blow Wilder away, but as Grey began to speak, even he couldn't keep himself from turning around to watch.

"You don't know her," Wilder said quietly to Ansel's back as everyone froze with rapt attention.

His lips curled up into a smile as she answered Danny's counting with her own words, girl on fire. "You underestimated her. And now you're going to lose."

Just at that moment, Grey smiled on the screen, as though she had heard him speak. The entire lab was dead silent as she spoke. "I'm the main character of a television show. And I quit."

Ben laughed out loud, and Carly let out a cheer. Mia gave a long, somber look back to Wilder, but then smiled and shrugged. "You did it, Loverboy."

Ansel was spluttering mad. "Cut the live feed! NOW! And get legal on the phone!" he ranted to one of his underlings, who immediately started scrambling to obey. "Grey has no right to quit. She's not an employee, she's my daughter. She can't quit!"

It was the opportunity Wilder needed. As Monroe spun towards the massive screens, turning his back on Wilder, he left his back pocket vulnerable. Wilder had a perfect shot for the phone inside.

Quick as a snake, Wilder plucked the phone out of his pocket and swiped the screen open.

Bruno Approval Needed, read a pop-up box. There was an image of a fingerprint below the words.

It was now or never.

Wilder grabbed Ansel's meaty wrist and yanked it back. He pressed the phone against the pad of his pointer finger.

Ansel whirled around to face Wilder, murder on his face. "What are you doing? Let go of me, you little—"

He cut off as the wall full of screens went black.

"Thank you for your cooperation," Wilder said with a smirk.

"Did you just..." Ansel trailed off, his mouth wide with horror.

Ben pushed off his pod. "The show's over, Ansel, and no matter how many lawyers you throw at us, you can't change the fact that Grey knows the truth now. She *knows.*"

Ansel reeled back, turning to his developers. "Grey's not connected to Bruno at all right now? She's seeing what's really around her?"

A broad-shouldered developer was the only person brave enough to nod.

Before Monroe could commit murder right in front of everyone, a tall man in a nice suit stumbled into the room. He was holding a tablet in one hand and his side with the other, leaning over to catch his breath.

"I was told to run here," he said, panting. "Two flights of stairs. Mr. Monroe, I have to urge you to not take any sudden actions right now."

"Legal," Ben said at Carly's confused look.

"Love myself a lawyer," Mia said with a salty grin. She was holding up her cell phone, recording everything.

Ansel took a deep breath. "Good. You're here. Security, why don't you take these criminals and lock them into a room while I talk to Redmaine."

The lawyer, Redmaine, cleared his throat. "Well, Mr. Monroe, it might be best not to hold them against their will," he said delicately.

"They're trespassing!" Monroe roared.

"This is a *highly* public situation, as evidenced by the cell phones that are out right now." Wilder looked around along with Monroe, and there were several people who were holding up their phones.

Mia winked at Wilder. "Book deal," she said with glee.

The lawyer glared at her. "Technically, they're not trespassing; Benjamin is an employee, and they were all let through the front gate. For now, let's send these kids home, and we'll figure out next steps."

Ansel turned to Wilder, his upper lip quivering with anger. "Get out," he growled.

Wilder didn't have to be told twice. He led the others out of the room and into the hallway.

As soon as the door closed behind him, he let out a loud whoop. "We did it!"

Ben shook his whole body like a dog shaking off water, releasing the tension. "As the only legal adult in this situation, I'm probably looking at jail time, and I honestly don't care," he said. "What do you say we go get her?"

"What?" Wilder asked. "Go get Grey?"

Ben grinned.

"She's close?" Wilder asked, hardly daring to breathe. "She's close enough for us to go now?"

Ben nodded. "A little over three hours east."

"I'm in," Carly said. "Let's finish this."

Mia grinned, wrapping an arm through one of Wilder's. "You ready to get your girl?" she asked.

"I'm ready," Wilder said. "I am so, so ready."

He immediately realized, however, that his words were a lie: he wasn't *totally* ready to go. "First, though, we should probably get Abe and clue in security about the murderer he's guarding."

Carly crossed her arms. "Did you just say murderer?"

Wilder shrugged. "It's kind of a long story."

realgreymonroe

WHAT JUST HAPPENED
WHERE DID THE SHOW GO
HOW COULD THEY DO THIS
TO ME
NOOOOOOOOOOOOO!

wilderbluebells

UM, EXCUSE ME? What just
happened? Was that
seriously Wilder Blue?!?!

ishipgreymarc

I am sobbing so hard right
now I think I'm about to
throw up. That was
EVERYTHING to me.

GREYWATCH

Grey

27

It was gone. Everything was gone.

Grey looked around at the empty field where the tents used to be, the flat ground where the mangled spires of the Ferris wheel still clawed at the sky. There wasn't even any grass anywhere, just packed dirt.

Looking behind her, she could only see her lonely car parked on the street. The street looked pretty intact, even complete with road signs. However, as Grey looked back at town, which was in her line of sight now that all the carnival booths were gone, she saw that some buildings looked much more plain than usual, with no bricks or decorations on the exterior. None of them had doors. Many were just plain gone.

All this time, LeMarc had been telling her nothing in her life was real. But *this*... How could she have possibly known, ever imagined... How could it all just be *gone*?

She felt just as empty as her world. If so much of her life was fake, did that mean part of her was, too? If she was just a character in a fairy tale, what happened to her when the story reached its end?

"At least the lights are still on," she said out loud. LeMarc had said that she was underground, but the lights must have been real, not a virtual lie. LeMarc had said that some of the people in her life were real, and they would have needed to see.

Her housekeeper. Victoria was gone, but her replacement was real. Grey ran to her car, pulling her keys out of her pocket. She needed to get home, find their housekeeper Sharon and beg her to explain everything.

Driving home was nightmarish. It was like someone had taken an eraser to Heringford and removed huge chunks of the town. She was relieved to see that the ice cream shop was still there, and her school, but many buildings were just empty shells.

Maybe she really was crazy. For so long that had been her worst fear, and now it felt like the only thing she could hang onto. Losing her mind was *nothing* compared to this. Were they watching her right now? Thousands—could it be *millions*?—of strangers' eyes, watching her eyes fill up with tears. She could *feel* them on her, the imperceptible pressure on every inch of her skin.

When she pulled up to her home and saw the garage door missing, she was already crying. The exterior of the house was similar to how it was before, the same siding and roof and windows, but with no grass or fake trees surrounding it everything looked completely different. The inside of the garage was empty, completely devoid of the shelves full of camping gear and sports equipment and boxes of Christmas decorations.

Suddenly, Grey had a horrible thought: What if they were going to just leave her here? Leave her trapped in this world until the air ran out? She could drive out, of course, but she was plunged into a world of panic at just the thought of leaving town. The town had already left her.

Her breath was coming in gasps now, but she *wouldn't* let them see her fall apart. The faceless voyeurs so hungry for her pain would have to look elsewhere for their sick thrills.

She got out of the car and opened the door to her home. Someone had taken all of the heavy furniture and remade it using lego-like blocks: There was a piano bench, but it was just a rough shape, not the elegant bench hand-carved in France that her mother had spent hours picking out. The dining room table and chairs were simple, wood-hewn. The piano was just a piano-shaped prop. Anything she could sit or lean on was there, keeping her from falling through them all these years, but nothing looked like it had before.

An avatar can't play real piano keys, she realized. They'd needed virtual keys for Danny's concertos. It was the same reason everyone else ate virtual food, according to LeMarc. The details of her life had to be virtual, so the fake people could interact with everything realistically.

The family photos were all gone, the wall empty.

Grey sat down on the hard, plastic sofa, lifting her hand to brush her hair out of her eyes.

Her hand stopped, however, as she realized in horror that there was something on her forehead. A node, LeMarc had said, feeding her sensory information and recording her every heartbeat.

Crying out, she tried to pull it off, but it must have been adhered to her skin somehow, because it hurt when she yanked on it. She quit trying, putting her face in her hands.

There in the middle of the stage she'd thought was home, she finally broke.

The sobs came like waves, ever cresting and crashing, unrelenting in their brutal assault. And beyond them, beyond the onslaught of panic and fear and pain, was an ocean so deep and cold she'd never survive it. Each time she began to calm, her heaving sobs slowing to a whimper, she'd catch a glimpse of the expanse of frigid water around her and the tears would come all over again. She would never see her parents again; they weren't even real. Who even were her real parents? Did she have any at all? And she'd never talk to Ellie and Kamilla at school ever again, or laugh with them at the ice cream shop, because they were ghosts and always had been. They were acting the *whole time*. The grades she'd worked so hard for, the clubs she'd joined, her track trophies... all of her efforts were creating keys to a door of future opportunity that didn't even exist. And Danny... She couldn't even think about Danny.

Another wave, another crest. Her thoughts were as chaotic and gnarled as the ruins of a Ferris wheel—a *fake* Ferris wheel. Round and round she went, rehearsing every lie, every tender moment that meant nothing, just dialogue in some psychotic play.

It was all a lie. *Everything, everything, everything.*

Eventually, she ran out of tears. The waves of panic and pain were still crashing, but she was too exhausted to keep breaking. She'd cried herself out.

After a while of sitting in silence, she wiped at her puffy, tear-stained face and stood up slowly. Turning in a circle, she took one last look at the empty house. *I thought this was my home.* She knew better now. She didn't have a home.

She returned to her car and climbed in, pushing down another rogue wave of tears. She'd planned on driving out of town right away, but instead she found herself taking the turn to go to the riverbank. She was relieved to see that the river was real, meandering along in the sunlight. Not real sunlight, she reminded herself.

She sat on the bank, watching the reflections dance across the gentle waves. She didn't have any idea what to do next. Should she take the east route out of town, or the west? Which led to the way out? And what would she find when she got there? The thought of leaving town sent a spiral of fear surging through her.

I've lost everything, she thought.

But then a pesky little voice, suspiciously similar to LeMarc's, invaded her thoughts. *Maybe that isn't a bad thing.*

Her bruised heart immediately pushed back against the notion, but it kept flickering in her mind, snaking through the despair and grief.

She'd never had anything to lose. The horrible things that had happened to her, the trauma she'd endured, was all a part of the act. Her life wasn't a lie, it was a cage. She was a zoo animal, a curiosity, a circus performer shackled to the ring.

"And now I'm free," she whispered, trying out the words on her tongue.

A lie, maybe. Perhaps the most true thing she'd ever uttered. Only time would tell.

She wasn't sure how long she sat at the river before she heard footsteps behind her, a few hours at least, but it was long enough for the waves to stop crashing, at least for now. It was long enough for her to find some semblance of peace.

She stood and turned around, watching as the stranger approached. He looked to be about her age, tall and striking with blonde hair and deep blue eyes, broad shoulders and narrow hips. His gait was graceful, like an athlete, and though he gave off an unmistakable air of confidence, his face was cautious as he approached.

"I figured I would find you here," he said as though he knew her, stopping ten paces back. She wasn't quite sure why, but she was surprised by his voice. She'd expected him to sound like LeMarc, though he didn't look anything like him. He had the same air of danger and recklessness, the same way of holding himself. She took a step back.

"Have they turned everything back on?" he said, taking a few lazy steps forward. "Or are you still seeing things as they really are?"

"Everything's still empty."

The boy just watched her with his blue eyes, and she was scared by the intensity behind his gaze. But then he smiled, a broad grin, and it changed his face completely. He had the kind of smile that made you want to smile back.

"We argued the whole way here about who should come talk to you. I thought it should be Danny, but I think he's worried you'll hate him for lying to you."

Even though the voice was different, the way he said things, the shape of the words as they left his mouth, it was so familiar she was finding it hard to breathe.

"Who are you?" she asked finally.

He raised his eyebrows, surprised. "Oh! Right. You don't know what I look like. I'm Wilder Blue." He held out his hand for her to shake. "It's me, Grey. I'm LeMarc."

She crossed her arms, leaving his hand hanging between them. "No, you're not."

His mouth quirked up on one side, and again she saw the boy she loved in someone else's features. "I'm not?"

"LeMarc is heavyset, with acne. He told me."

Wilder laughed in surprise. "I didn't... Oh wow, I did say that, didn't I? When you told me you hated blondes."

"I did not say I hated blondes!" she retorted, though she did prefer brunettes. Her eyes were filling up with tears again, and there was a nervous flurry in her chest. Wilder was the golden kind of attractive that made her feel self-conscious. He didn't have LeMarc's dark, wild curls and scrawny elbows. She missed his scar, his hooked nose, and his soulful eyes.

Wilder started biting his lip again. "So do I... uh, look okay?" he asked, holding out his arms and spinning around. "I've never really worried about that before, but all of the sudden I'm feeling self-conscious."

Grey circled around him, tapping her finger to her lips. "What's the name of LeMarc's dog? And I'll be able to tell if you read it off of floaty words."

"Trick question," he said, a smile playing across his lips as she came back in front of him. "I didn't have a dog on the show."

"What should the real name of raspberries be?"

"I'm *not* going to say redberries. I refuse to let you win that debate. Raspberry is a perfectly good name, and there are multiple varieties of berries that are red, and yes, I know that strawberries aren't berries."

He laughed, and it was LeMarc's laugh, his low chuckle. Grey couldn't keep herself from smiling at the sound of it.

"What did you get me for Valentine's Day last—"

"Grey," he interrupted, his voice deep. He took a step forward, closing the remaining space between them, and wrapped his arms around her waist. "Anyone who watches the show knows the answer to that question. You know there's a way for you to know for sure."

She reached up, tracing down his nose with her finger. She brushed her thumb over his top lip. "You used to have a scar here."

"I'm still me, Grey. I still love you more than anything else in the world."

She nodded and wrapped her arms around his neck. She was crying again, but these tears didn't hurt. "You know, I have heard of one method of determining if my boyfriend is really my boyfriend. Even if his personality and memories are transplanted into some blonde supermodel with perfect teeth."

He smiled again, and this time she smiled back. She might some-day learn to like this grin better than LeMarc's, even without the scar. She leaned in for a kiss.

She knew it was him the minute their lips touched. She put her hand on the back of his head, her fingers tangling in his hair, and he kissed her just like he always did, sweet and soft but spiked with danger.

"I can't believe I just got to do that for real," he said when she pulled away.

"It's nice to meet you, Wilder Blue," she answered, grinning up at him. "I think I love you."

He kissed her again, sweet and quick, and then took her hands, letting his thumbs run across her knuckles. "Danny and a few other friends are parked down the street. What do you say we go meet up with them and get out of this ghost town? I know you're scared of leaving Heringford, Grey, but the real world is waiting for you just outside."

She squeezed his hands in hers. "I'm not afraid. I can do this."

"Of course you can," he said simply. "You're Grey Monroe."

They started walking away from the river, hand-in-hand. Grey smiled as a sudden thought entered her mind.

"What?" Wilder asked, seeing the secret smile.

"I was just thinking," she started, pulling up their joined hands to look at them. They fit together perfectly. He raised a questioning brow.

"*This*," she said, looking at the boy she loved for the first time. "*This* is real."

THE
EXCLUSIVE INTERVIEW

GREY
MONROE

A RETURN TO *THE REAL LIFE*
5 YEARS LATER

STREAMING SEPTEMBER 6
8/7 CENTRAL ON MBS

Epilogue

G rey winced against the studio lights. When she'd agreed to this, she'd been picturing an intimate affair, a few comfy chairs set up in a muted room. There were too many cameras in here, soulless black eyes set up to catch every fleeting expression, every nervous tick. At least they'd agreed not to have a live studio audience.

Remember to smile, she recited in her head. *Don't start crying when they mention my agoraphobia—no one wants to hear about the weeks it took to finally leave the hotel room they put me in. Don't blink too much, but also don't forget to blink. If I'm floundering, look to—*

"You say the word, and we bolt." Wilder's husky whisper interrupted her increasingly frantic litany. "You've got the power here."

His hand snuck into hers, warm and familiar, and she held on for dear life, inhaling deeply. She wasn't alone in this.

Looking up into his sparkling blue eyes and roguish smile, she shook her head slightly. "No, I can do this."

"Of course you can. You're Grey Monroe."

She knew he didn't understand why, after a lifetime of cameras, she was so intent now on doing this interview with Liz Larkin, America's journalist. But after five years of hearing everyone from the supermarket clerk to her college professor tell her own story back to her (*Remember that tornado? That must have been terrifying...*), she was finally ready to write her own narrative.

She'd chosen a crisp pantsuit with clean, sharp angles, hoping it would make her look more adult, but she worried it had the opposite effect. Wilder, of course, looked as effortless and cool as ever in slacks and a shirt open at the collar. In this humidity, his hair was curling at the ends.

He raised an eyebrow at her staring. "Take a picture, it'll last longer."

Laughing, she shoved him playfully. He always knew what to say to relieve the tension.

Just then Liz Larkin arrived, her dark skin blurred with layers of heavy makeup and her hair styled into a voluminous mane.

"Thanks for being here, Grey."

And then, after a few minutes of nervous small talk, the interview began.

The first question was a softball, but Liz Larkin's aggressive empathy was still unnerving. "Grey, we're all so excited to have you and Wilder here today. Tell me, what was the most surprising thing about the real world after leaving the show?"

Easy. "The smell of grass." She realized she was unconsciously reaching up to touch the scar on her forehead where the node had been removed, a nervous habit, and quickly clasped her hands together to stop herself. "And the taste of mint ice cream. Bruno got a lot of smells and tastes right, but a few were wrong. Turns out I hate the taste of mint."

"That must have been disorienting."

"*Everything* was disorienting at first. Still is, sometimes."

"What was the hardest part?"

"Umm..."

Everything. Everything was hard. How could she trust anyone? The whole world had watched her cry herself to sleep, had listened in on every appointment with her therapist, every whispering kiss with LeMarc. They all knew her, or at least thought they did.

She'd refused to talk to anyone about how she was feeling, even Ben and Wilder. Especially Ben and Wilder, because they'd been the ones who she'd given her heart and fears and hopes to, knowing they would hold them safe. And all along, they'd been passing them right along through America's TV screens every week.

Wilder's hand snuck into hers again, and she realized there'd been too long of a pause.

"I felt alone," she said finally. "Really, really alone."

"No one in the world can claim to know what you've been through," Liz Larkin confirmed. "But I think your fans were thrilled to find out you had a shoulder to cry on." She smiled suggestively at Wilder.

"Eventually," he answered. "Grey understandably needed a little time."

"I knew I loved him, but I hated him, too. Same with my brother. It took me almost a year to be able to really talk to them about what had happened, and another year after that to finally go to a therapist without fearing I was being taped. That was a turning point for me, though. I stopped running from all of it."

"Neither of you have social media accounts anymore, but from what I've heard you've been incredibly successful since the show ended, Grey, getting your GED and working towards a degree. Is it difficult to feel like a regular student?'

"Yeah, the others are all jealous I'm dating a celebrity. Wilder's pretty famous, you know."

Liz Larkin raised her eyebrows in surprise, and it wasn't until Wilder snorted next to Grey that the journalist seemed to realize it was a joke.

"I'm studying social work. Unfortunately, there are a lot of kids in this country who have it worse than I ever did, and I want to help if I can."

"And you're living with your brother and his fiancé?"

"Yes, Sarah. She's absolutely wonderful. Once they get married, though, I'm going to get my own place."

"I'm sure Wilder's place is nice. Any wedding bells in the near future for you two?"

Wilder somehow managed to deliver the message "None of your business" with so much charm and charisma, Liz Larkin didn't even realize he'd evaded her question.

Liz continued on to probe about whether Grey had watched the show (*some of it*), whether she'd been able to make friends in the real world (*well, my new friend Mia is great, and she'd want me to mention that the soap opera she's starring in, "Passion Falls," is on every Friday at noon CST*), whether she had any idea who her biological mother was (*no, and I'm not going to try to find out—though I might feel differently in the future*), and whether she still got together with the old cast (*dinners with Oscar, my dad in the show, every second Friday, brunch with Kamilla when she's between movies, and even the occasional yoga class with pre-coma Ellie*).

Liz tried to ask a question about Michael Michigan, but Wilder helped navigate her away from dangerous waters on that one.

"Michael played a really convincing Yusuf, but what he and Grey had was never real. Not like us."

And then they came to the most difficult topic: Ansel Monroe.

Liz Larkin leaned forward, and her voice dropped low. "I'm sure it was difficult to see him during your civil suit, though if the rumors about the settlement are true, the money probably softens the blow. Did you attend any of your father's hearings for his criminal charges?"

She already knew the answer to that; if Grey had been there, it would have been plastered all over the news.

"No."

"You didn't want to see him? He's been sentenced to two years in prison in the same facility as Brooke Baxter, his alleged spurned ex-lover who killed Victoria Price. Do you agree with those who feel he got off too easy? How would you describe your feelings towards your father now?"

The word *father* was a stretch. With Ansel Monroe's high-priced team of lawyers and hard-fought influence amongst politicians and celebrities alike, she'd been surprised at any jail time at all. Maybe she would hope for more, if she were willing to waste her time thinking about the man.

"I don't know Ansel Monroe. I grew up with a different father, and I'd rather focus on the people in my life who do care about me."

With a nod, Liz turned to Wilder. "Speaking of people who care about Grey, the world was shocked when they found out you'd been visiting her virtual world at night, unbeknownst to anyone other than Monroe Studios developer Reggie Meyers, still at large."

Grey hid a smile. Reggie had never returned to the U.S., but occasionally Wilder got random Star Wars memes from unknown users in Turks and Caicos with handles like "SunburnedRedBull-Fanatic" or "TrickedByAnIdiot."

Liz Larkin continued, "Tell me, Wilder: What led you to risk everything to convince Grey her world wasn't real?"

Grey snuck a peek at him, and she wasn't surprised to find he was smiling at her. "I bet I can get you to blush with my answer."

Grey rolled her eyes. "Try me."

He chuckled, but there was a strange seriousness in his eyes. "I was in love with her."

He could have stopped there; Grey was already blushing. But of course he kept going.

"I was a dumb teenager, but even then I was able to see that Grey had the potential to either absolutely destroy me or make every moment worth it. A lesser woman would have been crushed by just a fraction of what Grey has gone through, but she's come out stronger, more compassionate, and more beautiful. I love you, Grey. Always will."

Now that she was surely the color of a fire hydrant, it was probably Grey's turn to whip up some romantic, flowery declaration, but all she managed was, "Thanks."

To wrap up the interview, Liz turned back to Grey. "My final question for you today is this: The show was called *The Real Life of Grey Monroe*. Do you think that was an appropriate title? Was any of it real?"

Grey looked again at Wilder, his long fingers twisted in hers. She thought of Ben, watching from his living room couch with Sarah tucked into his side. But most of all, she thought of that moment on the fairgrounds, the rush of confidence and triumph she'd felt in just two little words, reclaiming her power.

"The Grey the world got to see once a week was edited and manipulated. She was a character in a TV show. But I'm real, and my experiences might have been fabricated, but they made me who I am. The life I'm living now, that I'll continue living, is built off of those formative years inside the show. The name wasn't a lie, but I hope fifty years from now, *The Real Life of Grey Monroe* means much more than a TV show."

"I have no doubt they will," Liz Larkin finished.

Grey nodded. "I'm just getting started."

Excited for More?

Get an exclusive peek at *Dark and Dreary* and other free content when you sign up for Catherine's newsletter at https://www.catherinelyonbooks.com/

Please leave a review on Amazon!

DARK AND DREARY

A ROSIE CANTO MYSTERY
OCTOBER 2025

In the thrilling finale of the Rosie Canto Mysteries, Rosie faces a heart-pounding race against time to unmask a ruthless kidnapper and unravel the secrets behind her family's murders—before it's too late. Read an excerpt by signing up for Catherine's newsletter at catherinelyonbooks.com!

Acknowledgements

This book has had quite the journey (the original version had a supervillain who controlled the weather and a visit from Grey's time-traveling grandson, believe it or not), and countless people have made that voyage possible. Thank you to my many beta readers, critique partners, and ARC readers: Emily Rhodes, the first actual teenager I've enlisted as a beta reader, as well as Megan Thomson, Danielle Boleski, Kirsten Henry, Deb Brown, Jesse, Joseph, Mom and Dad, Steph Hong, Shae Driskill, Janeva Boker-Dopp, Tiffany Knowles, Stephanie Coniff, and Abigail King. I'm grateful for your keen eyes, your courage in giving incredible feedback and advice, and your enthusiastic support. In addition, thank you to everyone who helped put the music together for the *Grey Monroe* playlist: Joseph, James, Natalie Everhart, Kristi, Jesse, and Elizabeth. As always, thank you to Sarah, my writing partner-in-crime.

I realize this book has a lot of dysfunctional family relationships, but anyone who knows the incredible family I've been blessed with knows I didn't write from experience. Anthony, James, Aiden,

Kaylee, and Grayson are the best nephews and niece around, and I am so proud of, and grateful for, each of you. Thank you to Jesse and Kristi, Thomas and Amber, Elizabeth, and Joseph. I would sooner believe that my whole life was a TV show than that any one of you would ever do me wrong—Grey and I have that in common. And, of course, I always have to thank and honor the goodliest of parents. Mom and Dad, a thousand thanks for everything.

Lastly, I want to share my thanks and gratitude to my Heavenly Parents. In the immortal words of Albus Potter's namesake, "Always."

About the Author

Catherine has always loved the written word. She's been crafting novels since childhood, and some even say she's improved since then. She currently lives in the frozen wonderland of Southern Minnesota, where she works in education and assessment. Visit *catherinelyonbooks.com* to sign up for her newsletter!